# TONI MOUNT

# THE COLOUR OF SHADOWS

# The Colour of Shadows

A Sebastian Foxley Medieval Mystery
Book 8

Copyright © 2020 Toni Mount
ISBN-13: 978-84-122325-0-9

# M

MadeGlobal Publishing

For more information on
MadeGlobal Publishing, visit
our website
www.madeglobal.com

To history lovers everywhere
**Toni**.

Why not visit
Sebastian Foxley's web page
to discover more about his
life and times?
**www.SebastianFoxley.com**

# Prologue

T HE CHILD was screaming, attracting attention even on London Bridge, where there was noise enough to drown out any normal conversation. The little wretch wriggled in the man's grasp, doing all he might to break free.

Shrieking fishwives jostled them with reeking baskets; a scawager's dung cart that by rights ought to have finished its business before dawn forced them into a shop doorway as it negotiated its cumbersome route through the crowd of early risers, trailing a miasma of stench in its wake. A gaggle of geese up from Kent and destined for the poulterers added to the cacophony, their feet, painted with tar for the long walk, slapping the road as they waddled and honked and got in everyone's way. The fellow driving them along seemed oblivious, more interested in the wares for sale on the counter-board of a cookshop.

'Cease your bloody squealing. You sound like a stuck piglet,' the man said, giving the child a vicious shake. He was dragging him by the arm, but had to bend low so the child might hear him. 'Behave... son!' he added, seeing a fishwife frowning at him. Then he continued in a whisper: 'You want your Mam to suffer?'

The lad shook his head.

'Then be quiet and walk properly beside me. You try to run off again and your Mam's for worm-fodder. Understand?'

The lad nodded and trotted along at the man's side, sniffing and wiping his snotty nose on his sleeve. If it wasn't for eyes red with weeping and the blue egg of a bruise on his forehead, he could have been comely; a dimpled chin, a shock of golden curls

1

and a pretty mouth that would look well on a girl child. But that was what one particular customer wanted. If he was willing to pay an excess of coin for the lad, the man didn't care why.

With Parliament summoned by King Edward, now was a good time to acquire new 'stock'. Delicious, soft and enticing: innocents were just what were desired by those with jaded appetites, to add spice to their tedious lives. Whores and strumpets were all very well, but the brothel at the sign of The Mermaid in Bankside offered more delicate fare to those who could afford it. Now that London and Westminster were brimful of lords and shire-knights come to attend Parliament, men who would be requiring of some novel entertainment during their leisure hours, the man expected to have made a sizeable profit by the time the king was done with the sitting of that illustrious body.

Illustrious! Huh. The man grimaced to himself. There was naught 'illustrious' about what those rich devils did behind the shutters at The Mermaid. Nigh every vice and sin under the sun went on there. The man was delighted by the revenue brought in even as he disdained his disgusting customers. He informed the Lord God of all their names, if he knew them, but otherwise, he told not a soul. 'Make money and keep silent' was his motto. It had always served him well.

He glanced down at the lad as they turned to the right at the southern end of the bridge, beside the Bishop of Winchester's palatial residence. Aye, this one was special: good skin, straight of limb, and with decent teeth. Bessie would be pleased with this new apprentice to the trade. She would know how best to train him, to show him off to advantage to make the greatest profit. This one had the potential to fill their purses and the man knew just which lord was likely to stop by and appreciate such pretty merchandise. He had deep coffers and a liking for golden hair and soft flesh. Bessie said they had need of just such a boy and he would be kept aside until that particular lord came by.

# Chapter 1

**Saturday, the fourth day of April
in the year of Our Lord 1479
Crosby Hall, Bishopsgate,
in the City of London: the Residence of
Richard, Duke of Gloucester**

THE HALL was full of petitioners, supplicants and assorted folk, all seeking an audience with his grace, the Duke of Gloucester. Sebastian Foxley and Adam Armitage had submitted their names to the steward, as required, and now it was just a matter of waiting. And Seb knew the wait could be long indeed. He and Adam stood in a corner at the back of the hall to watch the proceedings. Adam, beardless now after the London fashion, took the opportunity to admire the sumptuous hangings, the coffered and gilded ceiling, the impressive display of silverware on a huge buffet and, most of all, the vast expanse of glazed windows overlooking the wind-swept gardens. Both men had had to hang onto their best Sunday caps on the walk from Paternoster Row to Bishopsgate in the gusting wind.

The duke, slim and lithe in his finely tailored doublet of murrey wool, did not dominate the gathering from the dais, but stood among the throng, although a discrete circle of space remained around him whenever he moved. It did not do to jostle royalty nor to step too close to those practical but expensive

3

noble shoes.

Seb began to wonder if their day to visit might be ill-chosen. When they entered the hall, Lord Richard was brandishing a sheet of paper aloft and a man was huddled upon his knees before him.

'What does he mean by this?' Richard said. He did not raise his voice – he had no need, for the company fell silent – yet the anger was apparent. 'Explain this wretched epistle to me.'

'Y-your g-grace, I... I...' The man stammered. 'My Lord Pierpoint... he...'

'Cease your nonsense. Tell me.'

'My Lord Pierpoint said... he thought... 'Tis not my fault, my lord.'

'This is not Imperial Rome,' the duke said, 'We do not slay the bearers of ill-tidings. Speak plainly, man.'

'I... I do not know...'

'I have not time to waste on this. Withdraw. Compose yourself. Return when you can speak coherently. Leave us.' The duke dismissed the man with a flick of his hand, as if swatting away a fly or brushing off a fleck of dust.

'I don't like the look of this duke of yours,' Adam whispered in Seb's ear. 'He has a face like thunder and the eye of an executioner.'

The man got off his knees, bowed excessively a half dozen times as he backed away before turning and rushing for the door in unseemly haste.

The mutter of conversation resumed.

''Tis said he has the temper of a true Plantagenet, but I have ne'er witnessed it afore,' Seb answered, keeping his voice to a murmur. In truth, the duke had never looked so forbidding. Seb had only ever seen him courteous and gracious; this was a man of another complexion entirely.

'Master Sebastian Foxley; Master Adam Armitage; step forward and present your business with his grace!' The steward stamped his staff of office on the floor, announcing them in ringing tones and far sooner than they expected. Seb hardly felt prepared now that the moment had arrived.

He and Adam walked in step towards the duke as a way opened up through the crowd to allow them passage. Bare-headed, they bent the knee and lowered their eyes in unison. It was surprisingly well accomplished, Seb thought, seeing they had not rehearsed it.

'Master Foxley. What a pleasant happenstance is this. Be upstanding, my friend, and make introduction of your companion.'

They both stood to face the duke. Gloucester was smiling, a sparkle in his grey eyes. This was not the man who had just sent a fellow scuttling in terror.

'Your grace. May it please you: I present my relative, Adam Armitage. He is from Norfolk but now bides and works with us at Paternoster Row.'

'Welcome, Master Armitage. 'Tis a pleasure to make your acquaintance.' Richard extended his hand, but not so that it might be kissed by lesser men – as could correctly have been the case – rather to shake them both by the hand as friends. 'And Sebastian, it has been brought to my attention that you are to be congratulated, having become a father. Is that the case? I trust I have not been misinformed.'

'Indeed, my lord. I have a fine son.'

The duke laughed.

'And no doubt he is a paragon, as are all sons until they be of an age to err. What is his name?'

'Er, forgive my impertinence, my lord…' Seb's pulse raced and he felt over-hot of a sudden. 'We named him Richard and call him Dickon, saving your grace.'

'Well, such a compliment is this. I heartily commend your choice. Mayhap, I shall find an opportunity to visit my illustrious namesake. Now, to business, master. What brings you here to my hall?'

'We have a gift, my lord, for your children.' Seb knelt and

held out the copy of *Aesop's Fables* that had taken so many months of work, complete in its protective embroidered chemise. The duke's face lit up as if a candle flame had been kindled behind his eyes.

'How very thoughtful. What is its text?' He accepted the book with such reverence and stepped towards a table to set it down and remove the chemise. Seb felt somewhat heartened.

''Tis the moral fables of Aesop. Instructive and amusing for young readers... I hope.' Seb's nervous state had not lessened despite the duke's apparent approval of the gift, thus far.

'Your goodwife embroidered the chemise?'

'Aye, my lord, and wove the ribbon to tie the covers closed and made the tasselled bookmark within to note the page. Adam penned the text; Jack Tabor carved the wood boards; Mistress Rose Glover made the white leather covering over the boards and embossed the gilding...'

'And you painted the exquisite miniatures,' the duke said, turning the pages with care. 'I recognise your style straightway.' As he leafed through it, he paused at a page and chuckled. 'Rob!' he called, 'Come see this: it will amuse you mightily.'

A tall, broad fellow with fiery hair came from a knot of courtiers standing by the dais to join Richard at the table. It was Seb's old friend, Sir Robert Percy.

''Tis a very fine book, Sebastian,' the duke said, turning back to his visitors. 'My children will love to see it – under close supervision, I warrant – but not until I have read it myself. The contents must be approved beforehand.' Seeing Seb's worried expression, the duke laughed out loud and patted the artist's shoulder. 'I too have a fondness for a moral tale and colourful picture. You cannot blame me if I delay in passing on your generous gift, wishing to peruse it first before less appreciative eyes see it and grubby fingers mar the pages.'

# Palm Sunday, the fourth day of April in the year of Our Lord 1479 The Foxley house, Paternoster Row, in the City of London

Saturday night had been wild and windy indeed but, as he opened the window shutters and looked out, the sky was an innocent pearlescent blue, as if naught of the kind had ever come to pass. Yet the street below was littered with spring-budding twigs, ripped untimely from bushes and trees, and terracotta shards of broken roof-tiles lay strewn around like a drunken mosaic. Wisps of thatch drifted past on the now-courteous breeze, evidence of yet more damaged houses.

'I must check upon our shutters and roof, Em, afore we be away to church,' Seb said to his wife as he bent to fasten the ties on his Sunday shoes.

'If we've lost any tiles after what that wretch charged us for repairs last autumn, you must demand our money be repaid.' Emily stood before the pewter mirror to adjust and pin her best veil. She caught her breath of a sudden and put her hands to her swelling belly.

'What is it, Em?'

'The babe. What else would it be? This one kicks like a horse, as Dickon never did.'

'A lively little fellow then. 'Tis good to know.'

'Only a man could think so; you're not the one being kicked about inside like a pig's bladder at a Shrovetide football contest.'

'I shall go see that no tiles have slipped. I'll be outside if you need me.'

'See that the privy is still standing. If it's not, God help me.'

Seb unbarred the door from the kitchen and stepped out into the cobbled yard. Debris from the storm and bits of broken fence paling were scattered about but the palings were not theirs, fortunately, but a neighbour's. Beyond, the back garden plot looked wind-blasted. Every last white petal was gone from the blackthorn tree. It had to be hoped the bees had done their work already, else the fruit harvest of sloes would be poor later in the year. Gawain snuffled about, investigating any new scents that might have blown in overnight.

Seb made for the end of the garden where the privy stood, ivy-shrouded and solitary, as a house of easement should. He made use of it and all was well as he had hoped since the ivy chained it to the ground as surely as a ship's anchor rope. The pigsty had suffered no hurt bar a mess of twigs blown into the water trough. He fished them out and the pig appeared, grunting and eager in expectation of breakfast.

'Later, later,' he assured her. 'We have none of us had time to prepare food.' He stepped back, turning to look up at the roof and gables of the house, almost falling over Gawain, who was right behind him. The dog yelped as Seb stepped on his tail. 'Sorry, lad. Give me space to tread, I beg you.' He fondled Gawain's silky black ears and was rewarded with a well-licked hand, so it seemed his clumsiness was forgiven. Seb squinted up at the roof, narrowing his eyes against the brightness of the sky. All looked well; no missing or slipped tiles and all the window shutters seemed to be undamaged. The single chimney pot still stood proud – which was as well since it, along with the glass in the window of the master bedchamber, proclaimed the Foxleys' improving place in London society.

Returning to the kitchen, Seb reported that all was in order at the back of the house. Rose smiled at him, her face as welcome as the sun. She always cheered him. She was giving little Dickon his breakfast of bread sops in milk, sweetened with honey. Emily's breast milk had dried up since she was great with child again, but Dickon seemed to be thriving on the goat's milk he was given instead. He had his own chair, now that he could sit up properly. Emily's father – a skilled carpenter – had made it for his first grandchild. It was finely carved with a row of ducks across the back, more of the same lined up along the removable bar at the front, which prevented the child from falling out. The turned legs were of such a length that raised him to the height of the table-board, so that Dickon could share mealtimes with everyone else. But the day being Sunday, the babe broke his fast alone. The household would attend church before coming home to eat.

Dickon, upon espying Papa, waved his hands excitedly, gurgling through a mouthful of food and sending the next spoonful, as Rose offered it, down his father's clean Sunday best doublet. Adam grinned and offered Seb a napkin.

'You'll be in trouble when Em sees you. She'll claim you bring her laundering skills into disrepute.'

'I know,' Seb said with a sigh, using the napkin to wipe Dickon's mouth. 'But how does my little man fare upon this fine morn?' The child chuckled and made babbling noises, for all the world as if he was answering Papa's question. Seb laughed. After a rough night with little sleep due to the howling storm, at least the day began on a merry note: Dickon content, Rose smiling, Adam jesting and the house intact. Things were better yet when young Kate bounced in.

'Do you approve my new ribbons, Master Seb? Are they not the finest shade of green ever made? Do you like them?' She tossed her flamboyant dark curls to show off the ribbons to best advantage.

'Indeed,' he answered, never knowing what to say when a woman asked his opinion on female matters.

'They're beautiful,' Rose said, laying down the horn spoon

she had been using to feed Dickon. 'Here, let me straighten that bow for you. There: perfect.'

'I can't wait to show Jack. He will like them, won't he? I chose green because it's his favourite colour.'

'Is it? I never knew he appreciated any colour particularly above another,' Seb said, being one to whom colour mattered so much.

'He'll favour the wearer more than the ribbons, if he has the least drop of red blood in his veins,' Adam added.

It was a known fact that Kate and Jack had what Seb referred to as "an attachment" to each other, which other less-mannerly folk called "a lusting" on Jack's part and "a fancy" on Kate's. It was a continuing anxiety to Seb that the relationship should go no further since he was guardian to both youngsters. Kate's father would never forgive him if his daughter's reputation were sullied but how to prevent it, short of keeping them locked in their separate chambers, he did not know. He had lectured, cajoled and warned them so many times but could words ever overrule nature? He had no choice but to trust them and hope common sense and propriety would win the day.

'I must check the shop and the roof at the front for any storm damage,' Seb said, recalling that his task was only half done. He kissed Dickon's head of soft ebony hair, so much like his own, and was rewarded with a crow of delight and a little fist catching him a buffet on the nose. 'Mind Papa's nose, little one. 'Tis a sizeable target, I know and I would have it no larger.'

'For certain, it gets stuck in everyone else's business as it is.' Adam jested. 'Has anyone seen those idle good-for-nothings yet, else they'll be late for church?' He meant Tom Bowen, one-time apprentice and now the workshop's journeyman-scrivener, and Jack Tabor, also a one-time apprentice but now learning a new trade as a joiner with Stephen Appleyard, Emily's father.

'Their door was still closed when I came down,' Kate said. 'I expect the storm kept them awake and they're sleeping yet.'

'It kept us all wakeful and that's no excuse. The rest of us will be at St Michael's in time for Low Mass this Palm Sunday and so will they if I have to give them a dousing with a bucketful of icy water to get them out of bed.' Adam's expression implied that he might well carry out the threat.

Meanwhile, Seb had unbarred the door at the front of the shop and gone out into Paternoster Row, to check the shutters on the parlour window and the roof that faced St Paul's across the way. As with the back garden, the street was strewn with storm debris but none that looked to have come from the Foxley house. The roof tiles were all in place and the window shutters hung straight. What a relief. A neighbour from further along the row, by Lovell's Inn, came running, chasing a hen that seemed the faster of the two.

'Catch the devil, Seb!' the man called out.

Just in time, Seb made a lunge and grabbed the bird. Squawking and lashing out with its sharp-taloned feet, it was all Seb could do to keep hold of the writhing bundle of angry feathers. He managed to tuck it under his arm, covering its yellow eyes with his free hand so it became calm.

'Damn storm brought down our old cherry tree,' the neighbour, Jonathan Caldicott, explained as he came puffing up to Seb. 'It smashed the henhouse... birds have gone everywhere... wife's spitting mad... says it's my fault.'

''Tis the fault of the storm, surely? 'Twas quite the tempest last night, Jonathan. You could do naught to prevent it.'

'Not how the wife sees it. Says I should've known the tree was like to come down and done something about it beforehand. You know how women are,' Jonathan added with a meaningful look.

'Aye, I suppose.' Seb handed the hen to his neighbour with care, not wanting to be pecked for his trouble.

'I'm grateful, Seb. I'll stand you a jug of ale in the Panyer later. Oh, and there are two more hens on the loose somewhere about, if you see them...'

Seb nodded and turned to go back within doors. There was still one more shutter to check at the east-facing window in the workshop, but that opened inwards and had a new latch, so would most likely have weathered the storm undamaged. He brushed a few stray feathers from his doublet and was dismayed to see that the fine blue cloth, previously spattered with milk sops, was now smeared with mud and chicken dung. Jonathan Caldicott was not going to be the only man in Paternoster Row to receive the sharp blade of his wife's scolding tongue this morn.

Hoping to avoid meeting Emily for a little longer – mayhap, the mud and dung would dry somewhat and brush off – Seb went straight to the workshop. The room was cast in deep gloom which was a good indication that the shutter remained in place and unharmed. In near-darkness, he felt for the wooden latch and lifted it from its hasp, opening the two halves of the shutter like the covers of a book. Spring sunlight flooded in, welcome and warm upon his face. No damage, the Lord be praised. Emily took pride in glass window panes and a tall chimney but, of all things, Seb took the greatest satisfaction in his workshop: orderly, well-stocked and a hive of industry on weekdays. Of a Sunday, it was still a joy to behold with everything set out: inks, pigments, parchment, paper and pens, awaiting an early start on Monday morn.

But there was something that did not belong.

Frowning in puzzlement, Seb wondered what on earth lay in a heap beside his desk. He went closer to look, but leapt back with a gasp, making the sign of the Cross.

'Sweet Jesu have mercy,' he said aloud. A second look confirmed it. 'Adam! Adam!' he called out. 'Come to the workshop.' He was still struggling to regain his composure as Adam came down the passage, followed by everyone else from the kitchen. 'Stay back, the rest of you,' Seb warned, 'Come no closer, Em. This be no sight suitable for a woman with child to see. Go back to the kitchen. Do as I say this once, all of you but Adam.' The womenfolk obeyed – even Emily – but Tom and Jack did no more than retreat a step or two back in the passage. 'You'll be my witness, Adam, but to what, I do not

12

know precisely. We must move my desk…'

'By all the saints, what is a lad like that doing here? How did he get in? Was a shutter broken?'

'No shutters were broken and I unbarred the doors myself this morn.'

'We have to get him to a bed, fetch the surgeon…' Adam knelt beside the lad.

'I fear 'tis too late for that. Whoever he be, he lies dead… in our house and no way he could have entered in. I know not what can be done.' Seb sat down on the nearest stool and sighed. ''Tis a mystery indeed and likely beyond my power to solve.'

Adam moved the body, rolling it onto its back.

'There's blood, Seb. We'll have to inform the sheriffs' office and your friend Master Fyssher.' Adam referred to the Deputy Coroner of London, who occasionally forced Seb to assist him at a wage of sixpence a day – an insulting recompense for the gruesome work often involved. And 'friend' was not the word Seb would use to describe the pompous, inefficient and downright idle overseer of unexpected deaths in the city. To have to be involved with Fyssher on any matter was a hateful prospect and concerning a death in his own home was worse yet.

'Later. I cannot face them now. After mass, mayhap. The dead will wait patiently. The body will not walk off, will it? But we must cover it decently. I would not have Em catch sight of it. Who can tell what effect it might have upon her unborn babe? You know the sight of a hare in a field can cause a babe to be born with a hare-lip, or so they say.'

'Aye, so I've heard, but I'm not convinced it's true.'

'I will take no chances, be it true or not. Em and the child must not be put at hazard in any way.'

'Of course not. But look here, Seb, he was a striking lad, was he not? Someone will recognise him, I'm certain. Why don't you draw a likeness of him while he's still fresh and wholesome – or as much as a street urchin ever is?'

Seb winced. Adam spoke of the lad as if he was a side of

mutton on a butcher's stall. Turning, he saw Tom and Jack were now in the doorway.

'Did I not tell you…' Seb began. 'Oh, no matter. One of you fetch an old blanket or sheet to cover the body, then you may both escort the womenfolk to church.'

'Tom'll do it,' Jack said.

'Don't you tell me what to do, you pissing jackanapes.'

'I ain't no such fing, you fat arse-wipe. I knows stuff wot you don't an' I might knows 'im, mightn't I?'

'Cease your foul language upon the Lord's Day. I will not have such words uttered in my house, as you know full well. Have you no respect? A Christian child lies dead there, and you two make Billingsgate fishwives sound like Paul's choristers compared to your filthy tongues. Tom, go fetch a covering and be certain 'tis not Mistress Em's best tablecloth.'

'Why me? I'm a journeyman now, not a 'prentice.'

'In either case, you do it because I be master here, and I tell you to.'

Tom slunk off like a whipped dog and Jack smirked.

'And you can cease gloating, Jack, and go wash your mouth out with soap and water.'

'Wot! But he said worserer than me.'

'And he will do likewise. Then you'll go to mass, make your contrition and light a candle – both of you – for the soul you have insulted.'

'But I never said nuffink 'gainst the dead un, did I?'

'Your behaviour was sufficiently disrespectful.'

'But, like wot I said: I might knows him, mightn't I, if'n you let me look proper. Adam says he's a street urchin, like I wos, so…'

'The lad be not of an age with you and you have been off the streets now for nigh unto four years. How would he be any acquaintance of a respectable young man as yourself?'

'Aye, well, I still sort o' knows folks, don't I?'

'You mean, you still consort with undesirables

behind my back.'

'Nah! But you said he wos a Christian soul, not a undeseribble – wot ever it is.'

'Every word you speak makes matters worse, Jack. Come. Take one good look at the poor lad and then be gone.'

Jack went over to the body where Adam had lain it out straight.

'Well? Do you know who he is?' Seb asked.

'Nah, but…'

'Then cease your gawping and get to church.'

Tom returned then with a rumpled sheet from the morrow's laundry pile and took the opportunity to see the corpse for himself.

'Do you recognise him, Tom? His hair be quite distinctive.'

'Never seen him before and I reckon I'd remember him if I had.'

'Aye, you would. Now, the pair of you, see the others safe to St Michael's. Be alert for any falling tiles or leaning trees after the storm. If he asks, tell Father Thomas that Adam and I will attend High Mass later.'


With Tom, Jack and the rest of the household gone to Low Mass, Seb and Adam were left with the problem of what to do about the body. For fully ten minutes at least, the two sat silent upon their stools, regarding the sheet-covered corpse, deep in thought. Gawain lay at Seb's feet, waiting for whatever should come to pass. In truth, Seb was not so much thinking as praying, but the Almighty must be too concerned with other matters on a busy Sunday because no divine response was forthcoming. He scratched behind Gawain's ear.

'We can't just sit, staring at it 'til it starts to stink, Seb,' Adam said at last. 'I'll fetch one of the sheriffs: we can't avoid it.'

'Which of them?' Seb asked. 'I have little faith in either of this year's sheriffs.'

Adam shrugged:

'Sheriff Byfield is less use than a blunt knife and I don't trust the other one no more than a cat with a sparrow in a bucket.'

'I agree. Byfield will probably be the more sympathetic to our case.'

'Our case? I don't understand, Seb.'

'Oh, Adam, can you not see how this may look to others: to the authorities? A good-looking lad found dead – most probably unlawfully killed – in a room within a house with windows shuttered and doors barred. There was no way he could have got in nor out without our knowledge, nor could any outsider have left him here for those same reasons. No one but us.'

'But that isn't true. He did get in somehow and we knew nothing of it, Seb. Are you thinking the sheriff won't believe our story?'

'Would you? Would any man of sound mind and logical reason?'

'Mm. In which case, what do we do?' Adam was pulling at his earlobe. In the past, he used to pull his beard when distracted but was now clean-shaven in the London fashion. At this moment, he missed his beard.

'I wish I knew, Adam, but I fear the truth may serve us ill.'

'Suppose we take the body to the river and throw it in. Nobody need ever know it was here in this house.'

'You would deny him decent burial? That be most un-Christian of you, Adam.'

'It would spare us a legion of unanswerable questions. What if they arrest us? Have you thought of that?'

Seb straightened his stained doublet as if by doing so he might straighten his confused thoughts also.

'Aye, the possibility had occurred to me. There be but one way of discovering the truth and that necessitates the acquiring of evidence and I cannot do that sitting here, maudlin and moping.' He stood up and the dog that had waited at his master's feet stood up also, hoping for a walk or a titbit. 'Let us examine the lad and this room more thoroughly afore Fyssher and his ilk come thundering in and destroy every clue. 'Tis all I can think to do: we must solve the mystery and then report it to the authorities. No doubt, they will have much to do elsewhere about the city in the wake of the storm. We must use our time wisely.'

'Where do we begin?'

'With the body. Out of the way, Gawain, 'tis no business of yours.'

Seb eased himself down to kneel beside the dead lad. His hip joint protested but he ignored it. With due reverence, he turned back the sheet, folding it down until only the shoes were covered. On second thoughts, he uncovered them also: no point in half measures. The feet were as likely to reveal a clue as any other part.

'What think you, concerning his hair, Adam? Unusual to see hair of so pale a hue in a youngster, is it not?'

'I knew a Dutch family in Norwich. Their hair was much the same as this. Could he be Dutch, perhaps?'

'We will keep it in mind. He has a good face: fine-featured. He would be accounted handsome, I believe. As you suggested, it will be worthwhile to record his likeness.' Seb made a few brief notes on scrap paper, using his thigh as a writing slope. 'Could you hazard a guess at his age?'

'Eleven or twelve years, maybe? Not much more than that.'

'I agree. What of his eyes? Dutchmen most commonly have blue eyes, as indeed do other fair-haired folk.'

He glanced at Adam who was, likewise, upon his knees. But Adam made no move to look at the closed eyes. Seb sighed and carefully raised the lid of one eye with his thumb.

'Mm, I fear 'tis hard to tell the colour with death's cloud now misting it. Mayhap, 'tis blue?' He made another note. 'The dead do not bite, Adam, nor do they protest. You may touch them without harm, unless they be dead of some pestilent fever.'

'Aye, I know. But it seems a violation somehow.'

'He was violated in life. Now he deserves justice and only he can guide us by allowing us to observe the details preserved upon his person. Your squeamishness will not aid in this.'

'You're right. How may I help?'

'Describe his clothing.'

'But you can see as well as I…'

'A second opinion always adds certainty. You may notice things I miss and *vice versa*.

'A jerkin: filthy but probably once a greyish shade of green. A linen shirt…'

'Unlace the jerkin and look to the seams: colour is oftentimes better preserved there.'

Adam obeyed and was surprised to discover the original hue had been a deep green.

'And what of the fit?' Seb asked.

'The fit?'

'Does the jerkin fit him well, or is it likely made for another?'

''Tis of a fair size in breadth, in that there is no sign of the laces pulling too tight and straining the holes, but it seems rather short for him.'

'And look to the belt also?'

'The belt is worn, with many holes having been used, but its present fastening has more use than any other. Seb: you think I'm getting the way of this searching business, looking for clues? The clothes have much to tell us, I see that now.'

'And what do they say to you?'

'That he's grown taller but no fatter of late. I suppose that is the way of lads his age. The sleeves of his shirt end above his wrists, which agrees with my deductions.'

'Or 'tis borrowed from someone else.'

'Mm… that could explain…' Adam slapped the back of his hand. 'Hey, I'm getting bitten here. Damned fleas.'

'More likely a louse. Fleas would have jumped from the scalp as soon as the body began to cool, whereas lice get trapped in the clothing. Now you have freed them, they too desert the dead.

Not an uncommon occurrence.'

'You could have warned me.'

'Searching out clues can be an occupation full of surprises,' Seb said, grinning. 'I once found a live frog within the damp folds of a dead man's cloak and as for those dragged from the Thames, the things I've discovered there...'

'Don't tell me; I don't want to know. I hope to eat a good breakfast when we're done with this.'

'Then let us continue. The jerkin be of good quality woollen cloth with no sign of moth damage nor repairs, yet it be faded and filthy. Therefore, much care has been taken of the garment until recently. It was made for the lad, as you supposed, but he is growing out of it in length yet not girth. Either his family has fallen on hard times, or they are no longer able to care for him.'

'How do you know it was made for him? Could be handed down from an older brother or bought from a fripperer or be, as you said, borrowed.'

'Neither borrowed nor second hand. See the faint lines of wear radiating from the armholes. The cloth still lies in those same worn furrows. If another had worn it, there would be other crease-marks now fading. The lad has always been the wearer, lacing and fastening it in the same way. I would surmise also that he is a scholar and carries his book tucked under his left arm. See? The wool has lost its knap there. But we must move on swiftly, else the others will be returning from church. Afore then, we must see what his wound can tell us; how the bloodstains lie...'

'Seb, I truly don't want to do that. I think I'll leave you to your notes, sketches and deliberations. I shall take Gawain for a walk...'

'Adam. Four eyes be far better than two. Your aid be much appreciated.'

'I know but my eyes would rather not see any more of this.'

With Adam departed, Seb gave the dead lad his undivided attention. The wound and bloodstains were examined in minute

19

detail. The rest of the clothing, particularly the good, though worn, shoes which were nigh too small for him, revealed more of his story. And his hands and fingernails told a great deal; a tale of misery and neglect. It was a sorry end for a fine young lad. And how had he come to lie in the shuttered workshop? Some measure of light was shed upon that mystery also, although not every aspect was made clear as yet. Mayhap, it never would be.

# Chapter 2

## Palm Sunday
## The Foxley house

B Y THE time Emily and the others came home from St Michael's, trailing a wake of curious gossips and those of a ghoulish turn of mind, eager to view someone else's misfortune, Seb had wrapped the body in the sheet and laid it out of sight in the storeroom. The church-goers were still carrying their willow 'palms' as tokens of Our Lord's triumphant entry into Jerusalem.

'Sweet Mary, but my feet do ache,' Emily said, flopping onto the nearest bench in the kitchen. 'See how my ankles swell? Pour me some ale, husband, if you have the least concern me.'

'Adam has gone to fetch a sheriff, or at least someone in authority,' Seb said. He was at the laver bowl, scrubbing vigorously at his wrists and hands, his shirt and doublet sleeves rolled up, using lavender-scented water in an attempt to dispel the stench of death and dried blood. Seb wiped his hands upon a towel and found a clean cup. Having served her ale, he knelt to unlace his wife's Sunday best shoes.

'Oh, Em, you poor lass. I'll fetch more water that you can soak your feet a while.'

'No time for that now. I have dinner to cook. But you can deal with the gawpers. I have no patience with their kind.'

'What are they doing here? Who informed them of the sorry

occurrence this morn? I said to say naught of it.'

'Who do you suppose? Jack, Tom and Nessie – she set it all off, sobbing loudly and making a dismal show. When folk asked what was amiss, the lads couldn't wait to spread the word, making the matter far greater and worse than it is. Now half the parish has come to see for themselves… Oh, how wretched I am.'

Rose entered the kitchen, little Dickon on her hip. Seb took the child.

'If I amuse him, can you and Nessie see to the cooking, please? Em needs to rest.'

'Aye. I intended to. You're right: Em shouldn't be on her feet, preparing food.' Rose exchanged her best Sunday apron for a work-a-day one hanging on the peg by the chimney-corner and began chopping a bunch of parsley.

'Cease talking about me as if I'm an unhearing piece of furniture,' Em told them. 'And don't tell me what I may and may not do in my own house. I'll decide…'

'Calm yourself, sweetheart. We be concerned for your welfare is all.'

'Don't you dare patronise me, Sebastian. I'll not have it!'

'Forgive me. I meant no…'

'And why did you not join us at church? Father Thomas wasn't alone in remarking upon your absence. Dame Ellen was most determined to point out my lack of a husband.'

'I had to attend to…' Seb lowered his voice to a whisper, '… the body; note any particulars, draw a likeness, make it decent, lay it straight…'

'So you've been working! And on Palm Sunday of all days. Have you no regard for such matters as observing the Lord's Day and Holy Week?' Emily was irate at the thought and more so at the penance her husband's activities would incur – of a financial kind, no doubt. 'Have you got rid of it yet? I can't have it in my house…'

'The poor child lies in the storeroom, out of sight, Em. But a thorough examination was better done now, afore Master

Fyssher destroys any evidence and a likeness drawn whilst the face be yet recognisable and...'

'He's the coroner; it's up to him what he does.'

'But I know well enough Fyssher will take no pains to discover the dead child's family. They have a right to be told.' Seb turned away from her, hoping to avoid further argument. 'Come, Dickon. Let us say 'good morn' to Mistress Piggywig in her sty, shall we? And were you quiet in church, eh?'

'Sebastian Foxley!' Emily screeched, snatching at his sleeve. 'What in the name of Our Blessed Lady have you done to your best doublet? Look at it. It's a disgrace. And how am I ever supposed to get it clean?'

'What?' Seb looked down at his attire and remembered: milk sops, mud and chicken dung. His clothing was indeed a thing of horror and, since then, dark smears of old blood, the taint of voided urine and faecal matter of the dying had been added to the unsavoury mess. 'Sorry, Em, I forgot... I never meant...'

'You never do, you unthinking wretch. You never concern yourself about how I'll ever get the stains out. You just don't care, so why should I? Go to mass stinking like a cesspit, looking like a midden-heap. See if I care, you vile, disgusting beast. And don't touch me... or little Dickon. Just don't touch... anything.' The tirade ended as Emily burst into tears, slapped his cheek – the child in his arms notwithstanding – and fled up the stairs. Running footsteps passed overhead as she hastened along the passageway to the bedchamber at the front of the house. Dickon began to cry, as he often did when voices were raised. Like his Papa, he preferred peace and pleasantness.

Seb rubbed his tingling face: out of favour yet again. All the same, Emily was correct: he should be cleanly clothed before Adam arrived home with the sheriff and the coroner. He ought to make some attempt to look like a respectable citizen on a Sunday.

'We shall visit Mistress Piggywig later, Dickon, when Papa be suitably attired, I promise you.' He kissed his son's cheek, soft as down, and put the little lad to sit in his cradle and play with the patchwork ball Rose had stitched for him, using scraps of coloured rags.

Dinner was nigh ready to serve: mackerel in a mustard sauce with herb bread. It being Lententide, fish was upon the board on Sundays also but at least next week, Easter Day would see the welcome return of meat. Emily had already planned the celebratory meal, having placed an order with her favoured butcher for half a side of best mutton. But today, they would enjoy the mackerel in its sauce, made to her own receipt with its secret ingredient – saffron. How she craved the expensive spice when she was with child.

Little Dickon was sleeping in his cradle, so they should be able to eat in peace. Seb reappeared from upstairs, more seemly clad. His spare doublet was worn and faded but at least it was clean. Mind you, the scent of lavender was so strong upon him, Emily wondered what unhealthful stinks it might be disguising. No matter.

'Come to the board,' Emily called out. Watching as members of the household materialised in the kitchen as if conjured by a sorcerer, she noted one was missing. 'Where is Adam?'

'Still searching out a sheriff, I suppose,' Seb said.

'The food will spoil if we wait for him.'

'He has been gone some little while; mayhap, a sheriff be hard to find, but if one cannot come, I be certain Adam will return anyhow. Since neither of us has yet broken our fast, he will be as hungry as I. That fish looks good, Em. What a fine wife I have...'

'Cease your honeyed words: I have not forgotten what you did to your best doublet and now you cause dinner to ruin because you sent Adam on an errand that could have waited until after our meal. You are so thoughtless.'

'I did not send him; he determined to go...'

'Don't try to shift the blame: this is all your fault.'

Aye, was it not always the case, Seb thought. Jonathan Caldicott had spoken truly.

Seb was saved by Adam's timely return. Although he was not accompanied by either of the sheriffs or the coroner, Thaddeus Turner was a far more welcome visitor and one who had Emily wearing a pleasant expression.

'Nessie, set another place at the board for Beadle Turner. He will dine with us. And fetch a pewter platter for him, not that dented one, you foolish wench.' Emily smoothed her apron over her ample belly, wanting to make a good impression. The beadle was a fine fellow with a ready smile and black locks that were ever unkempt but in a most attractive way.

'Greetings all and good health be upon you,' he said. 'Master Seb; Mistress Foxley; Mistress Glover. Master Fyssher is out of town, visiting relatives, both sheriffs seem, likewise, to be unavailable. I hope I can serve as well as they?'

'Welcome, Master Turner. I trust you will join us at dinner?' Seb said, shaking the beadle's hand. In truth, he preferred to deal with Thaddeus. 'Please wash, if you will: the water be hot.' He indicated the laver bowl and offered a fresh towel.

After Seb had said grace, everyone tucked in to the excellent repast. Over the meal, the talk was all of the last eve's storm and Thaddeus told of damage done to St Bartholomew's Priory within his jurisdiction. Officially, having been elevated to his new position as the City Bailiff, answerable to the Lord Mayor, Thaddeus' writ ran as far as Southwark these days as representative of the city authorities. With no sheriff available – and, in truth, Adam had not tried too hard to find either of them or the coroner – Thaddeus' services were preferable in any case and likely to be more courteous and friendly besides.

Replete with generous helpings of preserved apples and apricocks in a tart, the menfolk withdrew to the workshop since that was where the body was stored, to discuss less savoury matters.

'Adam has told me something of what came to pass, Seb, but I should hear the tale from you, how you found this body here.' Thaddeus Turner attempted to be comfortable upon a workshop stool, unsure where to put his long legs and great boots so none should stumble over them.

'Aye, Thaddeus, shall you see the poor lad now? He lies in the storeroom there.'

Thaddeus shook his head.

'In a while will suffice; I would digest that fine dinner first. Has he received the offices of a priest?'

'Nay. I regret to say, like the sheriffs, Father Thomas be overburdened with his Palm Sunday duties. He promised to come as soon as maybe. As for Surgeon Dagvyle, he has a number of injured folk to attend after the storm. Young Jack, whom I sent to fetch him, tells us that a mighty beech tree came down upon a busy tavern, The Barge, over by Bucklersbury and Walbrook, if you know it? A dozen or more have suffered various hurts. Dagvyle will attend here when he may. Is that not so, Jack?'

'Aye, but I can tells you sommat…'

'Later. You and Tom need to hasten. Archery practice will commence shortly. Warden-Archer Appleyard will be displeased…'

'Oh, he won't mind. He knows wot a master I am wiv a bow. Don't need no practice, do I? But Tom does. He couldn't shoot St Paul's door from ten feet, he couldn't.'

Tom promptly cuffed Jack's ear.

'I can. I'm better than you, toad's-breath. You shoot like a one-armed blind man. God help London if you ever have to defend us.'

'Enough. Fetch your bows. We'll all go,' Adam said, clouting the pair of them. 'Master Seb can speak with Beadle Turner in peace, without you disrupting the conversation.'

'But I…' Jack began.

'I said "enough". Now do as I tell you.'

'Can Kate come t' cheer me shooting?'

'If she wishes,' Adam said.

'Nay, Adam, I have a small task that requires Kate's assistance,' Seb interrupted. 'She may attend after.'

'She'll have naught to cheer, anyway,' Tom muttered as the three left the workshop, the quarrel continuing.

'I apologise, Thaddeus,' Seb said when they were gone, 'They never cease bickering, those two. 'Tis wearing on the spirit, I admit, but what to do about it, I know not.'

'Adam seems to have the best notion and a good beating wouldn't come amiss.'

'But would it make the least difference? They be like a pair of wild dogs chained together: 'tis in their nature to fight and they cannot do otherwise.'

'Aye, well, I must leave that problem for you, my friend. Now, what of this body? Tell me what you know. How in the name of the Devil – pardon me...' Thaddeus crossed himself, 'Does a corpse end up in your workshop? Adam said the shutter was closed and undamaged.'

'Aye, yet the poor lad came in that way, all the same. Permit me to show you. I pray you, come out into the yard and I will demonstrate my findings. If you leave first, then I may close and latch the shutter, for fear you may stumble in the darkness.'

Once in the yard, bringing Kate away from her task of drying pots and platters in the kitchen, Seb explained:

'See here, the upturned bucket, 'tis how I found it. Standing upon it, the lad would have been of a height to reach the window and climb in. Kate be much of a size with the lad, by my reckoning. Kate, if you would oblige us, please?'

Content to leave her domestic chores, the lass hitched up her skirts and climbed upon the bucket, smiling broadly.

'Like this, master, I can reach well enough, but the shutter... how to open it?'

'With this.' Seb picked up a rusted blade, broken and without a handle. 'This was lying beside the bucket.' Seb handed it to Thaddeus and took his own knife from the sheath at his belt.

'Now, take my clean knife and slide the blade betwixt the two halves of the shutter, Kate, and then move it upwards. Take care not to cut yourself, lass, but mine has a handle, at least.'

''Tis against the latch inside,' she said.

'Aye, but raise it higher.'

Another inch and Kate felt the latch lift and the shutters swung inwards.

'There! And to think I paid good coin for that new latch last winter, hoping to deter any would-be hedge-breakers. You will recall the spate of thievery from houses in this parish afore Christmastide, Thaddeus. I may as well have left the shutter open and a letter of invitation pinned upon it.'

'And you think he got in this way?' Thaddeus asked, still examining the rusty blade.

'He did. See here: mud from his shoes upon the window frame; rust from the blade upon the wooden latch...'

'And bloody finger marks on the shutter where he pushed it open,' the beadle added. 'He must have cut his hand on the blade.'

'Not so. There be no injury to his hands, but blood aplenty, I fear. The lad had been stabbed, Thaddeus.'

'Poor soul,' Kate said, tears glistening.

'Forgive me, lass. I should not have spoken thus.' Seb wiped her cheeks with the sleeve of his shirt. 'Dry your tears and return to your tasks. And my thanks for your assistance. Tell Mistress Em, I said you be deserving of an almond sweetmeat by way of reward. Then you may go watch the lads at archery practice, if you wish. '

Kate's smile was there, in its rightful place, in an instant and she ran back to the kitchen to collect her prize.

'With this blade?' Thaddeus asked. ''Tis rusted, but I see no blood. It looks to be unused for years; thrown away.'

'The wound was not fresh,' Seb continued now Kate was gone. 'It was made by a broader blade than that and was partially healing, but badly inflamed. I think the lad was seeking shelter from the storm, which explains why he closed the shutter behind him and latched it anew. He also wanted help. He was bleeding afresh, thus his hands were bloody.' Seb paused and sighed. 'He needed our aid. He may have known he was dying and was desperate not to be alone with his fears. We failed him. He died in the darkness of the workshop, too weak after his exertions to call out. Mayhap, a surgeon could have saved him, though I misdoubt it, but we could have given him comfort, a gentle hand, a soft word at the last. That a child so young died alone and afeared... it breaks my heart to think on it, Thaddeus, it truly does.' Seb felt salt tears burning his eyes and swallowed down a sob.

'Indeed. I suppose I have no choice but to see the body. I trust it will confirm all that you say, my friend. I should hate there to be any doubts...'

Seb nodded, understanding the beadle's warning. If the evidence did not wholly support his story, the Foxley household could be in deep trouble.

'A cup of ale first, though,' he said, feeling the need to wash down the threat of weeping.

Back in the kitchen, Seb realised Rose, Kate and Nessie were setting the place in order but there was no sign of Emily.

'Where be Em?' he asked.

'Upstairs, resting,' Rose said.

Seb nodded. There was no doubt she needed to rest but with a visitor in the house, Emily would have regarded it as her wifely duty to be present. She must feel weary indeed; this babe seemed to be causing her greater discomfort than Little Dickon had done.

Seb and Thaddeus took their ale cups down the passage, back to the workshop. Thaddeus required to hear the story yet again, delaying as long as possible the moment when he would have to look upon the corpse. He had no stomach for such things, especially when the deceased was a child. Sorting out a Saturday night tavern brawl, apprehending thieves and arresting adulterers: these duties he was content to carry out. Dead bodies, however, were another matter entirely and not at all a dish to his taste – worse yet that it was a youngster.

Seb opened the door to the storeroom. A faint but definite miasma of death wafted out. He waved away an unholy congregation of flies and turned back the sheet, preparatory to revealing the body. He glanced up at the beadle who was steadfastly gazing into his ale.

'You see the wound here?' Seb said. 'Observe its condition: severely inflamed, yet here… 'tis beginning to knit together. The injury be by no means inflicted as recently as last eve. 'Tis three or four days old at least, to judge by others Master Fyssher has caused me to examine in the past, though I be no expert.'

'Indeed. I believe it is as you say, but the surgeon must confirm,' Thaddeus mumbled, eyes averted, and gulped down the rest of his ale. Once Seb had replaced the sheet and closed the door, the beadle sighed and felt able to deal with business as he ought. 'I'll send for Surgeon Dagvyle. He'll have to attend my official summons, no matter what other business he may have. Then I'll arrange for the cart and have Master Appleyard prepare the parish coffin when he's done with the archers – a busy Lord's Day for him. We'll have it all done seemly and take it, er, him, to St Michael's. 'Tis a pity we have no name for his marker, but the Lord God will know His own, no doubt… if he was baptised a Christian, of course.' Both men crossed themselves. 'A pauper's burial, then…'

'Nay, Thaddeus, it will be done seemly, as you say. I'll pay for the obsequies. He died 'neath my roof; 'tis the least I can do. And I shall make every effort to learn his name and find his family. I owe the poor child that… and it will ease my conscience that I did not aid and comfort him in his pain.'

'You say you didn't know he was here, so you're not at fault… unless you lie?'

'Every word be true, I swear upon my soul, yet such a death lies heavy upon my spirit, though I be not to blame for it. To die alone so young...'

'Aye. Well, it can't be helped now. I'll be on my way; put matters in hand. My thanks for a splendid dinner, if you will give my compliments to Mistress Foxley? I hope she will be much improved after her rest.'

'I shall pass on your kind words to her. Thank you for your attentions this day, Thaddeus. I know not what we could have done without you, since no one else was willing nor available. I be most grateful for your time, given up upon the Sabbath. God give you good day, Beadle Turner.'

With Master Turner's departure, Seb returned to the kitchen.

'Surgeon Dagvyle will be coming by as soon as may be,' he said. 'If you would look out for him, please? And then Emily's father will be bringing the parish coffin along. In the meantime, I shall take Little Dickon and Gawain out for some sweet fresh air. I be in need as much as they, I confess. It has been a sorry day's work thus far.'

'Don't let Em hear you say that word – work – on the Lord's Day.' Rose smiled at him. 'Off with you; you deserve some respite. I'll deal with the surgeon and Master Appleyard if they come before you get back. And Seb... fear not: all will be well.'

His grey eyes, darkened with anxiety, met hers, soft and bright. He felt the burden upon his heart ease a little.

'Aye. You be correct, lass, no doubt. As you say: all will be well.'

## The Hart's Horn Tavern

Seb walked out of Newgate, hailing the gatekeeper who knew him well. At least the gossips and goose-necked idlers were gone from his door when he left, tired of waiting for juicy snippets of news and wanting their dinners, no doubt. With Dickon on his shoulder, he turned up the lane, passing the Hart's Horn where Mistress Fletcher stood upon her well-swept doorstep. He waved and encouraged Little Dickon to do the same. Mistress Fletcher waved back and called them over.

'Come in, Master Foxley, I have news. And an almond wafer for the little one. I must tell you: you will recall Sir Robert Percy – a good friend of yours and an eager patron of this establishment – well, he's back in London. Is that not marvellous news? I shall have to do extra baking on the morrow. You know what a good appetite Sir Robert has. Did you know he was here with Lord Richard?'

'I heard a rumour,' Seb admitted, not wishing to spoil Mistress Fletcher's merry tidings by saying he had already seen the red-headed knight at Crosby Place and spoken with Duke Richard – aye, and espied Lord Lovell, unfortunately. The dark lord also enjoyed the food here at the Hart's Horn; he would have a care to see their paths did not cross.

'And just see what I have found... a wafer for the little one, if he may have it?' The good woman lay the delicacy upon a spotless napkin on the board nearest the door. A few customers were taking a late dinner of bread and pottage, over by the hearth, but they seemed content and Mistress Fletcher lingered. 'Shall you take ale, Sebastian?'

'Why not, indeed. I shall be glad to.'

She made haste to serve him, bringing two cups, and sat upon the stool opposite him, across the board. Settled on his father's knee, little Dickon was sucking on the wafer, dribbling crumbs and making happy noises. Gawain sat watching, hopeful of a fallen titbit or two. Seb sipped his ale: renowned as the best in the city. It tasted good and he relished it, clean-tasting and fresh upon his tongue.

''Tis fine ale, mistress.'

'I know. I work hard to keep my reputation. But what of your news?'

'My news?'

'Don't be coy with me, Sebastian; we've been friends for too long. A dead body in your workshop, so they say. Now tell me the truth of it.'

Reluctant to think upon a matter he had hoped to put from his mind, however briefly, Seb related the barest facts, knowing Mistress Fletcher would not let him leave until he had done so. Some of her customers moved their stools closer, inch by inch, wanting to learn of other folks' misfortunes.

'What a turn of events! And you say you never saw the lad before.'

'Nay, mistress, leastwise, not as I recall and his colouring was quite distinctive. I be certain, I should remember him if I had.'

'You drew his likeness then.'

'Aye but I have left it at home.'

'But you mentioned his hair was white.'

'As this napkin afore Dickon made a mess of it.'

'There was a family over Holbourne way had children with pale hair and skin so like alabaster, they looked unreal except for their blue eyes. I know not if they bide there still. 'Tis some while since I saw them last. Could the lad in your workshop be one of them?'

'I cannot say, but if you know the family's name? Their house, maybe?' Seb sounded eager, anticipating a possible clue but Mistress Fletcher shook her head.

'Not sure I ever knew their name. They might have moved away. And they looked so frail, a gust of wind could have blown those children into the grave. No, Sebastian, I'm sorry; I can't help you. But if you bring your drawing…'

'Aye, I shall. My thanks for the ale.' He wiped Dickon's mouth and fingers on the napkin, then reached for his purse.

Mistress Fletcher stilled his hand and gestured to the taproom.

'No payment needed. Your story has brought in custom enough, as you see.'

Seb frowned at the crowd that had gathered, unnoticed, whilst he recounted the tale. He nodded a farewell, hoisted

Dickon onto his shoulder and continued on his walk to Smithfield, intent upon reaching the Horse Pool. There, in his most favoured place, 'neath the great oak, he could have leisure to think whilst Gawain chased squirrels and Dickon watched the ducks.

## The Horse Pool, Smithfield

Buds on the oak tree were swelling, pregnant with new leaves. The hazel and quickthorn bushes, impatient to begin the spring, had already burst forth with bright, verdant foliage. Amongst the grass at his feet, nosegays of pale primroses nestled and violets hid their royal purple attire beneath heart-shaped leaves, as if modesty had triumphed over imperial splendour. There were no squirrels this day; no red-brush tails for Gawain to pursue. Mayhap, the little creatures had seen him coming. No matter. He chased the butterflies instead – the first of the year, the colour of brimstone in an apothecary's pot.

As they sat on the grass, Little Dickon pointed and waved at the ducks, gurgling with delight as two emerald-headed males argued, splashing silver droplets, quacking as they fought for the attentions of the drab brown female, like a poor wench at a lordlings' feast.

'Aye, and see there,' Seb said, attempting to persuade the little lad to look further out, across the water, 'Swans. Are they not majestic birds? So elegant. They belong to the king himself, as seems only fitting for such splendid creatures.' Seb laughed at his own foolish talk, seeing Dickon was far more interested in a tiny spider that crawled along a blade of grass, watching it intently, following its endeavours until it disappeared in a clump of primroses. 'We could pick a posy for your Mam. That will surely cheer her.' Seb showed Dickon how to pick the stem as low to the base as possible but he preferred to pull off the petals and eat them. Primrose petals were edible but when Dickon found a worm that seemed destined for the same treatment, Seb swept him up in his arms and strolled further along the edge of the pool.

'Nay, little man, leave the worms for the birds. You shall have your fill of bread, milk and honey at home.'

Smooth as glass now the storm winds were gone, the quiet water reflected the clouds, drifting lazily, like scholars reluctant to attend their lessons. A red kite quartered the sky, searching for a meal. Then there were two of them, wheeling and diving, dancing on the air; aerial lovers teasing. Aye, spring was the season for love indeed – unless your name was Seb Foxley, in which case, quarrels and upbraidings were your lot in life. No wonder he sighed all the while.

Little Dickon was distinctly wet against Seb's arm, a damp patch appearing on his father's sleeve and spreading. Time to return home. Seb called to Gawain, who was investigating intriguing scents along the hedgerow.

As they returned to the city, Seb trudged beneath the arch at Newgate, heavy-footed. The prospect of Emily's displeasure these days, at the least of faults, did not encourage eagerness or haste. The dog was no keener than his master; his wagging tail stilled.

'A gift for your beloved, eh?' the gatekeeper said, nodding at the wilting primroses in Seb's free hand. 'Or a peace offering, more like.' He grinned and chortled, ending on a wheezy cough. He thumped his chest with his fist. 'Damned phlegmy humours'll do for me one o' these days.'

'Try horehound,' Seb suggested. 'My goodwife swears by it.'

'Good with remedies, is she?'

'Aye. She serves us well with her knowledge of herbs and simples. Drop by, if you will. We bide in Paternoster Row, 'neath the new sign of the fox. You cannot miss it.'

'Maybe I will.'

# The Foxley House

'Did you enjoy your walk?' Rose asked Seb as he entered the kitchen. Gawain, at his heel, made straight for his water bowl and lapped noisily.

'Aye. We all did, did we not, little man? I fear he be in need of a dry tailclout. Do you have a small pot for these flowers, please? I hope they may cheer Em.'

'That's a kindly thought, Seb... Oh! Remove your boots, for pity's sake. She will have apoplexy if she sees the mud you've brought in.'

'Mm.'

The flagstones were strewn with lumps of mud, but it was already too late to mend the situation as Emily came down the stairs at that moment.

'So! You've returned at last.' She stood, hands on hips, upon the third stair. 'Gracing us with your lordship's presence *after* I've had to deal with that disgusting corpse. Surgeon Dagvyle was most angered that you weren't here. I had to appease his wrath and then get that thing sent off to St Michael's while you – by the stink of you – sat swilling ale in some tavern or other all afternoon, introducing *my* child to the sin of drunkenness at such an early age. What kind of father does that? No decent, moral parent for certain. Ahh! And just look to my floor! You thoughtless, inconsiderate wretch. Here I am, indisposed, and you expect me to scrub the kitchen, cleaning up after you, even on the Lord's Day. St Mary, give me strength.'

'I brought you primroses...'

'What do I care for a few useless weeds? Get out of my sight and take your filthy boots with you. And your dog with his great muddy paws.'

'But that is all untrue, Em,' Adam said, coming from the workshop to wash his hands and overhearing her tirade. 'You remained abed whilst the surgeon was here and Rose served him ale and a kindly smile to temper his humour. Whatever you overheard, it was not *wrath,* as you say. It seems the fellow was somewhat put out that Seb had usurped his role and deduced the facts correctly. And then Rose and I assisted your father with the poor lad's body. You did naught to aid us; never so much as came to offer him greeting or a sip of ale. Don't blame Seb.'

'I'm unwell, Adam Armitage. And keep your nose out of matters that don't concern you.'

'They do concern me. Seb is my dear relative and I would have this house – *his* house – a place of harmony, where we can all live peaceably together. You're a shrew, Emily, not a wife. Seb is a saint to put up with you.'

'How dare you speak to me in this manner? Who are you to defend that idle, useless, stupid creature that calls himself a husband?'

The 'stupid creature' left the kitchen, dropping more mud, hating arguments and not wanting to hear the slanders heaped upon him. He was tired of his wife's ill-tempered ranting, heart-sick at what she thought and said of him. Seb was no hero but he did his best, yet that was never enough to please Em. He sat on the up-turned bucket behind the pigsty, his head in his hands.

How long he sat there, he did not know but dusk was gathering when Adam disturbed him from his melancholy brooding.

'I apologise, Seb. I made things worse, did I not? I just couldn't stomach listening to her any longer, treating you worse than a worm or something she trod in at the Shambles. It's not right. A wife must respect her husband. She's a harpy, Seb, and I couldn't put up with her as you do. Here, share my slice of pie. 'Tis all they had left at the Panyer Inn that looked the least bit edible.' Adam sat on the old tree stump and offered Seb a lump of pastry. It was burnt at one end and raw at the other with a grey filling oozing between.

Seb declined the offer.

'You went to the Panyer? Why?'

'What do you suppose? Em threw me out: no supper and no bed. Oh, and the same applies to you, I fear, in your case, *forever*. Or at least until tomorrow. You know how she changes like the weather.'

'Aye. Jude used to call her the Moody Mare.' Seb looked shocked by his own admission and shook his head. 'I should not have spoken thus. I pray you, forget my words, Adam. I do Em a grave discourtesy.'

'She does as much to you every time she speaks to you.' Adam inspected what remained of his supper. 'This pie is horrible.' He lobbed it at the ivy-cloaked privy, disturbing the sparrows that were settling to roost in the evergreens. 'You're her husband. As I said before: she should give you due respect as your wife.'

'Mayhap, I have not earned that respect.'

'Seb, you're a bloody saint where Em is concerned; anyone else – me included – would have given her a sound beating long since.'

'I cannot. I abhor such actions... cruelty of any kind. If only you knew what it was like to be a crippled child, you would never cause hurt to any. Do not tell me she deserves punishment, that I have the right to chastise her. It makes no difference. If I inflicted pain, it would hurt me far more than it would hurt her. And what good would it do? Do wives... children... apprentices.., any of them truly mend their ways after a sound beating? I think not.'

'So what will you do? Sit silent and let her abuse you?'

Seb made no answer.

'No matter,' Adam said at length, realising it had become dark and a chill in the air made him shiver. 'I suppose you'll be sharing my chamber again this night.'

'But Em forbade...'

'It's your damned house, Seb. Assert your rights as owner of the place, at least.'

'Aye. You be correct on that account, Adam. I refuse to share the pig's bed or Gawain's kennel.'

'Good man.' Adam clapped him on the shoulder. 'We'll show the Moody Mare who rules under this roof.'

'She does,' Seb said and they were both laughing as they climbed the outside stairs to Adam's bedchamber.

# Chapter 3

## Monday morn, the fifth day of April
## Southwark

THE SIGN of The Mermaid squeaked upon its pole in the sickly breeze off the Thames. The tall man pushed open the door of the tavern. Once painted blue, the door was warped somewhat and required a shove from his boot to get it open. He pushed the lad over the threshold.

'Got one for yer, Bessie. Just wot his lordship wants, I reckon. Better than the uvver one.'

An equally tall woman, scraggy and moth-eaten as an alley cat, came out of the gloom and stood, arms folded across her flat chest, looking the new lad up and down with a critical eye, hard as agate. There seemed to be a vague family likeness betwixt the pair, although the woman was most certainly the more frightening of the two.

'Aye. I suppose he'll do, Cain.'

'My name's Will,' the lad spoke up. 'Will Tha...'

A hefty swipe caught him across the mouth and he fell down.

'Nobody spoke to you. Keep quiet.'

'Hey! Easy, Bess. Don't damage the merchandise,' the man, Cain, said, holding up his hand to keep the woman from lashing out a second time.

'Stay out of this, brother.' She pushed the man aside. 'The little toad needs to learn his place from the start.' She gripped the lad's shoulder, her nails digging in. 'You listen here: I don't care what you was called before. You're mine now, 'til I say otherwise.'

'I want to go home. I'm supposed to be at Paul's School. The master, Dr Hawthorn, will beat me if I'm late for lessons.' The child's complaint earned him a kick on the shin.

'Shut your noise. You want feeding, you do as I tell you. Now get them clothes off yer back and let's see what we can offer his lordship. Fair curls an' blue eyes, he said, so you'll suit, I suppose. Bit skinny though… there's more flesh on a church mouse than you.' She pinched the skin at the top of his arm betwixt her fingers.

'Ow! I'll tell Mam what you did, you smelly old cow.'

'Cain! Bring the birch rod. This one needs to learn his manners, else he's no use to us. No lord will pay for a filthy mouth like his, so you'll have to beat some courtesy into him, Cain. See to it but be sure it doesn't show too much. I have business to attend to.' Bessie moved towards the door but turned to look back. 'And tell Cherry-lips to clean herself up a bit. She looks like a midden heap and Sir Giles has asked for her especially, for after dinner. I don't know why he always chooses her; she's old enough to be his mother. Peaches or Katerina would be more lovesome, I should've thought, but there's no accounting for a man's prick-fancies, is there? Like this string o' pork chittlins.' Bess gave the lad a hard look as he stood there shivering, his bag of school books at his feet. 'Who'd want him? But they say the customer's always right, so why should I wonder? As I said, beat him so it don't show, Cain, then dress him in that velvet stuff. I'll leave you to it. And you can sell them books; he won't be needing them anymore.' She wagged her finger at the lad. 'And don't you cause us no grief, you hear me?'

The lad gave a sullen nod, but eyed the door hopefully as the woman went out into the street.

'Don't even think about it,' the man said, seeming to read

the lad's mind. 'Bessie'll have yer back here afore yer reach the Bridge and tell me to give yer anuvver thrashin'. Yer want that? No? I reckon not then.'

'Did you mean what you said about Mam?' The lad felt braver now, seeing Cain was putting him into a doublet of worn velvet without having administered the punishment.

'What about her?' Cain began lacing the points, pulling the garment closed over the lad's own shirt, which was of fair quality and clean – unlike the doublet. Unfortunately, the garment was also over large and did not look as well as it might, if it had fitted more nearly.

'You said she'd be for worm-fodder if…'

'Forget about her. Bessie's yer Mam now.'

'But I hate her. I want to go home.'

'I think the doublet might need a few stitches, as will yer lips, if Bessie hears yer say such things. Keep silent and do as yer told; that's my advice to yer. Life here ain't so bad and, if I knows anythin', Peaches'll spoil an' pet yer like a lap dog an' Claudette – she's French – will feed yer up on sweetmeats. Katerina'll weep with envy over yer golden curls and Magdalene'll call yer her babe.'

'I'm nobody's babe. I'm ten years, eleven this summer coming. Even Mam has a new babe to fuss and coddle. I don't need it no more.'

Cain stepped back to admire his handiwork, see whether the lad would pass scrutiny under Bessie's sharp eye. He scratched at his lank hair that might have been fair if it ever saw soap and water.

'Yer'll do,' he said with a shrug and a sniff. 'Now let's see wot's in yer bag… good leather… might fetch a few pence. Books. No use to us but a stationer might take 'em.' He piled three books on the floor, uncaring of their condition. 'And wot's this? A fine, fancy piece, these rosary beads. Where did yer snaffle them from, eh?'

'I didn't snaffle them. They were my grandmother's, left to

me in her will. Please… don't sell them; let me keep them…'

Cain examined the beads of coral. The ivory crucifix that dangled from the end was well carved but looked to have suffered damage, as if it had been chewed. This would spoil its worth, though the beads were good enough to fetch a decent price alone. Seeing the lad's pleading look and tear-brimmed eyes, he relented, pity overcoming his better judgement.

'Aye, well, I s'pose yer can. Jus' don't let Bessie see 'em or we'll both be in trouble.'

'Thank you, Master Cain. I'll keep them safe. When can I go home?'

# The Foxley House

It was as though naught had come to pass last eve: Emily did not speak of it and, apart from a baleful look or two cast at Adam, she served the herb pottage and bread with good grace to both him and Seb. For which Seb was immensely grateful and relieved. Besides, he was hungry, having gone supperless to bed.

'Your feet and ankles, Em: be they improved this morn?' Seb asked, wiping the bowl clean of pottage with a piece of fresh-baked bread. 'That was delicious, my sweeting. I would have more, please, if it be to spare?'

Adam also held out his empty bowl, as did Jack, of course.

'None for you, you greedy hog,' Emily said, taking Jack's bowl from his grasp and putting it in the tub to be washed when the water boiled. 'You'll only outgrow yet another pair of boots. Now be on your way, else you'll be late for work and my father will have another cause to complain about you.'

'Master Appleyard don't complain 'bout me. I works hard, don't I? He let me do me first bit o' turnin' on the lave las' week an' it came out fine, didn't it? Two more legs an' I'll've made a stool. He says I'm good wiv me hands, don't he?'

'Out! And no more back-answering or you'll feel my broom,' Emily said, although the threat lacked substance; she sounded too weary to make the effort.

'The correct word be "lathe", Jack,' Seb said betwixt mouthfuls.

''S'wot I said, i'n'it?' And with a last, longing glance at the pottage pot – in which there remained more than enough for another helping – Jack slouched out of the kitchen door. He could be heard, scuffing stones in the yard, still dawdling.

'Be on your way!' Emily yelled at him from the back step.

'I'm goin', ain't I?' He went off, muttering.

Emily was sure she heard him say something like 'bloody woman' as he went out of the gate. She would box his ears come dinnertime – if she could reach (he was grown so tall these days); if she could be bothered. She took a deep breath.

'Tom. Kate. Workshop. Now,' Adam said, thinking Emily was preparing to administer another scolding to someone; probably Seb. He was mistaken, this once.

'I have to go out,' she said, easing onto the vacated bench, still warm from Tom's backside. 'I have those new skeins of silk to deliver to Beatrice and Peronelle and the new woman in Poultry. I can't manage the basket and little Dickon, so you'll all have to give eye to him.'

Seb looked up, knowing she meant *he* would have to care for their son. It being Monday, Rose and Nessie were already up to their elbows in wet linen clouts, soaking sheets, scrubbing at stains, washing and rinsing endless yards of cloth, dripping puddles of lye and water out in the yard. As if he did not have work of his own to do; a business to run. Ah, well, so be it. Since Rose was fully occupied, he had been intending to serve in the shop this morn. Little Dickon's presence was inclined to deter male customers but often encouraged women to stop by. The trouble was, they were mostly more interested in chatting than buying books but you could never tell. He set his empty bowl aside, wiped his fingers on his napkin and stood to lift Dickon from his special chair. Crafted by Stephen Appleyard – a besotted grandfather, if ever there was one – it was high enough that Dickon could sit at the board, of a height with everyone else, with the bars around to keep him from falling. An ingenious device, Seb had always thought.

'Come, little man. You can aid Papa in the shop; persuade reluctant customers with your angelic smile, even as you threaten to douse them in dribble. You too, Gawain. Come away from under your mistress's feet.'

Her kitchen was blessedly empty. She could hear Rose and Nessie laughing over the washing outside but in here was peace at last and Emily closed her eyes. The thought of walking across the city, as far as Poultry and back, seemed such a daunting prospect. She had never felt so tired. When she had been great with child before, she had not been so weary and out of sorts, even at the very end. And there were still five weeks at least – maybe more – until she could be rid of this burden. It was hard to imagine how she was going to manage, trying to do everything as she ought when all she wanted was to rest abed and sleep.

But even that was difficult. However she lay, she was uncomfortable; every bone ached. And, of course, there was no sympathy to be had from that wretch of a husband of hers; the useless creature, so enamoured of his damned precious manuscripts, he thought of naught else. He'd be more concerned for her if she were a ruled sheet of parchment. And she – may sweet St Mary aid her – was chained to him for life. But what could she do about it? Just suffer and make the best of it, she supposed. For a moment or two, lovesome memories of Gabriel Widowson brought a wan smile to her down-turned lips – what a fine man was he. All a woman could wish for in a lover, except that he was far away, sailing the Seven Seas. Then the memories were gone, driven away by a sudden spasm of pain. She stood slowly, easing her back, put on her cloak, took up her basket and went out into the soft April sunshine.


Peronelle's house was hard by St Peter's in Cheap. It was small but in good order, an asset for a young widow. Pen kept the place spotless: neither menfolk nor children to make a mess of her kitchen, Emily thought. The door stood open and Emily tapped upon it to announce herself and stepped within.

'Pen! Are you here?'

'One moment, Em. Help yourself to ale.' Pen's voice sounded muffled but she soon appeared, straightening her widow's wimple. 'I'll be glad when I don't have to wear this any longer. My year of mourning be at an end upon the feast of St George. My husband was a good soul but a year in mourning for him seems far too long when we were wed but four months. I've grieved for his loss, as I should, but I'd known him less than a year. We were not close.'

'But you have this house to compensate you,' Em said, pulling her skirts as low as they would go, to hide the fact that she'd kicked off her shoes. 'You'll have every eager bachelor at your door, wanting to share your widow's dower.'

'That isn't going to happen.' Pen put a fresh log upon the fire, stoking the flame to a blaze.

'Why? You haven't done anything so foolish as becoming a vowess, have you, Pen?'

'A vowess? What? And condemn myself to wearing a wimple forever? Turning every likely man away? No, Em. What I have done is – and you mustn't tell a soul until after St George's day – I've already accepted a proposal of marriage. Is that not the best thing? Oh, I'm so happy, Em, I could dance the whole length of Cheapside. And this time, my husband will not be some creaking greybeard but a lusty swain who'll take me in his strong arms and kiss me and...'

'Aye, well, my congratulations to you both,' Em said, attempting a semblance of enthusiasm. 'And who is this lusty swain? Are you allowed to tell?'

'I haven't told anyone, as yet, and I daren't tell Beattie, else the whole of London will know by suppertime, but… well… I hope you won't be put out, Em…'

'Just tell me. I swear I'll not be put out in the slightest degree, whoever he is.'

'Well, 'tis Bennett Hepton, the fishmonger; he has asked me to marry him. I know he held a candle for you, once upon a time, Em, but you always loved your dear Seb better… I've envied you your sweet, gentle husband all this while and now I shall have one of mine own, to cherish me. I hope I am as fortunate as you in my choice.'

'Fortunate? Mm.'


Having instructed Pen and left her a half dozen skeins of new silk to be tablet-woven into colourful braided edging for an altar cloth – ordered by a wealthy parishioner of St Margaret's, Lothbury – Emily left her friend joyously contemplating wedlock. She could but pray that Pen would not be disappointed in marriage a second time – she deserved better. Mayhap, Bennett Hepton would prove to be a good husband but there was never any certainty, as Emily had found to her cost.

Across the way, by Cheap Cross, Emily knocked upon Beattie's door.

'Come you in!' a woman's voice called from inside.

Unlike Pen's spotless house, Beattie's was untidy and unswept. Nonetheless, it somehow gave the impression of happy chaos: dishes awaited washing, babe's tailclouts festooned every hook, rafter and stool. Half-chopped pot herbs were piled on the board and dough, left to prove and rise, sat in a floury heap in the kneading trough. In the midst of all, Beattie sat, surrounded by her uncompleted chores, nursing her babe, seemingly unconcerned about her household duties. Annie was three months of age now and suckled noisily at her mother's breast.

'Find a seat, Em,' Beattie said, waving a hand at the disarray as if, by some miracle, the gesture might restore everything to its place. 'Shift Harry's old boots off that bench and rest. You look worn. I've got mead upon the shelf there: that will lift your spirits and give you strength for the day. Annie's almost done here and then we can talk.'

Beattie had just put her tiny daughter down to sleep in her woven basket when there came another knock at the door. Beattie frowned with impatience.

'Oh, what now? Who can that be?

She opened the door. A tousled lad with a freckled nose stood there in his scholar's garb. Beattie's frown deepened.

'Simon? What's amiss? What has Will done now?'

'Naught, Mistress Thatcher, that I know of. Doctor Hawthorn sent me to enquire if Will is sick. We're supposed to be making the sung responses – him and me – at the Passiontide services. If he's sick, we can't practise and master will have to replace him.'

'Sick? Will's not sick. I sent him to school as usual this morn. If that young scamp is skipping school after all the money it's costing me and Harry to pay for his learning, he's going to feel more than sorry for it, come dinnertime. Bread and water is all he'll get and his father's belt on his backside. Harry will be madder than a rabid cur when he hears of this. Tell me, Simon – and be honest now – has Will missed school otherwise?'

'No, mistress, never. Will likes school. He's the best pupil, Doctor Hawthorn says, sometimes at least.'

'Do you speak true, Simon? I don't want you defending him forwhy he's your friend.'

''Tis God's own truth, Mistress Thatcher. Will has only missed school that time when he had the measles and the day he broked his arm and it had to be splinted and never else since then, I swear.'

'You're too young to swear, Simon Hutchinson. Just tell the masters that... er... he's running an errand for me up

Houndsditch way and will be there after dinner.'

'Aye, mistress, I'll do that.'

Beattie closed the door on the lad and turned her attention to Emily, pouring mead for them both.

'What do you make of that, Em? What's that son of mine about, eh? When I get a hold of him… well, I don't know… What would you do, Em?'

'Take my broom to him, that's what. I wouldn't leave the punishment to Seb, that's for certain. He'd give him a few words of courteous advice and pat him on the head.' Emily sipped her mead. It was good and strong, just the restorative she needed.

'Mind you, it's not like my Will to be so disobedient. He knows how we scrimp and save to afford the fees. We reckon he'll make a lawyer someday and won't have to work his hands to the bone like we do. Then, God willing, he'll make a good marriage to a lass with a decent dowry… keep us in our old age.'

'You have everything planned then, Beattie.'

'Aye, but it'll all be for naught if he skips school, the young rascal. I wonder where he is and what mischief he's in to? It doesn't bear thinking on.'

# The Foxley House

Seb was in the shop, straightening a pile of pamphlets one-handed whilst balancing little Dickon on his hip with the other. Two customers had stopped by: one to browse, who had left without buying so much as a sheet of paper. Although Seb had shown him the drawing of the poor lad who had died in the workshop, the fellow had shrugged and said he'd never seen such a one. It was worth trying, Seb thought.

The other customer enquired as to the price of a book, concerning the game and rules of chess, which would obviously over-stretch his purse, as Seb judged by the tattered hose and down-at-heel boots he wore. But you could never be certain these days, when beggars bought from fripperers the cast-off attire of wealthy merchants, yet knights arrived in town so mud-bespattered they looked like vagabonds. So Seb gave the fellow a courteous greeting. He seemed much taken with the book, turning the pages with care and commenting on the images which Seb had drawn and young Kate had coloured in with red and blue inks, creating a bold effect.

''Tis a handsome volume,' the fellow mused, smoothing his hand across the tooled leather binding. 'I want it as a gift for my brother's coming of age but I fear 'tis somewhat too grand for his taste. Do you have something a little cheaper, perhaps?'

'Well, master, we do have a clothbound version of the same,' Seb said, shifting Dickon to the other hip so that he might reach up to a high shelf. It was difficult to manage without climbing upon a stool and Seb would not chance such an action with his son in his arms. He brushed away a cobweb. ''Tis not coloured but the drawings be much the same, as you see...' Seb turned back to the customer, offering him the alternative copy but the customer was gone. And so was the more expensive book. Seb hastened to the shop door and looked out. Paternoster Row was crowded as usual but there was no sign of the thief. If Jack still worked for him, he could have pursued the wretch but Seb was not a man for running, encumbered with an infant or not.

He sighed, sorry at the loss of so much work for no gain. But then he groaned, thinking what Emily would say when she learned of the cunning theft. The thievery was so blatant, with him right there beside the customer; Em would blame him, and rightly so, for their loss of income. But then, mayhap, discretion being the better part of valour, as they say: it would be safer to say naught of the incident to Emily. Seb almost succeeded in convincing himself that, in her present condition, it was best not to impart to her such tidings for her health's sake but, in truth, 'twas all for his own benefit. What a coward was he at the thought of facing his wife's wrath?

Yet matters looked up later in the morning, just as Emily returned from her errands and Seb had settled Dickon in his cradle. Mistress Caldicott arrived in the shop.

'God give you good day, mistress,' Seb said, smiling a welcome. 'Emily be resting in the parlour, if you wished to see her?'

'No, Master Foxley, I would not disturb your goodwife's rest. Rather, I have a commission for you.'

'Then may it please you to sit?' Seb put a cushioned stool for his customer and took up his silverpoint and paper to note the order. 'Oh, afore we begin, mistress, may I trouble you to look at this drawing? 'Tis of the lad who died here, during the storm a few nights since. Do you recognise him?'

'So the rumours were true then.'

'You heard of it?'

'All London has heard.' She glanced at the image and shook her head. 'And no, I've never seen him before.'

'Ah, well. I be asking everyone. Someone must know of him. My thanks, mistress, for taking the time to look. Now, what task would you have me undertake?'

Mary Caldicott took out a most battered volume from her basket and handed it to Seb. It was in a poor state, indeed. He saw that the spine was broken and pages had come loose from the binding, their edges frayed and dog-eared. Notes and annotations had been scribbled in the margins and throughout the text. It was an astrological and medical manual and Seb shuddered to think how it had been used, recognising the imprint of fingers on some of the surgical diagrams. Could they be marks of blood?

'Surely, your goodman can trim the pages and rebind it?'

'Aye, so he could but I want the whole thing recopied – notes and all – with illuminated initials. My brother Martin – a, er, barber-surgeon over by Bucklersbury – makes use of it so often but it's no longer fit for purpose. I would have a new copy made exactly, as a gift for him.'

'Will he not miss having it to hand?'

'Aye, soon enough, which is why the task must be done as swiftly as maybe. How long will it take you to complete?'

Seb frowned at the pages. It was difficult to decipher some of the scribbled additions and the text itself contained many unfamiliar terms, some in Latin and a few that might even be in Greek. Given a month or two to study it in detail, it could be done but to hasten the work would lead to errors in the transcription of so difficult a text and accuracy mattered. Had it been a book of poetry, what harm if a word was wrong? But in the case of such a text as this, a mistake in copying might cost a patient his life.

'The cost will be twenty pence for each gathering, whether parchment or paper; gold and large painted initials be charged at fourpence each; half-page images at sixpence and full-page ones at twelve pence. I shall itemise the reckoning for you as I work through the text but I fear it will cost you as much as five-and-thirty shillings, mistress, afore ever we consider the binding... But then again, your husband could do that; save you a few shillings.'

'I most certainly will not pay so much. I shall pay you five-and-twenty and call it a contract. And you have three weeks to complete it.'

'I fear, that be too soon, Mistress Caldicott. 'Tis no easy text to work with. With the binding, forty shillings at least would be...'

'Five-and-twenty or I take my commission elsewhere. It's your choice, Master Foxley.'

Thoughts raced through Seb's head: such a difficult book; so little time allowed; Em's anger if he turned away a commission – a good one, even if it was somewhat under-priced.

'I'll do it,' he said. 'It will be finished come May Day.'

'That is more than three weeks hence,' she argued.

'But less than four. 'Tis my best offer.'

'Done! And not a word of this is to reach my brother's ears. Understand?'

'Aye. Now, did you want the gatherings of parchment or paper?'

'Which lasts the longest?'

When all the details of the commission were noted down, Mistress Caldicott left the shop. Seb held the sorry-looking book in his hand and sighed. He would have to begin immediately, trying to comprehend the nigh-illegible handwriting and the customer wanted the annotations incorporated within the text, to give a more ordered appearance to the whole. As soon as he examined the first notes, he realised that was not so easily accomplished since it was hard to tell precisely where they should be inserted to make sense. The scribbler had not always indicated to which phrase or other each note applied and, not being a medical man, Seb was unsure whether his understanding was sufficient to decide correctly.

With Rose now serving customers, Seb took the book into the workshop. He put it upon his desk and sat down, puffing out his cheeks.

'What's amiss, Seb?' Adam looked up from his work, reshaping his quill with a couple of dextrous strokes of his penknife.

'The commission from hell, I fear. We have 'til May Day to copy this astrological text – 'tis so annotated and battered, 'tis a nightmare. I can barely make sense of it.'

'Then I hope you charged the customer a handsome price?'

'It could have been more but Mistress Caldicott drives a hard bargain.'

'She got the better of your soft heart, eh, Seb? You ought to have called me; I'd have got a fair price out of her. How much did you agree?'

'Five-and-twenty shillings.'

'That's all?'

'Aye, and do not tell me Emily will scold me, for I know she will. And 'tis not the morning's sole disaster. You recall the leather-bound copy of the book concerning the play of chess?'

Adam nodded.

'Did you sell that for a song, also?'

'Worse. I did not get so much as a bent farthing for it. It was stolen from 'neath my very nose by a devilish knave. I should have pursued the wretch...'

'Yet again, you did not call me or Tom. We would have caught him and got the book back and given him a hiding he'd not forget.'

'He was long gone, swift-heeled as a deer.'

'Even so. Now, what of this book is of such difficulty?'

Seb passed the astrological book to Adam. The journeyman's face screwed up in puzzlement as he squinted at the pages.

''Tis all Greek to me, Seb.'

'Aye, some of it seems to be of that tongue.'

'I meant it as a jest. Are there truly bits of Greek here?'

'I believe so. I have no comprehension of how such words should be translated, so in Greek they must remain and the strange letter shapes simply copied as accurately as I may do them. As I said: 'tis a nightmare.'


Dinner was once more of Lenten fare: shellfish in saffron sauce. The oysters, mussels and cockles were plump and juicy but everyone was weary of saffron at every meal. An expensive spice it may have been but too much of any luxury palls eventually. But no one commented, knowing Emily would eat naught that did not come with a saffron flavouring. Saffron was said to be the spice of jollity but Emily wore an expression of abject gloom.

'How went your morning, Em?' Seb enquired brightly, attempting to lighten her mood by expressing an interest in her affairs.

'Poultry was too far for me,' Em said, pushing her platter aside, the meal hardly touched. 'That new out-worker had better be worth my efforts, walking all that way. She seems competent enough, thorough but slow. She'll have to work faster…' Emily paused, wincing at a sudden spike of pain. Seb saw it; her discomfort written upon her face.

'Why not rest this afternoon, sweetheart. Take a nap.'

'You think I have naught else to do? I have a business to run, even if you don't bother overmuch with yours.'

'On the contrary, we have a new commission.'

'Oh? Well, I trust it's more lucrative than the last.' She referred to an order for five songbooks for St Paul's School. Seeing he was a chorister there, Seb had felt obliged to give the cathedral a special concession: five hefty, beautiful books for the price of four. Emily had had much to say upon the matter since: not one word of it approving.

Rose and Nessie were about to serve almond fritters and honeyed almond-milk custard to follow the shellfish when Beatrice Thatcher burst through the kitchen door, uninvited, screaming babe in arms, apron flying. Her cap was all awry and she wore neither cloak nor hood, despite the drizzle of an April shower.

'Oh, Em!' she cried, 'What am I to do? Our Will hasn't come home for his dinner. Where can he be? He never misses a meal. As fine a trencherman as any. Something's happened to him, I know. What shall I do?'

''Tis not so late, Beattie,' Emily said calmly, 'He may be home by now, wondering where you are; why you're not there to see him dine. Go home, Beattie. I'm sure you worry to no purpose. Will is safe and well but tardy. You'll see.'

'You think so?'

'Aye. Compose yourself, woman; you are a shambles. Here, borrow my cloak against the rain and be sure you return it later.'

'Em be correct most likely, Beatrice,' Seb added, rising from the table to help her arrange the cloak to keep the bawling infant dry as well as herself. 'But do inform us if we may aid you: we will help in any way we can. Try not to worry so.' With the woman departed, he resumed his seat at table to eat the fritters. 'I wonder why she be distraught at her son's lateness; 'tis barely passed the dinner hour. He was probably distracted on the way home from school, tossing pebbles in puddles or searching the sky for rainbows.'

'More likely trying to toss his fellows in the mud or searching for birds' nests to plunder the eggs,' Adam said, dipping a crisp fritter into the custard and munching it, appreciatively. 'That's what me and Noah used to do. What right-minded youngster takes time to watch ripples on puddles and look out for rainbows? Besting your fellows is far more important. "I have a redbreast's eggs; yours are but a sparrow's. My boots are muddier than yours. My father will beat me harder than yours." You know how it is.' He exchanged a glance with Seb whose eyebrows were raised. Aye, well, mayhap some folk didn't know how school fellows behaved. He'd forgotten that Seb, as a cripple-child, had never been allowed to enter any school but was taught by his father.

'Her Will never got to school this morn, the young miscreant,' Emily said as she picked up her spoon and put it down again with a sigh, as if it was too heavy to lift. 'But Beattie was certain he wouldn't miss dinner. I suppose that's why she's so frantic about his lateness.'

'You think he's run off somewhere?' Adam suggested.

'I would've, if me farver beat me too much, I would,' Jack added. He slurped custard from his spoon so noisily, eyes turned to Emily, expecting a sharp reproof. It didn't come.

'I did run away.' Tom sounded proud of his achievement. 'Twice. Master Eastleigh, that filthy old apothecary, was a bastard to work for.'

'Tom! Mind your language. This is no common ale-house and women be present.' The reprimand from Seb received an approving nod from Emily though Tom deserved a greater punishment.

'Bread and water for supper for you,' she told him but he just laughed.

'You can't treat me as an apprentice now I'm a journeyman. And I don't have to eat supper here. I'll eat wherever and whenever and whatever I please and there's nothing you can do about it, you fat-bellied sow.'

Emily gasped at the insult.

Tom's bench grated on the flagstones as he stood, flushed and defiant.

Seb leapt to his feet and faced him across the board.

'Thomas Bowen. You will make an abject apology to your mistress this instant.'

'I will not. You can't tell me what to do.'

'Journeyman or apprentice, I be your master yet. You will behave in a seemly manner in my house, or you may leave my employ...'

'It's not your bloody house!' Tom yelled. 'It's supposed to be my inheritance. You stole it from me, you thieving jackanapes. I'll take you to the law over it, when I'm come of age by Michaelmas. Then you'll regret it.'

'Curb your tongue. How dare you speak thus and so disrespectfully. I dismiss you, as of this moment, and there will be no letters of recommendation for you to any other employer. Get out. Be gone from my sight. Now!' Seb pointed to the back door. 'Take your belongings and go. I will not tolerate abusive words nor threats.'

'You owe me wages...' Tom protested.

Seb unfastened the purse at his belt and took out a handful of coins.

'One morning's work be worth threepence.' He slapped a coin on the board. 'Here. Have a whole groat: a penny extra that you do not deserve. I will not have any man accuse me of being an unfair master.'

Tom snatched the coin, kicked aside his bench and stormed out, slamming the door so hard the house trembled upon its foundations. No one spoke.

Seb left the kitchen and went down the passage to the workshop. After a moment or two, Gawain followed dutifully but his tail drooped. The dog had no more liking for discord than did his master.

Kate made to return to her work also but Adam gestured to her to remain at table.

'Give Master Seb a few moments, Kate,' he said.

The lass nodded, understanding. Silence ensued, then everyone flinched at the sound of crashing timber and smashing earthenware.

'He did well, this once,' Emily said, stacking platters ready to wash. 'It was time that young braggart was put in his rightful place: anywhere but under my roof, what with his mouth like a midden. Seb is to be commended.'

Seb was shaking as his anger ebbed away. He surveyed with dismay the broken pots strewn across the workshop floor – all empty, thank goodness. Even in a passion of wrath, he had made sure no precious pigments were wasted. His favoured drawing board was another matter: chipped, leaving a splintered corner, and now with a great crack across the middle. It was no use any longer for the fissure would show up as a line struck through the midst of any drawing. A sorrowful thing, fit only for firewood. He shook his head over the loss.

Adam came in, broom in hand, prepared to sweep up the debris he expected to find.

'Leave it. 'Tis my doing,' Seb said.

'As you will. You want me to take a proper look at that astrological book? See what I can make of it. I can work out the pattern of margins and start ruling up the pages at least. On parchment, did you say?'

58

'Mm?'

'Come back to us, Seb,' Adam said, clicking his fingers to gain his attention.

'What? Oh, aye. Parchment.' Seb took the broom from Adam and began sweeping. 'I have never been so angered at any man. Was I wrong to dismiss him, Adam? Did I go too far? Was I within my rights?'

'Of course, you were. No master could be fairer, not after what he said. Such insults are not to be borne without retribution. He got what he deserved. No man will dispute that. But what did he mean about this house being his inheritance? Such nonsense…'

'It has some element of truth though.' Seb swept the pot shards into a corner to be dealt with later, leaned the broom against the wall and sat at his desk. 'It happened some years back. My brother Jude and I worked here, under this very roof, as journeymen. Our master was Matthew Bowen, Tom's father… 'tis a long and convoluted story but, in short, Matthew was murdered; poisoned by his wife – Tom's step-mother…'

'What! Great merciful God. A woman did that?'

'She did and with the murder of one parent and the execution of the other, Tom, as a minor, came under the guardianship of his elder sister, Bella, and her husband, Dick Langton. He be Dame Ellen's son, by the by. They live in Deptford now, as they did then.

'This house stood empty, except for Nessie. No one wanted to live here forwhy it now had a dubious reputation, folk being suspicious of a place where murder was committed. Jude and I were in need of new employment and we had money enough from an important commission completed for Duke Richard to set up our own business. These premises were familiar to us and exactly what we required, so we made a proposition to the Langtons: we would buy this house and workshop and everything in it for a reasonable price – Jude drove a hard bargain, indeed – and I would take young Tom as my apprentice, giving him bed and board in his old home.

'The poor lad had suffered – as he mentioned – in serving as an apprentice to an apothecary in Ivy Lane across the way. There had been an accident of some kind in the still-room there. The apothecary was killed and Tom badly injured. It seemed a kindness to take him on and let him live and work here.'

'But he was no better as a stationer's apprentice than an apothecary's,' Adam concluded. 'But what of your purchase of this place? It was all done legal and above board, wasn't it? Tell me his threat to take you to court is groundless in fact.'

'The contract was drawn up by Duke Richard's own lawyer, Miles Metcalfe. It was signed by Jude, me, Dick Langton, Bella and young Tom. I suppose Tom may have signed unwillingly but, as a minor, his signature was not even required by law. It was a courtesy is all. The transaction was witnessed by the duke himself, as our patron, and Sir Robert Percy, whom you met at Crosby Place. Also, by my old master, Richard Collop, as representative of our guild. The document bears the duke's own seal and that of the Stationers' Guild. I doubt any man could contest its legality under the law, however much Tom may feel aggrieved. I suppose it would have been his inheritance if his father had not been slain, but his guardians acted with all propriety in the heir's best interests at the time. Rightfully, the price we paid for the house should be made over to him, by his sister and Dick, when the lad comes of age a few months hence. If they fail to do so, or if they have spent the money, his argument should be with them, not with me. And now you know the truth of it.'

'It's quite a tale, Seb. And where is this precious document?'

'Safe, lodged with the Goldsmiths' Guild, in their vault. 'Tis the most secure place in London.'

'And what of Tom now?' Adam threw down his pen, realising he had trimmed it away to nothing all the while. 'You think he'll come back, grovelling, begging your forgiveness?'

Seb thought, rubbing at his nose.

'No. I do not believe Tom will be of a mind to apologise or beseech pardon. He be too prideful and obstinate. Most like, I have made an enemy this day.'

'How does London treat its masterless men?'

'Harshly, I fear. No man will employ him without recommendation, not at a proper rate of pay, leastwise. He may end up as a menial, lugging ale barrels in a tavern, or as a scawager, emptying cesspits. Nobody wants that job. More likely, he will cross the bridge to Southwark. Folk there have little concern for reputation. I pray God, the lad does not turn to crime... Mayhap, I should seek him out; tell him I was over-hasty in dismissing him; ask him to return.'

'No, Seb. You should not. What he does from henceforth is his business; not yours. You cannot be responsible for another man's soul.'

'But what of his well-being and safety?'

'Not those either. He's his own man now and there's an end to it.'

# Chapter 4

## Monday afternoon
## Ivy Lane

TOM SWIPED at a clump of dandelions that dared spring up from betwixt the bricks of the fine house, decapitating the early blooms with a stick. Aye, and he could think of a few others he'd like to behead also – with a dull blade.

He kicked a stone at a wandering chicken, laughing when it squawked as the missile hit its mark. He watched it flutter over a fence in a shower of feathers, the damned, stupid bird. Didn't it know better than to cross his path?

He couldn't say why he had turned into Ivy Lane, nor why he now stood before the new goldsmith's shop that had been built upon the site of Master Eastleigh's old apothecary's place, where he'd been apprenticed for that eternity of misery. The chaos of charred timbers and the crumbled stone chimney were long gone, replaced by this brash building with its striped shutters and a doorway flanked by stone lions, as if it was some nobleman's palace. In truth, the real nobleman's house stood opposite. Its fashionable brickwork had mellowed with age beneath a layer of London dirt, its hideous gargoyles softened by ivy drapes.

The shutters were flung wide at Lovell's Inn, revealing gleaming eyes of glass that stared at him, knowingly. And, as he watched, the great door opened and a servant came out, to sweep the marble steps. The lord must be in town – or soon would be – to attend the Parliament after Passiontide. Tom shivered at the thought of that man.

He wondered whether the owner of the house had, likewise, mellowed in temperament these years past but he doubted it. He had suffered Lord Lovell's wrath in those horrible few weeks, almost four years since but, these days, he had an advantage. No longer a cowering 'prentice but a man grown at last: he knew things about Lord Lovell; was privy to his darkest secrets. It occurred to Tom, in that moment, that such knowledge might be used to advantage by a masterless man. Aye, "knowledge is power", as the saying goes. Mayhap Seb had done him a favour by dismissing him. He would make his own fortune. A spring in his step now, he shouldered his pack with his few belongings and made for the nearest tavern.

## The Foxley House

The workshop was a scene of silent diligence. Adam was stitching together the gatherings of a book of Master John Lydgate's poetry. The thin volume was to be added to the few they made, hoping to sell to passers-by, rather than commissioned by specific customers. It would be given a simple parchment wrapper, imprinted with the fox-head image. Adam was proud of their new makers-mark. His name might be 'Armitage' but he was a Foxley man, born and bred, more so even than Seb. A cheap little quarto book, such as this, received the same care in penmanship and stitchery as Seb's exquisite *Aesop's Fables* had done. The Foxley workshop was earning a reputation for its high quality of workmanship, whatever the book, and Adam knew he was playing his part to the full in regaining that good name – a name Jude had sullied so badly before walking away from it all.

Kate was grinding chalk to a fine powder, ready to whiten more parchment for the astrological book, over which Master Seb was frowning, sighing and making frantic notes at his desk. She had taken a quick look at the tatty pages and thought it seemed a horde of drunken spiders had dipped their hairy legs in ink and played knock-and-run across the text. No wonder master was vexed by it. With the chalk now fine and smooth in the mortar, she put down the pestle and hastened out, into the passage, before giving a mighty sneeze. That was the trouble with chalk dust and a sneeze could send it flying everywhere.

Jack had done that once, she remembered. Poor Jack. Nothing he did in the workshop ever seemed to go right but at least he was happier, working for Master Appleyard. She wondered if the sawdust in the carpenter's place also made him sneeze. Jack. Everything made her think of Jack. She hoped Master Appleyard wouldn't keep him working too late. The evenings were lighter now and, if it wasn't raining, after supper, there might come an opportunity for a kiss or two behind the pigsty.

In the meantime, remembering that Jack was always thirsty, Kate hastened to the kitchen for the ale jug. Masters Seb and Adam would, no doubt, appreciate a cup and the chalk dust had made her throat dry.

There was no sign of Nessie but Mistress Em sat alone, all ungainly upon a bench, half sprawled across the board, eyes closed.

'Mistress Em? What's amiss?'

Hearing Kate's voice, Emily made the effort to push herself upright and straighten her skirts.

'Nothing. Go back to your work.'

'I came for some ale. The chalk dust… Are you ill, mistress?'

'No. Cease fussing and take the ale. I'm tired; in need of peace, is all. And don't you dare say a word of this…'

'Of course not, mistress.'

Nessie came in from the garden with a basket of laundry

in her arms.

'Some's dry, mistress. The small bits, leastwise. What shall I do with the wet stuff? I knows you don't like washin' hangin' in the kitchen.'

Emily waved aside the question.

'I don't care. Leave it.'

Kate and Nessie exchanged glances. All the times mistress had instructed them never to leave damp linen in a heap for fear it would go mouldy. Nessie shrugged and put the basket on the hearthstone, thinking the fire would help dry the sheets and things.

'Not there, Nessie,' Kate whispered, nudging the elder girl. 'The fire may spit an ember into the basket and set all afire. Why did you not leave it spread along the hedge?'

'Rainin' agen,' Nessie grumbled, shoving the basket into a distant corner, far from the hearth. If the linen got black mould spots and mildew all over it that would be mistress's fault, not hers.

Kate took the ale jug and four clean cups back to the workshop. She served the masters, then took a cup through to the shop for Rose. Rose was singing softly as she tidied the display of books, giving an eye to Dickon, seated on the floor, playing with the colourful rag-ball she had stitched for him.

'Thank you, Kate,' Rose said but then, seeing Kate's expression, she asked: 'Why so gloomy?'

Kate frowned, thinking the matter through.

'In truth,' she said at last, 'Mistress told me not to say anything of it but I believe she's sick, Rose. She looks so weary and the wet linen has more colour than she. I'm concerned for her. She didn't even scold Nessie for putting the washing basket too close to the fire. She said she didn't care about it. 'Tis so unlike mistress.'

'I'm worried for her too, Kate,' Rose admitted. 'As you say, 'tis so many little things that seem amiss with her. And her poor feet: have you seen them of late; how swollen they are? Mayhap, we should ask Nell Warren or Dame Ellen about her, seeing they have aided more babes into the world than anyone can recall... but she'll be so angry if we betray her.'

'We could ask Master Seb; get his permission. Then mistress couldn't protest so much.'

'No, Kate; him least of all. This is hardly a man's business, is it?'

'But he'd want to know if she's sick, wouldn't he?'

Before Rose could reply, Adam appeared in the doorway.

'What's this? Women plotting how to get the better of us poor menfolk?' He laughed and grinned at them but realised the discussion had been of a serious matter. 'Mistress Em, is it?'

They nodded.

'Don't think I have failed to notice her unsettled humours, just because men aren't supposed to see such things. I'm not blind.'

'Is Seb aware also?' Rose asked.

'Of course he is. He's greatly troubled concerning her, but what can he do? He cannot exchange a word with her without upsetting her the more. We can but pray she'll be more amicable towards him once the babe is born. But enough: I came to tip the rain off the new awning afore it rips under the weight of water. You best return to your work, Kate: the parchment won't whiten itself, now will it?'

Despite his words, when Kate scuttled off, back to the workshop, Adam made no move towards the outer shop door, to go tend to the awning, but watched Rose awhile. If Emily was a fading, overblown bloom, Rose was as radiant as the midsummer flower of her name. Mayhap, it was time he found a respectable, kindly woman of his own, before desire overcame his better judgement and he did something improper. Resigned to loneliness and a solitary bed for the present, he went out to empty the bulging awning of its burdensome pregnant belly, careful not to drown any passer-by in the sudden deluge of water, nor to wet the books displayed on the counter-board beneath.

Not that there were any passers-by in the dripping, puddle-strewn street, nor much likelihood of any more customers unless the rain relented.

'Shall we close up the shutters and take down the awning, Rose? I cannot imagine we'll get more business this day and the damp airs will curl the books.' Such inclement weather was always the stationer's foe, moistening paper and causing the pages of pamphlets and any book without a stout and weighty cover to bend out of shape. And if the wet continued, then mould became a worse enemy still, spoiling stock and second only to fire as the utter ruination of the bookseller's business.

In the workshop, Seb remained engrossed all the while, attempting to make sense of the adulterated text, writing copious notes of his own on sheets of paper, of which there was now an unruly pile teetering on the edge of his desk. His ale cup had not been touched yet and he spoke, without looking up, as Adam returned.

'This book be all but impossible,' he muttered, laying down his pen and straightening the notes. ''Tis making me cross-eyed just staring at it.'

'Would the scrying glass aid you?' Adam suggested, pausing before resuming his seat at his own desk.

Seb held up a half-sphere of polished glass.

'It does but enlarge the letters without making them any easier to comprehend. I fear old age – if not blindness – will overtake me afore this task be done. I know not what I shall say to Mistress Caldicott but I believe this commission be beyond my abilities. If I had some little astrological or medical knowledge, I might make educated guesses as to the meanings of the text, but since I have naught beyond the everyday remedies for headache or itch, it may as well be written in the script of the Vikings or the Egyptians of ancient times. And speaking of headaches…' He massaged his temples before taking up his pen and a fresh sheet of paper.

'Drink your ale; it may refresh you.' Adam stood, looking

thoughtful. 'What if you took it to that surgeon fellow who was here to see the body? What was his name?'

'Dagvyle.'

'Aye. Him. Might he not help you?'

'Mayhap: for a fee. And Em will say I'm undercharging Mistress Caldicott as it is, without paying a surgeon to assist me.'

'Better than going blind over the wretched thing.'

'I cannot ask him to translate the entire book for me.'

'Just the most difficult passages, then.'

'Oh, Adam, every passage be a difficult one.' Seb put a scrap of paper to mark the page and closed the book. 'I be done with it,' he said, sighing. 'On the morrow, God willing, my eyes may be keener, my mind more alert. I shall try again.'


Tom sat in The Pig and Pipe, a seedy tavern by Paul's brewhouse in Knightrider Street. The ale was not of the best but Tom had his mind set upon other concerns. In leaving Paternoster Row, he had seen it as his due to take a few additional things, as well as his own belongings: a half ream of best paper, lidded pots of both red and black ink and enough quills to last a year or more. He had also purloined red wax and one of the workshop's two new seals with the fox's head. Since he had no letters of recommendation, he would write his own, if needs be. He couldn't forge Seb's beautiful signature but the seal would suffice. Seb would soon miss everything, no doubt, but he owed him that much, beside a few paltry pence. A man had to get by somehow and Tom had thought to offer his services to the illiterate, in taverns and inns, reading and answering their correspondence for them. But to continue as a journeyman would pay better if he could persuade a new master to take him on.

However, as it was, with his bold new notion, come to him in that instant of inspiration, he had a most important letter of his own to compose. If matters worked out satisfactorily, he might never have to bother about employment again. He dipped the pen and began:

'*From a Well-wisher…*'

No, no.

'*From a Concerned Acquaintance. Greetings be unto you, Lord Lovell…*'

No. That would not do either. Tom sipped his ale and chewed the quill. How to begin an extortioner's letter? His life of crime had never gone much beyond cheating at dice, lying to Seb and the odd petty theft. An attempted rape didn't really count, since it came to naught. Except for the stabbing… and that was what this letter was all about. Lovell had forced him to do it. Of course, Seb had never known who was his assailant in the dark church that eve, nor ever would. And Tom knew of other things, other crimes, Lovell had committed. Murder, for certain. Abduction. Arson. And Lovell had so much to lose: the king's trust, if the truth came out. Duke Richard's friendship and patronage. And, not least, his life, if found guilty by a court. The devil would pay handsomely for Tom's silence. The correct wording of this letter was vital to ensure that came to pass.

'*From a Knowledgeable Acquaintance. To Lord Lovell. Greeting.*'

He then described in detail, Lovell's deliberate actions which had caused the explosion in the apothecary's shop, killing the old man, so his lordship must realise that this was not just idle speculation but a full and certain knowledge of the event. By listening at doors, he had overheard Lovell's plan to abduct Emily Appleyard – as she then was – to bait the trap set for Seb. And he was convinced it was Lovell who had set a warehouse ablaze in an attempt to kill Seb.

The letter was long. Tom read it through before ending:

*'Twenty pounds is the price of silence. Bring the coin
to The Pig and Pipe in Knightrider Street upon
Wednesday next, at noontide. Leave the money
behind the holly bush.'*

Every tavern was supposed to display a green bough or bush beside its doorway to show when fresh ale had been brewed but, long ago, someone at The Pig and Pipe had planted a holly bush in a pot. In the past, the pot was only put out at the time of a new brewing but, these days, the bush had grown too heavy to move, so it stood by the door permanently, fresh ale or not. At The Pig, it was hard to tell the difference betwixt fresh and stale anyway – it always tasted sour.

Tom asked the tapster to bring a lighted wick, that he might melt the wax and seal the letter. He grinned as he imprinted the Foxley seal into the blood-red wax. If anything went amiss in this plan, Lovell would believe Seb was the guilty party, for he was the only other man living who knew any part of this.

When the wax was set, Tom packed up his writing stuff and put it in his bundle of belongings. Then he made his way back to Ivy Lane, as dusk was falling. At least the rain had stopped. Making certain no nosy neighbour was looking out, he slipped the letter under the door of Lovell's Inn, laughing to himself. Next, he had to find a bed for the night and he knew just the buxom wench to supply it for free.

## The Three Feathers Inn at Lambeth

Lord Pierpoint exploded like an ill-primed cannon.

'He what! How dare he?' he bellowed, flinging bread, cheese and the platter at Walter. 'The king will hear of this. I'll not abide some upstart lordling barely out of tailclouts refusing my petition a second time. How dare he?' he repeated, foam flecking the corners of his mouth. 'I fought at his father's side in France before he was born. How dare he refuse me?'

A gaming board and all its pieces flew at Walter's head but he ducked and avoided it. This was no uncommon incident. Lord Pierpoint was ever in choleric humour if his mess of eggs was cold, his shoes pinched his gouty toes, or the wine was not to his liking. Walter waited in silence, knowing it would pass and be soon forgotten. At least, he hoped it would but his lordship was particularly agitated about this ridiculous petition. No matter how many times it had been explained to him, he seemed determined to ride this horse until it dropped from exhaustion. And there was worse to come.

'Forgive me, my lord, but your son is here to see you,' Walter said, aware the statement would rekindle his master's ire like throwing gunpowder on a flame.

'I have no son! How many times must I tell you?' Lord Pierpoint thumped the floor so hard with his stick, splinters flew. 'The wretch is dead to me.'

'Sir Marcus awaits below…'

'Tell him to go to the Devil. I have no dealings with him, nor he with me.'

'He has been waiting patiently for an hour or more…'

'And he can go on waiting 'til Judgement Day, for all I care. I will not see him, so go, tell him so. Tell him to get out of my house.'

Walter didn't bother pointing out that this was an inn, not his lordship's house, but obeyed, leaving the chamber with soundless tread, as a good servant should. But as he closed the door, he heard another thud, a crash and the splintering of wood: more expenses would be due to the landlord for damage to his property and the Almighty alone might know where the money could be found to pay the reckoning.

Downstairs in the inn, Sir Marcus sat alone at a table in a gloomy corner, wrapped in his lawyer's robes, sipping his ale. It did not do to draw attention to his profession in such places as this and the lack of light suited his mood besides. A meeting with his father was never going to end well. He exchanged a weary smile with Walter.

'Have some ale,' he said, passing a cup to the servant. 'We both must gird ourselves for the battle to come.'

'Your lord father refuses to see you, sir.'

'As expected but, on this occasion, he will have no choice. He has to understand that he cannot have his way in this matter.'

'He nigh had apoplexy when I told him the Duke of Gloucester had refused a second time to even countenance the petition.'

'Aye, the duke knows the laws of inheritance as well, if not better, than most of my profession.'

'But there has been a, er, development, sir,' Walter said, putting down his empty cup, 'And a strange one it is. I know not what my lord means by it, but he says he has acquired a new heir to replace you; whatever miracle has occurred to make that possible. I thought I knew most of what goes on within that – forgive my bluntness and begging pardon, sir – that addled pate of his but, of late, he has had visitors of a most desperate kind and has sent me away, such that I have not been privy to what was discussed.'

'But you listened at the door,' Sir Marcus said, fully aware of the ways of servants of long standing. Walter had served his father for thirty years or more and was the only retainer left. Never paid a wage these days, the loyal fellow yet contrived to keep a roof over Pierpoint Hall and food upon the board. How he managed this feat when the coffers were not only empty but long since burned for firewood, Marcus thought it best not to enquire, being a lawyer and all. He did make contributions to his father's estate but Walter seemed to stretch a few marks to last for months, somehow.

'I did, sir.' Walter made no apology. 'What little I could make of the muffled conversations did not bode well, I fear. They spoke of 'suitable children' for your father's approval.

He sounded right merry. I heard him say that no poor child, taken from a life of want and poverty, would refuse his offer of a fine manor, vast estates, knightly training and the life of a wealthy baron,'

'A wealthy baron,' Sir Marcus snorted. 'Why ever do I strive as a lawyer when that marvellous prospect lies before me? Come, Walter, we have a mad old man to convince of the error of his ways. Landlord! Send a flagon of your best Gascon wine to Lord Pierpoint's chamber.' Seeing Walter's expression of concern, Sir Marcus patted him on the shoulder. 'Don't fret. I've paid my father's reckoning and more. I know you'll be hard-pressed to find the coin, otherwise.'

'Thank you, sir. 'Tis a weight off my mind.'

Together, the lawyer and the servant made for the stairs, resigned to confronting Lord Pierpoint with his own foolishness.


Seb, Adam, Jack and Stephen Appleyard had been the only mourners at St Michael le Querne's Church for the interment of the unknown lad. Seb had paid to see that all was done with due propriety, with a simple coffin, not just a shroud. This was no pauper's burial. Yet the funeral was a poor affair with so few mourners. Father Thomas did not stint the prayers and the drizzle had ceased. Perhaps the office had been as well done as it could be but the menfolk returned home in sombre mood.


After supper that eve, Emily had retired straightway, leaving everyone else in the parlour, taking their ease around a good fire, it being a chill night; a remembrance that winter's grip was yet reluctant to leave the land entirely in the gentler hands of spring. Rose was dandling little Dickon upon her lap. He was teething and fractious, disinclined to sleep, but she had such a way with him, only she could soothe and quiet him. Gawain and the cat, Greyling – now harmonious companions after a fraught beginning – lay entwined upon the woven-rush hearth mat.

Seb had been all around the house, checking every shutter, especially the one at the workshop window. Wanting no more unexpected intruders, Adam had affixed an additional bolt and hasp that would defy any hedge-breaker. Seb was about to bar the shop door when there came a frantic hammering upon the timbers and such cries that no man with a Christian heart could ignore. He removed the bar he had just put in place and opened the door.

Beatrice Thatcher stood there in such a state of disarray he had to keep her from falling across the threshold as she flung herself at him and burst out breathlessly:

'Oh, Master Seb, he never comed home… we've searched half London… an' he's not to be found nowhere. You've got to help. You're good at finding out folk…'

'Mistress Thatcher? Beatrice, steady now. Take a breath, I pray you. Come through to the parlour.' Seb guided her to the cushioned settle close to the fire. 'Warm yourself. Nessie, fetch another cup of spiced ale, if you will.' He said no more until the woman was calmer, swathed in a woollen blanket and sipping her hot, mulled ale as a restorative.

'I take it, your lad be missing from home still?' he asked, sitting on a stool before her.

'I don't know who else to turn to. We've asked everyone. Nobody's seen him. It's as if the faeries took him for their own, disappearing him off the street. Oh, Master Seb, where's my Will? Where's he gone to? What shall I do?' Tears cascaded down her cold cheeks and Rose passed her a napkin.

'We'll find him, Beattie, won't we, Seb?' Rose said, consoling her.

Seb gave her a doubting look but his words were more hopeful than he felt was warranted.

'Aye. As soon as it be light, we'll all join the search, make every enquiry we may. I be sure he'll not have gone far.'

'Oh, Master Seb, what a comfort you are. I know you'll

find my Will, if anyone can. Harry's said he'll even pay for a consultation with Master Hobbs, the famous man of medicine.'

'Aye, I know him. He has treated me in the past, most successfully. Why? Do you fear your son be injured or unwell?'

'No, not that. But he can draw up Will's horoscope, can't he? Physicians and their kind predict where lost things can be found, don't they? My cousin consulted an apothecary when she lost her wedding ring and thought it had been stoled. He used the stars to tell her it was lying hidden in a dark place and it was. She found it under the bed. But for my Will, we'll consult the best in town: the king's and duke's own physician. It'll be worth the expense if he can tell us where my poor Will has got to.'

'Aye. That will be of, er, much assistance, of course.' Seb was no great believer in the use of horoscopes to recover lost things but no turn should be unexplored when a child's life was of concern. 'Come now, let me escort you home. 'Tis growing late and we needs must begin the search early, at first light. You need your sleep, mistress, for the task ahead.'

'You think I'll get a single minute's sleep, worrying about him?'

'You can rest, at least, though slumber eludes you. I'll fetch a torchlight.'

'I'll come also,' Adam said.

'No need to trouble yourself, cousin. Gawain will be sufficient escort for my walk back after. 'Tis but to Cheap Cross.'

'I'll come, all the same; stretch my legs before bed.'

'As you wish.'


The rain was gone and a large moon hung like an ivory pendant in a clear sky, haloed, as betokened a coming frost. The wet streets would be treacherous by dawn.

Having passed Beatrice, still distraught, into her husband's care – though he seemed hardly more composed than she – Seb and Adam departed with reassuring words.

'You didn't mean what you said, Seb, I know.' Adam held the torch higher to illumine a large puddle already ice-rimmed. 'About the lad being safe.'

'What else should I say: that he'll probably be found in some filthy alley, stripped and robbed and frozen to death by morn? The poor woman be beside herself and, who may tell? He could be playing some prank; gone to stay with a relative just to vex his mother forwhy she scolded him.'

'Aye, that could well be the case. Me and Noah used to flee to Aunt Marjorie whenever we were in trouble at home. She would give us a good dinner, a hearty telling-off and send us back to our parents. You think young Will may have done the like?'

'Gawain! Leave be, you foolish dog.' Seb pulled the creature away from some unsavoury mess on the corner by St Michael's Church as they turned once more into Paternoster Row. 'In which case, his parents can make enquiries of the family. I'll draw a few likenesses of the lad and we can show them around, beginning here, nearby St Paul's, where he should have been upon his way to school. Someone must have seen him. Cheapside would have been thronged at that hour since the rain did not begin until later.'

'What are the chances of finding a lost child in London, Seb, if he hasn't run to a relative or friend? Truthfully now; tell me.'

'Matters may turn out well, if the Lord smiles upon our efforts; there be no knowing for certain…'

'But, the Almighty's miraculous intervention aside, you wouldn't chance a coin on a fortunate outcome.'

'I do not make wagers, Adam, as you well know. I shall say naught more than that. May I share your chamber yet again this night? I would not disturb poor Em's rest by clattering about and getting in bed beside her. She has looked so worn these past few days.'


Emily was not sleeping, as Seb thought. Far from it. Her

pain and discomfort made rest impossible. But worse than her bodily distress, she was afraid. She had never felt like this whilst carrying little Dickon. Then, she'd had a fat belly; but this time; her whole body was swollen like some monstrous thing. Tom had called her a fat sow. A vile insult indeed but, nevertheless, it was the truth. No wonder his words had hurt her so. At least Seb, for once, had behaved as a worthy husband and dismissed the wretch forthwith.

But where was Seb now, when she had the greatest need of a comforting gesture, a few loving words from him to prove his affection, even as she lay bloated and nauseous? His reassurances against her fears; consolation for her anguish: these he failed to give. He had abandoned her bed; abandoned her. Utterly unloved, she had never felt so alone. She sobbed silently into a pillow already wet with feverish sweats and salt tears, praying to the Blessed Virgin that her torment would be over soon.

Seb was no closer to sleep than his goodwife. Adam breathed beside him, deep in slumber but Seb's head was overfull, nigh unto bursting with more problems than he could count. He had hardly recovered from the shock of discovering a dead child in his workshop and now another lad was gone missing. He could well understand Will's parents' anxieties: if Dickon were ever lost, he would be mad with worry, he knew.

And what of the astrological text? Its convoluted diagrams and unintelligible words danced a crazed jig afore his eyes every time he closed them. What was he to do about that? Supposing the search for the lad took up all his time, that he could not complete the commission, as promised? Another blot upon the Foxley reputation would serve the business ill. It had taken so long to repair the damage Jude had caused to their good name, to lose it anew would be doubly regrettable.

And Tom… he felt he had been overly harsh, too swift in dismissing him. Where would he sleep this night? He hardly had coin enough to buy a bed and eat for more than a few days. If he was sleeping on the streets, huddled against the cold, hunger gnawing at his vitals… how could Seb sleep easy with that weighing upon his conscience?

And the greatest burden and the most disquieting was Emily. What to do to mend their marriage, he was at a loss to know. If only he could account for its failure. Was it his fault? Was he such a bad husband? Or had Em simply fallen out of love with him? He still loved her, mayhap, more deeply now than upon the day they wed, but there was no pleasing her any longer. Whatever he did was wrong in her eyes. The harder he tried, the more he seemed to displease her. Mayhap, matters would improve once the new babe was born.

And that was his greatest anxiety. Em was unwell; he knew that but she would not speak of it. He feared she felt worse than she would admit, struggling through her daily round of chores, a martyr to her ungainly body. If only she would talk to him, tell him the truth of it, mayhap, they could see a way through this time of tribulation, together. But he was the last person in whom she would confide her troubles. Rose, or Dame Ellen, or even Beatrice likely knew more of his wife than he did.

He could but pray to the Lord Jesu, during this sombre week afore His Passion, to aid in the resolution of all these difficulties. But what were Seb's minor sufferings compared to those of the Saviour? Such melancholy realisations certainly put matters into their relative degrees. He who had given His life for man's salvation was deserving of the fullest gratitude and adoration and thus, contemplating these higher things, Seb fell into a restless sleep in the watching hour of the night.

# Chapter 5

## Tuesday, the sixth day of April
## Cheapside

ADAM WAS at the Thatchers' door by Cheap Cross first thing that morn, to enquire whether young Will had been found, or any news of him. Beatrice was suckling her babe but seemed not to have been abed all night. Her goodman, Harry, was pacing the earthen floor, wearing a gutter there with his boots.

'You bring news?' he cried, leaping to a faulty conclusion as Adam entered their house.

'Nay. I fear not. I came to ask the same of you, Master Thatcher.'

'Oh.' Harry heaved a sigh, his shoulders slumped, his bald head drooping.

The babe, removed from the breast, began to whimper.

''Tis early yet,' Adam said. 'We will begin our searching directly. Master Seb is drawing Will's likenesses as we speak. We will show them wherever we go, that folk may know whom we seek. Do not be disheartened. We have the best chance of success with Seb's drawings.'

'Aye, I suppose so,' Harry mumbled, then turned to his wife, imploring. 'For pity's sake, Bea, can you not keep that child from bawling? My nerves be unravelling here.'

'You think mine aren't too?' Beattie yelled back and then

dissolved into sobs.

'I'll tell Seb that there is naught new. Leave you to...' Adam didn't complete the sentence, not knowing what to say to the frantic parents.

The frost was thawing, dripping from the eaves as the sun rose higher. Armed with copies of young Will's likeness, Seb and Adam waited by St Paul's as the congregation spilled out when Low Mass ended. There were far more folk than usual in this week of Passiontide and they showed the images to as many as possible. Some recognised the lad – proving it was a fair portrait – knowing him as a chorister in the cathedral. Others knew him from elsewhere and had heard of his disappearance. A few said they had seen him on his way to school but, upon closer examination, when pressed, they could not say for certain whether that was yesterday or some previous morn.

Despite their efforts, they were no wiser than before. Seb worked his way along the northern side of Paternoster Row and into Cheapside, knocking on every door, entering every shop, tavern and business premises, showing the portrait. Adam did likewise on the south side. It was heartening that most folk recognised the lad but none had any knowledge whatever as to his disappearance or present whereabouts. The fellow posted at St Paul's Gate, opposite St Michael's Church, said he knew the lad well, that he came through this gate most days, but he could not recall whether he had seen him yesterday for sometimes the scholars used St Augustine's Gate upon Watling Street.

'Paul's been busier this week,' he explained, 'So many folk wanting to atone for their wicked ways afore they take the Easter Eucharist, see. I can't remember 'em all.'

Adam thanked him and moved on to Mitchet's ale-house next door, famed as the smallest place of refreshment in the city with the smallest prices. Adam had discovered why soon after his arrival at Paternoster Row: the ale they brewed was the worst he'd ever tasted. Enquiries at Master Brook's girdle-makers and Mistress Routledge's most reputable cookshop, rightly renowned for the excellent pasties sold there, brought him to the conduit where the street widened into Cheapside.

Comparing information with Seb as they shared a hasty cup of ale at a tavern by Gutter Lane – so many questions made thirsty work – it seemed that no one had witnessed anything the least untoward occurring yesterday, betwixt Cheap Cross and Paul's School. But they weren't done yet.

Although Beatrice had insisted that her son always walked that way to and from school, going into Paul's Yard by any one of the three northern gates, there was the chance that he could have done otherwise. Recalling what the gatekeeper had said, Seb realised the lad might have turned down Friday Street, then made his way along Watling Street, or gone by the Bellhouse into The Old Change and, in either case, entered Paul's Yard by way of St Augustine's Gate.

Seb made enquiries all the way down Friday Street; Adam did the same for Old Change. Fewer folk recognised the lad here but, as Seb turned west into Watling Street, he caught up with a goodwife, struggling with a babe-in-arms, a wayward toddling and a basket of provisions from the market.

'God give you good day, mistress. May I assist you? You appear in need of another pair of hands.'

She turned, as if to give Seb the sharp edge of her tongue but, seeing he looked respectable and harmless, she managed a smile and gave him her basket.

'Thank you, kindly, master. I cannot tell you how vexed I am. This one has led me quite a dance all the way from Soper Lane.' She scowled at the toddling and clasped his hand more firmly now Seb had hold of her basket. 'A trial he is and not yet three summers of age. What'll he be like when he's grown, I ask. 'Tis not a merry prospect. But that is of no mind. Where are my manners? I must offer you ale at the very least for your trouble. I live in Distaff Lane on the corner of Old Change. I trust that doesn't take you too far out of your way. I wouldn't want to put you to any inconvenience.'

'Nay, mistress. I be on my way to meet someone in Old Change, so 'tis no inconvenience at all.'

'Do I know you from somewhere? You look familiar, if you'll forgive my 'pertinence.'

'Sebastian Foxley, at your service, mistress,' he said, touching his cap with his free hand. 'I run a stationer's workshop in Paternoster Row.'

'I've no need of books and suchlike. Could I have seen you elsewhere?'

'I sing in Paul's choir on occasion…'

'Of course! You're the one with the voice of an angel.'

Seb flushed at such praise.

'I would not go so far…'

'Aye. You sang at Christmastide, I recall. Beautiful, it was. We all agreed on that. Here. This is my house. Won't you come in? I have a fresh brewing of ale.'

Seb was in two minds. He did not want to miss meeting up with Adam, in case he had news and the woman's words had embarrassed him. On the other hand, it would be churlish to refuse and he was, again, somewhat thirsty besides.

Once within, the woman directed Seb to a bench by the hearth and put the babe in its cradle. Then, taking the basket from Seb, she set it on the floor and went to fetch the ale. The moment her back was turned, the youngster began poking through the basket, pulling out worts and onions and was about to drag forth a triplet of fresh herrings. Seb lifted the child away from his act of mischief and swung him in the air, just as he did with Dickon, to distract him and make him laugh. This child was a good deal heavier but the effect was the same. By the time his mother returned, he was chuckling with his new-found playmate.

'You have a way with children, Master Foxley,' she said, smiling.

'I have a little lad of mine own: Dickon. He will be one year of age, come midsummer.'

'I'll warrant, he's not such an unruly knave as this one.'

'No, not as yet, leastwise.' Seb put the child down and accepted a brimming ale-cup.

'Nicholas, have a care,' the woman scolded as the little lad barged into Seb's knee, jostling him and spilling the ale. She pulled him aside. 'Let Master Foxley drink in peace. Go play with your ball. 'Tis over there.' She pointed to beneath the babe's cradle.

Nicholas toddled towards the ball but then lighted upon a new mischief. He began rocking the cradle with all his strength, shaking the sleeping babe within. The babe awoke, howling in protest.

The woman slapped the child's hands away from the cradle and took up the babe to comfort it. Nicholas yelled loudly, going red in the face, and began to pummel his mother's skirts with his fists.

'Now, now,' Seb said, ''Tis no way for a fine gentleman to behave. Come, little man; can you play at catching your ball? Show me how skilled you be.' A game of catch – or rather 'lob and fetch' – ensued, distracting young Nicholas as his mother set all to rights once more.

After a while, the toddling was yawning and clambered onto the bench beside Seb, curled up and fell asleep, using Seb's thigh as a pillow.

'You've been a godsend, Master Foxley. How may I ever thank you?'

'No need, mistress… er, 'tis remiss indeed, but I fear I have forgotten your name.'

'In all the fuss, I don't believe I ever gave it. 'Tis Mercy Hutchinson.' She bobbed a little courtesy then, belatedly, offered Seb a napkin to blot the ale stains on his jerkin, though they were dried long since. 'I hope you'll have cause to pass this way again, sometime. Nicholas has quite taken to you and, by the saints, he has need of a man's hand occasionally, since my goodman was taken from us.'

'You have my deepest condolences, Mistress Hutchinson.'

She shrugged.

'Was a foolish mishap in May last. No one's fault. A boat overturned... he couldn't swim. May God assoil his dear soul.' She made the sign of the Cross and Seb did likewise. There came a pause as both considered the fragility of life that could be snuffed out like a candle at any moment.

'You mention my ever having cause to pass this way in future: in truth, I have a purpose at this time, which has nigh fled my mind.' From within his jerkin, Seb took out the folded drawings of Will Thatcher and gave them to Mistress Hutchinson.

'Aye, I know him,' she said. 'My eldest, Simon, goes to school with him. They're friends.'

'And did you see him upon yester morn? Might there have been any sort of incident to attract your notice?'

'No. Why? Has aught happened to him?'

'I fear Will Thatcher did not reach school and has not been seen since. His parents be distraught. If you recall anything amiss...'

'I did see something amiss, but not then. It was a little while ago, a week or more since. It quite upset me. A child was screaming and I looked out, thinking to be neighbourly. But the man deterred me. He was so vicious-looking, dragging the child along by his hair. And I remember that particularly forwhy the lad's hair was purest white, like a halo, almost. I prayed to St Mary to keep that poor lad safe. It has played on my mind ever since, thinking if someone ever did that to my Simon...'

Seb's heart skipped hopefully. He delved inside his jerkin once more and found the crumpled drawing of the murdered child in his workshop.

'Might this be the lad you saw with pale hair?' he asked, smoothing out the creased paper.

She considered, thoughtfully, pursing her lips.

'Maybe. I didn't see his face so well and he was in anguish and fear; not peaceful, as in this drawing.'

'You cannot put a name to him, then?'

'No. I don't think I'd ever seen such a one before and I'm sure I would have recalled him if I had. Is it important?'

'The lad has since died and been buried without a name. I would inform his family.'

'If the brute who was beating him was family, then I doubt they'll care. But 'tis a sorrowful thing, if he died of the hurts he received that morn. I'll light a candle for him at St Augustine's. There was naught I could do to aid him. The man was a powerful rogue...'

'No blame lies with you, mistress. If you had attempted to aid the lad, the rough fellow could have injured you, also, then what of your children?'

'Aye, you're right, Master Foxley. I never thought of that. There: you have aided me again, soothing my conscience.'

There came a gentle knocking at the street door. Mistress Hutchinson went to answer it.

'My apologies for disturbing you, good mistress...'

Seb heard the familiar voice but did not rise from the bench, not wanting to disturb the sleeping youngster beside him.

'Adam? We be well met,' he called out.

Any friend of Master Foxley must be a friend of hers, so Mistress Hutchinson invited the newcomer to enter and share the ale. Besides, he was a fine-looking man, this Adam.

'May it please you, mistress, this be Adam Armitage, my relative,' Seb made the introductions. 'We be upon the same errand. Adam: this be Mistress Mercy Hutchinson.'

The pair acknowledged each other courteously then Adam grinned.

'I see my cousin has made himself right at home. Seb, you secretive rascal, you never told me you knew of a beautiful woman living down Old Change. I'd have made enquiries here first, had I been aware such sweet mercy awaited.'

Seb frowned at this poet's wordplay. It was quite improper. Adam had yet to learn the appropriate London etiquette. It did not do to speak thus upon the instant of acquaintance.

'We met but an hour since,' he said and was about to make apologies on Adam's behalf. However, Mistress Hutchinson did not seem in the least offended, so he said naught. Adam was smiling broadly and she was laughing as she poured him some ale.

'You live in the city, Master Armitage?'

'Aye, in Paternoster Row, with my cousin… and his goodwife,' he added, casting Seb a meaningful, wide-eyed glance.

Seb, though, did not comprehend the look: a Norfolk gesture, mayhap.

'I believe we have yet to complete our enquiries along Watling Street, concerning Will Thatcher,' Seb said. 'My thanks for the excellent ale, Mistress Hutchinson, but we ought to be upon our task.' He gestured to the sleeping child and she lifted him away. He hardly stirred as she lay him upon a blanket in the opposite corner, as far from the babe's cradle as possible.

'I haven't finished my ale, yet,' Adam protested, raising his cup. 'You go on ahead, Seb; I'll catch up with you when I've drunk this. It would not do to waste such good ale, now would it?'

Seb nodded.

'As you will, cousin. Good day to you, Mistress Hutchinson. It was most pleasant to have made your acquaintance. May the Lord keep you and yours in His gentle care.' He touched his cap and departed. The last he heard as the front door closed behind him was Adam saying:

'Armitage is quite a mouthful. Why don't you call me Adam?'

Such forwardness was quite shocking. Did folk conduct themselves so differently in Norfolk? He would have a quiet word with Adam later; make him aware that Londoners behaved with more restraint than did their fellows from the shires.

Seb hastened back along Watling Street, retracing his steps to where he had first come to the woman's aid. Feeling discomforted, he quite forgot he was supposed to be knocking on doors, making enquiries along the way.

The hour for dinner was passed by the time Seb arrived home, having made good his earlier error in failing to enquire of the folk in Watling Street. Not that his efforts had borne any fruit. Mistress Hutchinson's tale had been the sole glimmer of hope on any account.

'I've kept dinner warm on the hearth for you, Seb.' Rose used a cloth to carry the hot bowl. 'Is Adam not with you? His meal awaits also.'

Seb unfastened his muddy boots and left them by the back door. It would not do to upset Emily by leaving a trail of mud across the kitchen floor – again.

'Adam is, er, making his own enquiries. What of Kate? Is she working alone? That should not be. The guild will have cause to reprimand me, leaving an apprentice to work unguided.'

'Fear not. The lass was in the shop with me all morn, either practising her letters or encouraging customers to buy. You know her smile works magick on the most reluctant of clients. We sold seven scholars' pamphlets, the Latin primer with the red cover, two reams of best paper and had an enquiry for an illuminated book of heraldry. Mind you, the last customer seemed so frail, I'm not certain he'll live long enough to accept the delivery when 'tis finished. I've persuaded him to return upon the morrow to discuss his requirements with you. He knew precisely what he wanted and a collection of heraldic beasts sounds most intriguing. You'll enjoy painting those, Seb. I made a few notes…'

'You are a veritable jewel, Rose. My business would languish without you.' Seb took up his spoon and tucked into his savoury pottage. 'This cannot be of Em's making,' he said, swallowing a good mouthful, 'Else, where be the saffron?'

'No. Nessie and I made it. Em went to visit Dame Ellen.'

'That be good tidings, indeed. She must be feeling better. I hoped an undisturbed night's rest would serve her well. All the same, I purchased this for her from Giles Honeywell, the relic-seller in St Paul's.' He took a tiny silken bag from his purse and gave it to Rose. 'What do you think?'

Rose loosened the drawstring and looked inside. A curling lock of golden hair lay within.

'Whose hair is it?' she asked.

'St Margaret's, the patron and helpmeet of women in childbirth. I thought it would aid and comfort Em in her coming travail.'

'It was a kindly thought. I'm certain she will be glad of it. Did you learn anything of young Will's whereabouts during your enquiries? You were gone quite some hours.'

'Aye, and they were mostly time a-wasted, I fear. However, a widow woman by Distaff Lane believes she may have seen the other unfortunate lad: he with the white hair. At least, she saw a child not unlike him being dragged along by a brutish fellow, a week ago or so. The lad's yellowing bruises could well have been caused around that time.'

'And could she put a name to him?'

'No, not his, but I think our Adam's name may well be upon her lips. They seemed quite taken with each other when I left them at her house, sipping ale together.'

'That isn't proper.'

'Of course it is not, but I could not drag him out by his jerkin. Such a scene would but attract more attention to the impropriety. I pray Adam will not bring yet more disrepute upon the name of Foxley. It will be as if Jude has returned to sully our hard-won reputation all over again.'

'Adam will be most discreet, I'm sure. Have you not considered that he might be lonely here, in London?'

'Lonely? But he has all of us to give him good company.'

'It may be that he needs the solace of a woman.'

'Oh. Aye. I suppose so. Just so long as he keeps within the bounds of acceptable behaviour.'

'Seb. Adam is a man grown; not a green youth. If he needs a woman, a decent widow is better than… than some poor lass forced to work, pleasing men, in order to earn her bread.'

Seb saw that Rose was close to tears, recalling her past life as just such a lass.

'Forgive me, I did not mean to…'

Rose dried her eyes upon her apron.

'You didn't. But of late… what's to become of me, Seb? Your brother abandoned me at the church door but I'm not of a mind to enter a nunnery; not yet.'

'You be lonely too, are you not, Rose? What an unthinking and unkind fool am I, ne'er to have considered your feelings? Dearest lass… any right-minded man in London would be glad to wed you and will have my blessing, so long as he treats you honourably and with gentleness. I will see you have a good dowry: 'tis the least I can do…' He fell silent, seeing the expression upon her lovely face. For the second time that day, the look on a dear one's face left him utterly perplexed as to its meaning.

'Forget my words. I have no complaint. I'm content here, helping Em, working in the shop, caring for Dickon, sewing a few gloves…'

'Aye, well the offer of a dowry stands, should the occasion arise. I'll not go back upon my word.'

Rose sighed as she put his dinner bowl to wash. For a man with so keen an eye for detail, it was a wonder he could be so blind. No matter. Hers was a hopeless cause, anyway.

Whilst they had been talking, little Dickon had been playing quietly, chewing his rag ball, but he crawled over to Rose and used her skirts to pulling himself upright.

'Such a clever little fellow,' Seb cried with delight. 'When did he learn to stand?'

'A few weeks ago but that isn't all he can do, is it, my sweeting?' Rose turned the child around, so he was facing Seb, holding both his hands until he was balanced. 'Now, go to your

Papa, Dickon. Show him how clever you truly are.'

As though he understood every word, the child tottered to his father, barefoot across the kitchen flagstones, arms waving madly. His little face was a study of concentration but having managed four steps before his father caught him and held him close to his heart, one huge smile lit his features.

'What a fine son. What a wonder you be, Dickon!' Seb kissed his soft, dark hair, hardly able to believe one so young could have achieved so much.

The child fought free of Seb's embrace, eager to repeat his new-found skill. Seb set him down, so he faced Rose and he took three steps, paused, then plumped down on his backside to play with his ball – as if that had been his certain intention all along – yet still beaming at his enthralled audience.

'Well done, little man,' Seb applauded. 'Your Mam will be so proud. Does she know of this?'

'Not as yet,' Rose said. 'He managed his first steps only yesterday. Em was too weary...'

Seb looked thoughtful.

'By Christ's sweet mercy, I realise one of my greatest fears has been unfounded, Rose. Little Dickon has not inherited my tendency to lameness, may God's Name be praised for it, indeed. Come Passion Sunday, I shall sing the *Jubilate* with more heartfelt gratitude than ever afore. Dickon will be able to run, jump, dance and play as I have never done. What a marvellous day is this: I shall give twelve pence in alms, on my son's behalf, to the next deserving beggar I see, in thanks for his straight limbs. Oh, Rose, such a blessing we have been granted in this child. Am I deserving of so much joy?'


Despite his delight at seeing Dickon take his first steps, Seb felt somewhat guilty on two accounts: their lack of securing any knowledge whatever on Will's disappearance and his failure to add so much as a single sentence to the transcription of the astrological text, despite Mistress Caldicott's insistence upon urgency. Reluctant to report the lack of progress on one account to the despairing parents – a truth he could do naught to remedy unless Dame Fortune chose to smile on their efforts – he determined to spend at least an hour in the workshop, transcribing the book – something over which he did have some iota of authority at least.

In the event, he became so engrossed in his work, more than the allotted hour passed and the excited voices in the shop did not alert him, oblivious as he was, poring over some convoluted passages on various distempers of womankind under the dominion of the planet Venus and the Moon. They made worrying reading.

'Seb!' Rose called out. 'Seb, this good fellow believes he saw young Will Thatcher yesterday. You must hear his tale straightway.' She ushered a ragged individual into the workshop before returning to the shop, where other customers required her attention.

Seb put down his pen, wiping the nib carefully upon a linen scrap before leaving his desk. The man stood, cap in hand, gazing around the shelves of pigment pots and stacked paper, as though he had never seen such objects in his life. Mayhap, he hadn't. There was likely little use for such things in a stable. With dung on his boots, straws in his hair and the strong stink of horses that swathed him about like a mantle, Seb had no doubt as to the fellow's occupation.

'God give you good day, Master Ostler,' Seb said. Though he was certain of the fellow's trade, he did not look to be master of anything. But Seb knew it was better to assume a man's more elevated rank than to demean him by assuming a lesser degree and giving offence.

The fellow's eyes were darting about. Did the paraphernalia of a stationer so enchant him, or could he not meet Seb's gaze?

'Ned,' he said. 'Just call me Ned. They all does.'

'Very well: Ned. You have information for me?' Seb tried not to sound over-eager; he had already been disappointed too many times during that morn.

'Aye. Like I told her in the shop. I seed him, the lad wot's gone missin'. Yesterday, They tooked him, this lad, Walter.'

'William.'

'Aye, him. They tooked him.'

'And who are 'They'?'

'Them. They swirled him about in their black cloaks, even as he wept and wailed, and bundled him away, ne'er to be seed again.'

'Sit down, Ned, if you will?' Seb moved Adam's vacant stool so the fellow could be easy. In truth, he seemed much agitated by what he had witnessed. And no wonder. 'Kate, lass, would you fetch ale for our guest, if you will. And wafers for us all, if there be any.'

Kate had been working at her desk, quietly ruling up pages, but Seb did not want her to overhear some grisly tale. He returned his attention to Ned. 'Now, good fellow, tell me all you may of this incident.'

'Well, I knowed it must be this lad, Walter...'

'William.'

'Aye. When me sister told me you was askin'. She lives in Friday Street; said you was askin' everybody 'bout a lad gone missin', I knowed it must be him wot they tooked.'

'And where did this occur?'

'Opposite the stables. That's how comed I seed everything.'

This interview was not progressing so well.

'And where be the stables?'

'Down a ways from the Big Owse, o' course. We keeps his lordship's extra horses when there's no more room in his stables.'

'Which big house? To which lord, do you refer?'

'Ned's brother. It's like he's my brother – wot I never had, just me sister – the king and me sharin' a name as well as bein' much of an age. Me and the king – both of us 'Neds', see?'

Seb nodded and rubbed his temples.

'Aye. So this occurred in Bishopsgate, not far from Crosby Place, the Duke of Gloucester's house?' Seb asked, unravelling the fellow's riddle-making.

'That's wot I telled you. You deaf or wot?'

Fortunately, Kate arrived, bearing a tray, and there was a brief respite from this tiresome interrogation whilst she served the ale and offered almond wafers. Both she and Seb were somewhat shocked when the fellow, instead of taking a single wafer, took the platter from Kate's hands and proceeded to devour them all, one after another. He then leaned back against the wall with his ale cup, settling in for an afternoon of pleasurable conversation, so it seemed.

'My thanks, Kate. Mayhap, Rose would welcome your aid in the shop? I hear more than one customer, I believe.' With Kate elsewhere, Seb resigned himself to suffering Ned's story-telling. 'To return to what came to pass, yesterday… describe what you saw, precisely.'

'Well, like I telled you already – if you wos listenin' – They tooked him, bound him in their cloaks, black as night they wos, and then 'pht!' He wos gone, disappeared into their secret portal, into their nether world, never to be seed again. 'Pht!' Just like that. Gone.'

'And where might I find this, er, secret portal?'

'Bishopsgate. Like wot I said.'

'And who was it that abducted the lad? Did you see their faces? Would you know them if you saw them again?'

'Aye, o' course I would. I'd know them black imps anywheres, in their black cloaks. Faery folks… they take pretty little maids. Everybody knows that. Leave changelings in their place. I seed them do it.'

'Imps. Faery folk. In Bishopsgate.' Seb sipped his ale, swirling it in the cup. 'And they take little maids, you say?'

'The prettiest ones. Like wot I telled you.'

'So, why do you suppose they took a lad instead?'

'Me sister said you showed her a picture of him, that he

wos pretty enough to be a maid. P'raps they made a mistook, thinkin' he weren't a lad at all.'

Belatedly, Seb showed Ned one of the drawings of Will Thatcher, but the fellow only shrugged.

'Never seed his face, did I now. They covered his head with their cloaks, them damned black imps, God curse them.'

'If I come to Bishopsgate with you, could you show me this secret portal?'

'Aye. I'd be glad to. Anythin' to vex them nasty faery folks.'

# Southwark

Tom, disappointed by last night's wench who was having none of a masterless man without prospects, although she'd been willing enough when he was a journeyman, had made his way to Southwark to find a bed. His claims that he would be rich come Wednesday hadn't persuaded her either. And then he'd been forced to waste a precious ha'penny to pay a rogue to row him across the river to the southern shore at Bankside, London Bridge being closed for the night by the time the miserable bitch had convinced him he was unwelcome in her bed. Ah well, that was her loss, wasn't it, he thought. Serve her right if her next bedmate gave her the burning pox.

He had found his way to The Mermaid. Desperate for some female company after his earlier frustrations, sloe-eyed Katerina had been everything he needed. Hot and exotic-looking, her lisping accented English tempted him to new follies and he had enjoyed every moment – until this morn.

He had taken Katerina for a willing and lusty tavern wench with a liking for his youthful manliness. And then, all unexpectedly, when he was about to take his leave after breaking his fast on ale and cheap rye bread, a witch of a woman with stone-hard eyes had demanded he pay a groat. A whole groat! For food, drink and services rendered. As it was, his purse contained a penny three farthings, so he could not pay. Even if his purse had been fat enough, he would have refused to pay such a sum for the use of some common Bankside doxy, which, he now realised, was Katerina's trade.

But the skinny witch gave him no choice. He had to work for her to pay off his reckoning. Thus, he was now emptying chamber pots. The indignity of it.

'This is bloody woman's work,' Tom complained loudly to a hefty fellow the woman called 'Cain'. 'I shouldn't be doing this: emptying other buggers' piss. I've got better things to do.'

'Ain't we all,' Cain said, scratching at a fleabite in his groin. 'And when yer've done wi' them pots, Bessie says yer can start washin' cups an' platters. There's plenty else to do an' all. After that, them stables round the side need muckin' out.'

'I'm not washing cups like a serving wench.'

Cain nodded.

'Then go to the stables. That's man's work, no mistake. And get muck-shovellin', or Bessie'll summon the bishop's bailiff and have yer clapped in the Clink for a debtor.'

'That's not fair,' Tom whined. Of a sudden, he seemed to have shed ten years and was a petulant child again. 'I only owe a groat.'

'Aye, an' that's four days' work, at least, prob'ly six, seein' yer'll want feedin' the while an' a bed. That's a week's work yer owe.'

## The Foxley House

'Faery folk!' Emily said. 'You spent the whole afternoon, chasing across London after faery folk? I cannot believe you could be so witless.'

They were at supper. Seb was content to allow Em to chide him, relieved that she looked somewhat improved since yestereve and had strength enough to mock his actions.

'I had to be certain there was no substance to the fellow's tale. With no other clues as to young Will's whereabouts, no stone can be left unturned. But I admit, I may as well have been chasing clouds or trying to catch sunbeams in a sieve.'

'The fellow was right though, about changelings,' Adam put in. 'A widow woman in Norwich one time, swore upon the Gospels that the faeries had stolen her good son and left a changeling in his place. Her neighbours agreed that the little lad had become a monster of late: kicking, biting and screaming, then holding his breath until he went blue in the face. And he but two years of age.'

'Did they find her real son?' Kate asked.

'I never heard what happened after. Me and Noah soon returned to Foxley village and heard no more of the matter. But it was the talk of Norwich for a week or more.'

'Well, there were no faery folk, nor black imps, nor secret portals in this instance,' Seb admitted. 'They were but the good sisters of St Helen's Priory, in their dark habits, taking in orphaned lasses to teach them of housewifery, laundering, cooking, sewing and suchlike. For some reason, the fellow has taken against the nuns. As for the secret portal, it was but the postern gate, through which the children enter the priory for school. There was naught untoward about it. No abductions. No inexplicable disappearances. Ned made it all up. Apparently, he hoped some monetary reward might be forthcoming. He was sore disappointed, especially when I gave the good sisters twelve pence towards their charitable work with the orphans, in lieu of their gross misrepresentation by him. Calling them black imps, indeed.'

'A cracked pot, by the sound of him,' Adam said.

'And you gave them a whole shilling? That fellow isn't the only cracked pot. Whatever possessed you to give so much, you fool?' Emily sounded horrified.

'I had pledged to give that sum in alms to a deserving beggar, to give thanks for little Dickon's straight limbs. The sisters' deeds seemed yet more deserving in the circumstances. I was right glad to do it.'

'Glad!' Emily echoed. 'You'll ruin us, giving coin away for no reason. And what has Dickon to do with it? Don't lay blame upon my child for your lackwit behaviour.'

'Did Rose not tell you? He took his first steps: strong and straight as you please... well, as good as any other babe may, at least. Is that not an occasion to mark with some joyous act of charity, to thank the Almighty for His blessings upon our little son?'

'But a whole shilling? Would a groat not have served to show our gratitude?'

'I will not be miserly in giving thanks to God. Our Saviour gave every last drop of His precious blood for mankind's sake. At this Passiontide, you would have me withhold a few paltry pennies for the betterment of a fatter purse? 'Tis not my way, Em, as you well know.'

She stared at him, then looked away. It seemed, for once, that Seb had won the argument.

'When supper be done, shall Dickon demonstrate to you his new skill?' Seb suggested, attempting to divert his wife's thoughts to a far more pleasing matter. 'You will be full of wonder, seeing him walk.'

''Tis what all children do...' she said, pushing aside her pottage bowl, having eaten little.

'But Dickon be so young. Jude once told me I was nigh unto four years of age without succeeding in taking a step.'

'You were a cripple.'

An uncomfortable moment ensued.

'Hence my generosity,' Seb whispered.

It appeared that despite his and Adam's extensive enquiries, they had advanced not a single step in their search for young Will Thatcher. Time could be running out for the lad. Seb was dreading making report to Beatrice and her goodman. He never knew how to deal with women's tears and that there would be a veritable Noah's Flood of weeping, he did not doubt. So, what next, he wondered?

# Southwark

Tom was curled up in the straw of an empty stall. A horse blew through its nose. Another shook itself and moved a hoof as it slept. The stink of animal-kind was overpowering but the straw provided a free bed. At least, he hoped that witch Bessie wouldn't dare to charge him for it. Where else he might sleep, out of the chill night airs, he didn't know. How he envied all those lucky bastards next door at The Mermaid, slumbering in warm beds or frolicking with the whores. Just thinking about Katerina set his manhood throbbing. It wasn't fair and curse Seb for dismissing him.

This was all *his* fault. Old Master Prim-and-Proper, God rot his soul. Tom seethed with suppressed rage. He would be avenged; pay him back for having to sleep in this filthy hole, for being forced to shovel horse shit all day with little prospect of anything better on the morrow. What would cause Seb the greatest misery? There were numerous possibilities; much scope for hurting that pompous, holier-than-thou, lame-legged fool and Tom fell asleep, plotting the gravest misfortunes that could befall his one-time master.

# Chapter 6

## Wednesday, the seventh day of April
## The Foxley House

DAWN WAS another hour away at least but Seb was in the kitchen, rekindling the fire, doing it quietly by rushlight, leaving the window-shutter closed so as not to waken Nessie, who was sleeping still behind her curtain in the chimney-corner. The thought of her mindless chatter was too much so early as this. As it was, her loud snores were torture enough to a man who had not slept all night.

Sharing Em's bed had been unwise. He had lost count of the times he enquired the reasons for her moaning and groaning, whether he might aid her or fetch ale, only to realise she did so in her sleep - if she truly was sleeping and not feigning it in order to avoid giving him answer. And lying beside her had been like unto embracing hot coals in a furnace until she pulled the blankets this way and that, leaving his nakedness exposed to the chills of night.

Unable to remain abed, he now sat at the kitchen board with a cup of ale, wrapped in his fraying night robe, watching the flames in the hearth dance around the kindling, gaining in strength. He yawned. This day would be a long one, for certain.

'What's amiss, master?'

Seb was startled into wakefulness just as he was snatching a few moments' rest, his elbows propped upon the board, his head in his hands.

'What? Oh, naught amiss, Nessie.' He fingered his eyes. 'Could not sleep is all. I bid you good day.'

'And good day to you, Master Seb. And you lit the fire already.'

'Aye. It was cold.'

'Are you going searching for Will Thatcher again?'

'No doubt. Unless he has come home of his own accord or been found.'

'You ask me, he's runned off to avoid a beating, I reckon.'

'His mother assured me there had been no occasion of late for any kind of family strife…'

'What Beattie Thatcher tells you and what's true mayn't be the same thing. Not everybody tells the truth like you do, master. I know that much and Beattie's a one for telling lies when it suits her to do so.'

'Now, Nessie, that be no way to speak of a respectable woman. Look to your manners, lass.'

''Tis true though, isn't it? Last year she told lies aplenty about Lizzie Knollys' murder, didn't she?'

'Enough, Nessie. We shall not rake over the leaf-fall of those events. They be over and done with.' Seb was aware that Mistress Thatcher had not been alone in telling untruths that previous summer, he and Emily as guilty as any. He would not think on such matters now. He stood and unbarred the shutter, letting in a shaft of pale spring daylight. 'You have tasks to be done, rather than wasting time on gossip.'

'I can do both at once,' she said, giving him a cheeky gap-toothed grin.

Seb shook his head. Why did his serving wench treat him with such discourtesy? Emily would take her broom to her if she knew.

'Come, Gawain,' he called to the dog sprawled under the board. 'At least I can expect good manners from you.' But even as he spoke, opening the door into the yard, Gawain rushed past him in such haste to be about relieving himself outside, Seb was knocked against the jamb, striking his elbow precisely where it most hurt. It seemed there was no courtesy to be had anywhere this morn. Rubbing his elbow, Seb thought again what a long day lay ahead of him and sighed. 'Pour some ale for Mistress Em,' he told Nessie.

'Shall I take it up to her?'

Seb thought of Nessie thundering up the stairs like a herd of oxen on the rampage, pounding along the passageway and hammering on the bedchamber door when Em might still be sleeping.

'Nay. I shall do it shortly. I need to dress anyway.'

Seb tip-toed upstairs, passing Rose on the landing with Dickon in her arms. Having exchanged greetings with them both and having his hair pulled by his son, he went along the passage to the chamber at the front of the house. In the bedchamber, all was quiet but for the early-morning sounds from the street below, Jonathan Caldicott's cockerel crowing – late, as usual – and hints of plainsong chant from St Paul's across the way.

He set down the ale and began to dress in the gloom with barely enough light to see by creeping around the edges of the window shutters. Pulling on nether-clouts, breeches and a clean shirt from the linen press, he decided he was sufficiently decent to waken Emily with gentle words and a draught of ale to refresh her.

'Em. Em, sweetheart. I have brought you ale.'

She did not stir.

'How do you fare, sweetheart?' he asked more loudly. He touched her cheek. It burned like fire. 'Em?' He put down the cup and took her hand, shaking it gently. Her skin felt aflame. 'Em, wake up, my dearest.'

His efforts served for naught. He could not wake her as fever consumed her.

'Sweet Jesu have mercy,' he cried, crossing himself. He stood, perplexed, his heart frantic, his belly churning. He went to the door, paused and thought to take the rest of his clothes. Then discarded them again, going to the bedside, touching Em's forehead. Hot and dry as fire. 'What must I do, Em?' he asked aloud. 'Fetch Dagvyle.' He answered himself. 'Aye... the surgeon... or Nell Warren, mayhap? Tell me, Em. Be you in need of the midwife?' What to do? What to do? Rose. Rose would know.

Seb ran along the passage and down the stairs to the kitchen. On the instant, all knew something was amiss since Seb never ran anywhere.

'Seb? What's wrong?' Rose settled Dickon in his chair at the board.

''Tis Em. I cannot wake her. She burns with fever...'

'Nessie, leave those fish; bring cold water and cloths,' Rose said, hitching up her skirts to retrace Seb's steps in haste.

Nessie abandoned the preparation of the breakfast meal to fetch what was necessary to tend her sick mistress and followed Rose.

Seb, standing in the midst of the kitchen, looked down at his hands. They were shaking like birch leaves in a gale. His whole body was atremble with anguish.

'What to do? What to do?' he repeated under his breath.

'Calmly, Seb,' Adam said. 'Rose will know what's to be done. Most likely 'tis some womanly distemper to do with the coming babe. A day or two of rest and she'll be well again. Mind you, that whitebait will burn if no one tends them.' He took up the largest ladle and pushed the tiny fishes around the pan on the fire.

'I'll do that, master,' Kate said, taking the ladle from him and exchanging it for a long-handled spoon of more suitable size. Adam possessed many skills but cooking was not among them.

Nessie came down the stairs, heavy-footed as a carthorse pulling a laden dray.

'Jack!' she screeched, hanging over the stair rope. 'Mistress

Rose says you've to fetch Mistress Warren. Now!' she added, seeing the lanky youth had yet to move from his stool where he sat, expecting to break his fast.

'Don't yell. I ain't deaf, am I?' He put down his spoon, arranging it just so. Not that he usually cared how the board was set.

'Get a move on, Jack. Mistress Rose said so.'

'Look: I'm goin', ain't I? Keep yer cap on, woman.' He rose, moving slower than treacle, and fetched his cloak from the hook by the door.

'Run, you great oaf!' Nessie cried, urging him out into the yard with her foot. She might have kicked his backside but he was too tall and she had to be content with the back of his knee.

'Leave off, yer stupid woman, else I won't be able to run anyways, will I?'

'Well, make haste then. Mistress Em's that poorly. Go.' Having made sure Jack was gone upon his errand, Nessie thumped back up the stairs and along the passage overhead, dislodging dust motes from the rafters which reflected in the light before landing on the board.

'The fish are ready,' Kate said. 'Shall I serve them, masters?'

'May as well, lass,' Adam said. 'No point having them all spoil but set some aside for everyone else. Seb, do you want bread with yours? Seb!'

'What do you say?' Seb was vague.

'Food: you want some?' Adam was wrapping a slice of bread around three or four whitebait.

'Nay. I be of no mind to eat.'

'You need to keep your strength up, cousin. Mayhap, you're going to be a father twice over sooner than you thought.'


Seb wandered up Ivy Lane, into the Shambles. Butchers were busy, setting up their stalls; goodwives gathering, hoping to be first to buy the best cuts the moment the market bell rang, chattered whilst they waited. For weeks, the butchery trade had been meagre, what with the Lenten season and meat not permitted. But Easter Sunday would see the long fast at an end and preparations for the celebratory feast were underway in most households.

Someone called out to Seb, knowing him for their neighbour, but he did not hear them. Gawain stopped, turned and trotted to Mistress Caldicott, who gave him a scratch behind his ear.

'Your master seems distracted. What's amiss with him?' she said to the dog – as if the creature might answer.

To Seb's eyes, London seemed bleached of colour this morn; all sounds afar off, as though fleece filled his ears. He could think of naught save Emily's beloved face, hot and puffy with fever, her eyes closed. With her sorry image before him, he reached Newgate just as the gates were unbarred.

A stream of carts, donkeys with panniers and folk with laden baskets came pouring into the city, bringing fresh produce from the countryside to London's many markets. Seb was pulled aside by the gatekeeper, out of the path of a cart, loaded with onions and little spring caboches, that he failed to notice was bearing down upon him.

'Watch out, my friend,' the gatekeeper warned. 'Surely, you see the cart?'

'Oh, aye. My thanks,' Seb replied even as he was knocked by a woman's hefty basket of new-sprouted alexanders, richly green, and the carter shouted at him, cursing him for a blind idiot.

'I tried the horehound, as you recommended,' the gatekeeper was saying. 'Got it from the 'pothecary in Cheap. Me cough's much improved since.'

'Oh.' Seb glanced around, wondering how come he stood by Newgate without any remembrance of getting there. Was he come for a purpose?

'Right grateful for your advice, master.'

'What? What advice?'

''Bout the horehound. I'll buy you an ale sometime... The

wife sent me to the 'pothecary for something for our young un's feverish chill and I saw the horehound on the shelf and…'

'Fever! Something for fever. Aye.' Seb was shaken from his bewilderment, recalling that he too should have been making for the apothecary's shop – in quite the opposite direction. 'I thank you for reminding me,' he called out as he joined the incoming flow of folk making their way to Cheapside, instead of battling against the tide. 'Gawain! Gawain, where be you?'

A wet, black nose and glossy coat came out of the crowd, carrying a juicy piece of mutton in its jaws.

'Have you been thieving, you bad dog? Oh, Gawain. You will be in trouble, if the butchers see you with your ill-gotten prize. Eat it swiftly, you foolish creature. I dare suppose the Lenten fast does not apply to dogs. 'Tis unfortunate we must go back through the Shambles to reach Cheap. Behave yourself this time. Keep close, Gawain, and your head low. I would not have them see any trace of blood upon your muzzle.'

Gawain obeyed, trotting so close to Seb's feet there was a danger he would trip his master, but they reached the apothecary's shop in Cheapside without mishap.

The apothecary, Master Lewis, was a merry Welshman with red cheeks, a beaming smile and a Celtic lilt in his voice. Such a fellow was a ready tonic for anyone feeling out of humour, even before they purchased a remedy. The place smelled sweeter than other shops of its kind that Seb had entered in the past, but Master Lewis's was a new business. Mayhap, Seb thought, it took time for the stinks of brimstone and Venice treacle to permeate the walls and rafters but, for the present, the scents of caraway, thyme and anise filled his nose.

'God give you good day, Master Lewis,' Seb said, ducking beneath the bundles of dry herbs that hung from the ceiling.

'And also to you, Master Foxley. How may I be of service to you? More pigments, is it? I have some fine ochres lately from Naples in Italy. First shipload of the season.'

'Nay. A remedy for fever. My goodwife, Emily, be in need.

Gawain! Leave be.' Seb pulled the dog away from a basket upon the floor, the contents of which had enticed him.

'Dried bullocks' testicles,' the apothecary said.

'What? For a fever?' Seb's horror was apparent as he stepped away from the counter-board, catching a dangling nosegay of dried lavender that showered its scented flowers upon his head.

'No, no,' the man laughed. 'In the basket. Your dog has found them out.'

'Oh. I was afeared you meant...'

'Your goodwife is great with child, is she not?'

'Aye. You know of her?'

'Certainly. She has been here much of late for various remedies for her swollen feet and hands, aches and pains and nausea. And now you say she has a fever?'

'I did not know of this. I was aware that she was nigh overcome by weariness and her feet were swollen but...'

'She has not told you of her indispositions? Well, I suppose that's the way with female problems: the husband is the last to learn of them. You haven't noticed her dizzy spells then? She was taken quite poorly by such a turn here just yesterday; had to sit upon a stool while I held a burnt feather to her nose, to revive her, and then took a draught of spiced wine as a restorative. You didn't know of this?'

'She ne'er said a word of it,' Seb said, shaking his head. 'Do you know of the cause? Be the babe in her womb the reason? She was not assailed by such afflictions last time she was with child. But this morn, I could not wake her and she burns so....'

A customer came in then, demanding something to ease his agony of a tooth worm upon the instant. The apothecary sold the man some oil of cloves but, with his jaw looking so inflamed, advised him to visit a barber-surgeon and have the offending tooth drawn. The man paid three pence for the tiny vial of oil, disinclined to argue the high price, but muttering as he departed something concerning the likelihood of hell freezing over, ere he would resort to suffering the ministrations of a damned, blood-thirsty barber-surgeon.

'He will, in the end,' Master Lewis said, putting the coins in a box on the shelf. 'They all do, eventually. Now: your goodwife's fever... I like not the sound of it.'

'The midwife has come. She has sent me here for pennyroyal, mugwort and white hellebore. Be those good for fever? I have not heard that such things are. I thought feverfew might be...' Was it Seb's imagination, or had the apothecary's ruddy cheeks faded somewhat of a sudden?

'Master Foxley, won't you come through to my still-room? We can be undisturbed there. I would speak privily with you.'

'But I was told to hasten. These things be needed urgently.'

'A few minutes won't matter.'

'What of other customers that may come?'

'As I say: a few moments only. Come through, I pray you, master.'

Seb followed Master Lewis into the poky still-room behind the shop, where various potions bubbled over braziers, stood cooling on the window ledge or awaited bottling and labelling. Here, the smells were not so sweet, and Seb's eyes watered as pungent, acrid steam wafted towards him.

'Sit there, if you will.' The apothecary removed a basket of green glass bottles from a stool and indicated that Seb should sit down. He appeared immune to the potent airs, taking a cup and a flagon from a shelf and pouring a generous measure. 'You may be needing that,' he said, handing Seb the cup.

''Tis Emily who be sick, not me. I have no need. What is it, anyway?' He sniffed the cup.

'Spiced wine: a good restorative; the same remedy I gave your goodwife yesterday.'

'But...'

'Just listen, Master Foxley. I think you must prepare yourself. Do you know of the uses of pennyroyal, mugwort and white hellebore?'

'Nay. I know little of the apothecaries' craft, except for inks and pigments, of course.'

Master Lewis sighed.

'I thought not. These plants are used by women to bring on the menses.'

Seb gave him a blank look.

'You know of women's moon cycles?'

'Somewhat. I know they cease when a woman is with child and begin once more sometime after. Is that what the midwife be about? But what of the babe in the womb? Emily says 'tis not due until the end of May...'

The apothecary remained silent.

'The babe is to be birthed now,' Seb said, drawing his own conclusion. 'But why? The child will die, if 'tis born so soon.'

'I fear there is little choice, Master Foxley. I have come across such cases twice before; one was my own sister. Something has gone awry betwixt mother and child – no man knows what, exactly – but your goodwife's body is poisoning itself. Removing the babe is the only way to save her life; God willing. In my sister's case, she recovered, though she will never bear another child. But in the other, the outcome was not so happy.'

'The woman died?'

'I'm sorry to give you such ill news but I thought you should be forewarned. I know midwives rarely take the trouble to inform husbands of what they're about. Drink your wine. Recover yourself, master, whilst I prepare the herbs for you.'

Seb walked home slowly, sorrow dragging at his heels, knowing what dire consequences lay within the twists of linen in his purse: life for Emily, but only if Jesu Christ was merciful; the certain end of life for an innocent babe that had ne'er even drawn breath. He almost regretted that the apothecary had told him.

Casting his gaze along Paternoster Row, it seemed the buildings, the cobbles, the folk going about their lives, everything was the colour of shadows, as if grey Death stalked the streets. And he feared that he knew which street Death was haunting now, the very house: his own.

# The Pig and Pipe tavern in Knightrider Street, midday.

Tom had sneaked away from the stables by The Mermaid, across the river. It had been difficult to elude Cain, who seemed to be everywhere at once but, having joined the throng on London Bridge, he felt safe. What was more, after this day, his debts would be no more, when Lord Lovell's coins filled out his skinny purse. The prospect of imminent wealth brought a smile to his face. When Lovell brought the money – as he surely would – leaving it behind the holly bush outside the tavern door, Tom would be waiting. Not too close, though. The last thing he wanted was a face to face encounter with the dark-visaged lord. That would be too terrifying, aye, and dangerous. Who could say what the man might do? Tom realised, belatedly, he really hadn't thought his plan through. Oh, well, it couldn't be helped now. He must make the best of it. If he hid close by the tavern and watched for Lovell's arrival, he could send a street urchin – with the promise of a whole penny reward – to collect the coins. Aye, that would serve. No point in risking his own skin.

St Paul's bell chimed the midday Angelus. Tom's mouth was so dry, he felt in need of another drink but his purse contained only a bent farthing. Besides, in a few minutes, he would be able to afford best Gascon wine by the jug full. He could wait that long and find a better hostelry in which to drink it. He picked up his bag of belongings and left the tavern by the back door, out into a noisome alleyway.

The alley served as the tavern customers' privy and smelled worse than the public jakes over the Fleet River. Tom gagged on the stink and tried to hold his breath until he'd rounded the corner, where the alley came out onto Knightrider Street, beside a harness-maker's shop three doors along. Peering out cautiously, he saw he had the perfect vantage point: the holly bush in its pot was in clear view. The wait should be a short one, he hoped.

Folk came and went along the busy thoroughfare. Some entered the tavern; others departed. But not one of them was Lord Lovell. Tom began to fret that his plan had gone awry. Mayhap, Lovell hadn't received the letter. Or he'd chosen to ignore the threat. So what now? He had no coin to live on.

Then he noticed a little ferret of a fellow glancing about, furtively. Having made sure he was unobserved, he dropped a heavy-looking cloth bag behind the plant pot and scurried off, head down. Tom laughed out loud. His plan had worked and, since Lord Lovell was nowhere in sight, he had no need to pay an urchin to collect the bag but could do so himself. Without taking so much as the precaution of looking around, as the deliverer had done, Tom strode towards the pot, eager to claim the bag before someone else should think to take it.

The weight of the bag thrilled him. He had no idea that the sum of £20 would weigh so heavy and the chink of metal within was the most joyous sound Tom had ever heard. He did his best to walk away as if this was a matter of no importance but he was so eager to open the bag, to see and touch the silver, that he almost ran to find some place where he could look inside without any prying eyes to see.

There was another alleyway betwixt the church of St Andrew-by-the-Wardrobe and a respectable house next door. Less vile than the one behind the tavern, this alley was narrow and dark beneath the eaves of the buildings on either hand. A feral cat hissed as he intruded upon her domain before she turned and fled, leaping over a high wall at the far end. This place seemed safe enough and secret: Tom could examine his prize at last. In his haste, he fumbled with the tied cords of the drawstring, getting them hopelessly knotted. He put down the rest of his belongings to try again, but the knot had pulled too tight. Frantic with impatience, he took his dinner knife from its sheath at his belt, cut the cords with it and dropped it to the ground, intent upon opening the bag.

It was hard to make out in the gloom but surely there should be a glint of silver, at least. There was none. Tom put his hand in the bag and drew out a length of rusted iron chain. Throwing the bag aside, he swore mightily and kicked at the stonework of the church.

'Bastard! Bastard!' he yelled. Only then did he look up.

A dark figure stood, hands on hips, blocking the alley, outlined against the brightness of Knightrider Street beyond. The figure was making an odd sound. Belatedly, Tom realised it was laughing.

'Thought to abscond with your master's ill-gotten gains, did you, you disgusting little worm?'

Tom felt panic rising in his gullet. This wasn't the ferrety-looking fellow. No. He recognised the voice, one he would never forget from those terrible days as the apothecary's apprentice. It belonged to the dread Lord Lovell himself. He darted towards his dinner knife, lying where he'd dropped it.

'Leave it,' Lovell growled, advancing down the narrow way to kick the small blade aside. 'You think it a match for this?' He drew a long-handled dagger from his belt. The ferocious steel caught what little light there was in the alley: an evil, deadly gleam. The lord wasted no more time nor words but stepped closer, grabbing Tom's shoulder and pulling him forward onto the blade.

Tom had no chance to struggle nor to cry out. His last sensation in this life was the icy spike of fine Toledo steel in his vitals.

'Fear not,' Lovell muttered, withdrawing and wiping his dagger on Tom's jerkin, 'You'll soon have familiar company in Purgatory. Your Master Foxley will be joining you before much longer. Reneging on our past agreement was unwise of him. I should have ended his miserable existence long ago. He ought never to have sent you on this errand, since you're utterly untrustworthy and incompetent as ever. 'Tis a pity indeed that Foxley did not come in person: I could have put an end to this problem once and for all. However, 'tis not too late; his days will be few.'

Lovell stepped away, noting with distaste a smear of blood upon his silken hose where the falling body had brushed his leg. Peasant's gore. The lord shuddered.

With a parting kick at the now-lifeless body, Lovell sheathed his blade, straightened his fine-plumed hat and strolled out into the sunlight, to collect his horse. The splendid beast waited patiently, tethered by St Andrew's porch. The priest was coming from the church and, seeing so finely dressed a gentleman, gave him a blessing. In reply, Lovell showed his teeth, but whether in a smile or a snarl was hard to tell.

# The Foxley House

All was quiet when Seb reached home. Kate was watching the shop. For once, her smile was absent; even her unruly curls were somehow subdued, having lost their bounce. Little Dickon sat on the floor, chewing his rag ball; he was also quieter and less lively than usual.

'Not one customer has come in, master, in all the long while since you've been gone,' Kate said. 'It is as if they know all is not well here. Mayhap, they have heard of Emily's fever and fear it to be a symptom of some contagion.'

Seb nodded but did not speak.

In the workshop, Adam, as ever, was working at his desk. It might seem that he was unaffected by events until he screwed up the paper he had been writing and flung it in the corner, where it added to a pile of similarly discarded sheets.

''Tis no good, Seb. I cannot concentrate this day. I've made so many mistakes, you wouldn't believe I was ever a competent scribe. Knowing… or rather not knowing what's going on above stairs: the comings and goings, the cries and outbursts...'

'All seems quiet now,' Seb said.

'Aye, and somehow the silence is worse. What are they doing up there? I can't enquire; I'm not her goodman, but you can ask, Seb.'

Seb made for the stairs, taking the twists of linen from his purse. His errand had taken far longer than it should have but, no matter the urgency demanded, he had found haste impossible. Both his heart and his feet would delay the delivery of those fearful herbs as long as they could. Even now, it was all he might manage to drag himself up the stairs, to hand them to Nell Warren that she might do her best – or worst – as a midwife.

When he knocked at the bedchamber door, Nessie opened it. Over her broad shoulders, he was shocked to see Dame Ellen, her friend Mary Jakes and Peronelle Wenham, as well as Rose and Nell, all crammed into the chamber, working by candlelight. The shutters still closed out the sunlight and two braziers glowed like devils' eyes in the gloom. A gust of hot air hit Seb's face, as though he had opened an oven. He wondered how Em's fever could ever be cooled in such a chamber and was about to ask. But Nessie took the herbs in their twists of linen from him and shut the door again, catching the toe of his boot upon the threshold. No enquiries could be made. He would have to suffer in ignorance.

'How is Em faring?' Adam asked when Seb returned to the workshop.

Seb shrugged as he set down the ale jug and cups, brought from the kitchen, onto Tom's unused desk. It yet bore the lad's initials that he'd carved into the oak years before.

'I had no opportunity to ask,' Seb replied, filling the three cups. 'The door was closed in my very face. What c-care they for our manly anxieties in such a case? The apothecary was more informative. In truth, he told me far more concerning the herbs I was sent to purchase than I w-wanted to know.'

'What did he say of them?'

'That they indicate a grave s-situation… that the b-babe be unlike to s-survive.' Seb dabbed his eyes with his sleeve and made an effort to compose himself as he carried a cup through to the shop. 'Kate, there be ale for you at your desk. I shall wait upon any customers and tend to Dickon.' He sipped his ale and surreptitiously wiped a stray tear. 'Mayhap, you could rule up some fresh pages for Master Adam; 'tis likely he will need them.'

'Aye, master. Is there any news of Mistress Em?'

'Nay. Not as yet. Go have your ale, lass.'

'What of dinner, master? 'Tis well passed the hour. I'm surprised Jack isn't here, chewing his thumbs for hunger's sake.'

'Oh, aye. I had not realised.' Seb fished in his purse. 'Here, take a groat. When you wish, go buy a pie from the cookshop.'

'No need. Mistress Rose sent me out earlier. She has taken care of all. An oyster pie awaits us on the hearthstone, keeping warm in the kitchen, when you permit, master.'


There were six persons, including little Dickon, sitting down to a belated dinner in the kitchen of oyster pie and flatbread – no one had time to spare to let it work and rise. Nessie, coming downstairs for more ale for the women, had told them to think themselves fortunate there was any bread at all on such a day. Jack had arrived with a sack of shavings and wood off-cuts for the fire, accompanied by Master Appleyard, who was invited to share the meal.

'They'll be needing extra kindling,' Master Appleyard was saying, speaking around a mouthful of oysters and sauce. 'Always need a good fire to warm a new babe. Leastwise, they did when my John and Em herself came into the world. And what of Emily? Any news of my daughter?' He swallowed and broke off more bread to mop up the sauce. 'I have to say, Seb, this is all your doing, this early arrival.'

'Mine? How so?' Seb pushed his platter towards Jack. He had

barely touched the food and knew Jack would not see so much as a mouthful go to waste. 'Whatever did I do amiss, Stephen?'

'She's afflicted because of seeing that murdered lad in this house. Everybody knows this is the likely outcome for a woman great with child. If she espies a hare in the field, her child is born with a hare-lip, so the Blessed Virgin knows what harm seeing a slain corpse might cause her. 'Tis your fault, Seb. You should have shielded my Emily from such horrors at this time.'

'But I did not bring the dying lad into this house. He came of his own accord. And no more could I prevent Emily from seeing him. I told her to stay away but she would not heed my words.'

'You're her goodman; as her husband, you should have insisted on her obedience for her own good.'

Seb sighed into his napkin. Did her father not know his daughter better than that? For certain, he must realise she was the most obstinate woman in all the city. She delighted in defying her husband at every turn, even upon occasion when obedience was to her advantage.

Before he could make any defence, someone knocked at the shop door, which was closed whilst they ate.

'A customer, no doubt,' Seb said, eager to leave the board. 'I shall go attend them.'

But it wasn't a customer. It was Beatrice Thatcher.

'Any news?' she demanded without giving any greeting, nor entering the shop.

'No, not as yet, mistress. Too early, I suppose,' Seb replied. Will you please to come in?'

'Too early? 'Tis nigh unto the hour of three after noontide.' The woman remained standing in the street. 'How is that too early? How are your enquiries after my Will coming along? Any word of him?'

Seb gaped at her, appalled. He had forgotten utterly regarding the missing youngster. What would the lad's mother think of him? What kind of uncaring man was he to have abandoned the search when time was of the essence?

'Forgive me, Beatrice, other matters have demanded my full attention this day but...'

'Other matters, indeed! Naught can be more important than finding my son.' Beattie burst into noisy tears. Folk in Paternoster Row stopped to gawp at this terrible fellow causing a goodwife to weep in public.

''Tis Emily... taken right poorly this morn,' he attempted to explain but Beattie wasn't listening.

'Hardly half an hour you gave to the search yesterday and then ceased troubling yourself with the task. You promised me you'd find him. What sort of idle, useless so-called neighbour are you, refusing to aid us at our time of greatest need and worry? You're wicked, Seb Foxley, abandoning my lad to who knows what terrible fate. I shall never trust you again.'

'Beatrice... 'tis not as you say...' But she was gone, hitching up her skirts and running back towards her home by Cheap Cross.

Seb returned to the kitchen.

'Anyone important?' Adam asked.

'Beatrice Thatcher, wanting to hear of our progress in the search for her son.'

'Oh, God Almighty save us, I had quite forgotten about the lad.'

'As had I.'

'I'll remedy the matter straightway, cast our net wider. I'll ask along Cheapside to the east and into Poultry. You have no objection, do you, Seb? After all, I'm worse than useless at scribing this day and the task may redirect my thoughts.'

'As you will, Adam. I feel 'tis my duty to remain here, in case I be needed. And Kate cannot work at her desk, nor in the shop, unsupervised.'

'I could wash these platters and start preparing supper, master,' the lass suggested, piling up the soiled dishes on the board. 'I know the pot herbs and worts to be added to the pottage. I can do that without you need to watch me.'

'And we'll be away to our own work,' Stephen Appleyard

announced, rising from the bench. 'Come along, Jack, shift yourself. You've another leg to turn for that stool you're making. My thanks for the pie and don't forget to send me tidings directly, if anything happens above stairs. I'm looking forward to being a grandfather again.' The older man kissed Dickon's dark downy hair as the child sat high in his special chair. 'And take care of this little one, also.' He said no more but Seb sensed the unspoken reproof: 'better care than you've taken of my daughter'.

Seb reopened the shop door, hoping for a few customers to cheer him. Gawain sprawled 'neath the counter-board and Dickon slept in his nest of blankets in the corner, under a shelf of cheap, scholars' pamphlets. He had outgrown his basket some while before and usually took his nap in the kitchen after noontide, whilst the women were busy there. But Seb felt the need of human company of some kind; even a sleeping infant was better than being alone.

Paternoster Row was bustling outside. An intransigent dray-horse, shying at a stray chicken, had provided a distraction, to be followed by a pair of curs fighting, urged on by passers-by who would wager upon the victor of this unexpected entertainment. Growls, barks and shouts grew louder.

Seb went out to intervene. So much noise would disturb poor Em in her sickbed above the shop. Of course, Gawain came also, joining in the barking with enthusiasm.

'Less noise, good folk, I pray you,' Seb shouted, attempting to make himself heard. 'Please… take these wretched creatures elsewhere. My wife lies ill above stairs.' He waved towards the closed window shutters. 'Can you not have some consideration…'

'How much you want t' wager?' a scruffy fellow asked him, quite mistaking Seb's meaning. 'Your dog going t' join in?'

'He is not.' Seb hauled Gawain back inside the shop and closed the door to keep him within. 'My goodwife be most unwell.'

'Aye, and a good scrap will cheer you. I'll wager a penny on the brindled dog. You want the same on that one-eared beast?'

'Nay. I want you to cease this unholy row for my wife's sake.'

Before the fellow could answer, the dog fight ended as suddenly as it had begun with the brindled dog turning and fleeing through the crowd, directly towards them, followed swiftly by his opponent. The tattered fellow was knocked off his feet and fell against Seb, taking them both down. The street was muddy and Seb slipped in trying to regain his balance. The fellow's elbow caught him upon the nose and blood flowed.

The crowd regrouped, thinking the fight was continuing with two men come to blows over a wager won and lost. Seb's neighbour, Jonathan Caldicott, once again searching for his wife's wandering hens, saw his friend in difficulty, suffering a bloody nose, and waded into the affray, thinking to assist. Others joined the fight on the scruffy fellow's side. Fists flew; blood sprayed; eyes blackened and knuckles bruised. A mishap had become a street brawl.

The window shutters above the shop were thrown open and Rose leaned out. A bowl of water was emptied on the heads of those wrestling on the cobbles below.

'Stop this!' Rose yelled. 'A woman labours with child here. Cease your quarrelling, you rascals, and give her some peace.' She withdrew her head and closed the shutters after.

The unexpected dowsing worked a small miracle. The brawlers, one by one, sorted themselves out of the heap of bodies and slowly dispersed to nurse their hurts.

'Not sure how that happened, are you?' said the fellow who had brought Seb down, offering his hand to help Seb to his feet.

'Nay. Be you injured?'

'A few knocks. I'll mend but you should get a surgeon to look at that nose. It might be broked.'

''Tis bruised, is all.'

'You'll likely have a handsome pair of black eyes by the morrow.'

'What were you fighting about?' Jonathan Caldicott asked,

licking his grazed knuckles and grinning. He enjoyed a good scrap as much as any man, no matter the cause.

'Naught,' Seb said. 'There was no fight betwixt us. We two were knocked down by a pair of curs. Others saw blood – as you did – and determined it must be an altercation. The brawl was of their making, not ours.'

'I was only thinking to aid you, Seb.' Jonathan sounded most disappointed. 'Your brother Jude would do so.'

'Jude be in some far land; Italy, so he wrote in his most recent letter after Christmas. And in any case, I did not require aid.'

'You certain of that? I thought I saw Jude last week in Southwark… when the bishop's business took me there,' Jonathan added by way of explanation. ''Twas a fellow so much like him and Christmas is long past. He could be back in England by now.'

'I be sure he would have returned to us, if he were here.'

With that, Seb went back into his shop. Dickon was wailing, having been frightened by the disturbance outside. Seb was about to take him in his arms to comfort him but then realised his jerkin was soaking wet and blood-stained, his hose plastered with mud and his nose was bleeding still. 'Kate! Kate,' he called out.

She came running from the kitchen.

'What was all that noise, master?'

'Console Dickon, would you, lass. I need to clean myself somewhat.' Seb sounded nasal as he blotted his sore nose on his sleeve.

'But whatever happened to you, Master Seb? I'll fetch a towel.'

'No need. I shall tend to it.' He went to the kitchen but found there was no water, the buckets and ewers must all be upstairs – where he dared not intrude. Out in the yard, a bucket stood by the pigsty, ready for the piglet's suppertime feed. It was half full of water and Gawain began to lap it up.

'Leave it, for pity's sake,' Seb told him. 'Your kind has caused me trouble enough this hour past.' He soaked a napkin and bathed his face. The cold water eased the pain in his nose but the white linen was soon crimson. How Emily would scold him when she saw his stained and soiled attire and one of her best napkins, ruined. He should have used an old one but, in his haste, had grabbed the first cloth to hand. His face hurt and his head was throbbing from the blow received, but if he asked her for her meadowsweet remedy, she would tell him the pain served him right; it was his own fault and he could suffer the consequences.

If, indeed, she ever told him anything... ever again.

The sudden thought horrified him.

Adam found him there, leaning against the wall of the pigsty, sobbing as though his heart was rent asunder.

'What is it, Seb? Not Emily?' Adam pulled his kinsman's hands from his face. 'God Almighty, what have you done to yourself? I've seen more heartening sights dead on a butcher's slab. I'm gone for an hour or so and return to find you thus. I daren't turn my back for an instant and look at you! Tell me what came to pass.'

'I tripped is all. Naught of importance. Caught my nose.'

'On some man's fist, it seems to me.'

'It was not thus.'

'As you will.' Adam shrugged. 'So, what of Em?'

'I know not. They tell me naught. Oh, Adam, I be so afeared for her. What if the worst befalls? I could not bear to lose her. What would I do? What of little Dickon?'

# Chapter 7

**Wednesday eve and Maundy Thursday,
the eighth day of April
The Foxley House**

ROSE CAME down the stairs. She looked weary indeed, her hair straying from her cap and a single long strand hung to her shoulder.

'How be Emily?' Seb asked.

'She is asking for you, Seb,' Rose answered. Her tired face betrayed no hint as to why he was wanted above stairs of a sudden but, since she was not smiling, Seb doubted the reason was a pleasurable one.

He rose to follow her but she saw his shirt and noted his bruised face for the first time.

'Oh, Seb, you can't let Em see you like this, all blood-spattered. Whatever befell you?

'An unfortunate mischance.'

'Take off your jerkin and put on a clean shirt, at least, else you'll affright Em.'

'All my linen lies in the clothes-press in our chamber. I have naught else to hand.'

'I'll lend you one of mine,' Adam said, sprinting out into the yard and taking the outside stairs two at a time, to his chamber over the workshop. He returned swiftly with a clean garment, still smelling of lavender.

'Seb, I'll put your stained shirt to soak overnight in the bucket, else the blood will never come out,' Rose said, sighing over the lamentable state of the garment.

'Give it here,' Adam offered, 'I'll put the bucket outside in the yard, out of sight. No need to affright Em, if she should see it.'

Now looking respectable – though naught but time would remedy his bruised and swollen nose – Seb went upstairs with Rose, his heart fluttering in his chest, fearful of what awaited him. He wanted to enquire of Rose, desperate to hear some reassuring words yet, expecting there would be none, he did not dare to ask.

He entered the bedchamber. The rank odours of medicinal herbs and perspiring female bodies nigh overwhelmed him, but he braced himself and, in the grip of apprehension, made his way to the bedside. The women drew back, to give him room and a morsel of privacy with his wife. He sat upon the stool and took Em's hand in his, hot and moist against his chill skin.

'Em, dear heart. 'Tis me; Seb. You asked for me.'

Emily's eyelids hesitated, fluttering like the wings of a butterfly, then opened. Her eyes were clouded, the pupils enlarged. No sign of the sapphire blue that he adored.

'Did I?'

'I was told so. How do you fare, sweetheart? If I may do the least thing for you... Do you have the lock of St Margaret's hair that I bought to aid you?'

'Just go away. Leave me in peace. I'm that weary.'

Seb tucked her hand beneath the coverlet and stood.

'Is the babe likely to be birthed soon? Did the pennyroyal work?'

'What do you know of such matters?' Nell Warren said, folding up a sheet.

'The apothecary explained the uses of the herbs you had me purchase this morn.'

'He had no business doing that. Men should keep their long noses out of women's matters.'

'Tell me, mistress – and I want the truth – is the babe coming now?'

'No. It is not; not yet.'

'And Emily herself? What of her?'

'Only God can answer that.' The midwife turned back to folding sheets.

Outside the chamber, Rose saw his forlorn expression and touched his arm.

'Em is a strong woman, Seb. There is always hope. We are all praying for her.'

'I know and I be that grateful, Rose. Do what you can to aid her.'

Rose did not mention that she prayed hardest of all for him.

## The Mermaid, Southwark

Will Thatcher lay curled up on a pile of smelly old sacks. Last eve, he had cried himself to sleep once again, clutching his grandmother's rosary so tightly that the coral beads made a chain of deep dents across his palm and the chewed cross of ivory scored his fingers. He wanted his Mam; he wanted to go home, to sleep in his own bed betwixt proper sheets. It seemed he had been here for weeks in this horrible cellar.

A stout oaken door, barred on the other side, blocked his way to freedom, although a sleek rat came and went, able to squeeze underneath it. The creature had been company for a while, bold enough to steal a breadcrumb left on Will's platter. It had then disappeared through a crack in the wall. The wall along that side was slimy and green and Will was sure he could sometimes hear the river lapping nearby. He could certainly smell its stinking mud.

In the opposite wall, furthest away from the damp, there was a narrow iron grille, high up, which let in the thinnest line of grubby daylight and the sounds of folk passing by. Thinking they might aid him, he had shouted until his throat was sore, begging for help but either they were all deaf to his cries or the noises of the street were too loud. Or, mayhap, such pleas were so common in this place, none heeded a young lad in need. Whatever the case, he was still here.

It seemed some other had been here before him also. Nasty brown stains upon the sacks that served as his bed and fine white hairs, like short pale lengths of his mother's silk threads, were left behind. It might even be that someone had scratched their name on the wall beside the bedding, or had begun to do so: 'E' was clear enough; then 'D' and, mayhap the start of a 'P' or an 'R' before the carver had given up the effort. The gouges looked to be quite recently made. Will wondered what had happened to his predecessor. He'd likely never know.

Cain brought him food every so often, unbarring the door to a flight of uneven wooden stairs. Will ate it, having a youngster's appetite, but it didn't taste like Mam's cooking. No white bread, only dark stuff of the cheapest kind he'd always thought was meant for horses. That's what Mam called it: horse bread. There was a slop bucket for his use in the corner. At home, one thing Mam was particular about was emptying the chamber pots first thing in the morn, but the bucket had yet to be taken for emptying. It just added to the stink.

## Maundy Thursday morn
## The Foxley House

The solemn office of the day had been conducted in every church throughout Christendom and everyone had attended. But not Emily. Seb and Rose had been fearful of leaving her abed, alone whilst everyone went to St Michael's, forwhy she might take a turn for the worse. However, even in her poorly condition, Em was not to be gainsaid. With her fever much reduced, she had insisted that she was well enough and would enjoy the peace of an empty house for a while, taking the chance to sleep. In truth, she was weary of their fussing and much relieved that Nell Warren and the other women had gone home, since the babe's coming was not imminent after all. Heaven alone knew what potions they had poured down her throat but they had eased her pain somewhat, although she felt as exhausted as one who'd climbed to the moon and back.

In St Michael's, Seb had been desperate to light candles for Emily's recovery but on Maundy Thursday, of all days, no candles were to be lit in church, signifying the darkest hours as the moment of Our Lord's greatest sacrifice approached. Father Thomas – usually so compassionate and obliging – had refused Seb's heartfelt plea that exception be made for Emily but promised to remember her especially in the daily prayers. Seb had to be content with that but his anxiety for Em took precedence in his mind, even outweighing any contemplation of Christ's coming Passion, upon which every Christian was required to fix his thoughts. For Seb, any attempt to envision the Lord's suffering was overridden continuously by the remembrance of the sights and sounds of Em's pain. Christ would rise again upon the third day; if she succumbed, his beloved would have to await Judgement Day afore they could be reunited. Life without Em… the prospect was unthinkable.

The moment they returned from church, Seb hastened up to the bedchamber, only to halt at the door. Supposing… No, that could not be. He pushed open the door. A smile lit his face. Emily was sitting up, propped against the pillows, combing out her tangled hair.

'Oh, 'tis you. Ask Rose to come, will you? My hair be in such disarray, I can hardly get the comb through it.'

'I shall assist you, sweeting; it would be my pleasure.' He sat upon the rumpled bed, took the ivory comb from her, lifted a long tress in his hands and began to tease out the knots. 'Your hair be ever a delight to me – the colours within enchant me so.' He stroked along the length of the strands, bringing back the gloss and sheen that had been dulled by fever. As he worked, gentle as though she was fragile as Venetian glass, he began to sing softly, the joyous words of the *Magnificat*.

Emily lay back and closed her eyes. Whatever his failings, Seb's voice belonged to the seraphim; the heavenly choir had lost one of their own the day Seb was given the gift of musick.

As for Seb, he would be content to comb her hair for as long as it gave her peace. He poured every ounce of tenderness into bringing back the beauty of her hair. If only he might restore her body with so simple an act. He rearranged the tresses so they caught the sunlight streaming through the window, watching how the slightest movement of his hand brought forth glints of copper, bronze and gold, chestnut and tawny. Even a hint of crimson lay under the shadows. None of his own efforts with inks and pigments had ever equalled the glories of Em's hair, the subtle changes of hue that sparked and glistened.

Little wonder married women were required to cover their hair by Holy Church, for fear of leading men astray, as Eve did Adam. In truth, Seb thought, if Em let her hair hang loose all the while, he would get no work done but gaze at her constantly. Aye, and threaten to blind any other man who looked upon her – of which there would be a multitude, no doubt, drinking in such beauty. Holy Church was wise indeed.

Eventually, seeing she slept, he smiled to himself and put the comb down. He kissed her brow, thankfully now cool against his lips, and departed the chamber with silent step.

# The Mermaid, Southwark

'Come on, get up,' Cain said. ''Ave yer bread n' ale then we got work t' do, places t' be. Make 'aste, yer young rascal.'

'Am I going home now, Cain?' Will scoffed his bread, eager to be any place but here.

''Ome of a sort, I reckon. Now straighten them hose, tidy yerself.' Cain assisted, finger-combing Will's hair, but it persisted in standing awry, sleep-dishevelled. The man stepped back, the better to see the results, then shook his head. 'That doublet's over large. I told Bessie to put a few stitches in it, but will she listen t' me?' He pulled the garment about and brushed it down, making no difference that Will could see.

'Mam'll sew it for me so it fits, when I get home. She's good with her needle.'

'I dare say,' Cain muttered. 'Now move yerself.'

Will was ready in an instant, bending down to retrieve his one and only possession: the rosary.

'Yer won't be needin' that.'

'But it was my grandmother's. You said I could keep it.'

'Leave it. Bessie won't approve.' Cain snatched the beads and tossed them in the corner. 'Now, come on… and stop that bloody snivellin'. They's only a few ol' beads.'

Will wiped his nose on his sleeve and sniffed hard.

Cain took his hand and led him out of the door and up the rickety stair.

Bessie awaited. Her stone-hard eyes looked the lad over, head to toe.

'Get him cleaned up, Cain. He ain't worth a groat in that state. And tell Claudette to give yer some o' that French scent and douse his clothes with it: he smells like a midden heap.'

A pretty woman who spoke strangely but kept smiling at him helped Cain to pin the worn velvet doublet so it seemed a closer fit. Will didn't like the fuss. She washed his face and hands in some flowery-smelling water, scrubbed at the cuffs of the shirt he'd worn clean to school so long ago and wet his fair curling hair before combing it into some kind of order. He hated that when Mam did it, never mind some woman he'd never seen before, even if she was pretty.

Bessie stood, arms folded, to inspect their handiwork.

'Aye. I s'pose he'll have to serve.' She fetched a shawl from a peg by the door to the street and led the way. 'Bring him, Cain.'

For the first time, Will noticed the likeness of a mermaid, swinging on leather hinges above the door as he went with Cain who held his hand so tightly it hurt. They turned to the right. Betwixt the buildings on the right hand, Will caught occasional glimpses of the Thames, its brown waters hastening towards London Bridge.

'We're going the wrong way, Cain. I live across the bridge.'

'Not no more yer don't.'

'But you said I was going home.'

'No, I never. Now shut yer mouth, else Bessie'll hear yer.'

It was a long walk. Gulls wheeled and oystercatchers piped along the water's edge, probing the mud. A cormorant dried its wings, perched upon the skeletal ribs of a decaying boat. The buildings of Bankside gave way to tumbledown hovels, draped about with nets drying and eel traps awaiting mending. Skinny women and children worked at the nets, repairing tears, whilst the menfolk were tarring and caulking leaky boats and all smelled of rotting fish and river mud, most vile at low tide, as now.

The water could be heard, sucking and slurping at rubbish washed up along the tideline where urchins scavenged, ankle-deep in grey mud, searching for driftwood for the fire, rags to sell or anything that might have a use or earn a farthing. The fisherfolk never so much as looked up from their work to glance in Will's direction.

The hovels, too, were left behind as the track led across

Lambeth Marshes. There was a better road, inland, but it wove a meandering way, avoiding the marsh. For those on foot who didn't fear to dirty their shoes, the trackway was more direct. The stumps of ancient hithes and jetties stuck out like blackened, broken teeth from amongst the marsh plants, the glasswort and eel grass and others that could withstand the brackish water. The tang of salt was in the air and the screech of black-headed gulls as they sailed effortlessly against the grey skies.

Will was surprised to see some kind of dwelling out in the marsh.

'Who lives there, Cain?' he asked, his youngster's curiosity overcoming his fear of where they were going.

'Nobody. 'Twas once a hermit's place, so they say, but no one bides there now. Look yonder, though and yer can see the Horse Ferry wot crosses t' Westminster.' Cain pointed. 'See it?'

'Hold your tongues, the pair of you.' Bessie cut in sharply. 'This ain't no Sunday stroll. This is business.'

A grand brick-built gateway, so new the red bricks still glowed, appeared to their left hand as the trackway and the better road converged. It was a huge place. No, Will thought, rather a palace. Mayhap, it belonged to the king, as well as his palace across the river at Westminster. The Horse Ferry would make it quite close at hand – if the king ever used a ferry like other folk.

'The Archbishop o' Canterbury bides there,' Cain whispered, seeming to know the lad's thoughts.

'Are we going there?' Will asked. To go within such a fine building would be an adventure indeed.

# The Three Feathers Inn, Lambeth

Lord Pierpoint was from his bed early, huffing and fussing worse than usual, much to Walter's annoyance.

'The day has dawned at last: my son is coming home. Home to his loving father's bosom, where he rightly belongs. Such a joyous day, Walter, a joyous day, indeed.'

'Is Sir Marcus joining us again then, my lord? He did not say in my hearing.'

'Forget that wastrel. He is no son of mine, gone for a bloody lawyer. I'll not have his name mentioned. No. I speak of my true son and heir, a most deserving boy. He shall be fetched to us this morn. 'Tis all settled and arranged. See the kitchen know to set an extra place at dinner. Can't have my son going hungry, can we? And see to it that his favourite dish is served.'

Walter cleared his throat.

'And what dish might that be, my lord?'

'Come now. You know as well as I.'

'Carp in a green sauce?' Walter hazarded a guess.

'Don't be a fool. What child prefers fish? Nay, serve him roasted beef, venison pie, capons and pigeons.'

'But it's still the Lenten fast, sir.'

'I don't care if the bloody pope forbids it. This is a day of celebration, my true son's homecoming, and we will have a proper feast in his honour.'

'If I might enquire, sir, what is the boy's name?'

'Henry, of course. What else should it be? The Pierpoint heir is always a Henry. Has been so since my grandsire's grandsire's day, as you well know.'

Sometime later, Lord Pierpoint was still fussing, flapping his hands like a washerwoman.

'Where is he? 'Tis nigh the hour to dine. The food will be ready to serve and he is not here. What can have delayed my son's arrival?'

Walter said naught. No one was coming. No fine repast was about to be served. In truth, he was at a loss, not knowing how to calm his fractious lord who was doomed to suffer a double disappointment: just bread, fish and a little of yesterday's wine and no new arrival to share it. Sir Marcus had business elsewhere and wouldn't have been a welcome visitor anyway, since his father loathed the very sight of him and was ever discourteous enough to state his feelings plainly.

The stairs creaked beyond the chamber, heralding a knock upon the door. Walter opened it. The tapster stood there. He removed his cap to reveal a head balder than any monk's tonsure.

'Beggin' pardon o' his lordship but there's folks below say they've got a 'pointment with Lord Pierpoint. Mind, they don't look the sort. I wouldn't trust 'em, if I was you.'

Lord Pierpoint bustled over, elbowing Walter aside.

'Well, show them up, you fool, and see to it that dinner is served directly. My son will be hungry indeed.'

Walter was shocked to see the callers. A hefty fellow with pale, dirty hair, clad in ragged attire, his face made ugly by the marks of too many brawls. A skinny woman with a gaze hard and sharp as a blade. She might have been pretty once, long ago, but a life in the seedier parts of Southwark had coarsened her features. Walter recognised her kind. Betwixt the unsavoury pair stood a young lad, wearing some once-fine cast-offs gleaned from a fripperer's hoard, no doubt. He looked afraid, hanging back behind the hefty fellow.

The woman pulled the lad forward and shoved him towards Lord Pierpoint.

'Here he is – as ordered. Fair of hair; blue eyes; straight limbed; pleasant of feature. Now pay up. Two marks, as arranged.'

Lord Pierpoint took the lad by the sleeve and turned him

about. Nodding and smiling, it seemed he approved of the youngster.

'Pay the woman, Walter,' his lordship ordered.

Walter's shock turned to outrage. They were purchasing a child? Surely, humans had not been bought and sold since mighty Caesar's time. But the fellow advanced, hand held out, palm uppermost.

'The money,' he said. He neither shouted nor made any threatening gesture but those two words and the expression upon his face were threat enough.

Walter opened the purse at his belt with shaking fingers, praying there would be sufficient coin remaining from the sum Sir Marcus had given him to pay his father's expenses. The last thing he wanted was to have to haggle the price with this pair. He sighed with relief when he counted out the exorbitant sum of twenty-six shillings and eight pence and still had a few pennies remaining. What they would live on or how they would pay the rent on this room, he didn't know, but seeing the fellow and the woman leaving eased his immediate anxieties.

'Walter. Go see why dinner is not yet served whilst my son and I are reacquainted. Come, Henry, greet your father as you should, for he has saved you from a miserable and unexhorted destiny. Come to me, Henry.' Lord Pierpoint held his arms wide, offering a hearty embrace.

The lad did not move.

'My name's Will, not Henry.'

Lord Pierpoint laughed.

'Mayhap, they called you Will but, now you are returned to me, your baptismal name is Henry. You were named for me, my father and his father before him. The Pierpoint heir is always Henry.'

'I'm not Henry. I'm William Thatcher. Though my father is Henry, my mother is Beatrice...' He began to sob, his shoulders heaving as he stood in the midst of the chamber.

'Nonsense. Your mother was my dearest wife, Yolande. Now,

132

cease your foolish noise. I see I have much to teach you of your splendid lineage and heritage. The Pierpoints are a family of great renown...'

Will had been scared of Lord Pierpoint at first. The old man shouted, even in talking to him when he stood hardly a yard away. The lad decided he must be deaf. Not only that but he was quite mad. A miserable dinner of mackerel stared up at them with cloudy eyes from a sea of grey-green, tasteless sauce, brought upstairs by the cross-looking tapster who had better things to do. Yet Lord Pierpoint kept asking him how he liked the roasted beef and was he enjoying the pigeons? Will thought to correct the old man but, before he spoke, he saw Walter's beseeching look, the slightest head-shake and had wit enough to understand.

'The beef is very good, sir, and the pigeons are the best I've tasted,' Will said, prepared to play along.

'There! Did I not tell you, Walter, my son Henry deserves the finest meats? He has a discerning palate as a lord should. I told you so.'

'Aye, you did, my lord.' Walter sounded weary.

Will wondered how long the servant had been playing this game of pretending. Too long, it seemed, but a merry jape appealed to Will.

'The capon is most juicy and tender,' he said, chewing on the stale bread that had been served with the fish.

'The capon? Oh, tender indeed, Henry.' Lord Pierpoint took a spoonful of sauce and beamed with pleasure. 'And this afternoon we shall enjoy ourselves. What do you say to an hour's hawking, eh? Sport of kings and all that. A fine pastime for a young lord. Fear not; I shall teach you the rudiments myself, if you have forgotten them. It's been a few years, I know.'

'I expect I shall remember how, once you show me, sir.'

'Of course you will, my son. What a marvellous day this is,

having you returned to me at last. Walter, order the grooms to saddle our horses. We shall ride out directly after dinner.'

Walter coughed discreetly:

'My lord, might it not be better to wait and go hawking tomorrow right early. You always advise that the birds are more eager to fly at dawn and the prey is more plentiful.'

'Do I advise thus?' his lordship pondered a moment. 'Quite right, Walter, quite right.' The old man opened the window casement and squinted at the clouds. 'I fear it may rain shortly anyway. In the morn, then, young Henry. You'll have to curb your impatience a little longer, but the sport will be better for the wait. We can play at chess instead. You haven't forgotten the rules, have you, my son?'

'I'm not sure, sir. Mayhap, you could remind me of them?' In truth, Will had seen a chessboard, ready set out with all the pieces, at his uncle's house one time, but he had no idea how to play. He hoped he could learn enough to convince the old man he wasn't entirely ignorant. If only he might please him well, perhaps the lord would let him go home. Mam must be worried about him after so long away. And his master at Paul's School wasn't going to be in the best of humours with him either. It would probably mean a beating but, so long as he could go home, Will would suffer the consequences with little complaint.

Walter set out the board. Will noticed that half a walnut shell served for one missing piece and a knucklebone for another. As with all Lord Pierpoint's possessions, the chess set had seen better days.

'Go fetch us wine and sweetmeats,' his lordship commanded the servant.

Will felt sorry for Walter, having to pretend his master was a great lord when, clearly, that wasn't so.

Lord Pierpoint began to explain all the chess pieces and how they could move upon the board. It sounded complicated but Will did his best to remember everything.

'What of the walnut and the bone, sir? How do they move?'

'Obviously, the walnut replaces the white queen and the bone is a black pawn… or is it the other way about?' The man scratched at his chin. 'Are you paying heed, Henry? The walnut is the black queen, as I said.'

'Aye, sir. The black queen.'

'And this is the walnut's bishop… here, which moves diagonally across the board. And this the knight which leaps as it will…' He took hold of a piece shaped somewhat like a horse's head. 'Gallop and gallop and off we go…' he shouted, leaping up from his seat and prancing around the chamber with the chess piece.

Will joined in, making neighing noises and clucking his tongue. The old man was enjoying himself. Will hadn't played such silly games since before he went to school. Such japes were for toddlings, he thought, but if it pleased the mad lord, then so be it.

At last, the old man fell onto his chair, breathless. Gradually, his eyes closed. His grey head nodded and he began to snore.


When Walter returned, at length, with a few broken almond wafers he had begged from the landlord's goodwife – she had required him to peel a heap of onions in payment – Lord Pierpoint was sound asleep in the chair by the hearth.

The window stood open wide, looking out across Lambeth Marshes to the river beyond. The first few tendrils of drizzly mist were weaving their way across the forlorn landscape, obscuring the towers of Westminster on the far bank and oozing over the window ledge, chilling the chamber.

There was no sign of the lad.

# The Foxley House

Seb was in the workshop. The showers of April seemed to have joined hands for a dismal dance and the drizzle had set in for the day. Thus, the daylight in the workshop was murky and it was more difficult than ever to make out the scrawling script of the annotations in the astrology text. Mistress Caldicott's commission looked ever less likely to be completed each time Seb thought to examine the task anew. He had been frowning for an age over an insertion mark – as he thought – but realised of a sudden it was the arrow symbol for the sign of Sagittarius. That made more sense. What he had previously taken for a capital letter M with a following slip of the scribe's pen, he now saw as the sign for Virgo, if he recalled it rightly.

He turned the page and was relieved to see a block of text unadulterated by scribbled notes. The rubric declared 'Upon prediction of proposed marriages'. He began to transcribe but found that what he read so intrigued him that he left off writing and set down his pen. Some folk would consult astrologers before setting out on any new venture, particularly if they planned to wed. Such matters as the union's happiness, how many children it would produce and which partner would outlive the other could all be revealed by consulting the stars. He and Emily had not troubled to do so, an astrologer's divinations seeming to be an unnecessary expense when they were both convinced their love for each other would be everlasting. Seb sighed, shaking his head. Mayhap, they should have taken the precaution.

He read on.

Towards the foot of the page was a list of inadvisable unions to be avoided at all cost and there it was, in stark black ink: 'Those whose natal horoscope lies within the dominion of the zodiacal sign of Sagittarius should most strongly be advised to avoid making marital contract with those whose natal horoscope lies under the influence of Virgo. Theirs will be a fraught and incompatible marriage, lacking harmony of feeling and without respect, the one for the other, any semblance of love betwixt them is but illusion'. Seb had been born a week before Christmas, thus he was indeed under the dominion of Sagittarius. Em's birth date in early September meant she was a daughter of Virgo. It seemed their marriage had been destined for failure from the beginning, foretold by the stars. And yet it was not entirely true, was it? He loved Em as deeply – deeper now – as he ever had and his respect for her was undiminished. Yet, from her side of the matter, it was all too true.

'Neath the list of those marriages to be avoided was another of those to be encouraged. Even as his eyes scanned down the words, he knew he should read no more; that he was inflicting torture upon his heart. But there it was: the union of those born under the zodiacal dominion of Virgo with those influenced by Pisces is the closest to perfection of any and to be favoured above all'. Aye, he thought, was it not inevitable? Gabriel Widowson, his one-time journeyman, was born under the sign of Pisces – Em's perfect partner in marriage. Curious and hoping to cheer himself, he ran his finger down the page and read: 'For those under the domination of Sagittarius, espousal should be most certainly considered with those whose nativity was influenced by the sign of Aries, in order to attain a union of contentment and delight to both parties'. He chuckled at the foolishness of his thoughts. Dame Ellen had celebrated reaching three-score years of age recently and must, therefore, have been born under Aries – it was hard to imagine her as his perfect soulmate.

'How is the transcription progressing?' Adam asked, setting a cup of ale on Seb's desk.

'I have realised that some of the incomprehensible letters I could not make out are the Signs of the Zodiac and planetary symbols. The text makes more sense now, at least in this chapter. But you will laugh at this, Adam: according to the stars, I should have wed Dame Ellen. It would be a union of contentment and delight, so the heavens predict. What do you make of that?'

'What a relief then that, as an unwed bachelor, I'm not of the same astrological sign as you. No disrespect intended, but the good dame is too ancient for my liking, though I know such unions have been made.' Adam perched on the corner of the collating table and sipped his ale. 'Do you recall when the queen's youngest brother, at eighteen years, was wed to the ancient Dowager Duchess of Norfolk, just so he could get his grubby paws on her wealth when she died? It was the scandal of Norwich for months.'

'Aye. It gave the London gossipmongers a deal to wag their tongues about too. And the youngster never had any benefit of his illustrious wife either. The Kingmaker had him executed, did he not? The elderly dowager outlived him. I wonder if the stars foretold that eventuality.'

'Have a look, Seb, and tell me: who is my perfect goodwife? Who should I be wooing? Who is she that is destined to be my soulmate? I can think of a fair few women who seem promising.'

'You be incorrigible, Adam. Why do you not make a start on a few more cheap Latin primers?'

'We haven't sold a single copy of the ones I did before. I fear Master Caxton's printing press is taking away our business on that score, Seb. His ugly pamphlets are flooding out of Westminster at a ha'penny a copy. No one wants to pay tuppence for ours, even though they're far better to look upon than his. Jonathan Caldicott told me he bought one, just to test its quality and the ink rubbed off on his fingers. He's going to report Master Caxton to the Stationers' Guild for producing shoddy workmanship, but I doubt anything will come of it.'

'Why do you say that?'

'Well, there's no regulation to apply to printed work, is there, seeing it's a new thing? And then Caxton has royal patronage. He could complain to King Edward himself, if the guild harasses him over much. Nay, Seb, I fear the printing press is going to prove the scribe's worst enemy. We'll have to turn our skills to tasks that devilish contraption cannot manage. Illumination, inn signs, coats-of-arms and portraits – and all of those make use of your talents, not mine. There's no other way for me, I fear: I'm going to have to wed a wealthy widow, cousin, so scour that star book and find me a suitable wife. And she must be a pretty one; money alone is not enough. Remember, I was born under the even-handed, lovesome sign of Libra.' With that parting remark, Adam slipped off the table, leaving his empty cup to make a ring on the spotless surface of wood, and went out, whistling.

'Tiresome, more like,' Seb muttered, taking up his pen once more.

# *Chapter 8*

## Later that Maundy Thursday
## Cheapside

HAVING STRAINED his eyes for too long over the astrology text in poor light, Seb felt in need of fresh air and the chance to stretch cramped limbs. The afternoon was dreary but he determined to go outside.

'Will you walk with me, Kate? We may search out some new inspiration for those comical creatures you invent so well.'

Kate had also been frowning in the gloom over a page of ornamented initials she was practising to perfect and was eager to unfurrow her brow as her master.

'Indeed, Master Seb. Shall we go to the Horse Pool? You always find something there to draw.' She wiped her pen clean on a linen scrap and closed the lid on the pot of red ink.

'Nay, lass. I think Cheapside and the market stalls might prove more profitable. Besides, along the way, I shall make more enquiries concerning the missing lad, Will Thatcher, and we still have the mystery to unravel as to the identity of the poor dead lad with white hair. Such matters will not be resolved by sitting here.' He handed Kate her green cloak and swung his own drab grey one about his shoulders.

Emily had been complaining of late that a master-stationer should not be seen attired in the garments of a pauper, that his Sunday best cloak should now serve for every day, seeing he had

140

worn it these four years past. Rather, he ought to purchase a new one for wearing upon the Lord's Day. She had been insisting that Easter Day would be the perfect chance to show off a fine new cloak but Seb had, somehow, failed to find time enough to visit her brother John's tailoring business and purchase such a garment. The old cloak was yet serviceable and had seen him through many an adventure. It would serve a while yet.

They departed, out into the bustle of Paternoster Row, Gawain loping along at Seb's side.

The dampness in the air soon turned Kate's dark curls to tight, black spirals but she refused to wear her hood, loving the feel of her hair flying free. All too soon, marriage would end that pleasure, since a wife must hide her hair 'neath cap and veil.

Marriage. Aye, Kate thought, some girls of her age were wed already, bearing babes soon after. She hoped her father would not hasten her betrothal to a suitable, respectable fellow. Jack! Well, one thing was certain: he would ne'er be the man that her father chose, but he made her laugh and his stolen kisses were sweet. For the present, she was content with that.

Seb saw her smiling broadly.

'What amuses you so, lass?'

'Naught, master.' She pulled her lips into solemn guise. 'I merely had an idea for a new piece of marginalia. I, er, wondered if a, er, tiny knight might joust with a giant grasshopper, or spar against a mighty tree that grows the full height of the margin? That might amuse the reader. It made me smile.'

Seb chuckled.

'Aye, lass. Why not do some sketches when we get home, to see how that might look upon the page. A joust with a grasshopper appeals to me; an entire tree trunk filling a margin might give too weighty an appearance to the page. And there could be no boughs nor branches forwhy they would interfere with the text. But I approve the grasshopper. And look, Kate.' He pointed at a cluster of sparrows, quarrelling and splashing in a puddle as they bathed. 'Would some such not make an amusing subject? Give the birds crowns, ducal coronets and bishops' mitres, perhaps?

'Oh, see there: 'tis Mistress Hutchinson of Distaff Lane. Mayhap, she has heard news of Will Thatcher, he being her son's schoolmate. Mistress Hutchinson!' he called, doffing his cap. 'Greetings to you. I bid you good day and ask that God's blessings be upon you and your little ones.'

The woman turned away from the market stall, arranging the fresh green stuff just purchased into her basket.

'Ah, Master Foxley. Greetings to you also. I know not about blessings upon this one.' Mistress Hutchinson kept a tight hold on the hand of her toddling, Nicholas. 'He's a very trial of my patience, running off and finding mischief at every chance, each time I let go of him to look at what's for sale or to take coin from my purse.'

Seb could see how difficult it might be for anyone to manage a babe-in-arms and a basket on one arm whilst keeping hold of a straying youngster with the other.

'Is this your daughter, Master Foxley?' Mistress Hutchinson smiled at Kate.

'Oh, I beg pardon of you both for my discourtesy. Mistress Hutchinson, this be Katherine Verney, my most talented apprentice illuminator and daughter of Edmund Verney of Walbrook, he that was lately made an alderman. Kate, meet Mistress Mercy Hutchinson, a recent and much-valued acquaintance from Distaff Lane.'

Kate bobbed a courtesy to the older woman. Mistress Hutchinson, so encumbered with children and multiple purchases, could but smile and nod in return.

'Have you found the missing boy as yet, master?' Mistress Hutchinson shifted the babe awkwardly upon her hip.

'I fear not. To be truthful, my purpose in addressing you just now was to enquire whether you or your son Simon had heard any rumour of him – William Thatcher by name.'

'No. His mother was asking here in the market earlier.

She said her goodman was making enquiries in every tavern, aye, and getting more drunk with every question asked. But I couldn't help her, or you, Master Foxley. Now, I must be getting home before little Mundy here begins bawling for his next feed. He's becoming restless already.'

'Forgive me for detaining you. I bid you good day, Mistress Hutchinson.' Seb touched his cap and was about to move on but Mistress Hutchinson called him back.

'Why don't you ask Old Symkyn? He sees everything.'

'Symkyn? The beggar, do you mean?'

'Aye. He's often to be found, hereabouts.'

'I used to see him nigh every day, by St Paul's, but I have not encountered him since my return to the city, in August last. I thought his soul might have been called upon to depart and was sorry for the loss of an old friend.'

'There he is, sitting at the foot of the queen's cross.' Mistress Hutchinson nodded in the direction of the once-magnificent memorial, erected by one king or another, long ago, to remind London of his dear departed consort: the Cheapside Cross.

'I be much obliged to you, Mistress Hutchinson. My thanks, indeed.' And touching his cap once more, Seb hastened towards the figure, bent over his begging bowl, seated on the crumbling stone steps. 'Symkyn! May God smile upon you, my dear friend.'

'Well, if it ent Master Foxley,' the old man said, smiling, showing toothless gums. 'Last I was 'earing, you was off up north a ways. Never thought t' see you back, young master.'

'My departure was none of my choosing, but a sudden necessity. But what of you? Why do you not sit at Paul's Gate in Paternoster Row these days? I miss you sorely; your kindly words of blessing no longer greet me of a morn.'

'Like yourself, master, I didn't choose t' go. The bishop, in his great wisdom, deemed us unfit – an eyesore, his clerk said – t' clutter up his grand gateway. I was told t' move on, else they'd take away me beggar's licence.'

'But that be against all charity,' Seb said, outrage making his usually quiet grey eyes blaze.

Old Symkyn shrugged.

'And don't I know it. Takings here are meagre, indeed, compared t' there.' He shook his cracked wooden bowl. Two farthings and a pebble chinked together, a dismal sound. 'Folk a-marketing have more thought fer spending their coin at them stalls, not fer making charity's gifts fer the good o' their souls.'

'I would not have you go cold and hungry one instant longer, my friend. Come with us. I shall see you fed and warm afore anything else.' Seb took the old man's good arm and aided him to his feet. 'Neath the threadbare cloak and sleeve, he could feel the beggar's bones. 'Bring the bowl, if you will, Kate: no reason to leave such charity as there be to the benefit of thieves.'

Seb led Symkyn into the nearest place of refreshment: The Cardinal's Hat Inn. A good fire blazed in the hearth; a welcoming warmth. Mayhap, though, it was not the most appropriate place to take a withered-armed beggar, the rest of the customers being merchants, higher class craftsmen, minor officials and such like. The main room of the inn was busy with a group of prosperous-looking merchants – clad like noblemen in their fine furs and brocades – discussing a contract over a jug of Burgundy wine. A noisy dice game was in progress in the far corner. Other customers, all well dressed, were chatting and laughing over their cups and bowls of food.

The innkeeper came over to the three as soon as they entered. But this was not to imply efficient service. Rather, the innkeeper sniffed significantly and pulled a face, wrinkling his nose.

'We don't serve that kind here.' He addressed Seb but gestured with his chin towards Symkyn. 'This is a respectable house. Take your custom elsewhere.'

Symkyn nodded and turned back to the door. Such words were a daily occurrence and he was used to them.

Seb had, in the past, as a lame youth, suffered the same, being taunted as a cripple. Those times were not so long since that he had forgotten the sting of such rejections. He kept hold of the beggar's arm to prevent his departure.

'When comes the time for your licence to be renewed?' he demanded of the innkeeper. 'Be sure, if you fail to be of service to all who request it and be able to pay, as the city ordinances state, I shall be speaking to my good friends, Alderman Verney and Bailiff Turner in that regard, and the alderman and Lord Mayor Gardyner himself be fellow mercers. Serve us with good grace, or they shall all learn of the discourtesies at this establishment.' Seb spoke with authority, giving the innkeeper pause.

'He can't pay,' he said, dismissing Symkyn with a wave of his hand, 'So I'm within my rights to refuse him.'

'But I can,' Seb replied, taking a newly minted half-angel from his purse, valued at three shillings and fourpence, and holding it under the fellow's nose. It was Mistress Caldicott's down payment for the new astrology book – a significant sum indeed. 'And this good man be my guest,' Seb continued, 'So you will treat him with due honour and respect or…'

'Aye, of course, master.' The innkeeper bowed and beckoned to his tapster and serving wench to come wait upon this wealthy and, of a sudden, much-valued customer.

It seemed, as ever, that money commanded more respect than persons. A lamentable situation, Seb thought, but that was the way of the world, was it not? He also noted that Kate was gazing at him with a look of wonderment. Aye, well, it was not often he stood up to bullies but Symkyn deserved to be treated better and the look of disgust on the innkeeper's face had fired his anger on the old man's behalf.

Symkyn had once been a thatcher by trade, but served as an archer in King Edward's army, where his right arm had been injured beyond repair at the battle of Barnet Field and his knee had taken a spear-point. Unable to ply his trade any longer, Symkyn was reduced to beggary, discarded and forgotten by the king for whom he had fought. Seb hated such unfairness.

They were served decent ale – well-watered for Kate – and a bowl of thick, steaming pottage for Symkyn, accompanied by soft white bread, which was all his toothless gums could manage. A dish of honeyed oatcakes was provided, *gratis*, the innkeeper wishing to make amends for previously upsetting someone who might spend more of his coin at The Cardinal's Hat in the future. Upon request, a bowl of water was provided for Gawain.

'So, what've you been about, young master?' Symkyn asked as he wiped the last trace of pottage from his bowl with the bread and sucked on it. 'Looks to me like you been in the wars.'

Seb put his fingers to his bruised face. It was yet tender under his eyes and his nose felt far too large to fit the rest of his features. He swallowed his mouthful of oatcake which, he grudgingly had to admit, was delicious and washed it down with a sip of ale.

'A mishap was all. An accident. Some fellow's elbow caught my nose. Why?'

'I've seen the like on those who took a strike from a poleaxe shaft in battle, through their helm.'

'Doesn't look so bad as that, surely?' Seb glanced at Kate as he spoke but her pitying look said otherwise. He changed the subject: 'We be in Cheapside for a double purpose. Kate here be in search of inspiration for her comic marginalia. She be most talented in drawing. Is that not so, Kate?'

The lass blushed and nodded.

'So master insists,' she said, laughing.

'Then it's likely true,' the old man said, with a wink, knowing Seb well enough in times past.

'It is indeed the case,' Seb went on. 'Our second purpose lies in making enquiries concerning a young lad gone missing: Will Thatcher. His family bides just close at hand, by Cheap Cross. I wondered whether you might have heard any word of him, or seen anything untoward upon Monday last. Right early, it would have been, forwhy it seems he disappeared upon his way to Paul's School. The lad ne'er arrived there and none has seen him since.' Seb delved into his purse and took out a much-folded paper. 'I have a sketch of his likeness here that may jostle your memory of him.'

He moved aside the empty pottage bowl and laid the paper on the board, smoothing out the creases.

'Aye. I know the lad. His father's a thatcher, as was I. I see Will often enough, running errands for his mother. When not in haste, he sometimes stops to share a word or two. He likes to hear my tales of adventure and great feats of arms.' Symkyn chuckled throatily. 'Few o' them wholly true, but it passes the time.'

'And when did you see him last? Can you recall?'

'I went t' Low Mass in St Peter's across the way upon Sunday. The Thatchers were there also. I lingered by the brazier, fer it had been a cold night, and Harry Thatcher gave us 'good day' and a farthing for ale. Young Will was with his father, begged us t' tell him more of Agincourt, but Harry told him the Lord's Day wasn't to be passed with such foolish tales.'

'You were at Agincourt? But that was so long ago, wasn't it?' Kate asked, awed by the thought. She was munching oatcakes and sharing them with Gawain, secreted beneath the board.

'It was, aye, and no, lass, I didn't bend me bow fer that one. I wasn't so much as a twinkle in me father's eye, not quite. But one war is much like another and Will Thatcher loves a good story.'

'What of Monday? Did you see the lad set out for school?' Seb asked.

Symkyn considered a while, scratching at a flea within his tattered clothing.

'Aye. Mayhap I did. He waved his hand to his mother as he flew out the door, then to me. He ran along Cheapside, towards Paul's, as usual. I watched him, saw him turn down into The Old Change, by the Bellhouse. I b'lieve he has a friend lives down that way. He often tells us of his mischiefs with, er – what's the lad's name, now – oh, aye, Simon, if I recalls it right.'

'Simon Hutchinson, that would be. Aye, I spoke with his

mother. Mistress Hutchinson said Will failed to call for Simon that morn. Of habit, they enter the school together. Simon waited overlong for his friend and was nigh late to school but Will ne'er arrived: not at the Hutchinson house nor at his desk. Did you notice anyone following young Will; any suspicious characters in the neighbourhood?'

A burst of raucous laughter from the dice-players turned heads and brought Gawain leaping to his feet. Seb soothed him with a pat on his glossy head, and the dog settled once more.

Symkyn leaned forward, scratched at his shaggy grey hair under his cap, then propped his bearded chin upon his fist, close to Seb.

'I saw naught that day, young master, but I tell you this: I did see some odd goings-on a few weeks past. A fortnight ago or more it was. I saw this tall fellow. From a distance, fer a moment, I was thinkin' it was your Master Jude but when he turned around, it weren't your brother after all. His face was scarred and I'd seen him before, over the Bridge. I'd gone there t' try me luck with the beggin' bowl but them in Southwark are either poor as church mouses themselves or else hold their purse-strings tighter than the Devil holds onto sinners. Any road, I seen this tall fellow there a few times, coming and going from this place...' Symkyn cupped his hand around his mouth and whispered, not wanting Kate to hear. '...from a house of er, entertainment, called The Mermaid.'

Seb wondered why a house of entertainment had to be spoken of so discretely. Nobody flinched from saying "ale-house", did they?

'And the tall fellow followed Will?' he prompted.

'No, not that I saw. But, as I was sayin', a while before all that, I saw this fellow manhandling another youngster down a ways from the Bellhouse. By Distaff Lane, if I recalls it aright. O' course, the lad might've been his son, fer all I know, or his 'prentice, but he was bein' o'er harsh, I reckon. The lad was kicking and crying out and the man was beating him, such that I'm sure he was bleeding. The blood showed up red enough on the lad's white hair. Then the fellow picked him up, threw him over his shoulder like a sack o' grain. Reckon the lad was senseless by then, since he lay quite still as the man carried him off along Watling Street.'

'A lad with white hair, you say? Symkyn, this may be of great importance. Could you describe the fellow to me? Hold, hold. I have an image of another lad here, a youngster with hair so fair 'tis white as frost on a glass windowpane.' Seb took the drawing of the dead lad, discovered in the workshop, and showed it to the beggar.

''Tis hard to say. I weren't so close and the pair was tussling, but could be. Who is this white-haired lad?'

'I know not,' Seb said with a sigh. 'I found him dead of a knife wound, in my workshop, the morn after the storm. Sunday last, that would be. None can name him, as yet. I fear they never will.'

'You think the death o' this lad and young Will's disappearance be linked in some way?'

'Mayhap, Symkyn, mayhap. But this fellow you saw, the one who looked somewhat like my brother, the one who beat the child so sorely... it could be that you have given me the first clue towards unravelling both mysteries. I be so grateful to you.'

''Tis I who am grateful to you, young master, fer this good food, fine ale and a warm hearth.'

'Would you be willing to cast your mind back to the occasions when you saw this tall fellow? Might you describe him to me?'

Symkyn nodded.

'I can try, master.'

'Tapster!' Seb called to the man pouring ale for other customers on a bench near at hand. 'I pray you bring me pen and ink, if you will? There be an extra ha'penny for you, if you do.'

The servant scuttled off and returned swiftly with what was requested, his hand already held out for the promised coin.

Seb paid up, turned over the image of the white-haired lad to show a blank page, dipped the quill and was ready to draw.

'Like unto my brother in build, you say?'

'Aye, tall and broad in the shoulder; fair-haired like him, 'cept the hair was somewhat longer, unkempt and dusty looking. Not clean. Neither were his clothes. When he turned around though, his face was very different; not good-looking as your brother. He had a scar on his cheek...'

'Left or right?'

'Er, left, I reckon... aye... that's it, young master, like you've drawed. But his nose was all out o' shape, like it had been broked more than once... and a scar on his lip – not big but made it look like he was sneering all the while... p'raps not so much as that.'

Seb made some adjustments.

'Was his face thinner or broader? Was he square-jawed?'

'Thinner.'

Seb added cross-hatching to give shadow under the cheekbones.

'And the chin?'

'More pointed, I think.'

Seb put in a few more lines.

'What of the eyes?'

'I was too far away to see their colour.'

'But you noticed the shape of them? Narrow? Wide-open? Heavy-lidded?'

'Small. Sneaky-looking, as I recall. Not so certain on that now. It was a while ago since I seen him.'

'You have done marvellously well, my old friend. And you say you saw him in Southwark, also?'

'Aye, at The Mermaid... one of *those* sort of houses, as I told you.'

Seb showed Symkyn the sketch.

'That's him, the nasty piece o' work. I'd know him agen from that.'

'My thanks again. You have been of more help than any other in London. On the morrow, I will go to Southwark in search of him.'

'Don't go alone, young master. There's too many like him south o' the Bridge.'

'Fear not. I shall take a friend.' Seb pushed back his stool and stood, beckoning to the innkeeper. 'The reckoning, if you will, landlord?'

'Aye, well that's tuppence for the ale; tuppence for the pottage; a ha'penny for bread; a ha'penny for pen and ink…'

'But that be extortionate!' Seb burst out.

'You got the oatcakes for free; you can't complain. That'll be five pence farthing, all tallied.'

'I only reckon at five pence. Whence comes the additional farthing?'

'Water for your dog.'

'Water be free…'

'But it has to be fetched and the bowl needs washing after.'

Seb sighed and paid the reckoning.

'Robbery. Thievery in broad daylight,' he muttered. 'Stay here by the fire, Symkyn, and drink every last drop of the ale remaining in that jug. We deserve our money's worth, at least. And you, master innkeeper, will leave my friend to drink in peace for as long as he wishes. Do not dare drive him out the moment I turn my back, or the bailiff and the alderman will learn of it. Come, Kate, Gawain, we have work to do.'

Outside, in Cheapside, they passed the Thatchers' house. Had Beatrice been watching the street? It seemed so as the door opened and she rushed towards them, stumbling in her haste, so Seb caught her up to prevent her falling to the miry cobbles.

'Slowly now, Mistress Thatcher,' he said, setting her steady upon her feet.

'Have you found my Will yet… any trace at all?' she said, breathlessly. 'Oh, Master Seb, I fear the faeries have snatched away my comely child.'

'I misdoubt that, mistress. Is London not far too busy a place for such secret folk to dwell?' He held her arm in a firm grip. 'Afore we account your son's disappearance to magick, I believe I have a clue to his whereabouts that takes a human form. Upon the morrow, I shall extend my searching south of the Bridge. Now be of good heart, I pray you.'

'Southwark? You think my Will's been taken to that viper's nest of cut-throats, thieves and whores? Oh, no, not there… my poor innocent lad, with naught but his grandmother's coral rosary with its ivory cross to protect him. Will it be enough? You must find him, master.' She clutched at his jerkin. 'You must.' Then she broke down, weeping.

Seb never knew what to do with a woman in tears but Beatrice's near neighbour and friend, Peronelle Wenham, had heard the exchange across the way and rescued him from his difficulty.

'Do you really think Will is in Southwark, master?' Kate asked him as Peronelle led her distraught friend back home.

Seb removed his cap and ran his fingers through his dark locks.

'I know not, Kate, and that be the truth of it. But Old Symkyn's revelations open up an entirely new chapter of possibilities. His astute observations may aid us greatly in the search. At least, I pray they do. With the Good Lord's blessings, we may yet find the lad safe.'

Kate nodded but her master's brave words were unmatched by his bleak expression.

''Tis Eastertide after all,' she said, smiling up at him. 'If Our Lord Jesu would give us a miracle, most surely there cannot be a better time to do so than now?'

'If we all had such faith as you do, lass, this world would be a holier and better place, indeed. Come now, you have notes to make and sketches to do and I have a manuscript much in need of decipherment. You also, Gawain. Take your nose out of there and heed me.'

# The Foxley House

'Master Appleyard sended me 'ome, didn't he?' Jack was explaining to Rose in the kitchen as Seb, Kate and the dog returned from Cheapside. 'Broked me thumb, I reckon.' Jack held up his injured digit for all to admire. It looked as though he had a blue-black apple there, instead of a thumb. 'Can't work wiv it like this, can I now?'

'Oh, poor Jack,' Kate said, tears welling. 'It must hurt you so much. Can I fetch you some strong ale to ease your pain?'

'That'd be welcome. It throbs like Satan's balls...'

'Jack! Mind your tongue. Let me see it.' Seb took a sturdy hold of Jack's wrist and led him out into the yard, where the light was brighter. 'How did you come to injure yourself?'

'Well, I wos bangin' in pegs, weren't I, to 'old a stool t'gevver. An' the 'ammer missed, didn't it? It weren't my fault. The 'ammer must've slipped, mustn't it?'

'So, the hammer was at fault?' Seb raised his eyebrows in question.

'Course.'

'And the workman was neither careless nor distracted?'

'I told you: the 'ammer... Ow! That 'urted.'

''Tis a poor craftsman who blames his tools, Jack. You have bruised your thumb severely but I do not believe bones to be broken.'

'You sure?'

'As may be. You can move it, which I doubt you could if it was broken.'

'Don't it need a splint or somefink?'

'And how would that ease the bruising? Nay, lad. Ask Rose to give you some violet oil to smear upon it. Three days away from the carpentry bench – with Master Appleyard's agreement – should see considerable improvement in your case.'

'Is that all? O'ny free days? But t'morrow's Good Friday when we don't work anyways, Saturday's an 'alf day, then Sunday, so that ain't 'ardly no time off at all.'

Seb shrugged.

'We will observe the progress of healing. Go see Rose about the violet oil. Or daisy oil may serve as well, if she has that instead.'

'I'll get Kate t' do it for me.'

'As you will.'

Jack slouched off, muttering something about his master being a hard man.

Back in the kitchen, Emily had come downstairs from her bed and was seated by the hearth.

Seb smiled at this welcome sight and hastened to kiss her brow. Her skin felt warm but not feverish. She seemed brighter in herself too. He took these to be good signs.

'Why are you not at your work with my father, Jack, you idle wretch?' she asked. She had taken up the ladle to stir the pottage pot but waved it at him in ominous wise.

In answer, Jack held up his thumb, glistening with the oil Kate had been smearing upon it. It glowed red as a hot coal.

'You clumsy great oaf,' Emily said, 'Don't think that spares you your chores. We need more wood for this fire, if you expect to eat supper, so go fetch it now.'

'But mistress....'

'Don't whine. You get no sympathy for your carelessness from me. Tell him, husband.'

'Aye. Your mistress be in the right, lad, and I be as implacable upon the matter as she. You still have one fully-functional hand and two good arms. See to your task.'

Jack wasn't sure what 'inplakerbal' meant but the look on both master's and mistress's faces left him in little doubt that he'd better do as he was told.

''T'ain't fair,' he grumbled.

'I'll help you,' Kate said, leaping to her feet. 'You hold out

154

your arms, Jack, and I'll stack the logs upon them. You won't need to use your hand at all.'

'S'pose so but not too many cos I'm still hurtin', ain't I?'

Outside, in the yard, they went to the lean-to where the firewood was neatly stacked, and Kate began to unhook the canvas that further shielded the heap from the rain. As testament to its worth, a cascade of water ran down. Kate leapt back, laughing, as the fall of water just missed soaking her shoes, although the hem of her gown fared less well, getting thoroughly wet.

'Leave the damned logs,' Jack said, pulling Kate around to the far side of the lean-to. His voice dropped an octave, becoming more manly and husky. He held her pressed close against him, his injury forgotten as he held her in his embrace, tight as he could. He kissed her hard upon the mouth for a long moment. 'Betterer than med'cine is that,' he said, pausing for breath.

Kate put her arms about his neck, having to stand on tip-toe to return his kiss but he lifted her off the ground, as though she weighed no more than dandelion fluff. His strength impressed her, as always.

'I think we should see about the logs,' she said breathlessly when he set her down.

'Bugger the bloody logs. Let 'em wait.' Jack stooped for another kiss, his hand fumbling for her breast beneath her gown and squeezing. Kate pulled back, giving a little squeal but whether of pain or delight, he couldn't tell and, at that instant, didn't much care. But his passion ended with a mighty clout across his ear.

'Whatever do you think you're doing?' Adam grabbed him by the scruff and yanked the amorous pair apart. 'Get your hands off her, Jack, you stupid young fool. Kate, go inside. And straighten your clothes; you look like a strumpet. As for you...' Adam dragged Jack by his jerkin, down to the end of the garden plot. Such action allowed time for him to recover his temper, somewhat, and Jack to get over his passion.

'I never seed yer there.' Jack said, his eyes downcast, his arms hanging slack.

'Obviously. I came through the gate. What possessed you? She's an alderman's daughter, not a street-walker. Do you not value your place here? Master Seb could throw you out in the gutter for this.'

'Kate loves me.' A hint of defiance crept into Jack's voice. His head came up. He could look Adam in the eye, almost.

Adam scoffed at the notion.

'You're both too young for that. You think her father would let her marry your sort? Think again. Kate will wed a rich merchant's son, not a young scallywag like you. It's called "having prospects" and you have none. Don't drag Kate down with you. You ruin her reputation, she'll have nothing either.'

'But we loves each uvver, don't we?'

'If you love her, Jack, respect her and leave her alone; unsullied.'

'I never unsullered her, whatever it is?'

'Just keep your grubby hands to yourself.'

'You goin' t' tell Master Seb 'bout us then?'

'I ought to. His good reputation will, likewise, be flown, if he cannot keep his apprentices from such immoral behaviour. And I most certainly shall if, in future, I even suspect…'

# Chapter 9

## Good Friday, the ninth day of April
## St Michael le Querne Church

THE MOST pious citizen in London was at St Michael's Church at first light, as required upon this, the most solemn morn of the year, along with Adam, Rose, Kate, Jack, Nessie and all the other parishioners. Seb knew he should be contemplating the Great Cross of rough-hewn wood, carried before them and now set in place in a mound of earth constructed for the purpose – Golgotha. Two lesser crosses were already set either side.

They shuffled forward on their knees, heads bowed, jostled by the rest of the congregation, likewise making their slow progress. But Seb could not keep his mind upon his Lord's suffering, but rather upon someone else's. She who should have been here but lay abed, alone: Emily. She had been most unwell during the night and Seb's concerns were all for her. Aye, and his prayers; may God forgive him.

'She'll not be long by herself, Seb,' Rose whispered to him, knowing his thoughts. For women, there was always the additional hazard of long skirts to hamper the creeping to the Cross and she held hers bunched up and over one arm even as her hands were pressed together in prayer.

'I know, but I worry, all the same. She be so poorly.'

At last, they were allowed to stand and there was much

rubbing of knees, easing of backs and straightening of skirts. Until a few years since, Seb had always been excused the act of creeping by reason of his lameness but that was a thing of the past and, having recovered so well, he now saw it as an act of personal thanksgiving, as well as meek contemplation. Yet this year, his heart, like his mind, was elsewhere. Even as Father Thomas read from the Gospels by the light of a solitary candle, all others having been extinguished, Seb could not concentrate upon the words. The old priest read the Latin in solemn tones, telling of Christ's last journey through the streets of Jerusalem, bearing his burden of the Cross. Occasionally, he paused, taking a moment to steady himself and dab his eyes with his surplus sleeve. Few of the congregation could understand every word – as Seb could – but all knew the story well enough and the gloom concealed many a sob and a deal of tears as they contemplated their Saviour's crucifixion. Seb felt choked also but knew his sorrows this day were not for Our Lord Jesu – as they rightly ought to be, but for his beloved Em.

## Crosby Place, Bishopsgate

Francis Lovell was annoyed. Duke Richard had ordered his entire household to attend St Helen's Church in Bishopsgate, close neighbour to Crosby Place, to do penance, creeping to the Cross, and now Francis' blue silken hose were ruined at the knee. Curse the duke. They could have done the same in the little chapel at Crosby Place, in which case, the crawl would have been a few yards and no more. But Richard deemed that an insufficient degree of humility and subjugation, so they were forced to attend St Helen's with the length of its nave second only to St Paul's, to wear out their knees in the name of Jesu Christ.

And a decent breakfast was then further delayed by a long, miserable sermon, harping on endlessly about sinful mankind, undeserving of the Saviour's sacrifice of blood. Francis did not care. He'd heard it all before and, to his mind, the promise of Heaven as mankind's ultimate reward was not especially appealing. The place would be crowded with pious, mealy-mouthed do-gooders, eternally at prayer. Where was the pleasure in that? Hell sounded more enticing, with assorted whores and loose women, gamblers and gamesters. That was more to his taste.

Further disappointed upon return to the duke's hall to find a fasting board of only bread and ale had been provided, on Richard's orders, Francis had suffered enough of Good Friday's dour aspects. Determined to find some more suitable occupation for the remainder of the day, he begged leave of Lord Richard and departed in haste. Revenge would make a more rewarding employment and he had a deserving victim in mind.

## The Foxley House

Seb greeted his visitor upon the doorstep.

'God give you good day, Bailiff Turner. Please to come in. Will you partake of ale? How may I be of assistance to you, Thaddeus?'

'This is not a social call, Master Foxley. We are here to serve a warrant.' The bailiff gestured to the two burly fellows behind him: constables. Both wore the most severe expressions and Thaddeus himself looked as though someone was holding him at sword point, his discomfiture plain.

'A warrant? Against whom and for what crime? None here has offended; I would swear my oath to that upon the Gospels.'

Adam joined Seb at the street door.

159

'Anything amiss, Seb?' he asked, seeing three dour faces.

'Thaddeus says they be serving a warrant.'

'I think you should address me as Bailiff Turner, under the circumstances.'

Seb raised his eyebrows. He had known Thaddeus long enough that they might use each other's baptismal names.

'And what circumstances might that be?'

Bailiff Turner cleared his throat and waved the constables forward.

'Sebastian Foxley, I am arresting you upon the charge of murder; that you did feloniously and with malice aforethought slay one Thomas...'

'Hey! Hold off now.' Adam elbowed one of the constables aside and pulled Seb back into the passageway. 'Seb never slew a fly, never mind some fellow. You're making a grave mistake here.'

'Stand aside, Master Armitage, or I'll cause my men to arrest you also for obstructing the Lord Mayor's officers in the rightful execution of their duties.'

'Show me the warrant then,' Adam demanded. 'I cannot believe such a monstrous accusation is being made against Seb.'

The bailiff handed over the warrant and Adam read it.

'Thomas Bowen!' he blurted out. 'That foul-mouthed rascal? He's not dead. Seb dismissed him and rightly so. I expect you'll find him in some low-life tavern, dead drunk. That's all. This is nonsense.' He made to tear up the document but the bailiff snatched it back, ripping off a corner.

'We have a corpse. And evidence enough to implicate Master Foxley.'

'Dear God in Heaven.' Adam looked at Seb, who was frowning so deeply that his dark brows met across his forehead. 'Well, say something, cousin. Tell them this is a bag of lies.'

'Aye, of course that be the case,' Seb answered, chewing his nether lip. 'But if Tom be slain and I did naught to harm him, then a murderer be at large in our city. Such a situation requires investigation.'

'But not by you,' the bailiff said. 'Bind his hands. Escort him to Guildhall for questioning. And you keep out of this, Master Armitage. You have been warned.'

'Leave it be, Adam. I shall go with them peaceably and delve deeper into this matter.'

'The only thing you'll be delving into is your own grave', one of the constables said, glaring at Seb.

'Hold your tongue. Just do your duty, as I instruct.'

Seb had never heard Bailiff Turner sound so assertive and yet the man's true nature was still evident. As the constable bound Seb's hands before him with a length of rough, hempen rope, Thaddeus leaned close. 'I'm sorry about this, Seb, but I have my orders, whether I like them or no,' he whispered.

Seb nodded.

'I understand; 'tis no fault of yours.'

Nevertheless, a crowd had gathered as if summoned by magick, jostling each other in Paternoster Row. Scandalous rumours would run swiftly around the city. Seb's heart was heavy. This would assist neither his business nor his reputation, being marched off to the Counter. Nor his wife upon her sickbed. This matter must be swiftly resolved.

# Guildhall

Thaddeus Turner had the use of a small room at Guildhall by reason of his new office as the Lord Mayor's Bailiff. Previously, he had served in the post of Beadle for the Prior of St Bartholomew's and worked alongside Seb to solve a few crimes during last summer's Fayre. In performing the office for the Lord Mayor – with a respectable increase in wages – he had never thought to be arresting his friend. Seb Foxley was not the murdering kind, in his opinion, but what of the evidence? It looked damning indeed.

They were alone in the room, although the constables stood beyond the door, at hand if the prisoner should prove troublesome. Thaddeus sat on a stout chair beside a table. Seb was perched on a rickety three-legged stool opposite and the warrant with its torn corner lay there betwixt them, bathed in a shaft of watery sunlight that penetrated the narrow window from the courtyard outside. It was as if the light illumined not so much a solitary document but a wall, a barrier betwixt friends, yet Thaddeus' earlier whispered apology gave Seb cause for hope.

Outside, a trumpet sounded. Some person of importance required folk to make way. Someone shouted out in a shrill voice. Horses' hooves clattered in the cobbled yard beyond the window. Harness jangled. When the noise faded, Bailiff Turner began the questioning.

'Adam mentioned that you'd dismissed Thomas Bowen from your employ,' Thaddeus said, fidgeting upon his seat. 'When was that?'

'What has that to do with my arrest?'

'Just answer my question.'

'Monday, I believe. Aye. 'Twas at dinner. Matters came to a head. I told him to go.' Seb spoke, soft and clear, his grey eyes steady, holding his old friend's gaze.

'Why? Young Bowen was your indentured apprentice. You would need to present your case to the guild before dismissing him, would you not?'

'Nay. His term of apprenticeship ended at Christmastide last. I kept him on as my journeyman, which was a mistake, I fear.'

'How so?'

'Tom was ever somewhat unruly but, of late, being no longer bound by the regulations of indenture, he frequented taverns and lost money at dice. He gave customers ill words, too frequently sat idle when he ought to work and his slovenly penmanship did naught to sustain the workshop's hard-won reputation. I knew he could do better if he bothered.

'At dinner upon that Monday, he insulted my goodwife,

used abusive language and made threats against me and my household. I could not permit such behaviour 'neath my roof.' Seb looked thoughtful. 'I was within my rights, was I not? I dismissed him, there and then, although I permitted him to collect and take his belongings. I also paid him his wages for the whole day, though he had not earned them. I fulfilled my obligations towards him.'

'Were you angry?'

'Of course. Any man would be. Such words as he gave Emily upset her so and she being unwell, I took greatly against his ill-manners.'

'Did you strike him? Or do him assault by any means? Was there a fight?'

'Oh, you have noted my bruises.' Seb touched his face with care, his hands yet bound. 'Nay, there was no fight. These result from an innocent mishap. But, had I struck him, I should have been within my rights, should I not? But, in truth, I did naught of the kind.' Seb tried to ease the rope around his wrists. 'I have ne'er done him the least harm; ne'er raised my hand to him. Mayhap, that was how I failed him. Could a few beatings have made a better man of him?' Seb shrugged at his own question. 'I know not. I sent him on his way without any letter of recommendation. I suppose that injured his future prospects for employment but he deserved none. I did him no hurt otherwise. He left my house hale and whole as ever, if in vile humour.

'But tell me, Thaddeus, of the circumstances in which he was found. What had come to pass?' Seb leaned forward, across the table, eager for information. The feeble light no longer fell upon the warrant.

'Well,' the bailiff folded his arms and sighed. 'A letter was delivered to the coroner this day, telling of a body found in a narrow alleyway, off Knightrider Street. It must have been there a while. It was not a pleasant sight. Rats... stray dogs... who can say? Master Fyssher claims...'

'The coroner has returned? I thought he was gone to relatives in the countryside for Eastertide.'

'He did but a disagreement arose...'

'Why does that not surprise me?'

'Unfortunately, upon his return, he learned of the lad's dead body lately found in your workshop and now this: two youngsters murdered, both of whom can be connected to you, in some way and some damning evidence was discovered with this more recent corpse and, er, elsewhere. Who do you suppose issued this wretched warrant for your arrest?' The bailiff fingered the document, rustling the paper.

'Oh, aye. That would appeal to Fyssher's nature. He holds no fondness for me; never has.'

'Because you solve crimes he doesn't even realise have been committed and outwit him at every turn. You show up his incompetence. No man likes to be seen for a fool.'

'You speak honestly, Thaddeus. Why do we not think this crime through together, you and I. Mayhap, we shall outwit the coroner once more.'

The bailiff hesitated, rubbing his chin – Seb recognised his friend's old habit as denoting indecision.

'Do you truly believe I killed Tom Bowen?'

There followed a time of silence whilst Bailiff Turner considered the question. To Seb, it seemed to last for hours but was probably no more than a minute, or less. Footsteps passed by in the ante-room but no one interrupted them.

'No. I don't believe you did. Hold out your hands.'

Seb obeyed. Thaddeus took out his knife and cut the hemp.

'There is not a grain of evil in your soul,' he said.

Seb rubbed his wrists to get the blood flowing again and quirked an eyebrow.

'My thanks for that but I be no saint, particularly where Coroner Fyssher be concerned. Now, you say this body in Knightrider Street had lain a while and was no pleasant sight: be you certain it is Tom Bowen? And why do you not describe this supposed damning evidence against me? Let us set about solving this murder, at least, although I admit to making no progress in discovering the name of the pale-haired child found in my workshop, nor his killer.'

'Mm, well, for one thing, there is the matter of a blood-stained shirt belonging to you, which has been brought to our notice. The victim was stabbed, so there was a deal of blood, without doubt.'

'B-but that be outrageous!' Seb leapt to his feet. 'There was a gory shirt, 'tis true, but how do you know of it? Last I saw, it lay soaking in a bucket in the courtyard. Who brought it to your attention? None in my household, I wager my life.'

'No. Coroner Fyssher received the letter concerning it.'

'From whom?'

'It was unsigned, so he said, but he determined to pay a visit to your premises.'

'He never did. I have not seen him; was unaware of his return – as I said.'

'The visit was, er, unofficial.'

'Snooping. The rascal came hedge-breaking, entering our yard, grubbing around to see what he could find to incriminate me. Despicable. The Lord Mayor should hear of this.'

'Aye, Seb. Fyssher behaved in an unseemly fashion but, you must admit, a bloody shirt raises many questions and arouses suspicion. Can you explain it?'

Seb resumed his seat. Losing his temper would gain him naught.

''Tis easily accounted for. Upon Wednesday last, a disturbance arose in Paternoster Row, before our very door. Two curs scrapping, is all, but they drew a noisy crowd. Emily – as you may have heard – lay in her sickbed in the chamber that overlooked the street. I went out to ask them to have pity for an ailing woman and disperse quietly. But, at that moment, one of the dogs bolted, fleeing straight towards a bystander and me, sending us tumbling. The fellow caught my nose with his elbow as we fell. Hence the blood upon my shirt... and this bruising to my face.'

'I was about to ask how you came by those injuries. Were there any witnesses to this misadventure?'

'A good many but the only one I can put a name to is Jonathan Caldicott, my near neighbour, and, of course, Mistress Rose Glover who observed the incident from the bedchamber window above.'

'Mistress Rose... aye, I shall enquire of her,' Thaddeus said, smiling at the prospect of a conversation with an attractive woman. 'So that explains the soiled shirt... and your bruises. The second piece of evidence will be harder to dismiss. Some of your property was found right there, beside the body of Thomas Bowen.'

'If it is him? And, if that be so, the property must have been stolen from me.'

'Have you reported to the authorities any items going missing?'

'Nay. A book with a fine cover was filched from the shop a few days past. I cannot recall which day it was; I had forgotten it 'til now. Was the book found there? I shall call its title to mind... it concerned the playing of chess.'

'There was no book but a half ream, or thereabouts, of fine paper, quills and covered inkpots...'

'Why would they be mine? Such things can be purchased from any stationer.'

'But not a seal with a fox's head...'

'My seal?'

'Indeed. And you have not reported so vital an object gone missing? You must be aware that the guild has to be informed of the loss, for fear it may be used to authenticate false documents by outsiders who do not belong to the fellowship.'

'I had not realised it was gone. Matters at home be somewhat in disarray with Emily sick, I have hardly had a thought for such things as seals, never mind paper and pens.'

'But its discovery at the scene of a crime incriminates you.

In truth, it was the seal that aided the identifying of the corpse as Thomas Bowen's, making the connection to you.'

Seb said naught. Something was amiss with such assumptions, if only his mind could determine how Thaddeus' arguments were awry.

'Might we have some ale and pause a while?' he asked, 'I cannot make use of logic for the present, I be befuddled by weariness.'

Thaddeus obliged. So much talk was dire work. He instructed one of the constables standing guard outside the door to fetch refreshments. The fellow stomped off, his disapproval of providing ale for a prisoner evident in his demeanour.

'So, what be amiss with your Emily?'

'Some difficulty concerning the babe, so Nell Warren says.'

'The midwife?'

'Aye.'

'Is she near her time then?'

'Not so close. Another month, so Emily believes. Or so she tells me. I was sent to procure medicaments to hasten the babe along, but naught came to pass, so I suppose the time be not yet at hand. But what do I know of women's matters? Yet, truth be told, I be that anxious for her health, I can think upon little else.' Seb sipped his ale. 'This new problem you have thrust at me comes at the worst of times. I should be at home with my wife.'

'I'm sorry, Seb. If I had a choice, you wouldn't be here, but Fyssher has forced my hand – he and his anonymous informant, whoever he may be.'

Seb nodded.

'I understand. Do you think there be an informant? Or did Fyssher come to my house, hoping to find something – anything – to incriminate me and then invent an informant?'

'Oh, there was certainly a letter, written upon expensive paper, saying your place in Paternoster Row would be worth the searching as well as telling of the body. Fyssher showed it to me.'

'Do you have it? May I see it?'

'Fyssher kept it, I fear. So, are you refreshed?' Thaddeus asked, having drained his cup. 'Then let us return to the criminal matters at hand.'

'Aye, as I see it,' Seb said, gazing into his cup, still half full, 'The finding of my seal and other items beside Tom's body only serves to confuse us. You must realise that, if I be guilty, I would have been the greatest fool in London to leave my own seal at the scene of the murder. Why would I be so stupid? And what of his purse, boots and belt?'

'What of them?' The bailiff spread his hands, perplexed.

'Did you find them?'

'Aye, not that there was much left in the purse: a farthing is all. No more than that.'

'And the body had lain there a while but no one had robbed it?'

'The alley was narrow, dark and hardly used since the far end was blocked off by a high wall. The letter said the body was only found because a member of St Andrew's congregation next door was caught short and hoped to be discreet about it.'

'The letter said that?'

'Aye. But it was unsigned.'

'Your informant be literate, then and not alone in knowing of the body. The killer knew of it and the parishioner who discovered it, unless all three be one? And why did the killer not take the coin? Also, the paper and pens could be sold and Tom's boots were purchased but a few months past. They would fetch a good price, being little worn. You realise what this means, Thaddeus?'

The bailiff pulled a face, frowning in puzzlement, rubbing his chin again.

'What does it mean?' he asked after a little thought.

'Tom's death was not the result of a chance encounter with a foot-pad, some penniless rascal or other. The murderer be a man of substance and standing who has wealth enough and no need to filch a dead man's possessions. Tom was killed for a purpose, the killer's intended victim. I fear the murderer may be your mysterious informant also.'

'Then what of the rusty chain? How does that signify?'

'Rusty chain? You did not mention that.'

'Oh? Maybe it isn't important anyway.'

'Tell me of it. Describe it to me, if you will.'

''Tis just a length of old, rusty iron chain – of some weight – yet in a good cloth bag. It lay beside the body. The drawstring on the bag was open, a few rusted links showing.'

'Mm. Tom – or his killer – had probably opened it but I misdoubt an iron chain was what he expected to find within. What did he think was in the bag and where did it come from? How did he come by it?' Seb took a sip of ale. 'How much coin did you say was in the lad's purse?'

Thaddeus rubbed at his chin.

'Er, a farthing, I think.'

'Then the lad had need of money. I should hazard a guess that he thought the bag contained coins. Did it rattle like money?'

'I don't know. It might have. I never shook it to hear how it sounded.'

'And where be the bag now?'

'Coroner Fyssher has everything in his keeping – including your seal.'

'Has he, indeed? 'Tis unfortunate, for I should examine everything, including the body. Where is Tom lain?'

'In St Andrew's-by-the-Wardrobe, being the nearest church. Are you certain you must see it? As I said before, 'tis not a heartening sight.'

'Aye, I have to, if only to pay my respects. Besides, I shall bear the cost of his funeral, for his sister's sake. Has she been informed yet?'

'I wasn't aware he had family.'

'Aye. His sister Bella be wed to Dame Ellen Langton's son, Dick. They live downriver, at Deptford, where Dick works as a shipwright. She will be sorrowful, indeed, to lose her only brother. Tom visited her regularly. It was one trait to be much admired in him: his affection for his sister and his little niece, Janey, and a new nephew. We know them well. Emily and I stood as godparents for Janey. It might be kindly if I went…'

'No, Seb. I must forbid your leaving the city. And how will it look if I allow the accused – even though I believe you innocent, you yet stand thus – to inform the victim's relatives?'

Seb sighed.

'Aye. I suppose. But I beseech you, Thaddeus: see to it the ill-tidings be gently given. Bella be a woman of sensitive feeling.'

'I can make no promises on that score, my friend. Fyssher will send whomsoever he chooses.'

'Forgive me. 'Twas foolish of me to think your writ ran as far as Deptford. I see that now.'

'But, fortunately, it does run as far as Paternoster Row. I'm releasing you on your own word of honour, that you'll not leave London. Will you give me your word, Seb?'

'Does it run south of the Bridge into Southwark?'

'Why? Surely that disgusting den holds naught of interest to you?'

'It may do. We yet be searching for the lad gone missing, young Will Thatcher. I have a clue which points that way, to The Mermaid in Southwark.'

'Aye, my authority stretches that far but no further. And have a care, Seb, someone out there – beside Coroner Fyssher – doesn't like you. Watch your back.'

A while later, when Seb departed from Guildhall, free for now to make his way home to his ailing wife, if he was watching his back, as Thaddeus had advised him, he wasn't the only one.

# The Church of St Andrew-by-the-Wardrobe

Seb had gone home but briefly, just long enough to enquire as to Emily's comfort and to be assured by Rose that she was resting quietly, as well as collecting his purse before making his way to St Andrew's Church in Old Fish Street, off Knightrider Street. It was drizzling again, a fine mist of moisture turning the afternoon to untimely twilight. A rat skittered away as Seb approached the priest's house next door to the church. He had a lengthy wait before anyone heeded his knock upon the door, time enough to note its peeling paintwork that might once have been green but was now a smoke-grimed grey, and the rust-freckled hinges sorely in need of attention.

The priest who opened the door, at last, looked most displeased at being disturbed by someone who was not even a parishioner of his.

'What do you want? Every good Christian should be on his knees, praying, this day of all days, as was I. Now get you gone, you rogue. I want none of your kind with your brawler's bruises and black eyes. Trouble: that's what you are. Trouble. Go away.' The man stepped back into his hallway and was about to slam the door in Seb's face – until he saw the glint of coin in Seb's hand. 'What do you want?' he repeated.

Seb removed his cap courteously and glanced towards the church. The house of prayer – once a royal foundation but no longer – looked to be in sore need of reparations also.

'Forgive my impertinence, father, your church appears to require work be done upon the roof.'

'If you're a tiler after business, I remind you 'tis Good Friday. Now be on your way.'

'I do not tout for work, father…' Seb held his coins more prominently, 'But would be willing to contribute to the cost of your repairs.'

'And why would you do that when my flock is reluctant to contribute so much as a clipped ha'penny? St Andrew's used to be a fine church in my father's day. I can recall when it…'

'Aye, no doubt it was,' Seb interrupted, uninterested in any such reminiscences. 'But I would have you recall more recent times. These few days past is all. In exchange, I be willing to donate two shillings to church works. Does that seem a reasonable request and fair exchange to you?'

'Depends. I suppose you best come inside.'

Did not money always work better than magick, even with clergymen, Seb thought, dismayed that it was so often the case. He signed to Gawain to wait outside.

The priest's house was as dusty and ill-kept as he was and no less reluctant to provide welcome. The fire in the hearth gave off wisps of smoke but no heat, its coals dull and probably damp. The rushes strewn on the floor were long ago trodden down flat and compacted. Seb was sure he saw cockroaches clambering among the unsavoury mess of crushed stems.

The priest sat on a bench with frayed cushions. Chicken feathers puffed out of a torn seam when he eased down upon them.

Seb remained standing. Neither comfort nor refreshment were offered.

'Well? I don't have the day to waste in idle chatter, like a country goodwife. What do you want? I shan't ask again and you can go to hellfire and damnation for all I care.'

'Yester morn, a body was discovered in the alleyway running beside this house.'

'What of it? 'Tis naught to do with me except that it now lies stinking in my undercroft. Have you come to remove it?'

'I fear not, but the unfortunate soul was slain a few days ago. I wish to enquire whether you saw or, mayhap, heard anything untoward upon Tuesday or Wednesday last?'

'I have better things to do than attend my neighbours' comings and goings.'

'The young man who lies 'neath your church was not your neighbour but lately in my employ; my journeyman...'

'Then you can take him away, can't you? And remove the offensive stench that turns my belly and causes my parishioners to gag.'

'I shall do so, in good time, but he was brutally murdered, so I have been informed by the authorities, and deserves to have the killer who slew him brought to justice. Any information you may provide, father, will not only hasten the entire process along, but earn your church twenty-four pence to aid its repair. I can see that be dear to your heart.'

Indeed, the priest's eyes gleamed at the sight of silver in Seb's palm. He reached for it but Seb closed his hand.

'What did you see upon Wednesday last or Tuesday? Any observation may help.'

The priest turned away to gaze into the lifeless hearth.

'You did see something,' Seb prompted. 'That be the case, is it not? What was it? Tell me.'

'I may have seen a man...'

Seb waited. Had not everyone in London seen a man?

'Wednesday. Just after the chiming of the Angelus bell at noontide. Dark hair, quite long and curling, as young lords wear it nowadays. Not so tall but broad in the shoulder. Although that could be down to the fashion for padding. His attire was most expensive, I would say. He wore such feathers in his hat from some bird or other. Who knows?'

'A swan?' Seb suggested.

'No. Brightly hued. Most ostentatious.'

'A popinjay, mayhap?'

'Not that. The one with a thousand eyes.'

'Ah. You describe a peacock.'

'That's the one. Foolish great plumes they were. Then he mounted and rode away, in haste, upon a very fine steed. He had tethered it at the church, beside the porch. Out of courtesy, I gave him blessing but he chose to ignore me.' The priest sniffed, disdainful of such irreverent behaviour. 'And now you have promised money in the sight of God and I would have it...'

Seb passed coin into the priest's over-eager hand, hoping the man's observations were not invented and his recollections true.

'I be most grateful to you, father, and apologise for keeping you from your prayers.'

He was shown towards the door.

'And don't forget to remove the stinking corpse, as you said you would.'

The door slammed shut. No blessing had been given.

Seb turned into the alleyway next door, said to be the place where Tom had met his sorry fate. The light was poor but Seb would look, all the same. Quite what he hoped to find, he could not say.

The ground was wet, awash with mud; any clues scoured away by the rain long since. No footprints, no sign of a scuffle and any bloodstains there might have been were now just part of the mud but Gawain nosed around, finding the empty shell of a sparrow's egg, ejected from a nest under the eaves of the priest's house.

Seb spent a fruitless half hour searching for who knew what. He was about to give up but turned his eyes from the ground to the wall of the house. Its easterly direction, and the eves above it, protected it from the prevailing west wind and rain. Seb spotted several rust-coloured splatters at shoulder level. Blood. It had to be. And Tom had been stabbed to death, so Thaddeus had told him. But that was not all: adhered to the wall by a splash of gore was an iridescent filament. Seb examined it with care. To his mind, there was little doubt that it came from the feather of a peacock. It must have become stuck when the blood was fresh spilt. Did it, therefore, identify the dark-haired wearer of the plumed hat, the rider of the fine steed, described by the priest, as Tom's killer? It seemed most likely. He tore a corner from a piece of paper in his scrip and folded it around the filament, putting it in his purse for safe-keeping.

His next task was to call upon Stephen Appleyard as keeper of St Michael's parish coffin, to arrange collection of Tom's remains. Then to Father Thomas, to prepare for the funeral of one-time journeyman-scrivener Thomas Bowen, late of Paternoster Row. A sorry end for one barely yet come to manhood.

# Chapter 10

## Saturday, the tenth day of April

IT BEING the last day of Lent, the housewives were out early, everyone wanting first choice of the fresh meat, spring worts, butter and cheeses. The stalls in Cheapside were already crowded even before the bell rang for trading to commence. However, business for those like Seb and Adam, who were not involved in the victualling trade, was likely to be slow indeed. Saturday was only a half-day for working in any case; the afternoon expected to be spent in contemplation of the Lord's Day upon the morrow, so Seb had little hesitation in announcing that the shop would remain closed.

Besides, they were all weary, having seen Tom safely into his grave in St Michael's churchyard last eve. Few had attended – Tom was not well liked, so it seemed – but Seb and Adam had stood by him, as was expected of the men of the household to which the deceased had lately belonged, except Jack, who claimed he would not pretend a respect for such a wretch. Stephen Appleyard had stayed but only to retrieve the parish coffin when Father Thomas had finished the committal. They had all departed once Seb had paid the Sexton to fill in the grave. They were sombre but no tears were shed.

God be praised: it was a beautiful spring morn – a rare thing of late – the sun glinting on muddy puddles and slick cobbles, turning all to gleaming silver. The breeze bore the promise of fresh green life and held a definite hint of warmth. Sheep's-fleece clouds gambled across the azure meadows of heaven. Finding a clump of golden stars of celandine to greet him by the privy door had further raised Seb's spirits. The better weather had also brightened Emily's spirits and she had risen from bed to join the household, breaking their fast in the kitchen. Seb thought she was much improved, stronger than of late.

Thus it seemed a propitious day to go to Southwark, in search of the scar-faced man and, hopefully, find some trace of young Will Thatcher.

''Tis a long walk to London Bridge,' Adam said. 'Would it not save us a deal of time, if we hired a boat from Paul's Wharf across to Southwark?'

'I feel the need of the exercise,' Seb replied. 'Yesterday's creeping to the Cross quite cramped my knees. Besides, Gawain has little liking for boats.'

Adam laughed.

'Oh, aye. I recall now: 'tis not Gawain but you who hates the water. I had nigh forgot how you get seasick just watching the boats bobbing upon the waves.'

'I require to have firm ground 'neath my feet, is all. I cannot help that. You may hail a boatman, if you will. Come, Gawain, we have places to be; matters to attend.' Seb walked off apace, hastening through St Paul's precinct, pausing for a heartbeat only to bow his head before Paul's Cross and making for the Watling Street gate.

Adam ran to catch him up.

'No need to be like that, Seb. Was a jest is all.'

'Aye, I know. Forgive me. 'Tis an affliction most annoying. You be right. A boat would be far more swift but I shall walk, all the same.'


Candlewick Street and East Cheap were bustling. Everyone, it seemed, was tempted forth from their fireside by the clement weather. Fish Street and the Bridge were thronged and most folk were coming into the city. Thus, Seb, Adam and the dog had to struggle against the human tide. Feet and paws were trodden on, ribs were elbowed and knees were bruised by laden baskets of wares for sale. People shouted, cursed and argued. Carts creaked and donkeys brayed. A flock of geese, on their way to the poulterers, honked their disapproval of being crowded. Beneath the cacophony, the Thames thundered ceaselessly, roaring betwixt the stone starlings of the Bridge. Enticing scents from the cookshops mixed with those of fresh dung and rotting fish and amidst the disorder, a troop of urchins played a riotous game of knock-and-run.

Seb danced aside as a bucket of chitterlings was sent flying, threatening to engulf his shoes in a slippery mess. Gawain was not dismayed and helped himself to a yard of entrails to break his fast for a second time that morn.

## Southwark

At last, they fought their way across and paused by the great church of St Mary Overy to catch a clearer breath of air. They checked that they still possessed their caps, scrips and purses intact and all was in order.

The way beside the Bishop of Winchester's house and the Clink prison was just as busy as anywhere else in the city across the river. Bankside was, likewise, crammed with folk, coming and going.

'I think we ought to split up to make enquiries,' Adam suggested. 'That way, we can both show the drawings to more folk. Then, if we meet back here, by the church porch at midday and compare our findings, we may decide what's next to be done.'

'Be that wise? Symkyn warned me that this place might well hold danger for us, particularly if we meet the scar-faced fellow. Mayhap, we should stay together.'

Adam shrugged.

'Then our enquiries will be halved. Besides, you'll have Gawain to defend you.'

'But what of you? If you cross his path first or that of any other rogue or rascal?'

'When did you last see me step away from a brawl, Seb? I'm as handy with my fists as the next fellow. You worry overmuch. I'll see you here as the Angelus rings. Just keep a sharp watch and all will be well.' Adam turned away, taking his copies of Seb's drawings from his scrip, ready to show to passers-by.

Seb saw him approach a woman, a huckster hawking bread from her tray, and engage her in conversation, showing her the papers. He felt so uneasy, he almost called Adam back but, looking around, he realised there were mostly ordinary folk going about their daily round, a few clergymen and two Dominican friars in their dark habits. Mayhap, they were from the monastery of the Black Friars across the river. The denizens of Southwark did not appear so threatening as he had been led to believe.

Calling Gawain to heel, Seb chose an old woman, bent-backed and shuffling, as a suitable person to ask. She must live close at hand, being unlikely to walk far abroad. He doffed his cap courteously and asked for a moment of her time. Perhaps lonely, she was willing enough to talk but Seb's efforts were wasted. The old woman frowned at his drawings, screwing up her eyes, holding the papers at arms' length. Eventually, she admitted that she couldn't make them out; her eyes weren't up to seeing things close to these days, so she said, not like when she was a young seamstress. She began to tell him about how she had sewn linen for the Bishop of Winchester himself, praised for her invisibly-fine stitchery.

Seb had to harden his heart and cut short her recollections.

He gave her a penny, thanked her, touched his cap and moved on. Espying a priest, he approached the cleric and was surprised when, upon seeing Seb, he cast down his eyes and scuttled off, giving the impression that he had been engaged in some nefarious practice or other. A foolish thought, of course.

Seb spoke then to a comely, dark-haired woman.

'God give you good day, mistress.' He gave a little bow. 'If 'tis not too much to ask of you, if you might spare a few moments and take the trouble to...'

'For you, it will be no trouble,' she said. She eyed him, up and down, from his cap to his dusty boots, assessing. Her voice was honey-rich but with a foreign-sounding lisp, those dark eyes inviting as charcoal in a brazier on a winter's eve.

'I-I wonder if you might look at these drawings? Have you seen this fellow with the scar? He be tall and well-built. Fairish hair. Or this lad with golden curls... or another youngster, here, with white hair...'

Was it Seb's imagination, or did the woman take a sharp breath, startled by the pictures?

'Nay. Never seen their like,' she said, clutching his arm, running her fingers down the front of his jerkin. 'I'm Katerina. Why don't we go somewhere less crowded? You've shown me your drawings, now I could show you a thing or two.' Of a sudden, Seb felt a bold hand caressing his manhood, there, in the midst of the street.

'No!' he cried, pulling away.

Katerina just smiled and shrugged, turning her back. She walked off, swinging her hips, back the way she had come. Rejection meant naught to her. But, though Seb could not see it, her expression was one of alarm and, once out of his sight, she broke into a run.

Seb stood still, shocked. Not so much by Katerina's brazen behaviour but by his own body which had leaped, all against his will, at her touch. His face burned, his loins stirred by lust and guilt overwhelmed him, bathing him in sweat. He had betrayed his beloved Em, even as she suffered at home, if not upon her sickbed. What a wretch of a husband. How could he ever forgive himself? Symkyn was correct: Southwark was a place of danger, not only physical but moral. He must be more vigilant.

Katerina made her way, in haste, to The Mermaid.

'Mistress Bessie,' she cried, flinging wide the door and stumbling over the threshold. 'Trouble is come upon us all.'

'Hold your noise, you fool. We've got customers.' The tall woman with eyes like agate pebbles ushered Katerina up the stairs. 'Cherry-lips, Magdalene, men need more ale here. See to it.' A woman of middle years with painted mouth and cheeks obeyed, flaunting herself as a strumpet half her age, pulling her bodice lower. Another younger woman, pale but buxom, followed her.

'Now, what's amiss, Katerina, that you make such a fuss?' Bessie demanded, hands on hips at the top of the stair.

'There's a man, coming along Bankside, showing drawings to anyone who cares to look. He has likenesses of Master Cain and both the lads we had here – all to the life. He's asking if anyone's seen them. Sooner or later, somebody is bound to say they know Master Cain, if not the lads as well.'

'You should have brought him straight here.' Bessie was angered. Wrath hid her deeper concerns.

'I tried but he wasn't to be persuaded. He pushed me off. I didn't want folk to take too much notice. They might be the more eager to see his drawings.'

'Aye. Maybe your sort don't appeal to him. Peaches! Get yourself dressed up in your country maiden's clouts. He'll not resist an innocent lass, new to the city and scared half to death of the crowds.'

Peaches appeared to suit her name: fresh of face with a bloom in her cheeks, wholesome as spring water.

'But mistress, you know I got the burnin' sickness,' Peaches whined. 'If I'm found out to have the pox, the bishop'll close us down.'

'He won't bloody dare, being one of our best customers. Besides, no one's going to find out. Just entice this knave with the damned drawings here. I don't care how you do it.'

'But how will I know him?'

'That's simple,' Katerina said. 'He's showing his pictures to everyone and both his eyes are black from fighting and his nose all fat and out of shape. You can't mistake him, Peaches.'

Meanwhile, Seb had hardly moved from the spot where he had encountered Katerina. There had been no reason to, since a constant stream of folk ever flowed towards and around him. A pair of housewives had cooed over young Will's pretty curls but moved away abruptly, shaking their heads in unison, as soon as he showed them the likeness of the man with the scars. A baker had been far too busy to look but his lad took the time to glance at the pictures. He paled visibly at sight of the man and bounded off after his master. No one knew nor had ever set eyes upon the scarred face. Seb did not believe them all. Some knew the man, he suspected, but were too afeared to admit this was so.

He was wondering whether his quest was to prove entirely in vain when a young lass ran straight into him, knocking his papers out of his hand. She was full of apology, tears welling as she retrieved the picture of the boy with white hair from a puddle. The drawing was ruined, tearing apart as she returned it to Seb before bursting into tears.

'Oh, good sir,' she sobbed, 'I be that sorry, I know not what I be about. This place scares me so. So much noise; so many folks... I be all perplexed, sir.'

'You be lately come to London then?' Seb felt pity for the lass.

'Aye, sir. Up from the shires but yesterday and at a loss. I miss my home so. I should ne'er have come but dare not return, or my Papa will beat me... yet more,' she added, glancing at Seb from betwixt wet lashes, gauging whether she had yet landed her fish or no.

'You poor lass. When did you eat last?'

'Can't recall, good sir, truly I can't.'

'That much, at least, I can set aright, though I fear I know Southwark no better than you. We must take our chances. I saw a cookshop back a way. Its wares smelled good to me.'

Gawain gave a yap and wagged his tail in agreement. 'My dog seems to approve my proposal,' Seb said, chuckling.

'Nay, nay, I know a better place where the ale is strong and food fine indeed, at the sign of The Mermaid. Come with me; 'tis this way.'

Seb frowned.

'You told me you be newly come to the city and have not eaten for days. How then can you know of this place and recommend its fare? I fear you tell me untruths. I cannot believe you. You appear plump enough; hardly a starvling wench. Be off with you, hussy.'


Peaches returned in failure. Bessie slapped her hard across the face.

'You useless bloody bitch. You couldn't tempt Satan himself to sin. Get out o' my sight before I mark you so you'll never work again. I know not why I give you bed and board and roof over your head, you pox-ridden maggot.'

Peaches fled. Her tears were real enough this time.

'Katerina! Where's John? Tell him to come.'

'I believe he's in the stable with Peter Tanner. You told him never to bring the stinking fellow within doors again but John earns regular coin from him, all the same.'

'Just fetch him.' Bessie's scowl was sufficient to affright the stoutest soul.

A young woman, tall and graceful, came in from the back of the tavern.

'What do you want, Bess? I was busy. You shouldn't interrupt me when I'm working.'

'You stink, as you always do after consorting with that damned tanner. Go change your gown, John, I have a more important pizzle for you to entice.'

'A handsome one, I trust?'

'Neither Katerina nor Peaches were to his taste, so I can only hope the knave has a liking for your kind, John.'

'When will you remember to call me Eleanor when I play the woman's part?'

'You're just an out-of-work mountebank. Don't get ideas above your estate. Now fetch Black-eyes back here in haste, before he brings the Lord Mayor's authority down on us all.'

'Oh, very well,' John sighed. 'Katerina, help me comb the straw out of my hair, will you? I must make myself beautiful for this new fellow. I only hope he's blessed with a bull's prick; I feel the need.'


Seb was enquiring of a huckster selling eggs from her straw-filled tray when he noticed a fine lady. Unattended? Admiring the wares at stalls along Bankside? What manner of lady would e'er risk her reputation in such a place? Yet Seb was intrigued. There was no question that she was beautiful; Seb's artist's eye had to admire the perfect curve of cheek and chin, the wild-rose tint of skin and the lustre of curls – worn loose under a veil of gossamer silk – the hue of Spanish chestnuts. He grinned to himself, imagining her as having won an hour of freedom from the confines of her father's house. Mayhap, her maid was playing her part, resting in her chamber 'neath the coverlet, pretending a headache. Could this be her last opportunity afore being wed to a husband who would assume her father's role as gaoler? In which case, her spirit was as much to be admired as her beauty.

The huckster, seeing her possible customer now had other matters upon his mind, went on her way, crying: 'Fresh eggs for sale! Newly laid!'

Whilst Seb was thus employed, day-dreaming, composing the lady's story to please himself, the lovely damsel had moved closer. Once, so he imagined, she had glanced at him, yet seemed not to see him. And why should she notice him, some fellow so ordinary? He watched, like one under an enchantment, as she swished her gown of emerald velvet, threw back her head and laughed at the antics of a street urchin who had been unmindful of her skirts. It was the laughter of tinkling bells, a joyous sound, indeed. Who could fail to be entranced by such as she?

The lady came closer, stopping beside a haberdasher's stall to admire some ribbons, running them through her fingers, laughing at the pleasure of so simple an act.

Seb, forcing his thoughts back to the matter in hand, turned to a matronly woman, basket-laden, asking if she might take a moment to look at his drawings. She obliged but, after some consideration, shook her head.

'No, I don't know these folks. I can't help you,' she said and went upon her way.

'May I see?'

Seb was surprised to find the lady before him.

'M-most certainly, m-my lady,' he said, instantly chiding himself that the proximity of such loveliness turned his tongue to that of a stuttering fool. 'Do you recognise this f-fellow or these young lads?' He held out the drawings to her.

For some reason, quite unaccountable, Gawain growled, a low, menacing rumble, deep in his belly.

Seb nudged the dog to silence with his foot.

'You may call me Eleanor,' she said, her voice melodious as birdsong to his ear. 'Now if you would hold them closer for me?'

Her gloved hand brushed his ink-stained fingers – the graceful and the workmanlike.

'You may have seen this man with the scars. 'Tis said he frequents this part of Southwark.' Seb did his best to keep his mind upon his task.

'He looks quite the rascal,' she laughed. 'I am certain I should remember him if I'd ever seen him. But this lad...' She paused, taking the likeness of Will Thatcher and studying it more nearly, putting her finger to her lips, thinking. 'He seems somewhat familiar and such a pretty lad.'

The little gesture distracted Seb and he watched as her hand ran lower, down her throat, white as a swan's, then down her shapely bodice. The drawings were forgotten, fluttering to the ground.

Gawain growled but his master didn't hear.

She took his hand in hers, guiding it lower, into a split betwixt the folds of emerald velvet, then forcing his fingers closed upon...

'God save us! Seb cried, jumping back, snatching his hand away. 'Y-you be no lady. You b-be a-a man.' He crossed himself repeatedly, as one who had there encountered Lucifer himself.

'If you wish, dear heart?' She – he – it laughed again. Gone were the tinkling bells. The voice was unmistakably male. 'I can be whatever you want. I can ride you like a horse, or you can fuck me like a stallion, whatever you desire?'

'L-leave me be, you... you unnatural creature.' Seb stepped away, tripped over Gawain, who yelped, and tumbled on his backside in the muddy street. Bankside echoed with merriment. It was a situation not to be borne.

The lady – so-called – enjoyed the hilarity more than any and no one else seemed shocked at the revelation of 'its' true nature.

'Your loss, dear heart. There's plenty who come willingly: priests, monks, lawyers, artisans and lords.' With a sweep of velvet, 'it' was gone, disappearing in the crowds.

Seb was shocked, left trembling. No hand was offered to assist him to his feet. He was simply an object of jest, humiliated and scorned. He clambered to his feet. His hip hurt, adding to his awkwardness.

'Come, Gawain. I be in need of a restorative,' he muttered, retrieving his mud-stained drawings and tucking them in his scrip. They were of little use now. His hose and breeches were not much better, advertising to all his misadventure.

Close at hand, he espied the sign of The Mermaid, swinging from its leather hinges, creaking softly in the April breeze. 'Twas the same 'house of entertainment' where Symkyn said he'd seen the man, somewhat like Jude but with the scarred face. It was worth the attempt.

So, now a customer greatly in need of refreshment and a bench on which to sit and rest his aching hip, Seb entered The Mermaid.

The place was quiet within and in gloom after the sunlight outside but it smelled as though someone had lately scented the rushes underfoot with dried lavender. Mayhap, this was done to disguise less pleasant odours but Seb did not care. The predominant aromas were of malted ale, fresh-baked bread and vegetable pottage and his belly informed him that the dinner hour was at hand. There would be time enough for a restorative cup and a heel of new bread afore he made his way back to St Mary's, to meet with Adam.

As his eyes adjusted to the lack of light, a woman came through a curtained doorway at the back, wafting further enticing smells into the room. Not that she had the appearance of one who ate good food. She was scrawny and unappealing as a fog on the river: grey from her grubby veil and wisps of hair to her well-worn shoes. Except, Seb noticed, for her eyes: flint-sharp.

She came towards him, gestured he should take a bench by the fire, then spent a moment observing him closely. Reckoning his worth as a customer, most likely, Seb thought.

'What's your pleasure, master?' she asked, after sufficient scrutiny.

Gawain retreated, tail down, behind Seb's boots and scrip, trying to cram his great self under the bench. But he was grown too big these days for such timid pup's behaviour.

'Bread and ale would be most welcome, mistress, if you

please? And water for my dog. He be in need as much as I, after the morn we have endured.'

As she returned to the kitchen, Bessie – for it was she – spoke to the only other customers, two men seated by the open window shutters. Seb could not hear what was said but the pair left their ale and departed.

'Right. He's here,' Bessie announced once she was behind the curtain. 'Black-eyes hisself, in person, come to us of his own accord. See he gets the best service. Colette, give him generous measures, a free cup to welcome a new customer. Oh, and water for his damned dog. Don't waste your time trying to entice him; we know he doesn't like women and it seems John had no better success, but we must keep him here 'til Cain gets back. Be friendly to him, Colette, speak of whatever interests him whilst I prepare a special helping of pottage.'

'For you, master.' A young lass set a brimming flagon and a cup on the board before putting a bowl of water among the rushes for Gawain. 'We serve the first cup for free to new customers, to welcome them. There will be no charge, so drink deep as you will.'

''Tis most generous. I have not heard of this custom north of the river but, in truth, I cannot drink so much ale alone. Would you care to share the flagon? I see none other here to demand your service at present.'

'Perhaps. Just half a cup or mistress will not be pleased.'

She fetched another cup, poured ale for them both and sat upon a stool, facing Seb across the board.

'You be from elsewhere,' Seb said, content at last to find a lass – or any other in Southwark – who was not attempting to lead him astray. 'France, mayhap? Your accent be not unlike that of merchants from those parts.'

She grimaced.

'I am not and never shall be French. They are filth, liars all.'

'Pardon my error. I meant no insult.'

'I am Bretonne.'

THE COLOUR OF SHADOWS

'Ah. From Brittany.'

'Of course.'

'Have you been in London long? Your command of English be excellent.' Seb sipped his ale. It was good and strong; he must not drink too much, nor too swiftly but it was an excellent restorative for ill-humours, as he had hoped.

'Long enough,' she answered cryptically. 'I am called Colette.'

'A pretty name.'

'It serves.' She shrugged the matter aside. 'But what of you? You are London born, I think?'

'Not quite but I have dwelt in the city for most of my life.'

At that moment, Colette was called to the kitchen. She returned with two bowls of steaming pottage, one with half a loaf of white bread balanced across the rim. This she placed before Seb; the other bowl she put upon the floor for Gawain.

'I did but order bread and ale, Colette, not pottage also.'

'As you see, we have few customers and good food should not go to waste. Mistress says it's for you and your dog.'

'That be a kindness, indeed. Is it not, Gawain? I had heard tell that The Mermaid be a place of entertainment?'

'Aye, of a sort.'

Seb took his bread and steeped it in the pottage. It was delicious, if a little peppery for his taste, but the portion was generous and he would not complain. Under the table, Gawain was devouring his helping with equal relish and far less grace.

'Do you have songsters, acrobats, fire-eaters and the like? Or mummers' plays?'

Together they discussed such matters. Colette did much of the talking whilst Seb ate until he could eat not another mouthful. 'That was a fine dinner.' Seb pushed his bowl aside, blew out a breath and patted his belt, now tight indeed. 'Was it not, Gawain?' He prodded his companion with the toe of his boot. The dog was asleep; not surprising after such a meal. 'My thanks, Mistress Colette, for a fine meal. I shall recommend The Mermaid to friends. Come, you idle dog, you cannot laze away the day. We must be at St Mary's to meet with Adam afore the Angelus. Get up, Gawain, I say.'

But Gawain didn't stir.

Seb stood up from his bench and bent down to pick up his scrip and rouse the dog. Of a sudden, the room began to sway; his head swam. Too much ale. And that was his last coherent thought as a dark cloud of nothingness engulfed him.

'What of the dog?' Colette asked.

'Reckon it's dead. You and Peaches chuck it on the midden heap behind the stables.'

'Huh. He's very weighty, the great fat lump,' Peaches complained as they dragged the dog through the curtained doorway.

Colette stumbled, going backwards through the kitchen to the outside door.

'That's far enough,' Peaches said, dropping Gawain's tail end before ever they reached the midden. 'I'm not lugging it any farther. Master Cain can shift it later. I'm blown.' She puffed out her cheeks and wiped her hands on her gown before the two returned indoors.

Bessie stood, hands on hips, then poked Seb, slumped half off the bench, and watched as he slowly toppled sideways to lie amidst the rushes.

'We'll get him down to the cellar. Cain can get rid of him after dark. The river will oblige us. Peaches, Colette, take his feet. Katerina, get a hold of his other arm,' Bessie instructed, seizing Seb's limp left arm by the elbow and wrist. 'Cherry-lips, go before us, light the way and open the door.'

'What shall we do with the bag of stuff?'

'Put those damned drawings on the fire and make certain they're nothing but ashes. Can't have anyone else seeing the wretched things. Then bring the bag. We don't want any sign that he was ever here.'

# The Church of St Mary Overy

The Angelus had rung some time since. Adam waited, pacing up and down outside its grand porch, but there was yet no sign of Seb. Having passed the morn in fruitless endeavour, discovering nobody who recognised – or would admit to recognising – either of the lads or the man in the drawings, he continued to wait, wasting yet more time. His patience was stretched as his anxiety increased. What was Seb doing? Perhaps it had been a mistake to split up. Yet he was a man, not a child. Did he need a guardian to hold his hand at every step? No. So where was the tardy fellow?

Adam began to push his way through the crowds along Bankside. The noise was such that there was little point in calling Seb's name. He would never hear above the hucksters' cries, the shouts of costermongers and haggling goodwives. But dogs have sharper ears, so Adam yelled out Gawain's name instead, every few yards, hoping the creature would come trotting towards him with Seb trailing behind.

His voice was becoming strained and worry gnawed at his vitals, like a rat at a grain sack, before a familiar, black furry head with drooping ears appeared through the forest of legs. But it was plain that Gawain was not his usual lively self. His coat was filthy, bits of onion skin and parsnip peelings clinging to his fur. His head and tail were down and he seemed unsteady on his paws. Adam thought, had Gawain been a man, he might well be accounted a drunkard.

'What's amiss with you, eh?' Adam crouched to make certain the animal was unhurt. There was no sign of any injury. 'Where's Seb? Lost your master, eh? Why is he not with you? Where's that foolish cousin of mine?' He fondled the dog's ears and Gawain responded with a half-hearted tail wag. 'Gawain, go find Seb!'

TONI MOUNT

The dog looked up at him with lack-lustre eyes, as if questioning the need.

'Aye, go on now. Find Seb,' Adam insisted.

Gawain turned back, along Bankside, walking as though he had aged a decade in the last few hours. All Adam's chivvying could not make the creature hasten in the least. He feared the dog was sickening but Seb's absence was a far greater concern.

## The Mermaid

Seb opened an eye. It was an effort, indeed. A drum pounded in his head. Ale. However much had he consumed? Where was he?

The most foetid stink made him gag. Reaching out, he felt cold, packed earth beneath him, a few straws. Forcing his unwilling eyes to open made little difference. Wherever he was, it was dark. Panic threatened as he recalled an earlier time of horror, when he had been lost in the Stygian blackness of the tunnels snaking 'neath the Tower of London's forbidding fortress. That had been terrible, indeed. He shuddered at the memory.

But, as his eyes became accustomed, he realised there was light, casting a faint, striped shadow on the floor which flickered, coming and going, although the stripes remained the same.

Seb pushed himself up into a sitting position but even that made his head spin. Refusing to give in and lie down again, he shut his eyes and waited until the feeling passed. Probing with careful fingers, he discovered painful bruises all along the back of his skull and wondered how he had come by them. Behind his right ear and above the nape of his neck, he felt the stickiness of blood. Did someone set about him with a cudgel? If they did, he had no memory of it.

192

'Gawain?' he whispered into the darkness. 'Be you here, lad? I cannot see you?' No answer came and Seb sensed he was alone. But all was not silence. At length, as the clammouring in his head became less, he realised he could hear footsteps, going to and fro, above him. Also, the narrow band of light cast upon the floor carried sounds: muffled voices, a neighing horse, the trundling of wheels. The light and noises came through a barred opening at the top of one wall. The passage of folk going by outside was the cause of the flickering shadows. The gap was as wide as the length of a man's forearm but rather less than that in height. Short iron bars were affixed into a stout oak lintel above and went into the earth of the street at the bottom. He must be in a cellar.

Listening hard, he could make out a huckster's call: 'Fresh eggs for sale! Newly laid!' Had he not spoken to that egg-seller, earlier? In which case, he must yet be in Bankside, mayhap, still at the sign of The Mermaid. Shakily, he got onto his knees. From there, it took several groggy attempts to get to his feet but, at last, he was upright, if inclined to dizziness. The beams above him allowed but the space of a few inches above his head.

Used to the gloom by now, he could make out four uneven walls, a small but stout wooden door off-set to one side. Opposite the door lay a heap of filthy sacking and soiled straw – a bed, mayhap? In the far corner was a bucket, more than half full of reeking human ordure; testament to another occupant of this nasty, little cell and not so long ago, either. No wonder it made him retch.

He tried the door. It was barred on the other side. He hammered on it with his fists and shouted. Kicked at it and yelled. Unsurprisingly, no one came. He was a prisoner.

He stirred the pile of bedding with his foot. Dark stains on the sacking, rust-coloured at the edges, looked suspiciously like old blood. They did not bear thinking upon too deeply. The bar of light was shifting as the sun beyond the window moved westerly. It illuminated the bedding and glinted off something shiny.

Seb stooped over to look closer. The giddiness came again and he thought better of it. Crouching instead, he pulled from the foul straw a set of rosary beads. Their bright coral beauty seemed so out of keeping with the grim cellar. At the end of the beads hung a pendant crucifix of bone or ivory, misshapen and somewhat damaged but recognisable all the same. And he knew to whom it belonged for, certainly, 'twas unlikely there could be another quite like it.

Young Will Thatcher.

Seb's heart leapt. Could Will have been brought here?

As if to confirm his deduction, low upon the wall beside the bedding was scratched a line of letters: Wm. THATC. Will had begun to carve his name into the crumbling stone. But that was not all. Below Will's name, closer to the floor... Seb knelt. The lettering was faint and the shaft of pale sunlight did not reach so low, but tracing it with his finger, he made out ED, then a space, then a P or, mayhap, an R. He wondered who Edward P or Edmund R might have been and then he saw something else: a few strands of pure white hair clung to the sacking.

With naught else to occupy his mind, Seb sat on the floor, to think through and consider the meanings of what he had found; the story they told.

# Chapter 11

## Saturday afternoon
## Southwark

ADAM FOLLOWED Gawain along Bankside. The crowd was thinning now, Saturday being but a half-day for most traders. Stall-holders were stowing their wares, those that would keep until next week. Only those selling fresh foodstuffs remained but, what with housewives buying up so much for tomorrow's Easter feast, they had little left to sell and would be gone soon enough.

Gawain stopped outside a tavern.

'Are you telling me Seb's in there, drinking himself stupid?' Adam said. 'I'll have words to say on this if he is. Leading me a fine dance, worrying for his safety. 'Tis not like him.'

But Gawain passed by the doorway and began digging with his paws.

'What have you found, lad?' Adam knelt in the mud of the street to see what had caught the dog's interest. There was a gap in the wall of the building at ground level. Five vertical iron bars blocked it. 'Seb? Seb? Are you down there? Answer me.'

'Adam?' A familiar voice, muffled, called back. 'Can you get me out of here?'

'We'll try.'

Seb moved to the window and recognised the wet black nose that poked through the bars.

'Gawain! You found me.' Seb watched as the dog began to dig at the ground around the bars. 'Adam, can you loosen the bars? Mayhap, I can then climb out.'

''Tis a small gap, Seb. How skinny are you? You'll never get through there. How did you get down there?'

''Tis a long story. This bar be rusted. I may be able to loosen it from this side.' Seb looked to his belt and realised his dinner knife had been taken from him. He found his scrip and brought it closer to the light, rummaging within. He discovered his penknife and a palette knife, used for mixing pigments. The latter was more sturdy. 'Dig, Gawain. Good lad,' Seb encouraged, adding his own efforts from inside the cellar.

Adam began working on another bar from outside. It was strange, indeed, that nobody stopped to ask what he and the dog were doing but Adam did not see the expressions on the faces of passers-by. Whatever went on at The Mermaid was none of their business.

The earth was soft after days of rain and the iron bars were nigh rotted through with rust. It did not take long before four bars were broken off but the fifth, towards one end, was far more stubborn.

'Never mind that, Adam,' Seb said. 'Here, take these.' He handed the coral rosary through the gap, then stuffed a bundle of stinking sacking into Adam's waiting hands, followed by his scrip. 'I be certain the rosary belongs to Will Thatcher. He was here but no longer. If he slept on that sacking, it will have his scent upon it. Let Gawain put his nose to it. Mayhap, he can find a trail to follow. Go, find the lad. I shall continue to work at this final bar.'

'Oh, no, Seb. We split up this morning and see what trouble you landed in. If we're to find the lad, we'll do it together. Take off your belt, your boots, your jerkin, as much as you can. Let's see if we can pull you through the gap as it is. So long as your head comes through and your shoulders...'

Seb did as Adam instructed, handing out items of clothing,

one after another.

'Where's your cloak? You'll need that. 'Tis getting cooler as the sun slides lower.'

'I don't have it. I suppose someone here thinks they have more use for it than I.'

Standing upon his toe-tips, Seb could get his arms out up to the elbows.

'Is there anything you can stand on?' Adam asked.

'Nay, I fear not. Oh, there be one thing.' Reluctantly, Seb went over to the reeking slop bucket. He braced his senses, held his breath and upended the foul mess in the corner.

Outside, Adam heard the sounds of coughing and retching.

'Dear God in Heaven, what's that terrible stink?' Foul miasmas wafted out through the gap.

Seb returned to the window, his face pallid.

'I shall stand on the upturned slop bucket,' he managed to say before gagging and gasping again. 'A moment…'

After a few minutes, he was back. The bucket raised him high enough that his head was at the gap in the wall. It took three attempts but his head, capless, came through. Mud matted his hair and smeared his face but merely added to the black of the bruises there already. He got his right hand free and wiped the mud from his eyes. Now, his feet were no longer able to touch the bucket. He could only push with his toes scrabbling for purchase against the stones and one elbow on the ledge of the gap. Adam took a firm grasp of his right arm and pulled. It was quickly apparent that Seb's shoulders were too wide to pass through.

'Hunch your right shoulder and drop the left,' Adam said. 'We'll get them through one at a time.'

There came a nasty point when Seb seemed wedged tight, unable to go forward or back. His head and arm were free but the rest of him was stuck fast.

'Let go of my arm,' Seb said. 'I think I be caught up somehow.' With a great deal of grunting, he was able to retreat inside the cellar. He moved the bucket closer to the fifth, last and most stubborn of the iron bars. With a brute strength he had not known he possessed, he succeeded in bending it a little. It yet refused to come loose but he had given himself an extra inch or two of space.

They repeated the process. This time, first one shoulder, then the other was squeezed out of the gap. Seb's narrow hips slid through without difficulty. He was free at last.

Having breathed deeply of the fresh air, Seb dressed swiftly and pulled on his boots, leaving them and his jerkin unfastened. They hurried away, no matter where, so long as it was somewhere other than The Mermaid tavern.

A little farther along Bankside, Adam paused and crouched down beside Gawain. The creature seemed well enough now.

'Whatever happened to you, Seb? How did you end up in that vile place? Did they drag you there?'

'I hate to admit it but I went in of my own free will. What a mistake that was, Adam, but how was I to know what would come to pass? Symkyn said The Mermaid was a place of entertainment. I ne'er suspected it could be the very Devil's den of horrors. Both Gawain and I were given a strong sleeping draught, I suspect,' Seb explained whilst lacing up his jerkin. 'It was put into our pottage. Little wonder they gave us the food for free. Poor Gawain succumbed first. I thought he had dozed off after a large dinner but then I too became affected; awoke to find myself in that noisome hole.'

'Gawain seems well recovered now. He was swaying like a drunkard when first I saw him. But what of you?'

'Aww, a few more bruises to add my tally – as if I needed them. I have some bumps at the back of my head that I know not how I came by. Those aside, I do well enough. I understand why Gawain was as a fellow in his cups. I felt likewise but the feeling be past now.' Seb fastened his second boot and buckled on his belt. The little leather sheath for his knife hung empty – as was his purse, so he discovered – but at least he still had his scrip. 'The drawings be gone,' he said. 'I believe they were the reason for our troubles at The Mermaid. Someone to whom I had shown them must have informed that cold-eyed proprietress.'

'We yet have the copies you gave me. Put them in your scrip in case we need them later.'

'Young Will Thatcher was in that hateful hole at some time. I not only found the rosary that I be nigh certain belongs to him but he had commenced the carving of his name upon the wall. I pray you, Adam, waste no more time. Give the sacking to Gawain that he may take Will's scent.'

'How do we know whose scent he may find upon it? Dozens could have touched this disgusting piece.'

'Aye, that may well be so,' Seb sighed, 'We can but pray that the lad's scent, being recent, is the strongest. 'Tis the only chance we have of finding him, unless you can think of another?'

Adam held the sacking to the dog's nose.

'Go, find,' he said. 'And let it be that you follow the right smell.'

Seb stuffed the sacking into his scrip, watching as Gawain searched the muddy street, nose down, questing for the trail.

''Tis too muddy. The street has been churned up by so many feet. He's not going to find anything.' Adam had little hope of success. Twice, Gawain appeared to discover something but then lost it, coming back to them again.

Seb took out the sacking once more to let the dog have another sniff. He wrapped the rough cloth around Gawain's nose, covering his eyes and ears also, so that there was naught to distract him from the scent.

'I know you can do it, Gawain,' he said, removing the cloth. 'Now go. Find Will Thatcher.'

After another false beginning and a deal of sniffing around, Gawain finally moved on, tail up, nose down, heading farther west, along Bankside.

'You think he's found it?' Adam asked. 'Let us hope he's not following the scent of a housewife's basketful of sausage and ham.'

'Have faith, Adam. Gawain will do his best. And if we find naught, at least we shall have tried. We shall be no worse off than afore.'

Adam remained unconvinced.

Gawain picked up the pace, once they were beyond Bankside. The trail was clearer as the way became less used. In truth, apart from a line of ramshackle fisherfolks' hovels, there was little of note. Barefoot wives and children sat outside their homes, mending nets. Eastertide might bring joy to others, but folk here looked forlorn. Ragged and thin, their poverty hung like a shroud around the cluster of dwellings.

'What is this God-forsaken place?' Adam asked.

'I do not know that it has a name,' Seb replied. ''Tis spoken of as Lambeth Moor but I think that refers to all this area of mud and marshland.' He gestured with a broad sweep of his arm. 'There be tales of quicksand that has swallowed horses and riders whole, of marsh spirits glowing with a blue light at night – an unwholesome, evil place. Mind, there is also a story of a hermit who once dwelt out there, somewhere, so holy that even the marsh lights aided him, guiding him safely across the treacherous bog in the dark. I know not if that be true or just a fisherfolks' tale.'

'Well, we may be about to find out.' Adam pointed to the dog, which had left the most obvious track and was trotting towards a clump of straggling brambles. 'Watch your step, Seb.'

They had been walking for nigh an hour, since leaving The Mermaid, although it seemed longer to Seb whose aches and bruises were growing more troublesome as the air chilled and he without a cloak. The sun was low now, not long until dusk. Across the marsh, the royal palace at Westminster should have been visible on the other side of the river but a white veil hid its turrets and the tower of St Stephen's Chapel. The mist was rising. Seb shivered.

Fortunately, Gawain had followed some path, invisible to the unaccustomed eye, that skirted the edge of the marsh and they came back to the original trackway just as it reached an imposing gateway, brick-built in the newest fashion.

'Very grand. Who lives here, then? The King of Barbary? Or Prester John, himself, maybe?' Adam gazed up at the portal, topped with a gilded coat-of-arms.

''Tis the Archbishop of Canterbury's Palace, I believe. We must have walked all the way to Lambeth. But why would Will be here? Still, if he is within, at least he should be safe.'

'I don't think he's here, Seb. See? Gawain is still upon his quest.'

But the dog didn't go much farther. He stopped before the door to an inn. The place had seen better days. In the fading light of dusk, it was barely possible to make out the name inscribed in flaking paint upon the board: The Three Feathers Inn.

They were about to enter, already savouring the possibility of a warm fire, food and drink and, if Fate was smiling, the end of their long search – if the lad was here. But Gawain was sniffing beyond the door, beneath a window in the upper storey. Then he was off again, making directly for the marsh. Their quest was not yet done.

# Lambeth Marshes

Gawain was following a path of woven withies that had, perhaps, once been the foundation of a causeway. It was a wonder the willow branches had survived when the planks that used to provide a firm walkway upon them had long since rotted away. They built well in olden times, Seb thought as they made their way with care, Gawain trotting ahead fearlessly.

'We can't take over long, Seb,' Adam said, pointing towards the glassy grey waters of the Thames. 'That boat out there is turning with the tide and it looks to me as though the water may cover this causeway at high tide. Besides, the lad cannot be out here, else he would have drowned, long since.'

It was at that point, just where seaweeds and barnacles displaced the samphire and marsh plants, Gawain stopped. The scent he has pursued thus far was no more. The animal turned around, circling, then gave up his quest and sat, looking to his master for guidance.

'Now what's to be done?' Adam asked. 'The scent has disappeared, washed away by the last high tide, no doubt. I think we should go back to that inn. We can't find the lad in the dark anyway.'

But Seb had keener sight, even in the mist at twilight.

'Out there,' he said, pointing. 'Do you see it? A building of some kind. Mayhap, 'tis the hermitage I told you of.'

'And, mayhap, 'tis your imagination, or the mist playing tricks upon your eyes. There's naught out there but the river.'

'This causeway must have served a purpose once. It must have some destination. The lad has to be hiding somewhere and why not there?' At that moment, Seb slipped and would have fallen if Adam had not grabbed him.

'Have a care, cousin. These withies are treacherous indeed. See how the mud squelches up betwixt them as they take our weight. I hardly dare trust them.'

'Come now. They have lain here for centuries. I be certain they may last one more day, at least. Do you not see it now?' Again, Seb pointed. ''Tis but a hovel yet seems to be raised upon a little island above the mud.'

'Aye, I see something, long abandoned, ruinous.'

'But Will could be there.'

'Perhaps, but I don't like this rotting wood underfoot. 'Tis well enough for you and the dog but I am the heavier by a goodly few pounds. I like this not, Seb.'

'Come. Be of good heart. The hermitage lies close at hand now. 'Tis but a little way farther.'

Malodorous airs wafted up from beneath their feet as their tread disturbed the tidal mud below.

'The farther out we go, the farther we have to walk back and I doubt the lad would have come to this stinking place. No wonder the hermit left. It smells worse than any midden.'

Of a sudden, a grey heron that had stood, still as stone and unnoticed, took to the air with a flap of its great wings, startling the men more than they had affrighted the bird at its fishing post.

Adam flinched and ducked instinctively as it seemed to fly so close as to catch his hair with its trailing feet. He took a step back, his boot scraping the edge of the causeway. The ancient withies gave way. He lost his footing and slipped sideways. Arms waving like a windmill, he struggled to balance but his other boot found no purchase and he fell into the marsh.

Seb threw himself towards Adam, grabbing his cloak. But the fastening tore through the cloth and Seb was left, holding the garment but not the man. He sprawled on his belly and looked down.

Adam was a yard away, over his belt in ooze, spitting and spluttering.

'Get me out. I'm sinking!' he yelled before a paroxysm of coughing robbed him of his voice.

Seb stretched as far forward as he dared and caught hold of Adam's arm. The dog barked frantically, as if that helped.

'Pull! For pity's sake, Seb. Pull.'

Seb obeyed but to no effect. Rather, Adam sank lower, dragging Seb with him. Seb managed to get both arms around Adam's chest and laced his fingers so his hold was sure. He pulled and wriggled but to no avail. His own position became more precarious and Adam remained clasped just as surely by the mud.

'I'll not let you go, Adam.' Seb tried to sound reassuring but, at every breath, the stench was nauseating. 'Lean back, into my arms, then try walking your feet through the mud. Try to bring your legs to the surface, so you lie less deeply.'

Adam struggled to do as Seb instructed but the sheer weight of mud around him made movement impossible. The marsh was claiming him, inch by inch, and would smother the life out of him soon enough.

From his position, Seb could see farther than Adam and realised another danger: the tide was flowing. The river waters were snaking across the mudflats, making islands of every clump of marsh plants and protrusion of rotting timber before covering them. Only the few leafless, spindly trees around the hermit's hovel remained dry.

'Try again, Adam,' Seb said, refusing to give in to panic. 'Push, if you can.' A deal of straining and gasping made no difference. They paused to catch their wind. Another mighty effort and another achieved naught. 'Try walking through the mud once more. Mayhap, you will loosen its grip.'

Adam only sank lower, the mud now covering his chest and Seb's arms.

'I can't move. I'm done for, Seb. I can see the tide coming in... Pray with me...'

'No breath to spare for prayers. Come on. Push! Kick out.' Seb pulled and grunted, straining every sinew. His arms were nigh wrenched from their sockets and his muscles screamed. His jaws ached as his teeth clenched tight. Using elbows, knees and the toes of his boots, Seb retreated an inch or two from the edge of the causeway but the water was just a few feet away and rising fast. The mud was now over his fingers and he could feel his grip around Adam might fail any moment.

As the brackish river water reached Adam, swirling over his shoulders and around his neck, Seb screamed:

'Kick, damn you,'

Adam writhed, putting every last ounce of strength into moving his legs. He felt the colder water of the river flowing into the loosened mud. He thought Seb was making way in pulling him out but his cousin's grip was slipping.

'Pull harder. Harder,' Adam urged. And with a vile slurping, sucking noise, like a hideous serpent regurgitating its prey, the marsh spat Adam from its maw.

Both men fell back, sprawled across the disappearing causeway, lying in the deepening waters. At first, neither could move. Only Gawain ran up and down, barking. Utterly exhausted, their breath laboured, Seb was the first to roll onto his belly and struggle to his knees.

'Quiet, Gawain. Cease your noise. Get up, Adam, else we both shall drown. I did not save you for naught. Get on your feet.'

Adam obeyed. Seb handed him his cloak, now sodden by the rising tide, but it alone did not reek of the foul mud.

'I lost a boot,' Adam said, looking down.

'But not your life. I shall buy you a new pair. Come. The hermitage stands above the tide; 'tis closer. We cannot get back to the road until the tide ebbs. Hasten, Adam. We be yet in peril. I do not want to be swept away.'

They waded through the icy water towards the hovel, standing on its little island, isolated in a sea of grey now surging in over the marsh mud. In places, Gawain had to swim to follow his master.

The door hung askew on what remained of its hinges. Inside, the wattle walls were green with slime and the daub that once covered the wattle to keep out the weather had crumbled away long since. At one end of the single room was a large puddle but an area of packed-earth floor survived at the other, a heap of debris in one corner. Seb dipped his finger in the puddle and tasted it. He nodded.

'Rainwater, not salt. We should be safe here,' he said,

suppressing a shiver. He wished he had his cloak. No doubt, by now, that wretched woman at The Mermaid had the benefit of its thick woollen weave, aye, and his money.

Gawain slaked his thirst, lapping at the puddle.

Adam lay on the floor, staring up at the overcast sky through the holes in the reed thatch. He began to laugh.

Seb could not help but join in, though he knew not any cause for merriment. The pair laughed until their ribs hurt.

'You saved my life, Seb,' Adam said at last, having run out of strength to laugh anymore.

Seb sat on the dirt floor, making marks in the damp dust, drawing vague circles with his finger.

'I could not let you die, cousin. Where would you have gone? Neither Heaven nor Hell nor yet Purgatory would let you in, you stink so abominably.'

Adam grinned at Seb's effort to make a jest.

'I doubt you smell any better; you're plastered in that tainted swill as much as I am. And I'm perishing of cold here.' Adam pulled his wet cloak tight around him and rubbed at his upper arms. 'Is there anything in this miserable hole dry enough to make a fire? I need to get warm somehow.'

'Probably not, unless you find something in the rubbish over there.' Seb turned on his side and curled up into a shivering ball, hugging himself in the filthy sacking from the cellar. It was better than naught and he'd grown accustomed to its stink.

Gawain was barking again, running to the heap of detritus and back again.

'Stop that, you silly creature. Come here and give me some of your warmth.'

Gawain obeyed but was too restless to remain at Seb's side. He preferred to lie beside the mound of rubbish.

'Now, Seb,' Adam insisted, hauling his cousin to his feet, 'Let's dance, sing, clap our hands, come on. We must keep warm, dry our clothes. Dance, I say.'

'Do not be foolish. You know full well I cannot dance. And

I be far too weary.'

'Nay, you'll do as I say. I did as you instructed out in the marsh. You told me to kick and it let the water loosen the mud. How did you know to do that?'

'I did not know but could think of no other way. It was Almighty God's doing.'

'Aye, well now Almighty God is telling me to make you dance; elsewise, you'll die of the chill. Come, Seb, point your toe and away we go. Come on, faster. Heel and toe. Take my hand and circle left... now to the right... pick your feet up. That's better. Remember how we used to prance like idiots in the tavern at Foxley.'

With Adam's unceasing encouragement, they leapt around, skipping and cavorting like a pair of moon-struck madmen destined for Bedlam Hospital. Seb was now sweating, adding another stink to the miasmas arising from his tired body and filthy attire but at least he felt warm.

As they sank to the floor, panting, Adam picked caked mud off his sleeve.

'See? We're drying out already. How long before the tide turns, do you reckon?'

'Hours. More than six hours betwixt high and low tide, if I recall aright. Boatmen live and work accordingly, so they say. It will be beyond midnight afore the tide uncovers the causeway once more. And finding our way back across without a light would be perilous indeed.'

'Seb, you sound like ol' Job. We'll simply wait until moonrise, when we can see our way.'

'If the clouds oblige us and clear the skies. And if not, by dawn the tide will be rising again. We shall have to wait another half day at least.'

'That's too bad. I'll die of hunger ere then. I'm famished now,' Adam complained. 'And naught to drink either.'

'Now who be sounding like Job? There are a few small stones strewn around the floor here. If we may find ten, I shall give you a game of knucklebones; distract your thoughts from your rumbling belly.'

'I don't know, Seb: it's rumbling pretty loud...'

But any noise Adam's stomach might be making was masked by Gawain, barking at the rubbish heap.

'What's amiss with him?' Adam asked.

'Rats, most like. Let be, Gawain. Leave the rats in peace. We do not want them scampering about us. Let be, I say.' Since the dog took no notice, Seb bestirred himself to see what so attracted him.

The heap was not as chaotic as first appeared. It seemed to have been fashioned into a little cave, a hiding place, the entrance blocked by the remains of an old barrel. Seb pulled the barrel aside. Something stirred within, setting Gawain barking again.

'Fetch it out, if you will, whatever it be?' Seb told the dog.

Gawain was willing but his quarry was not, shouting and squealing. Nevertheless, Gawain dragged forth a grubby little arm, clad in threadbare velvet.

'Let me go, you great devil. Let go of me.' Dirty fists hit out at the dog but Gawain was determined upon his quest as any knight errant ever was. A lad crawled out of his hiding place. 'Don't take me back there. Don't beat me. I want to go home.' The child dissolved into tears.

'Will? Will Thatcher? Seb queried. 'Be that you 'neath all that filth?'

'Don't beat me, please...' the lad sobbed.

'No one is going to beat you, Will. 'Tis me: Seb Foxley. You know me, do you not? And Adam and Gawain?'

The child scrubbed away his tears with the back of his hand and stared at Seb, bewilderment writ plain upon his features.

'Master Foxley?'

'Aye, Will. I know we must appear like a pair of vagabonds but we have been searching London for you, then Southwark and, finally, here at Lambeth. Half the city has been looking for you.'

The lad began weeping in earnest.

Seb gathered him into his arms, stroking his tangled curls.

'You be safe now, Will. We've got you. Hush, hush, still your tears.'

'Can I go home now?' the child sobbed into Seb's damp jerkin.

'Aye. As soon as may be. When the tide ebbs, we shall take you home to your Mam. Be afeared no longer.'

'I thought that mad lord had sent men and dogs after me. Or Cain. Or that horrible ol' sow Bessie. I hate her. That's why I hid, 'cos I thought you'd come to take me back to his lordship, or to that place where they locked me up. I didn't know it was you, master.'

'Your Mam asked us to find you. I be sorry it took us so long. Did they hurt you, Will?'

The lad shook his head.

'No, not really. Bessie told Cain to beat me but he never did. But he threw away my grandmother's rosary and took my school books to sell. Mam will be angry with me when she finds out, then I likely will get a beating for losing them but I won't mind that.'

'Your mother will be too glad of your return to beat you for a few lost books. As for the rosary – be it of coral beads and ivory?'

'Aye, it is.' Will's young face lit up like a candle flame. 'Did you find it?'

'I believe we did. Adam?'

Adam unfastened his purse and went to draw out the contents.

'Oh, ugh. It's full of stinking marsh mud but at least I didn't lose it in the bog.' Adam tipped everything onto the floor in a little heap of black slime. Pennies and groats were unrecognisable but he lifted a length of small round objects and its pendant lump, taking it to the puddle of rainwater. He washed it with care, rinsing off the mud.

Will pushed away from Seb's consoling embrace and went to watch as Adam's efforts uncovered the coral beads and crucifix of ivory with its corner chewed away by teething babes.

'That's it! That's the very one.' The lad pranced about with delight, holding the washed beads to his cheek. 'But what was all that noise and goings-on just now?'

'Er, aye, we were, er, dancing; were we not, Adam?' Seb sounded embarrassed and stared at the floor. 'To warm ourselves after a soaking.'

'And why's Master Adam only got one boot?'

'I fear your secret be uncovered, cousin.'

'Oh, very well, I admit it: I fell into the marsh.' Adam flushed red beneath the smears of dried mud on his face. 'My boot was sucked off; gone forever.'

'Well, I knew you had from the stink.' Will's eyes began to twinkle with mischief, now he knew he was safe at last and would soon be home.

# Chapter 12

## Saturday night – Easter Sunday,
## the eleventh day of April
## Lambeth Marshes

AS THE tide began to ebb, in the small hours of the night, it seemed the retreating waters dragged the mist away with them. The skies cleared and the milk-hued moon rode high with her attendant spangle of stars. The air was chill and the three possessed but one damp cloak betwixt them.

Young Will, though, was unconcerned. His youth and the excitement of returning home warmed him like a brazier from within.

Adam constantly moaned about having to tread the uneven withies with his left foot, bootless.

Seb said naught.

'What day is it?' Will asked, skipping along in the moonlight. Haste was the best armour against the cold.

'It must be Easter Day by now,' Adam said, gauging the hour from the turn of the constellations in the sky.

'Easter? I didn't know that was come already. I lost count of the days. I couldn't ask Lord Pierpoint; he wouldn't have known what month it was.'

'Lord Pierpoint? Who's he?' Adam asked.

'He bought me. Paid Cain and Bessie two marks for me, or rather Walter did.'

'He bought you? You were sold like a sack of turnips? Dear God, what is this world coming to, when children can be traded like merchandise?' Adam's disgust was so overwhelming that he forgot his bare foot, sore and cold. Such things would never happen back home, in decent, civilised Norfolk. 'What say you, Seb? We must speak with the authorities; prevent such fearful occurrences.'

'Aye.' Seb was too weary for more words. Mayhap, he was suffering some belated effects of the sleeping draught, though Gawain was well enough recovered. Every step was an effort like unto scaling St Paul's spire. He no longer had strength even to shiver. But at least he was too numb to feel his bruises and aching bones any longer. Only by the power of his will did he continue to put one foot before the other, following Gawain back along the causeway.

'Watch your step here,' Adam warned, turning back to look at Seb. 'I think this is the place where I fell in. If you see a lost boot...'

'You're about to lose more than a boot, you meddling bastards.'

'Let go of me!' Will screamed.

Before them, stood a man. He held Will by the arm in one hand and hefted a great cudgel in the other.

Adam recovered his wits first.

'Let the lad go!' He leaped forward but was undecided as to whether to pull the child free or grab the hand that wielded the cudgel. His momentary confusion meant he succeeded in neither but caught a blow to his shoulder, sending him sprawling. He managed to get a hold of the withies to keep from sliding into the mud a second time.

The brief distraction allowed Gawain to bite the man's ankle but he was kicked aside.

Will did likewise, burying his teeth in the man's thumb.

All was chaos on the slippery causeway: two men, a child and a dog, hitting out, biting and squirming.

Seb was slow to realise what was happening. Shouts and confusion were all he could make out. Then the tall figure of a man turned in the moonlight. Seb recognised him from Symkyn's description and the drawing he had made: the scars. It was Cain. Shedding his lethargy like an outworn garment, Seb threw himself into the fray. He, grabbed Cain's cloak and, skidding sideways, managed to wrap it around the man's outstretched arm, rendering the cudgel of little use.

Cain struggled to free his arm, trying to unwind himself from the folds of cloth. He had to release Will to do so.

'Run, Will!' Seb cried but did not see if the lad obeyed.

Gawain jumped at the man, sending him staggering.

Seb added his weight and the man tottered backward. The withies creaked and gave way. Seb tried to grab the man as he fell but history repeated itself: he was left holding naught but the cloak.

Cain fell into the sucking mud but, unlike Adam, for him there would be no reprieve since he went face first. The mud closed over his head and Cain was gone.

Adam stood, rubbing his shoulder.

Will and the dog were attempting to aid Seb to his feet.

'At least you now have a cloak to warm you... and it's dry,' Adam said, helping Seb to stand, though he swayed like an aspen in a gale and had to be held steady. 'I don't suppose you managed to save his boots for me, did you? Nay. Too much to hope for.'

Slowly, they made their way out of the marsh. Adam was of a mind to rouse the folk at The Three Feathers Inn but a great deal of banging upon the door and shouting of insults at the windows had no effect at such an hour. Besides, Will made clear that he would not enter that place again. They must forgo any chance of respite and a restorative there.

They trudged back along the way, towards the dwellings of the fisherfolk. Adam hoped they would have pity on them, forwhy he was taking all Seb's weight now, dragging him along.

His cousin might be skinny indeed but Adam was in no fit condition himself to carry him much further.

Fortunately, the fisherfolk were early risers. Dawn was yet no more than a fading of stars, low in the eastern sky, but the fishermen were from their beds, preparing for the day.

Adam was doubtful, of a sudden, whether they would help, it being Easter Day and labour of any kind forbidden. He need not have feared. The fisherfolk were of rough speech but when he explained that they had rescued the child from the marsh – having neither the strength nor the time to tell the story in full – the wives supplied ale and blankets and two men agreed to row them across the river, downstream with the outgoing tide, as far as St Paul's wharf.

It was as well that Seb slept throughout the river crossing, else he would have objected at every turn. The fishermen had to help them out of the boat, onto the landing stage.

'Seb! Seb! Come now. Wake up. We have to walk home.'

Seb blinked, leaning on Adam, but pulled himself upright on a wooden mooring post.

'Forgive me. I must have fallen asleep. Where are we?'

'Oh, aye, indeed you did. I'll tell you everything later. For now, we have to walk up Paul's Wharf Hill. Can you do that?'

'Then I can go home,' Will said, a grin so wide adorning his grubby face. Then the grin faded. 'You will come with me, masters, won't you? I'll never be able to explain to Mam where I've been. She'll never believe me.'

'Of course we shall,' Adam said, 'But before that, you must come home with us and wash your face, else your Mam will think some strange urchin has come to her doorstep, claiming to be her son. You don't want to affright her, do you?'

# The Foxley House

Home at last. And such a fuss was made of them all. Where had they been all night? Everyone was frantic with worry but relief was come.

Rose, Kate and Nessie hastened to and fro, heating water, warming towels and finding clean linen. Jack filled the bathtub. The laws against working on the Lord's Day had, of necessity, to be set aside.

By the time the sky was blue overhead and Emily had heaved her cumbersome body down the stairs, her errant husband, Adam and Will – now clad in Jack's cast-offs of two years before – and even Gawain were clean and presentable. Also against custom, though it was the one day in the year when all should partake of the Eucharist, sharing the Body of Christ, they had swallowed a few morsels of bread. Rose had insisted, seeing they were all faint with hunger.

Emily was angered at their thoughtlessness. Why had they not sent word? But what was the point? Her husband would never mend his ways. Their saving grace was that they'd found Will Thatcher. Once he was returned home, Beattie would have no more excuses for falling behind with her silkwork, as had been the case this last week past.

Now wearing a pair of boots – his Sunday best pair, appropriately, although they were now the only ones he had – Adam took Will home to his mother in Cheapside, by the Cross. Seb was asleep at the kitchen table and it seemed a pity to wake him, so they left him there. Young Will, though, couldn't wait to get home, which was understandable. So it was Adam who knocked at the Thatchers' door.

'No need to knock; I live here.' Will shoved the door wide

and bounded over the threshold. 'Mam!' he yelled. 'Mam! I'm back.'

Beatrice came through from her kitchen and stopped. Her mouth fell open with wonder at the miraculous sight of her missing son.

Will ran into her arms and the pair were soon hugging and weeping for joy.

Harry Thatcher bestirred himself, still fastening the laces of his doublet.

'Well, I ne'er expected this,' he muttered. 'Where did you find the young rascal, Master Armitage?'

''Tis too long a tale to tell in full at present,' Adam said, 'Else we'll all be late for church. 'Tis enough to know that there's naught amiss with him that his mother's arms and a good dinner won't mend. I'm sure Will can tell you himself, better than I, what befell him but Bailiff Turner will have some questions for him later, once we make our report to him. May I wish you all a joyous Eastertide. Oh, and Seb asked me to give you this.' He took the coral rosary from his purse and gave it to the lad's mother.

'What a miracle is this...' she said, clutching the beads to one ample breast whilst embracing her son against the other.

Adam was about to leave but Harry Thatcher seized his hand and Beatrice set her son aside for a moment to weep on his chest, unable to put her relief and gratitude into coherent words of any kind.

'Don't know how we'll repay you and Master Seb,' Harry grunted.

'We ask for nothing. Seeing Will home is thanks enough.'

# St Michael le Querne Church

St Michael's was crowded for Low Mass, the first office of the day. The little church soon became warm and stuffy and Seb kept dozing off, leaning against the ornate font cover.

'You're snoring.' Emily prodded him in the ribs with a sharp finger. 'Can you not show more respect to the Risen Saviour? You're a disgrace.' She was seated on a stool, a concession permitted for those unable to stand for the duration of the service.

Seb jerked awake but the snoring continued. The culprit was Gawain, lying at Seb's feet. The sleeping draught yet afflicted them both to some degree and a night out upon the marsh had not helped. Even Adam was yawning and he had not eaten the drugged pottage.

Jack wasn't paying much attention to Father Thomas's sonorous droning either. He too hadn't passed a peaceful night, although it had naught to do with concern for the masters not returning home. Now, in church, he remembered what had kept him awake.

He had lain, restless, in his attic bed above the workshop. In the past, it used to be cramped, having to share it with Tom and, of course, Little Beggar, his much-loved flea-bag of a dog. Beggar had been the closest thing he'd ever had to a friend. They'd been together on the streets: a pair of mangy vagabonds. Even now, the remembrance of the day Beggar died, taking on a vicious mutt twice as big as himself, brought the ache of tears to Jack's throat. The attic was a lonely place without company. That wretch, Tom, had been company of a sort. Always complaining and arguing, they'd oftentimes come to blows. Still, there had been moments. Their farting competitions in the dark of night were the stuff of legend. But Tom was gone too now, knifed in an alley, so Master Seb reported. Jack wasn't sure whether he felt sorrowful about that or not. Knowing Tom, he'd probably been in a drunken fight and deserved what he got.

But Jack didn't like being alone. And he knew who he wanted to have close. Not a dog, not some useless fellow. He wanted a wench. Not just anything in skirts, tumbled amongst the barrels at the back of a tavern.

He wanted Kate.

He dreamt of unruly dark curls, deep brown eyes and a merry laugh. He saw those every day as she went about her chores and working at her desk. But they were not enough. Stolen kisses behind the pigsty only made matters worse. Jack wanted – no – he needed to have Kate close, skin to skin, here in his attic, sharing his bed.

He wondered if he could even be in love with Kate, seeing he felt about her as he used to about Beggar. Was that possible? To be in love? Him? Jack Tabor? It didn't seem likely but there it was: a hole in his heart and an ache in his loins and only Kate could mend his ills. Not that they'd ever get the chance.

In church now, he kept looking at her, hoping she might cast a glance in his direction. Their eyes would meet and she would smile at him, sending shivers of longing through his balls and his prick would rise in readiness. But she didn't look up. And, anyhow, a stiff prick would serve no purpose. Kate was an alderman's daughter and he was – what? – of no account.

# The Foxley House

Breakfast was a joyous affair. The whole household, even Mistress Em, had attended the early mass on Easter Day, shouting 'Allelujah! He is risen!' at the tops of their voices. Everyone they met cried the same wondrous greeting.

And there were bacon collops, succulent and juicy, topped

with melting cheese. Coddled eggs, a tart with sweet herbs and clotted cream were set upon the snowy linen cloth before them. To Jack's mind, Rose, Nessie and Kate had performed a miracle as great as the Saviour's Resurrection. Not a fish scale in sight. Lent was ended at last and all the forbidden foods returned, much to the delight of all. If Jack ever saw another salted herring or a smoked eel, it would be far too soon. For once, he washed his hands at the laver bowl without being reminded.

Master Seb said a Latin grace – taking far too long about it, Jack reckoned, whilst the dishes went cold – then everyone set to, helping themselves, laughing, exclaiming over the first delicious mouthfuls.

'Oh, Jack,' Rose said, wiping the last morsel of cheese from her platter with a piece of fine white bread, 'I know 'tis the Lord's Day and a Holy Day and all but, last night, the window in our chamber stuck fast, half open, did it not, Kate?'

'Aye, 'twas fortunate it didn't rain but the wind howled in and blew the towel off the hook. We were chilled, indeed,' Kate said.

'Since you now know of wood better than the rest of us,' Rose went on, 'Would you mind taking a look at it; see if you can get it shut, at least, in case it rains? We'd be so grateful, wouldn't we, Kate?'

'For anuvver slice of tart, I might.' Jack held out his empty platter.

'You're incorrigible,' Rose said, cutting a large slice and lifting it onto his dish.

Jack didn't bother asking what 'ingoridable' meant, so long as he got second helpings.

'Greedy; that's what he is,' Mistress Em said but it was a mild rebuke and she didn't add the usual threat of taking her broom to his backside. Easter had cheered them all, even her, the Moody ol' Mare, Jack realised. He had never forgotten when Master Jude had called her that and the name fit her so well he always thought of her so… because she was. Jack had no liking for Mistress Em. Mind you, he didn't mind admitting she was a good cook but these days, Rose did most of the cooking, so the mistress wasn't no good for that anymore. Scolding and moaning was all she did: to himself or Master Seb mostly. And she dared call him greedy when she was fatter than a sow in farrow. Not that he saw her eat much. She must scoff sweetmeats in secret in her bedchamber.

An hour later, Jack was wrestling with the peg-and-groove window in Rose and Kate's chamber at the back of the house, above the kitchen and overlooking the garden plot. It was a pleasant room that had once been Master Seb's and the Mare's, well furnished with hangings of blue worsted. There wasn't much amiss with the window that a few days of dry weather wouldn't mend. The wood was swollen with damp but a bit of lard or some such and brute strength should get it closed. He was about to return to the kitchen for a blob of bacon grease – just as well Lent was done with – when the chamber door opened.

'I need a clean cap for High Mass,' Kate said, although the cap she was wearing was her Sunday best and looked perfect to Jack. But what did he know of women's headwear? 'How's the window? Can you mend it?'

'Well, it ain't easy t' fix, see? It'll take a fair bit of fettlin'. Might take me a while, mightn't it? The groove needs clearin' out, don't it? An' I might 'ave t' fetch me 'ammer an' chisels from Appleyard's.' Jack hoped Kate was impressed.

'But you can't do all that on the Lord's Day. I suppose we'll just have to shiver until the morrow.'

'Come 'ere.' Jack stepped close and took both her hands. 'Yer knows I c'n keep yer warm, if yer want?'

Kate giggled and moved into his arms. There was no need for words. The kiss lasted until they had to part to draw breath but resumed, hot as a first passion ever was. There was naught to be done but give in to raw lust. Neither gentle nor graceful, they tumbled onto the bed fumbling, grabbing and gasping. Jack fought his way through too many skirts. Linen tore, lacings knotted but he ripped them asunder.

Slippery with sweat, Jack got what he had wanted for so long. Kate's fingernails gouged his forearms as she clung to him but he didn't care, pounding away. Then, with cries of ecstasy – or pain – it was all over. He collapsed beside her, panting but triumphant, in a haze of pleasure.

They never heard the chamber door opening.

'Jack! Kate! What are you thinking of? How can you be so foolish?'

Jack tried to jump off the bed but his hose were entangled around Kate's foot. He saw that Rose looked appalled, as if she'd just seen a murder happen in front of her eyes.

'We woz on'y...' he began.

'Don't speak. I know exactly what you 'was only' doing. This day of all days...' Rose stood there for a long while, so it seemed, shaking her head. 'Get yourselves decent,' she said at last. ''Tis nigh time we went to church again for High Mass.'

Jack straightened his nether clouts, fastened his hose and breeches, slunk out of the chamber and down the stairs like a whipped hound. His moment of victory turned to disaster... wasn't that always the way of it? Jack Tabor was ever the loser in everything. God alone knew what would happen now, when Rose told Master Seb, or worse yet: Mistress Em.

Rose sat on the edge of the rumpled bed, sheet, blanket and coverlet dragged to the floor, watching as a tearful Kate attempted to pull a comb through her tangled curls. The eyelets of her bodice were ripped and a seam gaped, showing her shift beneath.

Rose stared at the sky beyond the window – half-open still. She hardly knew how to begin but something had to be said.

'Kate. You do know how a woman gets with child, don't you?' No answer.

'A woman may conceive by... well... by doing what you and Jack were doing. Did you know that?'

'My sister told me it happens if you lie with a man but... we weren't lying and Jack's... just Jack, not a man.'

'Man enough, I fear.' Rose put a hand on the young lass's arm. 'Tell me, Kate: did he force you to do it? For I know how it can be. At your age, I lived with my parents in Canterbury. My father was a glover, one of the best in his craft. I showed some skill at fine stitchery and, not wanting the expense of indenturing me to another, he took me on as his apprentice. But he already had an older lad serving an apprenticeship in the workshop. His name was Philip. I'll ne'er forget his face.'

Rose took a shuddering breath, crumpled her apron in her hands.

'He forced me against my will, Kate. He raped me. 'Tis not true, what is said: that a woman can only get with child if she takes pleasure in the act. I was terrified; hated every moment. I tried to fight him off and had broken fingers to show for my struggles against him. Yet I conceived a child all the same.

'When I could hide my dreadful secret no longer, I told my father. He called me a whore, a harlot, a slut for leading Philip astray, tempting him into sin. He said I had brought shame upon his house and upon his good name. He threw me out into the street, whilst Philip looked on, smirking. Not a word was said against him. As I wandered towards West Gate, my mother came running after me, pressed a few pennies into my hand and told me to make for London to seek my fortune. That was all and not a grain of comfort did she offer.

'You can tell me true, Kate: did Jack force you into doing this?'

Kate bowed her head so her hair hid her face.

'No. I was willing enough. I wondered… was all.' She spoke so softly. 'We both just… did it. We never planned anything; it just happened. But what of your babe, Rose? What became of it?'

'Edward. That was his name. My tiny treasure. He was beautiful. I always wondered how something so innocent, so sweet could come of an act so vile. But my Edward was the most perfect and most dear.' Rose wiped away a tear.

'Where is he now?'

'In his grave. Too good for this world. Now come, dress yourself, Kate. You must try to look the part of a maiden, at least.'

'W-will you tell M-master Seb of us?'

'No. That will be for you and Jack to do, if the worst befalls and you are with child.'

'But I'm not. See?' Kate stood, smoothed down her gown, patted her flat belly. 'See, there's nothing there.'

'You foolish child. It will take weeks before you can be certain, one way or the other. Your monthly courses will cease long before your belly shows, if you are.'

'Oh. I didn't know that. Is that how you can tell? What will I do, if I am, Rose? What will my father say?'

'We – the three of us, for I'll not let Jack escape his responsibilities, as Philip did – will climb that hurdle when we reach it, if we have to. Until then, Kate, I advise you to pray harder than you've ever done that your sin will not make itself known, revealed to all.

'Wash your face now. Change your gown, for I hear Master Seb and the others below, readying for church. Make haste and join us, Kate. And, if any should ask, say you splashed your gown with egg at breakfast and put on a smile for all to see.' Rose left then, her footsteps firm on every stair.

Kate washed her face in the bowl, hoping its lavender-scented water would soothe her flushed skin. That was easily done. She dressed in her second best tawny gown but putting on her smile was more difficult.

Slowly, she realised those few moments with Jack could have ruined the rest of her life. The promise of a rose-tinted future turned to dross might be the terrible price to pay for five minutes – or less – of pleasure. It wasn't worth it.

Jack wasn't worth it.

It had all been a dreadful mistake.

# St Michael le Querne Church

Seb was greatly recovered. All that had been needed was a good breakfast to overcome the lingering effects of yesterday's sleeping draught. This meant that during High Mass, he was more sensible to the subtle changes among those of the Foxley household. Was it the case that Kate seemed subdued? Even her unruly curls looked dull and sad and that should not be upon this most joyful day. The lass stared at the floor and never once raised her eyes, even at the ringing of the Eucharist bell. How unlike Kate.

Rose, too, appeared downcast.

He would needs enquire, after the office was done, as to what was amiss. After all, what with it being Easter Day and young Will Thatcher now found, what cause could there be for such solemnity?

Emily was finding this second attendance at church too tiring. That was plain to see. Her face was lined with weariness and he saw the way she tried to ease herself, wincing at the discomfort.

Seb moved close to her, gripped her slumped shoulders as she sat upon her stool, pulling her back gently against his body that she might use him as a pillow.

'Rest easy, sweeting,' he whispered. 'I shall waken you, as required.' He was gratified that she did so without argument. Gawain lay betwixt her and the church doorway. It was as if he would keep the niggling draught from her poor, swollen feet, aiding her in comfort.

Meanwhile, Jack was sulking, though that was not so unusual these days.

Seb wondered what he might do to raise their spirits. Much had weighed upon his mind of late but, this day, his heart was lighter. It seemed wrong that the rest of the household did not share this lifting of oppression. Mayhap, they could spend the afternoon in Cheapside, where, it was promised, a mummers' play was to be performed. That would surely cheer them all.

Dinner was as fine a repast as anyone could have desired and Seb was further concerned to note that some at the board were not relishing it as they ought.

Adam did justice to the roasted mutton that Rose and Nessie had laboured long to cook to perfection. It was served with a rich butter, mint and rosemary sauce. The new season's alexanders – a favourite of Seb's – were served crisply fried with a breadcrumb topping and blanched almonds. A simnel pudding followed, decorated with marchpane figures: one each to represent Christ and those Apostles who stood by Him. In honour of the day, they had spiced wine instead of ale.

Yet Emily hardly took a bite before making her excuses, saying she would rest abed for a while. Her pale face and evident weariness concerned Seb but she waved aside his attempts to help her climb the stair, insisting she could manage well enough.

Kate appeared to have little appetite and Jack never asked for a second helping.

'Jack, will you not have more mutton?' Seb asked. ''Tis a pity to let such excellent meats go cold upon the dish after Rose and Nessie have gone to so great an effort. Help yourself.'

Jack did so but took only a morsel and no more.

'Well, I won't see it go to waste,' Adam said, spearing three or more slices on his knife. 'I commend the cooks' skills heartily. And who decorated the pudding?'

'That was me,' Nessie said. 'I made all them 'postles meself. That big one's St Peter 'cos I reckon he was fat. The skinny one's St Mark and him with the little hat is Luke. I gave Our Lord Jesu a halo, so you can tell which He is. Hey! That's not fair, Jack,' she protested as he grabbed the marchpane Christ and bit it in two. 'You're s'posed to leave Him 'til last.'

'S'only marchpane. So what?' Jack said, swallowing the rest of the figure.

'No tears, Nessie,' Rose said, 'Your marvellous artistry has to be eaten some time.'

'What of you, Kate?' Seb asked, attempting to coax the lass. 'Will you not have St Luke or one of the others?'

She shook her head and frowned at her napkin.

'Well, since Luke be the patron saint of our own Stationers' Guild, I shall devour him myself,' Seb concluded, 'And delicious he be, indeed. I say we should all drink to the health of those who prepared this most excellent dinner for us, to show our great appreciation: to Rose and Nessie!'

The accolade was repeated around the board, half-heartedly by some, but little Dickon made sounds of delight as a marchpane saint was sucked on and squashed beyond recognition in his chubby fist. Gawain barked his approval before tucking into a juicy mutton bone. Grayling, the cat, received leftovers aplenty too.

Seeing what yet remained upon the board, Seb selected some mutton and a large helping of simnel pudding, including an unnamed marchpane Apostle, wrapping the food in a napkin. He hoped he would see Old Symkyn later, by Cheap Cross, and give him a share of their Easter dinner.

# Cheapside

As Seb intended, once dinner was done and everyone had helped clear the board and wash the dishes – even he, Adam and Jack dried the best pewter cups and platters and arranged them back upon the buffet in the parlour – those who could be persuaded went out, along Cheapside, to watch the mummers' play. Emily did not join them. When Seb had looked in to see how she fared, she was sleeping. Rose insisted on remaining at home, in case Em should have need of anything, but Adam and Nessie were eager to watch the performers. Kate and Jack were less keen, although they too would rather be out in the city at this time of celebration than sitting at home.

Yet Seb realised the two youngsters, who usually laughed together and joshed one another, remained as far apart as unwelcome strangers and ne'er so much as glanced at each other. What was amiss there, he wondered. Even before the entertainment began, Jack had sloped off somewhere, disappearing into the growing crowd, and Kate was definitely not her usual bubbling self this day.

Seb, with his little son perched on his shoulders, was ever on the lookout for subject matter for his illumination work, observing the crowd. Noting Old Symkyn sitting high upon the steps at the foot of Cheap Cross, he pushed his way through the merry bystanders to deliver the napkin full of mutton and simnel pudding.

'This is welcome, indeed, young master,' Symkyn said, taking a bite of tender, sauce-smeared meat. 'May Our Saviour bless you for your kindness.' The old man enjoyed his food for a while, then said, 'From my good vantage point, I see your noble patron has come to watch the play.'

'Duke Richard? I heard no fanfare nor cavalcade of fine horses.' Seb rearranged his best cap, which little Dickon had pushed down over his eyes.

'It seems he's come unannounced, to mix with us common folk. Not that his friend will ever be inconspicuous 'neath those peacock plumes. See them? They stand in the shadow of the doorway into Edmund Shaa's goldsmith's shop over yonder.'

'Aye, I see them now. Sir Robert Percy hides within the door. With his great height and fiery hair, he would be hard to miss, if he came out into the light. But you be correct about Lord Lovell's hat; he be showing it off to best effect, as ever. I believe he cannot help himself but make a display. Lord Richard should not have come with those two, if he hoped to pass unnoticed.'

'Lovell? Is that his name? Is he the owner of Lovell's Inn, around the corner from you, in Ivy Lane?' Symkyn handed Seb the stained napkin that had held his dinner.

'The very same, unfortunately.' Seb put the linen square in his purse.

'Why so?'

'He and I had a certain 'involvement' some years since. They were not happy times for me but we made a pact, never to speak of the matter to anyone, ever. I have kept my oath on that and so has he, insofar as I can tell. Though I would never account him a man of honour, 'tis in his best interest also to stand by his oath.'

'That sounds a most solemn contract, young master.'

'Aye, it is indeed. I hope the players begin shortly,' Seb said, changing the subject, 'for the sky be clouding over. I pray it does not rain afore the play be done. We would rather keep dry, would we not, Dickon? Ow! Let go my hair, lad, else your Papa will be bald as an egg afore too long.' He untangled the toddling's plump fingers from his hair, losing a tuft of dark strands in the process.

Even as the City Waits blew upon their trumpets and the Chief Cryer rang his bell announcing the mummers, Seb continued to watch the duke and his friends as best he might through the bobbing heads and waving arms of the crowd. He experienced a moment of grave disquiet as he observed Lord Lovell put an arm around the duke's shoulders. They laughed together, clearly sharing a jest, as close friends do. That the duke felt thus about Lovell and trusted him worried Seb. It was hard to credit that Lord Richard could yet remain unaware of Lovell's true nature, his capacity for heinous acts of arson, abduction, aye, and of murder. Did the duke truly not know?

An outburst of merriment and a great guffaw of laughter at his side brought Seb's thoughts back to Cheapside and the play.

'That was a fine jest, was it not?' Adam nudged Seb in the

ribs, chuckling.

'Aye,' Seb agreed without having heard what the players were saying. He must pay more attention. The duke's friendships were no one's affair but his own.

The crowd cheered as their favoured hero, St George, bested a devilish knight. The villain made a great show of dying in agony only to have a black-garbed physician rush in to revive him with a magick potion – at which the spectators hissed their disapproval. The maiden, with hands bound, cried out for succour, to be saved ere the devilish knight could rise and do his worst with her. George flourished his wooden sword but the evil one turned of a sudden, tripped him and knocked him down with a cudgel. A cowardly act. The crowd gasped as it seemed George was vanquished, although they all knew the play well enough; that it never ended thus. The physician capered on once more, this time teasing the crowd – will he give our hero the reviving potion or no? Of course he did. The fight resumed. George slew the devilish knight. The physician's potion bottle was empty. This time, there would be no revival for the evil one. St George had the victory, as was right and proper. Only the good prevailed to be resurrected for eternity.

Everyone cheered and applauded as the quartet of masked players made their bows and a hat was passed around to collect coins and just in time. During the performance, the sky had grown darker with the first hint of rain. Folk began to disperse.

As they did so, Seb noticed a tallish fellow who, like himself, bore a child upon his shoulders much in the manner that St Christopher had carried the Christ Child. And it was the child who attracted his attention for the little one had hair as white as frost on a winter morn. The man was approaching, coming along Cheapside, weaving through the throng, towards Seb.

'Master Seb, God give you the best of all blessings this day.' Beatrice Thatcher caught him by the sleeve. 'I hoped we'd see you here at the mumming. We can't ever thank you enough for fetching our Will back home. He's told us such tales as seem unlikely but says you'll be telling the same. You must come an' share supper with us sometime soon an' explain it all. We'll be glad t' hear what really came t' pass across the Bridge. And Emily, too, of course, when she's feelin' better. In the meantime, here's a gift of thanks from us all.' She pressed a package into Seb's hand and was gone before he could say a word in reply.

'That was thoughtful of her,' Adam said as Seb handed him the little package.

''Tis yours as much as mine, by rights,' Seb said as he was scouring the crowd, hoping to spot the man with the white-haired child on his shoulders. Either the fellow was gone into some side street or other or else, mayhap, he had simply lifted the child down so that she – for Seb thought it was a lass – might walk home, there being a spectacle to see no longer. 'Did you note that fellow, Adam? The one with the child sitting high? Did you observe the child's hair, pale as milk? 'Twas the very colour of the murdered lad's. Did you mark where the man went?'

'No, Seb. I was watching the players. Well, this is a fine gift, indeed,' Adam said, unwrapping the cloth around the package. 'See? A gilded leather bookmarker for each of us, to note the page as we read.'

'He was there after the play was ended. He was but a few yards from us when Beatrice came.' Seb ignored the gift.

'I was finding coin to put into the players' hat. I noticed you did not – I saw that much. Will you have the blue marker or the red?'

'We have to find him. There surely cannot be two white-haired youngsters in London, yet they be unrelated. We must find that fellow.'

'Aye, but not now.' Adam pulled up his hood and they all returned homeward, breaking into a run before they should be soaked as the clouds released their burden and the rain came down in strings.

# Chapter 13

## Easter Monday, the twelfth day of April
## The Foxley House

EVERYONE HAD been woken early forwhy a great cavalcade of noble lords had clattered through the city streets at dawn, trumpets sounding to clear the way. As if such was required at so early an hour.

'What was all that racket then?' Nessie asked no one in particular as she dished out a mess of eggs and herbs for breakfast.

''Tis the opening of Parliament at Westminster this morn,' Seb said.

'Well, do they have to make such a noise about it, waking decent folk when it's still dark? Gave us quite a start, they did, trumpets blaring an' all, shouting and yelling. They got no right to make such a din.'

'At least it means we've made a good start on the washing, Nessie, earlier than usual.' Rose was spooning bread sops and honey into little Dickon's eager mouth. 'We may be done by dinnertime. What a boon that will be. How is Emily faring this morn, Seb?' she asked, changing the subject.

'Sleeping still. She did not pass a restful night, I fear.'

'So what of you? Did you manage to sleep at all?'

'Somewhat. Enough for what must be done this day. I have to return to deciphering that text for Mistress Caldicott. I have left it over long. And…'

'De-sifoning? Wot's that then? Sounds like it'll 'urt.' Jack seemed to have recovered from his sulk of yesterday and was his usual self once more. Without waiting for his master's explanation, he grabbed a heel of fresh bread and rose from the board. His platter was wiped clean of every last smear of egg. 'Me an' Master Appleyard've got a settle t' put t'gevver t'day, now me fum's better. Be back fer me dinner.' The kitchen door slammed behind him.

'Never known him so eager to work,' Adam observed. 'Is he sickening or what? In love, maybe? Love can do strange things to a man.'

'I be certain you know everything concerning the matter, Adam,' Seb said, a wry grin on his face.

'I'll have you know I'm most skilled when it comes to wooing fair ladies. In fact, I have a fair lady who, this very day, would have me dine with her at her house, so I shan't be here for dinner.'

'Oooh,' Nessie squealed. 'Tell us who it is, Master Adam. 'Who's your lady-love?'

'Never you mind.' Adam tapped the side of his nose. 'I'm saying naught at present. You'll have to curb your impatience, lass. Now, to work, else I'll not be earning my wage. Come, Kate. You too. What's amiss, eh? You've not spoken a word this morn.' Adam and Kate went along the passage to the workshop, he cajoling her the while.

'Adam be correct,' Seb said. 'Rose? Do you know what ails our Kate? She was not so merry yesterday and is no better this day. Has some matter upset her?'

'Why ask me?' Rose made much of washing little Dickon's face and hands before lifting him down from his special chair. 'Why would Kate confide in me?'

'Why would she not? You be the closest to an elder sister in this house. I know you share a friendship.'

Rose turned away to busy herself, stacking dirty dishes in

the bucket to soak.

'Why don't you ask her; you're her master.'

'But if 'tis a womanly difficulty...'

'What makes you think that?' Rose spoke sharply.

Seb shrugged.

'Well, she has said naught concerning any problem with her work and, so it seems to me, her disquietude began yesterday, when we worked not. So, what else could it be but... Ah! I have it. 'Twas a lovers' quarrel... she and Jack. Aye, 'tis that, no doubt.'

'No doubt,' Rose echoed but would not meet his eye.

## King's Way, the road to Westminster

The Duke of Gloucester led the colourful procession of lords bound for Westminster, pennons flapping, harness jingling and Lord Lovell, mounted on a fine steed, was at his side.

'I have in mind a new commission for Master Foxley,' Duke Richard was saying as they rode along the Strand beside the grand townhouses of various barons, bishops and abbots. The impressive facades were mostly upon their left hand, such that the gardens behind ran down to the River Thames, so convenient for travelling by barge.

'You ought to acquire one of these places.' Francis Lovell gestured towards the grand construction of new red brick and gleaming marble of Exeter's Inn. A servant was using a hoe to jab at a weed that had dared raise its white blooms, like a many-headed hydra, beside the grand portal. He was having little success in removing the interloper. 'I'm sure Bishop Courtenay would sell it to you. I hear he's short of coin at present. You could rename it Gloucester's Inn. So much better to have your own place, instead of renting Crosby Place from some miserable merchant's widow. For God's sake, Dickon, it's unseemly for a duke of royal blood.'

'Take not the Lord's name in vain, Francis, I beg you. As for purchasing some over-grand palace, as you suggest, as I have said before: 'tis not worth the trouble nor cost of upkeep when I come to London so infrequently. Crosby Place serves my purpose more than adequately. However, I was about to say concerning a new commission: John, Lord Howard, has a fine new coat-of-arms above his gateway. You may have observed it last week when we joined him for an oyster supper, if you recall? The craftsmanship was of such rare quality, I should not have been surprised when John told me the artist was none other than Sebastian Foxley. You may remember him?'

Lovell growled an answer but the duke could make out no words.

'So I thought it might be a suitable addition to Crosby Place,' he continued, 'Now we have such fine new iron gates, to commission my own coat-of-arms to adorn the gatehouse – not permanently, of course, but when I be in residence. What do you say?'

'I say you're too late.'

'Too late, Francis? How so?'

'Word has lately reached my ears that your precious dauber of paint has been arrested and charged with murder. What have you to say to that, eh?' Francis's voice sounded gleeful indeed.

'Sebastian arrested? That cannot be so. And on such a serious charge? You must be mistaken, for certain. Mayhap, you misheard.'

'No mistake and there's naught amiss with my hearing. It's you who are mistaken, my friend, in your grave misjudgement of character. The fellow's a scoundrel, a thief and now a murderer. What else is to be expected of his kind? Have your grand coat-of-arms above the gate by all means, but find an artisan with a worthy reputation to paint it. A man from York would be a more honest choice.'

'I find it hard to believe this of Master Foxley,' Duke Richard admitted, 'I shall make enquiries concerning him.'

'I wouldn't bother; the wretch isn't worth the trouble. Let him hang and be done with it.'

By now, they had reached the king's palace at Westminster. King Edward would open Parliament at nine of the clock, when the abbey bell rang for the office of Terce, and the duke was required to turn his thoughts toward courtly etiquette and matters of state.

## The Foxley House

The morning was chill and the workshop cold, having been unused and unheated since Thursday last. Seb had lit both braziers but the charcoal in the iron baskets, set upon their stone plinths for fear of hot ashes causing a fire, had yet to glow and give out any noticeable warmth. He had begun afore breakfast, making notes of all that came to pass in Southwark and Lambeth, whilst the facts were fresh in his mind.

He shivered now as he set out fresh pens, ink and paper, preparatory to delving once more into the nigh-illegible mysteries of the astrology text. He should not complain: at least he had warm feet, as Adam and Kate did not, with Gawain supplying a fur blanket across his boots. Kate was grinding yellow ochre pigment, pounding with the muller on the marble slab as though crushing the Devil himself, perspiring with the effort, her tongue poked at the corner of her mouth in concentration.

Seb had suggested she work on her recent ideas for marginalia. The image of a tiny knight jousting with a great grasshopper had appealed to him and he hoped designing the piece would cheer her but Kate's enthusiasm for amusing sketches was quite lacking. Her sombre air of determination upon working the pigment to a fine powder was, somehow, sorry to behold.

Adam sat at the collating table, stitching the pages of yet another cheap Latin primer. More dreary labour, as Seb thought, yet Adam was singing some snippet of song under his breath and he alone appeared merry at his work.

'I meant to ask you, Seb, after yesterday's homecoming, how did you enjoy our boat ride across the river?' Adam snipped off a last linen thread and folded the leaves into book form.

'Boat ride? I did no such thing.' Seb frowned over some cramped words squeezed betwixt the lines of text in the exemplar. He turned the page, back and forth, realising his reading was hampered by marks showing through from the other side of a particularly thin area of parchment. 'I told you: I ne'er go near a boat or ship, else I become queasy.' He returned the old book to its stand and reshaped his pen.

'You survived well enough, yester morn. You slept all the way across.'

'Nay. I should remember such a torment.'

Adam laughed.

'It seems we've found a cure then for your seasickness: a sleeping potion from a mermaid. How apt: a mermaid? *The* Mermaid.'

'I comprehend your jest, cousin, but it will be the Day of Judgement afore I touch anything from that Devil's den again. Which reminds me, I must find time to report to Thaddeus Turner, concerning the goings-on there. Will you come with me, Adam, during the dinner hour?'

'Not this day of all days. As I said before, I've an appointment to dine with a lady.' Adam's grin spread wide.

'I pray she be a good cook. Does she know what a hearty trencherman you be?'

'Ha! I shall be the soul of restraint, relishing and appreciating every mouthful.'

''Tis most like to be a dinner hour of considerable duration, then. I'll not expect your return to your desk until when?

Nones, mayhap?'

'Aye, that will be time enough for me to make a good impression. She has a broken window shutter in need of a man's hand. I shall mend it for her... ingratiate myself.'

'You have wiles and cunning sufficient for a true Foxley, cousin. I hope your carpentry skills be up to the mark. I should not want the lady to be disappointed in your abilities.'

'She won't be. My woodworking isn't bad, either.' Adam laughed but then looked to Kate. Such talk was unsuitable for a lass's ears but her head was down as she concentrated upon pounding another piece of ochre into the finest powder. She wasn't listening, he hoped, or did not understand his meaning. None were aware of her uneven breathing and chewed nether lip.

## The Three Feathers Inn, Lambeth

Lord Pierpoint had been in a towering, but pointless, rage ever since the lad had disappeared by climbing out the window.

'Do something, Walter, you imbecile. And don't tell me 'tis another holy day or some such as an excuse for inaction. Those terrible people have abducted my son back again; I know it. You didn't pay them enough, Walter.'

'I paid them what they asked, my lord,' Walter insisted – not for the first time. This conversation had been repeated, time and again, since the boy's escape on Maundy Thursday, four days since. The repetition was mainly because his lordship forgot he had expressed his outrage many times already but why, Walter wondered, could the old man not forget that there had ever been a boy?

'Go and fetch my son back, Walter. Don't stand there dithering like the fool you are. And this time, get that petition to Parliament. I want this matter sorted out, so my son Henry inherits. Tell Gloucester I insist his inheritance is confirmed legally and to be quick about it. I won't live forever, you know.'

Walter sighed. One did not tell a royal duke what to do. He, a mere servant, could not instruct Parliament nor advise so eminent an institution on how to conduct its business. Gloucester had already rejected the petition as nonsense once and the look in the duke's eye at the time wasn't one Walter ever wanted to see again. Besides, his knowledge of the law was rudimentary at best. If his lordship required someone to argue the intricacies of the case, then he must instruct – and pay – a proper lawyer. And therein lay the problem. Lord Pierpoint would never employ one of that loathsome profession since he blamed the law for his state of penury – whenever he could recall the truth to mind – and, if he did employ a lawyer, he could never afford the extortionate fees. Add to that the fact that this situation, his desire to replace his truly begotten heir with another, had come about because Sir Marcus defied his father's intention of his becoming a noble knight and studied the law instead and the whole affair became one enormous, convoluted and circular argument, going around and around. And he, Walter, was caught amid the whirlpool. There was no escape.

'My lord...' Walter began hesitantly, knowing he ventured into lands unknown, 'I'm not sure those dreadful people did take the boy. I suspect he may have run away. The window was wide open. A lad like that would have little difficulty...'

'Don't be preposterous. What boy would run from the possibilities of an illustrious future with a barony, manor houses, horses and all the trappings of knighthood? You speak as a lackwit. The boy was bright, eager. Why would he flee? No, Walter, those devils stole him back. They broke our contract and I'll not stand for it. I'll report them to the sheriffs, to the Lord Mayor, to King Edward himself, if I have to. I want Henry returned to me. I care not how much it costs. Go, damn you! Fetch him home to his doting father. Now!'

It was all nonsense. His lordship was quite mad if he believed anyone in authority would sympathise with him. Paying for a child to be abducted from his family was a criminal offence, no matter the intentions behind such an act.

Walter took up his cloak and left. With no coin to spare to pay a boatman to row him across the river, he had a long walk ahead of him, through Southwark, across London Bridge, then all the way to Ludgate, out along Fleet Street to Chancery Lane, where the lawyers had their chambers. He could but hope to find Sir Marcus at home after he made so much effort.

# Guildhall

Thaddeus Turner was in his little chamber at Guildhall, scoffing a spicy beef pasty, when an usher knocked and announced the arrival of Seb Foxley. Thaddeus felt surprise at the visit, thinking his old friend would wish to remain far distant from the place where he was lately accused of murder. Mayhap, he was come to report that he had uncovered the true culprit. At least, Thaddeus hoped that was the case.

'Come in, Master Foxley. Be seated though you're just too tardy to share my pasty, I fear, but there is ale in the jug.' The bailiff brushed the last few pastry crumbs from his jerkin.

'No matter.' Seb smiled. 'I ate my dinner in haste afore I came.'

'Then how may I help you, Seb? Have you discovered who killed Tom Bowen?'

'Nay, although I have my suspicions concerning the matter. I would not accuse another of the crime without firm evidence, or else a confession, so I shall not speak of that, as yet.'

The two friends exchanged a knowing glance. Thaddeus nodded.

'Aye. Fyssher ought never to have leapt to conclusions and

accused you.'

'What did he have to say when informed of my release?'

'He cursed and fumed – much as you'd expect of him – but he acknowledged, eventually, that the evidence against you was all circumstantial, flimsy as old cobwebs and your logical explanations hard to refute. Mind you, he likes you now even less than he ever did.'

Seb shrugged.

'Then let us hope he refrains forever from summoning me to assist in his duties as City Coroner. 'Tis a miserable imposition I may do well without. His six pennyworth of payment, which materialises but rarely, be little in the way of compensation for the horrors I have seen, the stinks I have endured on his behalf. But I have come to you upon another matter: the lad who went missing on his journey to school a week since. We found Will Thatcher, cold, hungry but unharmed. He was returned to his parents yester morn.'

'Well, that's welcome news, for once. These walls hardly ever hear good tidings. Well done, my friend.' Bailiff Turner stood and shook Seb's hand. 'Now tell me all.'

'I had a deal of aid from my kinsman, Adam Armitage and, not least, from my dog, Gawain, whose nose sought out the lad's whereabouts. But something needs to be done about The Mermaid Tavern in Southwark for the folk there were at the heart of such villainy as you will find hard to believe.'

'I doubt that, Seb. Southwark is full of thieves, cutthroats and prostitutes… Have some ale.' Thaddeus blew dust from a spare cup and filled it from the jug before topping up his own. 'Discussing crime is ever thirsty work.'

'Aye and, reluctantly, I must tell you that women of loose morals are much involved in my report. Young Will can give you more names than I but a woman of middle years, whom I heard them refer to as "Bessie", seemed to have charge at The Mermaid. I disliked her for her cold eyes, even when she played the part of treating me kindly. She be untrustworthy, I know, but the real villain was a fellow called Cain. 'Twas he who abducted Will and took him to Southwark.'

'I shall see he's arrested forthwith…' Thaddeus began but then frowned as Seb shook his head. 'Why not?'

'Cain has suffered for his crimes already and cannot commit another act of villainy… ever.' Seb sipped his ale and set the cup down, careful that it stood precisely upon the previous wet circle where the bailiff had slopped the drink as he poured it.

'What happened? Do you mean to say you slew him?'

'Of course we did not. Cain was doing his utmost to kill us – Adam and me – to get the lad in his clutches once more. We were out in the dark, in the salt marshes by Lambeth. Cain attacked us but the causeway – such as it be – collapsed 'neath his feet. He fell, head-foremost, into the quagmire. The mud swallowed him down like a ravenous beast. He was gone afore we so much as gave thought to any means of pulling him to safety. He must have suffocated in moments. Any efforts we may have made would have been in vain to save him and, in truth, we were in no fit condition ourselves to wrestle him from the marsh. If we could have, we would have done so, if only to spare him for the hangman's rope, yet it was not to be.'

'Tell me everything, Seb,' Thaddeus told him, refilling the cups.

'To spare my tongue as well as your ears, I wrote the sorry tale down, in full, this morn, afore dawn.' Seb took a pile of papers from his scrip. 'I have included sketches of those involved, so you may know them when you see them, and other details I recall. If my account be muddled and vague in parts, I make my apologies but they drugged my drink, or my food, or mayhap, both. Young Will Thatcher and his parents have been forewarned that you may require to question him. A brave lad, indeed, is he and will furnish you with information unknown to me. All the same, my friend, treat him gently for he has been roughly handled and scared halfway to death.'

'You know me better than that, Seb.'

'Aye, I do. What I truly mean to say is, I pray you, keep Coroner Fyssher away from the child, if you can. The lad does not deserve to be tormented further after his ordeal. I trust my notes will be sufficient for you to act upon. If other queries arise, you know where to find me.'

'I'm grateful to you for this.' Thaddeus tapped the sheaf of papers. 'In truth, the city owes you a debt for making it a safer place for our children. May the Lord God keep you in His care, Seb.'

As Seb departed from Guildhall, he saw a face familiar from times past. He removed his cap and bowed to Duke Richard's lawyer, Miles Metcalfe, who had once done his best to get Jude's neck out of the executioner's noose by legal means. His efforts had been unsuccessful and another way required but the lawyer was not at fault. Seb had liked the grey-haired Yorkshireman.

'Well met, Master Foxley,' Metcalfe said. 'This is a fortuitous happenstance, indeed.'

'How so, Lawyer Metcalfe? I trust you be well?'

'Well enough, I thank you, though the years could be kinder. I came to Guildhall on the Duke of Gloucester's instruction. He was informed this day that you were under arrest upon a charge of murder and, if it proved true, I was to look into the matter. But I observe you are at liberty. The duke will be much relieved, for he has in mind a commission for you. Mayhap, you will find time to attend upon his grace in the near future? You will, of course, have to fit your visit around the duke's business in Parliament.'

'It will be my pleasure to be of service to his grace once more, Lawyer Metcalfe. Thank you for your time. And, I pray, express my gratitude for Duke Richard's concern in sending you to enquire of my situation. I was detained but briefly and hope the matter be settled now.'

They parted with due courtesies and Seb should have felt a burden lifted from his shoulders, having handed the problems in Southwark to Thaddeus Turner and received the possibility of another royal commission, yet there came no sense of relief. He had not resolved the mystery of the white-haired lad. The sighting yesterday of a child with hair likewise lacking any hue only served to remind him how long it had been since he found that sorry little body and the family remained ignorant of his loss – if there was a family to mourn him. And then there remained Tom's killer, still at large. His sister, Bella, and her goodman, Dick Langton, deserved to see the perpetrator pay the price and Tom's soul – whatever his shortcomings – cried out for justice. Seb's work in uncovering the truth was not done.

As he walked down Milk Street, the sky was clouding, the herald of yet another April shower, no doubt. He turned into Cheapside, a bustling place in the early afternoon. As he passed St Peter's church, it seemed a shadow fell upon him. He twitched, as if to shrug it off. Foolish – 'twas but a cloud passing overhead.

The street was full of busy folk: housewives with baskets, intent upon their purchases, or coping with unruly children. Apprentices yelled their masters' wares for sale or scuttled through the crowd upon their errands. An over-laden donkey brayed in protest and refused to move another step, blocking the way of two merchants on horseback, despite the pair laying about the unfortunate beast with their riding whips. It only brayed the louder. A man with live hens strung, feet uppermost, along a pole, added to the chaos by barging through, setting his birds fluttering and squawking and showering the angry merchants with a cascade of feathers. Folk were laughing at the commotion but Seb did not join them, calling Gawain to heel for fear he would be trampled 'neath so many hooves.

A pricking sensation betwixt his shoulders would not relent. He adjusted the strap of his scrip, thinking that to be the cause. It was not. Impossible to prove in such a throng of folk, Seb was becoming convinced that one alone among them was following him. He looked back more than once but could espy no furtive actions behind him. No one ducked into a doorway or peered from an alleyway entrance. Nobody skulked, prowled, or appeared otherwise engaged in any stealthy act of pursuit. It must be his imagination playing tricks, as in a game of hood-man-blind.

A last glance back along Paternoster Row, before turning into the narrow alley that led to the side gate of his own house, showed no felons lurking, just a huckster with her tray, now empty, going into St Paul's precinct and a group of urchins playing some rough-and-tumble game, shrieking with laughter. Gawain gave no hint of anything amiss, his tail wagging.

Seb entered the kitchen. Rose was putting little Dickon down in his nest of blankets under the board, that he might sleep, safe from the hearth and out from underfoot as she and Nessie went about their after-dinner tasks.

'Has Em come down to eat?' Seb asked Rose.

'No. I took her a bowl of pottage, bread and ale but she said she had no appetite. I bathed her face and hands but I think she was asleep again even before I had dried them. She seems restful enough, Seb, but I'm worried.'

'As am I,' he admitted. 'A woman so full of life to now lie listless and uninterested in the doings of her household... 'tis so unlike Em. Mayhap, we should fetch Mistress Warren once more, or Surgeon Dagvyle, to advise us?'

'I'll open the shop first,' Rose said, 'Though we are late in doing so.'

'Is Kate not there?'

'She said she had much to do in the workshop. Adam, of course, has not yet returned from his dinner.'

Seb had not expected that he should but he was surprised to see Kate, muller in hand, back at the grinding slab, working on green malachite this time. By right, apprentices ought not to labour unsupervised, so he had thought to find her in the kitchen with Rose and Nessie or sitting upon a stool in the shop, awaiting custom. After all, she had been pounding pigments assiduously all morn and it seemed a young lass would surely want some other task to occupy her through the afternoon.

'Kate, lass? So much hard toil? Would you not rather serve in the shop? Your arms must be aching by now.'

The lass shook her head but said naught.

Seb felt a sudden surge of anxiety: was Kate suffering some contagion, taken from Emily? Was the household infected with some debilitating miasma or other? Would they all suffer it, or did it only affect women? In which case, what of Rose and Nessie? They appeared lively enough for the present but what if... He shook off the thought. What was amiss with him this day, imagining the worst at every turn? It must yet be caused by the remnants of that filthy potion, upsetting his humours.

No one had been following him; Emily was ailing because of the babe she carried and Kate... well, Kate was of that age when a child becomes a woman, there were bound to be changes in her demeanour. Tom had certainly changed at that age and Jack was yet continuing to do so – mostly for the worse. For men, it meant a deeper voice and fluff upon the chin and, more unfortunately, ill-temper, sulks and an eagerness to fight. He wondered what it meant for women, apart from the obvious newly growing curves and an inclination to think of love. He could only pray that Kate's merry disposition would return as suddenly as it had departed. The house was not the same without her smile like a summer's day, warming them all and bringing colour to the workshop.

Adam strolled in, grinning. One was happy, at least. He returned to the collating table to resume his stitchery but there was no mistaking the gleam in his eye.

'Dinner was good as you hoped, then?' Seb asked.

'Better. And I mended the shutter. It didn't take long.' Adam threaded his needle afresh.

'But the lady would not permit you to leave? Much against your will, of course.'

'Her belt had a bent clasp. She asked me to straighten it for her, such that it might fasten properly once more. By then, she had made honeyed wafers and would have me sample them.'

'You will grow fat, Adam, if you visit Mistress Hutchinson too frequently.'

'How do you know that I did?' Adam swivelled on his stool to face Seb. 'You followed me,' he said, pointing an accusing finger.

'Nay. I had other matters to attend. I was at Guildhall, making report to Bailiff Turner, you will remember.'

'Then how come?'

'It was merely supposition. I know you have a fondness for her. But now you have confirmed its truth.'

'Aye, well, it's no secret: I like Mercy Hutchinson very much and she likes me... at least, I think she does. And she's a fine cook... so, why not?'

# Crosby Place

The ceremonial opening of Parliament was ended before dinner. King Edward had no further inclination to linger over matters of state when there was a fine meal awaiting – not to mention a most comely, eager and lovesome mistress. She was wife to a goldsmith but, since the fellow was in Flanders, attending to business, the king had no time to lose in attending to Mistress Shore. Parliamentary concerns could wait until the morrow.

Duke Richard returned to Crosby Place out of humour. Government of the realm involved more than a crown-wearing, a blessing and an opening speech. That the king had left the Chapter House at Westminster, where the Lords sat, even before approving the Commons' choice of a Speaker meant nothing had been achieved at all. This was typical of Edward, though Richard would never say so much aloud, to summon the Lords and Commons by royal writ, as required, and then decide he had more important things to do. A new mistress of all things! It was a disgrace. The kingdom might erupt in revolt or the French invade *en masse* and the king's only interest was bed-sport with someone else's wife.

Richard was more skilled than most Plantagenets at keeping that infamous temper in check but sometimes – like now – it was nigh impossible.

'What an utter waste of my time,' he growled, striding this way and that before the fireplace in the Great Hall, like a caged beast in the Tower Menagerie. 'He drags me all the way from Yorkshire and for what? To tell me governing the realm can wait. And where's Lawyer Metcalfe? I require an answer to my enquiries.'

'Lord's sake, Dickon,' Sir Robert Percy put a restraining hand upon the duke's arm. 'You only sent him to Guildhall half an hour past. Here, have some ale to cool your humours.'

'My humours have no need of cooling. What I need is information. Why is London full of idlers and dawdlers and nobody does a decent day's work? At least, in the North, folk get off their backsides…' He took a deep breath, trying to calm himself. ''Tis no wonder I loathe this city so. I be of a mind to ride home upon the morrow and Parliament be damned.'

'But you won't.' Rob handed him a cup of ale, which was accepted.

'No, I do not suppose I will, forwhy I know where my duties and responsibilities lie. Unlike some.'

Rob agreed but named no names. Everyone knew who the duke meant.

'My lord,' a servant said, softly, 'There are two men outside, hoping to speak with you, concerning a petition.'

'And is this petition of significance, Matthew? I was not expecting to deal with such matters today.'

'In truth, one of them came to you last week and you gave him short shrift for presenting a piece of nonsense and wasting your valuable time.'

'I did? So, what has changed that he dares return?'

'He comes with a lawyer, a man of some repute at the Inner Temple, my lord, and... a heavy purse was wagged beneath my nose.'

'Ah! And money ever shouts louder than human voice.' Richard left his cup and took his seat upon the dais. 'Tell them I shall spare but five minutes to hear their case. I believe I recall that foolish petition, concerning someone hoping to flout the laws of inheritance. If they think they can present the same again, they have wasted their coin. Bring them in, Matthew, and let us get this matter dealt with. I am certain I have better things to do.'

Before the petition could be presented, Lawyer Metcalfe arrived, breathless, from Guildhall. At least his welcome tidings, that Sebastian Foxley was not under arrest, put the duke in a better humour to listen to the unexpected petitioners.

He was further mollified to learn that the lawyer and the old servant – the fellow who had quailed before him last week – were come to apologise and beg pardon for ever having troubled him with the ridiculous petition. The lawyer, Sir Marcus Pierpoint by name, wished instead that the duke might endorse a document confirming him as his father's guardian. Richard agreed, in principle, but insisted he should meet the parent, to make his own judgement on the matter before setting his seal to such a document.

# Chapter 14

## Tuesday, the thirteenth day of April
## The Foxley House

NELL WARREN, the midwife, was above stairs, in the bedchamber, attending Emily. Poor Em had suffered much all through the night, though whether her time was at hand, no one seemed to know. The menfolk and Kate sat, breaking their fast – Seb seeming to chew rather upon his thumbnail than on the food set before him. Dark blotches beneath his eyes, denoting his lack of sleep, enhanced the fading bruises recalling last week's mishap. He had held Em's hand, bathed her face and sung to her, soft and low, but towards the end of a long night, none of these had given her any ease.

Meanwhile, Rose and Nessie were upstairs, then down, to and fro, ever in haste, carrying hot water, cold water, fresh sheets, warm towels, oil of lavender, oil of roses, ale and almond wafers. Then down they came with soiled linen, dirty water, empty cups and bowls.

Seb felt exhausted just watching so much activity and wondered at its purpose. Was the babe coming or no? No one thought to keep him informed.

'Come on, Seb,' Adam said, patting his cousin's shoulder. 'This is no place for us. Let's leave the women to their business. We have our own work to do. Jack: get you gone to Master Appleyard. Did you finish making that settle – or whatever it was – yesterday?'

'Almost done, ain't it?' Jack said, taking the untouched oatcake from Master Seb's platter and cramming it into his mouth.

'Well, get to it, lad.'

'But I ain't finished eatin' yet, 'ave I?'

'Indeed, you have, you young glutton. You eat more than the rest of us together. Go!' Adam insisted, tossing Jack the cloak hanging on a peg by the kitchen door.

'Don't need that. Ain't rainin', is it?' He kicked the garment aside, into the chimney-corner where Nessie had her cosy bed behind a curtain.

'It'll most likely rain later.'

'Don't care.'

'Have it your way then, Jack. You'll be the one as gets a soaking. Now hang it up, if you're not going to wear it.'

'No. You taked it off the peg. Why should I 'ave t' put it back?'

'You insolent pup. Pick it up.'

'No.'

Adam's hand caught Jack a hefty swipe across the ear.

The lad hardly flinched, although his scowl did credit to the Devil himself, but it was Kate who, unaccountably, burst into tears and fled the kitchen, running to the workshop. Jack stood up from the board, helping himself to a further stack of oatcakes no one seemed to want. He dropped one in his haste but Gawain got to it first and wolfed it down before it could be retrieved. Jack was about to kick the animal but, seeing Master Seb watching him, thought better of venting his anger on the creature. Master Seb put up with a deal of bad behaviour and rarely said much about it but two things could have serious results: insulting the Moody Mare was one, as Tom had found out to his cost. Causing pain and injury to his dog was the other and, despite his moans and complaints, Jack was too fond of his food and a warm bed to risk being thrown out of the Foxley household. He slouched off, muttering and banging the kitchen door so the beams shook.

Adam snatched it open again, grabbing Jack by the back of his jerkin and hauling him over to the water trough and dousing his head.

'Cool your temper, you thoughtless great clod. There's a sick woman trying to rest above stairs. Master Seb may not reprimand you forwhy the poor man's too weary to trouble with you but I'm not.'

Jack turned, unkempt hair dripping, spitting out water. He struck out at Adam, knocking him sideways so he caught his shoulder on the wall of the kitchen.

'You're not me master; I don't 'ave t' do as you say, you Norfolk prick. Why don't you go back where you comed from? You ain't no Londoner, yer straw-eating bloody shite-monger.' Jack manhandled Adam and threw him, bodily, over the low wall into the pigsty, to land among the dung and set the young pig – bought but lately for fattening over the summer and autumn – squealing like a demon.

Realising Jack was a child no longer, having now a man's strength, Adam took his time about climbing out.

'Just mind your manners,' he said, wiping filth off his face with a sleeve so soiled, it only served to make matters worse. 'I want no quarrel with you, Jack. Just have a little consideration for others.'

Belatedly, Seb came out into the yard, roused to action by the pig's noise, if not by the shouting of insults.

Jack was already leaving but he had grace enough to close the side gate quietly.

'Adam! By heaven, what has come to pass? You be in such a mess.' Seb led Adam to the trough and used the old bucket to help him wash the muck from his face and hair.

'A disagreement was all. 'Tis over now.' Adam said sheepishly. He wrung out a length of his hair then shook his head, like a rain-wet dog.

'Did you fall? Or were you pushed?'

'Thrown more like. I knew not the lad had such strength.'

'He has grown much of late. The way he eats, he should have the strength of Hercules.'

'Well, he's not got far to go on that score. In all the brawls we ever had in the Lower Tavern back home – do you remember? – only Cousin Luke, may God assoil him, could out-match me, yet Jack picked me up like a bundle o' kindling wood. We'll have to watch the lad, Seb. I fear he may not realise the harm he could do if someone rouses his wrath.'

'As you did?'

'I suppose so but he could have done me far more hurt than he did, I'm certain of that.'

'I shall speak with him later, concerning this. But, as for you, if you be dining with Mistress Hutchinson...'

'I'm not. We decided 'tis best if we don't besmirch her reputation. I'll go only when there is some legitimate purpose for my visit: if a door-latch sticks or a stool-leg snaps, or such like. Otherwise, we'll meet only in some place open to view. I would not want rumours to start.'

'So, we can expect a degree of clumsiness to ensue in Distaff Lane, then,' Seb said.

'What do you mean?'

'Broken stools, detached pot handles, jammed keys in locks...'

Adam laughed.

'I hope so.'

'In the meantime, cousin, even though you are not intending to visit your lady, Kate and I will appreciate it greatly if you change out of those reeking garments afore you join us in the workshop. And I will have words with Nessie also. The pigsty should have been mucked out hours ago. I be aware the women have their hands occupied, coping with poor Em, but if Nessie had done her chore first thing, you would have fallen onto clean straw and there would not now be your soiled attire in need of attention, adding to their work.' He shook his head. 'This household also has a reputation to maintain and, at present, I fear 'tis endangered by declining standards. Emily keeps us all up to the mark and to let matters slide whilst she lies upon her sickbed be an insult to her and all her past efforts. When she recovers, I would not want her appalled to observe how slip-shod we have become whilst she has been unwell.'

'Phew. That's quite a rant, coming from you, Seb.'

'Aye, well… forgive me but…'

'No. No apology required.' Adam held up his hands in mock surrender. 'You're quite right, cousin. We should all look to our behaviour of late. I'll tell you what, since it was partly my own fault that I ended up in the sty and I'm filthy already, I'll see to the pig. Nessie is too busy with fetching and carrying at Mistress Warren's command to stop and do such foul work. Then, I promise I'll wash and change, so as not to assault your delicate sense of smell.'

'There be naught delicate about it. In truth: you stink worse than the public house of easement over the Fleet River.'

'As bad as that, eh?'

Seb wrinkled his nose, making no answer, but returned within doors. There was work to be done at his desk; customers to attend in the shop – hopefully.

Adam pulled a face, collected the spade and the barrow and set about shovelling the ordure out of the sty and trundling it down the garden plot to the heap behind the privy. There, it would rot down, to be used to replenish the earth around the leeks and worts. He had no intention, though, of making a habit of doing Nessie's vile chores. And, to judge from the clucking protests and frantic scrabbling noises coming from the chicken run, she hadn't fed the hens either.

Having washed himself down and changed into sweeter-smelling clothes, Adam was ready to face the day. Seb had his head down, still puzzling over that wretched astrology text and Kate, wearing a less than joyous face, awaited customers in the shop.

'I shan't be gone for long, lass,' Adam told her as he went out. 'I need more thread to stitch those primers. I'm that tired of the very sight of them. I'll be right glad when the last one is done – for now, leastwise.'

'If you're going to Paul's,' Kate said, managing a smile, 'Master Seb said I was in need of a new squirrel-hair brush, one with a very fine point to it.'

'I'll see what I can find for you. If what I get 'tis not fine enough, Master Seb will show you how to trim it to suit.'

# St Paul's Cathedral

St Paul's nave was busy as a beehive, though a deal noisier as the voices of tradesmen, hucksters calling their wares and choristers practising their scales all echoed and re-echoed to the high roof above, combining in a cacophony of sound. It had taken Adam a while to get used to London's crowds and ceaseless racket, after the quiet Brecklands of his Norfolk home. He was certain there were more folk here, in the cathedral aisles, buying and selling, than the entire population of Foxley village.

Adam went to Giles Honeywell's stall, the best for any stationer's needs, although the old fellow also had a licence to sell holy relics, some of which looked suspiciously like ancient chicken bones, scraps of rags and horse hair.

'Good day, Master Honeywell. I trust you are in good health?'

'Bearing up, Master Armitage, bearing up.' Honeywell gave a toothless smile. 'What are your needs this morn?'

'Linen thread. 'Tis only for stitching cheap primers, so not your expensive bleached stuff. Unbleached will serve the purpose. And a fine brush of squirrel hair, if you have one?'

'Of course I have more than one. When has Giles Honeywell

ever failed to supply your requirements? I pride myself upon…'

'Aye, no doubt you do but my thread, master? I am somewhat in haste this day.'

Honeywell pulled a face. He liked to gossip with his customers; it generally encouraged sales.

'And I have pounce – the most finely ground in London, for whitening parchment and boards.'

'I have no need.' Adam was growing impatient, tapping his foot as the old man turned away to sort through his storage baskets and boxes piled behind his stall. Just then, an apprentice arrived.

'I've come to collect Master Collop's order,' the lad announced without the least pretence of courtesy or any acknowledgement that Adam was there before him.

'Hey. Stand back and take your turn, you unmannered young rascal,' Adam told him.

'But I'm on Master Richard Collop's business. He's Warden of the Stationers' Company.' The lad puffed out his skinny chest and held his head high.

'I don't care if he's the Archangel Michael. You'll await your turn as others do.' Adam knew exactly who Richard Collop was but reckoned that no excuse for discourtesy.

'His order is most urgent.' The apprentice sniffed significantly. He wasn't so tall but gave Adam such a look of disdain, Adam wondered if the stink of the pigsty yet lingered about him. He was in no mood for this. Having been humbled by Jack earlier, this scallywag-apprentice wasn't going to win the contest. Adam grabbed the youngster by the ear, pinching it hard, and dragged him aside. He'd had his fill of unmannerly youth for one morn: first Jack and now this rapscallion.

'One more word from you and your master will learn of it. I have the ear…' Adam pinched harder to make his point, 'Of Master Sebastian Foxley who, in turn, has the ear of the Duke of Gloucester… understand me?'

The lad muttered a reply. Adam released his hold and gained

satisfaction from seeing the ear so vivid a shade of vermilion. He grinned. It was a wonder what the mere mention of a royal name could achieve. It seemed to work on Honeywell too as the old man had lined up a half dozen bobbins of linen thread of varying qualities and a selection of his best brushes for Adam to make his choice. The apprentice was ignored, shuffling his feet and mumbling obscenities under his breath whilst he waited.

Adam was taking his time to choose his purchases. Despite insisting before that he was in haste, he now took pleasure in forcing the apprentice to wait longer still. Amongst Honeywell's clutter of so-called holy relics, he espied a carven figure.

'What's this?' he asked, picking up a likeness of a horse, whittled from limewood and of a size to fit in the palm of his hand.

'Carved by Our Saviour's own hand whilst he worked in St Joseph's carpentry shop, so 'tis true to life, as you would expect of the Creator himself.' Giles beamed, hopeful of another purchase. 'Of course, being Our Lord's own handiwork, it doesn't come cheap.'

'How much?'

'Sixpence.'

'Thruppence.'

'Nay. Five pence at least.'

'A groat.'

'Fourpence ha'penny and it's yours.'

'Done.' It was a high price to pay and Adam was under no illusion as to it being the work of Jesu Christ but it was well done and finely made. Neither was it a relic to warrant prayers being offered up but Adam had in mind that the little wooden horse was, in itself, a perfect offering.

With his other purchases stowed safely in his scrip, Adam bade Honeywell 'good day' and left him to serve the red-eared apprentice who gave him a glowering look as they parted.

# The Hutchinson House, Distaff Lane

Somehow, Adam's footsteps did not take him back to Paternoster Row but rather out of the door in the cathedral's south transept, across the precinct and through the gate onto Watling Street. He turned down The Old Change opposite St Augustine's church and found himself standing before a particular door on the corner of Distaff Lane. He knocked but feared of a sudden that there might be no one at home. His fears proved groundless.

'Master Armitage! What a welcome surprise. Come you in.' Mercy Hutchinson ushered him through the door. Her smile proved a candle as kindled gladness in his heart. Such a pleasant change after the sorrowful airs of the Foxley household. 'What brings you to my door, sir?'

'I happened to be passing.' The lie slid easily from Adam's lips.

'You must be in need of my excellent ale and wafers then?'

'Aye, those too, if you have time to spare?'

He glanced around the homely kitchen. The youngest of the Hutchinson brood was well swaddled, bound to a board and the whole hung by a loop of rope from two pegs high on the wall, out of harm's way. The tiny lad cooed and gurgled, waving his little fists at Adam, watching all that went on. Adam went to him, giving the babe his finger, which was gripped firmly.

'Well, little fellow, that's some considerable strength you have there.'

'Aye. My sister reckons our Mundy will be a rich man someday, keeping a tight hold upon every penny he makes.' Mistress Hutchinson served her unexpected visitor with his refreshment and sat upon the stool across the board from him to share the wafers.

''Tis no bad thing. I could likely learn to my advantage from his fine example.' Adam wasn't thinking so much of money as of

257

his life back in Foxley village, which time and distance made all the merrier than it probably was. 'Where are the others?' Adam asked to make conversation.

'Simon is at Paul's School. He will be overjoyed now Will Thatcher is back upon the bench beside him. We all are. You must tell me all that came to pass.'

'I told you all about our misadventures in Lambeth Marshes at dinner yesterday.'

'I know but such a fine tale deserves more than one telling. I would hear it again, Master Adam.'

' Adam will suffice. Another time for certain. But where is young Nicholas?'

'Sleeping in his cot, heaven be praised.' She sighed. 'He leads me such a merry dance every hour that he is awake, I welcome the moments when he sleeps.'

'I've brought him a gift.' Adam bent down and opened his scrip. ''Tis something I hope will amuse him and keep him from mischief for a while.' He handed her the carven horse.

'Oh, Adam, it's beautiful.' She examined it closely. 'I can see every hair in its mane and its little hooves are quite perfect. But 'tis too good for Nicholas. He would snap off its legs and tail as soon as he had hold of it, I fear. With your permission, I shall put it upon the shelf, out of his reach, until he has learned to take more care – if he ever does. Meanwhile, I can look at it every day and treasure it, knowing you carved it with your own hands out of affection for us.'

'Aye, well…' Adam had not thought to claim the artistry as his own but, somehow, the denial never quite reached his tongue.

'I did not realise you had such skill. Thank you.' She kissed him on the cheek.

'It was a pleasure,' he said, as she brushed against him.

'I beg pardon.' She pulled away and straightened her bodice, revealing damp patches upon the cloth. 'Forgive me. 'Tis nigh the hour for the babe's nursing and I leak milk worse than any she-goat.' Mercy was clearly embarrassed by her body's overabundance. 'I could likely feed an army of babes.'

'Then I'll leave you in peace.' Adam stood and took up his scrip. 'My thanks for the ale and wafers – good as ever, mistress. May God keep all in this house.' Touching his cap, Adam departed. It had been a satisfactory morn, indeed.

## The Foxley House

'Ah. Back at last,' Seb said upon glancing up and seeing Adam before returning his eyes to the pages of notes upon his desk.

'Aye, well, some matter arose…' Adam hoped his cousin wouldn't enquire further. 'I'll get back to my stitching, now I have the thread.'

He was about to sit at the collating table when a great outcry above startled them.

Seb was off his stool and down the passage to the kitchen as if his boots were afire. Up the stair, he flew, along the upper passage to his bedchamber door. And there he stopped.

'Em? Rose? What be amiss?' he called, not daring to enter.

No answer came from within.

'Rose! What goes on? Tell me, I pray you.'

At last, Rose opened the door and pushed Nessie through.

'Go and get dry linen, you clumsy creature,' Rose said, her face flushed and her cap askew.

Nessie was in tears, an empty pewter basin in her hand as she edged past Seb.

'What occurred, Rose? Has aught happened to Emily?' Seb asked, twisting the laces of his jerkin around anxious fingers.

'Nessie upended an entire bowl of water, soaking all the clean towels we had.' Rose was shaking her head.

'I could enquire of the neighbours whether they might spare us one or two towels,' Seb suggested. 'Was that all that happened?'

'The bowl clattered as it hit the linen press.'

'But we heard a scream.'

'That was just Nessie, over-playing her part, as usual. Fear not, Seb, I didn't take Em's broom to her, though she deserves it for her carelessness.'

'And how does Em fare?'

'Mistress Warren has made her comfortable.'

Seb was not sure what to make of that vague reply.

'What of the babe?'

'Not yet.'

He nodded. Those answers would have to suffice, he supposed. He was but an ignorant man, even if he was her husband and father of the child.

'I shall go, ask the neighbours for towels,' he said as the bedchamber door was closed to him.

Seb first went to the Caldicotts, being their nearest neighbours, Gawain trailing in his wake. Mistress Caldicott was obliging and said she would take some towels next door as soon as she had sorted out what might be spared. Unfortunately, she also seized the opportunity to ask Seb how the new version of the astrology book was progressing.

''Tis my brother Martin's birthday next month, don't forget,' she reminded him.

'I be doing my best, mistress,' he said, 'But what with it being Eastertide, a lad going missing and my goodwife continuing unwell...'

'Don't give me excuses, Master Foxley. I want that book finished in good time. Now go to, or you'll not get another penny out of me.'

'Aye, mistress,' he said, wishing he had asked elsewhere first.

'And take that dog with you; last time he filched my cheese.'

'My apologies for that. Gawain has ever been partial to the

stuff. God give you good day... and my thanks for the towels.'

Along Cheapside, he called upon Dame Ellen, who supplied a goodly number of towels but at the price of hearing every detail of his goodwife's plight. She was unimpressed by Seb's lack of knowledge of poor Emily's condition.

'You menfolk just don't trouble yourselves to find out, do you? 'Tis not sufficient to say you care when, quite obviously, you don't give a jot. Now be careful to mark which are *my* towels; I want them back – clean and laundered, mind – when you're done with them. And tell Nell Warren she's to come here and give me a full report as soon as possible, since you cannot be bothered. Emily was my best apprentice; I deserve to know how she fares.'

Seb left with a pile of towels, having been thoroughly taken to task for his abject failings by two women. He could but hope Peronelle Wenham would not chastise him further.

Thankfully, she didn't. What was more, she said she would deliver the towels and some spare sheets, in person, and assist the Foxleys in any way she could. Her only complaint was that Seb should have asked for aid before now.

Having given Old Symkyn greetings and put a penny in his bowl as he sat at Cheap Cross, Seb's last call was upon Beatrice Thatcher. She had little linen to lend and, what with a husband and two children, even less time to spare but she gave what she could: three fraying towels that were so thin they would hardly serve to dry finger tips. But Seb was grateful for those and even more thankful that Beatrice had not a single word of admonition to speak against him.

He was making his way back along Cheapside, his scrip, emptied of his own scrivener's bits and pieces, now bulging with acquired towels, when he noticed a man, pushing an empty handcart, one wheel squeaking at every turn. He had seen him previously, had he not? The fellow had been of interest for some reason but, for the present, Seb's thoughts were all of Emily, women in a flap, towels, astrological notations, moody youngsters and Tom's unsolved murder that he could not call to mind why that was. Even so, he noted that the man turned into Bladder Street and the butchers' Shambles. If and when he remembered the reason, he knew to make enquiries there and, mayhap, of his friend the gatekeeper at Newgate, if the man passed through.

For now, Seb hastened home with the borrowed linen.

Peace had been restored. Rose sat in the kitchen, changing little Dickon's tail-clout upon her lap.

Seb emptied his scrip, piling the clean towels on the board.

'Mistress Wenham says she will bring more,' Seb said, 'And has offered her aid in any way, which is kindly, indeed.'

'Aye, Pen's a good soul,' Rose said, tying the lacings on the infant's smock and setting him down on a blanket under the board to play with his rag ball. 'If she can take my place, assisting Mistress Warren for a while, I may set to preparing us some dinner.'

'Can Nessie not do that?'

Rose's look of despair told him the answer.

'Nessie is in such dither over Em being unwell that she's worse than useless. I sent her out to buy bread, seeing we've had no chance to make our own dough.'

'I shall tell Kate she may help you. Adam and I can manage the shop betwixt us. Oh, and Dame Ellen demands a report on Em's progress from Mistress Warren some time. You know how she has a deep regard for Em.'

'I can't see that happening very soon, Seb. Em is most unwell but the babe seems in no haste to make its appearance. I know not even whether the babe be the cause of it or no, but it cannot be helping her situation. I wish we knew more about what's going on. Nell Warren seems as mystified as anyone, despite having been midwife to at least a hundred confinements, so she says, but none quite as this one.'

Dinner was a thrown-together affair but tasty for all that, owing to Rose's skill with last year's dried herbs. The new season's were barely showing green shoots as yet. However, food was of small interest to any but Jack who was eating his third helping of frumenty – a vegetable pottage, thickened with wheat grains instead of oats, Nessie having forgotten the latter at the market.

'Master Appleyard wants t' know 'ow she's doin',' Jack said, speaking around a mouthful of bread. 'An' wants t' be told soon as his new gran'child comes, don't 'e?'

'She? Is that any way to refer to your mistress?' Adam said sternly. He was about to say more and cuff Jack's ear but thought better of rousing the lad's anger after this morn's debacle.

During the meal, Thaddeus Turner arrived and was offered a share. Since Seb, Rose and Kate had little appetite, there was food enough and to spare.

'I'm going to Paul's School this afternoon, to speak with the Thatcher lad,' the bailiff explained. 'When I tried to ask him questions at his home yesterday, his mother gave answer on his behalf to all my enquiries and fussed about him as though he had barely recovered from some grave sickness. The lad himself begged her not to make so much of his past encounters but she did not cease in her over-agitated concern for him. I realised I was uncovering no new information and determined to continue my questioning at his school. The master has been informed and is agreeable to stand *in loco parentis,* as is right and proper, but I wondered if your friendly presence, Seb, might not only reassure the lad but, mayhap, jog his memory on certain points. And you're skilful at judging whether folk speak true or false. Will you come with me?'

'Ah, I know you well enough, my friend,' Seb said, laying down his spoon, though his bowl was yet half full. 'What you truly ask for are my services as a scrivener and note-taker. You ought to insist that the city hires a secretary to aid you; some idle clerk with naught better to occupy him.'

'So you won't come?'

'I ne'er said that. Of course I shall come, if only to be certain your interrogation does not overstep the mark and distress the lad. To my mind, his mother has the right of it, to be concerned for his state of mind. Nonetheless, I do believe you have need of a scrivener to record your enquiries – other than myself.'

'Aye, but none can better you for speed and neatness of penmanship, Seb.' Thaddeus hoped a little flattery would encourage his friend.

'Your fulsome praise be unnecessary. I have said I will accompany you. I shall fetch my scrip directly.'

## St Paul's Cathedral Song School

The Song School was attached to the Bishop's Palace, on its southern side. The entrance to the two-roomed building opened off Bowyer Row, hard by Ludgate. The schoolroom, with its tiered benches for the scholars on either side, had seating enough for, perhaps, forty lads, to learn to read, write and sing in St Paul's choir. The master's canopied chair upon a dais at the far end was an impressive piece of furniture. A rack of birch rods, looking well used, stood as an ominous testament to past – and future – punishments, placed conveniently at the master's right hand.

When Seb and Bailiff Turner walked into the schoolroom, the younger pupils were reciting second conjugation Latin verbs. The older lads, on the higher forms behind, were scribbling diligently with chalk upon their slates whilst the uppermost bench on either hand had each a pair of scholars sharing a battered volume. Seb noted that the spines of both were broken with long usage and, in one case, missing entirely. Surely such a venerable institution could afford better than that? If the opportunity offered, he would speak with the master concerning rebinding, or even replacement of the old books, perhaps offering a discount – a small one, lest Emily berate him for his generosity. The room smelled of chalk dust and grubby youngsters with a faint tang of urine, as if someone had suffered a mishap of Nature's calling.

Seb's brother Jude had attended here, sitting on those same forms, reading those same battered texts, but Seb had been refused a place, being lame and bent of back in those days. The Bishop of London had deemed him unfit, as though his misshapenness was a contagion that might infect others. Even his father's offer to pay an additional fee and pointing out that young Seb's voice was sweeter than any other chorister's had failed to change the bishop's mind. Thus, Seb had been taught his lessons at home by his father. He had never felt any lack in his learning for all that, although he had wanted, more than anything, to sing those glorious anthems, harmonise the beautiful psalms and give those clear responses with the cathedral choristers. But he had made his mark on that score since, though not so often of late. The precentor had sent him a stern reprimand, in writing, for having failed to attend choir practice on Saturday last but Seb hoped his performance of the *Jubilate* at Vespers on Easter Sunday had made amends. Of course, the precentor had said not a word of approval after – that was never his way – but at least he had made no complaint of Seb's singing.

The master rose from his throne-like seat behind the lectern on the dais.

'Bailiff Turner,' he said in greeting without offering his hand since both were out of sight, tucked within the wide sleeves of his academic gown. The books might have seen better days but the master's gown looked new and of high-quality woollen cloth.

'Doctor Hawthorn, I thank you for agreeing to this meeting.

This is Master Foxley. He will be joining us. He is known to
William Thatcher and found the lad after he was abducted. He
is also acting as my clerk.'

Clerk, indeed? Seb thought.

Doctor Hawthorn gave a curt nod.

'Thatcher!' he bellowed. '*Veni mecum*.' He turned without
waiting for the lad to join them and led the way through the
door behind the dais, into the master's private inner sanctum.
The smell here was quite different.

Seb breathed in the familiar scent of old books, parchment,
and ink for the room also served as the school's library and
scriptorium. If anything, it was larger than the schoolroom,
but the shelves, with every volume chained in its place, took up
much of the space. Seb looked longingly at those shelves. How
he would enjoy an hour or two, leafing through the pages of
books unknown to him, taking pleasure in the feel of them, the
weight of knowledge in his hands.

Doctor Hawthorn cleared his throat meaningfully, drawing
Seb's attention back to the matter in hand.

'You can do your work there,' the master told Seb, directing
him to a desk in the far corner. Hawthorn sat behind a large
table with books piled upon it, indicating that Thaddeus should
take a lowly stool. Will Thatcher was to stand before the table,
facing the master.

Seb was displeased. The desk would make his task of note-
taking easier but from there he was unable to see Will's face,
only the back of the lad's head. How was he to gauge whether
the youngster's responses were truthful, or his degree of distress,
if the enquiries became too much for him?

'Are you well, William?' Bailiff Turner began.

'You may answer in English for the benefit of the bailiff,'
Doctor Hawthorne put in.

'Aye, thank you, sir,' Will said, his voice so soft, Seb hardly
heard him.

'Don't be afeared, lad. I do but want to hear your story, in your own words,' Thaddeus said. 'Tell me about the man who abducted – took you away. Take your time.'

Seb saw the master scowl at that. No doubt he did not want to waste a moment more on this matter than was necessary.

'Well, sir, it was Cain who took me. I didn't want to go, but he told me Mam had said I should go with him, that he had something to show me. But by the time he was dragging me across the Bridge, I knew it wasn't true 'cos Mam said I mustn't ever go there without her or Pa.'

'Had you ever seen this man Cain before?'

'Oh, aye. We – the other scholars and me – had seen him a few times, usually as we were arriving at school. He used to speak to some of us. Before Eastertide, he'd talked to Albus a few times 'specially. I think he liked Albus but I don't know what happened to him. He hasn't come to school of late.'

'Who is Albus?' Thaddeus asked, looking at the master.

'Edward Robbins. His fellows here have given him the by-name "Albus" because of his hair.'

Seb had put down his pen and was searching in his scrip for the copies of the likenesses Adam had given him in Southwark after his own were removed whilst he lay senseless at The Mermaid. His heart had lurched upon hearing "Albus", knowing it meant "white" in Latin.

'Pardon my intrusion, Doctor Hawthorn,' Seb said, speaking for the first time. He approached the table, offering the sketch of the white-haired lad who had died in his workshop. 'Might this be Edward Robbins?'

'It may have a resemblance,' the master said after a cursory glance. He did not take the paper forwhy that would require taking his hands out of the sleeves of his gown.

'What do you think, Will?' Seb asked, giving him the drawing and wondering why he had never thought to ask here, at the school, afore now, nor shown the drawing to Will. In truth, he had not thought the death of one lad and the abduction of another to be connected.

'I've never seen Albus asleep but it looks like him, without his grin. He always grins and laughs.'

Seb did not correct the lad's supposition that the drawing was of a sleeper. Better that than knowing it depicted the face of a friend now dead. It was a solemn realisation that the poor sad corpse he had found upon Palm Sunday morn had been grinning and laughing not so long ago, yet now lay cold, interred in St Michael's churchyard. At least he had a name at long last: Edward Robbins.

'Go on with your story, Will. What more can you tell us of this man Cain?' Thaddeus said, gesturing Seb back to his place at the desk with a nod of his head, as if to a lackey.

Seb obliged and took up his pen once more. At least one mystery had been solved.

# Chapter 15

## Tuesday afternoon
## St Paul's Cathedral Song School

THE INTERVIEW with Will Thatcher continued with Bailiff Turner teasing out information from the lad.

Seb was impressed with Thaddeus' methods, surprised and relieved at his gentleness of manner.

Will told them of the woman, Bessie, and the others who lived at The Mermaid. Seb recognised, from the lad's descriptions, some of those he had encountered in Southwark: Peaches and Katerina had been kind to him, Will said, and the others less so. But it was hard-eyed Bessie who had charge of the tavern – or house of ill-repute as Seb now knew it to be. She ordered the rest, including the infamous Cain. But Will made no mention of that strange creature Eleanor who had turned out to be a man, so, hopefully, the lad had not crossed the path of that one. Otherwise, this part of the tale tallied with Seb's own experiences. But the second part of the story was new: that Will had been bought and sold like a sheep at market.

'Two marks they paid to Bessie for me,' Will said. 'Just two. Like that was all I was worth. Mam would've paid a fortune for me, if she had it. But his lordship had hardly any money anyway, I heard his servant saying. And he was mad as a cat with its fur afire. Kept calling me Henry, though I told him my name was Will. Said I was his son and heir but, of course,

269

I wasn't. He pretended to be a horse and wanted to play chess with walnuts 'cos some of the pieces were missing. Oh, and we had to pretend that the stale old food was a fine feast. I escaped the first chance I saw.'

'Do you know the name of this so-called lord?' Thaddeus asked.

'The servant, Walter, called him Lord Pierpoint. And they spoke of someone called Sir Marcus, though Lord Pierpoint said of this Sir Marcus that he was no son of his. So I don't know if he was or not. If he was, then why did his lordship want me? I think they're all mad. And then I ran away. Trouble was, I didn't know how to get home. I'd never been to Lambeth before. I didn't want to go past that place again, where Bessie had kept me in that horrible cellar, but Cain had said something about a Horse Ferry and I wondered if I might get home that way but I had no coin for the fare.' Will's voice was quivering of a sudden.

'There now, 'tis over and done with, lad,' Thaddeus said, patting the youngster's shoulder. 'You're safe now. But can you tell us… do you know whereabouts in Lambeth you were?'

Will nodded and swallowed down the threat of tears.

'Aye, sir. We were at The Three Feathers Inn. When I asked Cain about the grand gateway nearby, he said it was the Archbishop's Palace. And he told me, too, about the ruined place out on the marsh being once a hermit's house. So that's where I hid so they wouldn't find me. But you found me there, Master Seb,' Will said, turning round, the beginnings of a grin upon his face. 'You and Gawain and Master Adam.'

'*Sufficit!*' the master bellowed, coming to his feet. 'Thatcher, *ut de.*'

Will bowed to the master and returned to the school-room, half running, which brought forth another order to walk, as the regulations required.

'I beg pardon, Doctor Hawthorn, but I had other questions,' the bailiff objected.

'I said that was enough. I cannot waste any further time

on this matter and the boy has his lessons to do, having fallen behind due to unauthorised absence.'

'Unauthorised? The child was abducted.' Thaddeus was aghast.

'*Valete.*' The master turned his back and stalked out, gown rustling, expecting Seb and Thaddeus to follow.

Seb packed his writing stuff back into scrip, along with the well-thumbed sketches, and hastened after.

'Who does he think he is?' the bailiff muttered. 'God?'

'Likely he seems that way to his *discipuli,*' Seb said.

'Disciples?'

'Pupils. The word is the same in Latin.'

'Oh. No wonder I hate foreign tongues, if they can't tell a saint from a schoolboy.'

'You required more information from Will? Mayhap, I can supply it, or Adam may know.'

'No… I think I have more than enough for a warrant of arrest for those whores at The Mermaid. This Pierpoint fellow, who paid for the abduction, maybe more difficult, especially if he truly is a lord, though a mad one.'

'Discrete enquiries could be made. The Duke of Gloucester's man of law, Master Metcalfe, be known to me…'

'That might be a help, Seb, if you could.'

'I shall, if the opportunity arises. Yet I also had a question to ask here, not of Will but of Doctor Hawthorn.'

'Prickly as his name, damn him,' Thaddeus said, fastening his cloak. 'What is your enquiry?'

Seb lifted his scrip and made for the door that led out into the school-room.

'I would ask where Albus – Edward Robbins – dwelt. I may close that sorry episode once his family has been informed of his death and I have shown them his grave in St Michael's, that they can put a name upon his marker. I shall ask the master as we leave.'

'Then you're a braver man than I, Seb.'

271

Seb's approach of the master's chair on its dais was met with a ferocious scowl. Doctor Hawthorn's piercing eyes glowed like coals in a furnace but Seb bowed and removed his cap with utmost courtesy.

'*Quid nunc?*' the master growled, so Seb asked his question in faultless Latin, explaining why he needed to know Edward Robbins' address. The master appeared to mellow slightly and, despite a deal of muttering, in Latin, of course, he deigned to return to the room where they had questioned Will, beckoning to Seb. There, he fetched a large ledger from a locked chest behind his table, thudding it down thereon, raising dust. He leafed through the pages. The ledger contained details of every scholar, past and present – including Jude Foxley, no doubt – their parent or guardian and records of fees paid. '*Hic.*' The master tapped the page with his long fingernail.

Seb read, in Latin, that Edward Robbins' schooling was being paid for by his father, John Robbins, a basket-weaver of Holbourne, who lived by the church of St Andrew, beside that stretch of the Fleet River known as Turnmill Brook.

'*Gratias tibi ago, magister,*' Seb said, earning a nod that might almost have been of approval. It never did any harm to render thanks appropriately, he thought. '*Vale, domino.*'

'You were showing off your knowledge there, my friend.'

Seb was unsure whether Thaddeus was disapproving or not.

'Indeed, I was and attained the result as I hoped. If I ingratiated myself to some small degree, I make no apology. Some day, I may wish my own son to attend here and, having impressed upon Doctor Hawthorn that I be more than a humble clerk, hardly able to write my ABC, mayhap, he will prove more agreeable to educating my child.'

'Sorry. I irked you, didn't I, calling you my clerk? Making you sound like my paid servant.'

Seb shrugged indifference but Thaddeus had hit the mark.

'No matter. Shall we share a jug of ale? So many questions and a deal of note-taking deserve a respite and refreshment.'

# The Panyer Inn

Thaddeus was somewhat surprised when, instead of returning home, as he would've expected, Seb led the way to The Panyer Inn, farther along Paternoster Row, towards St Michael's. He was more alarmed when, by the way, Seb ducked into the door of that dire ale house opposite, Mitchet's, the one every sensible man avoided like a case of plague. Fortunately, he did not purchase any of their suspect wares that few dare drink.

'Whose eye were you trying to avoid, Seb?' Thaddeus asked as they found a pair of vacant stools in the far corner of The Panyer.

'Mary Caldicott's. My transcription of an astrological text she has commissioned from me be proving a bane, indeed. Merely thinking of it causes me eye-strain and a headache. I know not if it will e'er be finished afore I go blind. Yet she has driven a hard bargain. I shall reap little reward for my painstaking labours.'

'Tell her it is indecipherable. Be honest: say you can't do it.'

'Mm. It may come to that but I'll give it one day more. It would be a pity to waste what I have managed to untangle of its arcane language. And so many deletions, insertions and annotations…'

Thaddeus succeeded in catching the attention of a tapster and ordered a jug of the best ale, bread and cheese.

'Sounds like a nightmare to me. Why ever did you agree to do it?'

'It did not appear so bad at first glance. And, I admit, somewhat of vanity on my part, thinking I be a better transcriber than be truly the case.'

'Serves you right, then,' Thaddeus said with a laugh. 'Drink your ale; it'll cheer you before you must resume your labour of Hercules. And don't forget, I shall be needing a neat and legible version of this afternoon's notes.'

Seb groaned and pulled a face.

'And I have the unenviable task of visiting the Robbins family at Holbourne, to deliver my sorrowful tidings concerning their son.'

'You want me to come with you?'

'Nay. The sight of the City Bailiff may affright the neighbours and set tongues a-wagging, although...'

'What is it?'

''Tis just foolish fancy, no doubt, but of late, I have had this notion that someone be following me. Not always but... 'tis likely so much nonsense.'

'Then it's a good thing you have Gawain to protect you.'

At the mention of his name, the dog bestirred himself from lying at their feet, sat up and looked at his master with beseeching brown eyes.

'Now see what you have done, Thaddeus. Oh, very well, you artful creature...' Seb cut a piece of cheese and held it out. Gawain took it from betwixt his fingers with the grace of a lady and swallowed it down without chewing. He then gave Seb's hand a thorough licking to be certain not a crumb was missed. 'The thing with having Gawain as my bodyguard,' Seb said, stroking the dog's silky ears, ''Tis not to be relied upon. Any would-be assailant need only offer him a tit-bit and gains a friend for life.'

Gawain put a great muddy paw on Seb's knee.

'No more, not after your antics last eve, you greedy scamp.'

'What happened then?' Thaddeus broke the remaining bread in two and munched on his share.

'Oh, Nessie was her usual careless self. We were to have leeks in a white sauce for supper, the dish to be dressed with crisp-fried bacon pieces. She set the pan aside on the hearth to cool for a moment...'

Thaddeus laughed aloud.

'And the dog got to them first?'

'Aye, and ate every bit, licking the pan clean of every last trace. He knew he was in the wrong. When I spoke his name right sharply, his tail went down, his ears drooped and he took himself away into the farthest corner.'

'I trust you beat him. He sore deserved it.'

'Nay. How could I? The expression in his eye was that sorrowful... if he had speech, he would have begged pardon, I know. Besides... there be too much pain and suffering in this world; I cannot bring myself to add to it.'

'You know your trouble, Seb? You're too soft-hearted.'

'So they tell me.' Seb sighed and refilled their cups, draining the ale-jug.

'I warrant, you'd be willing to cause suffering to any miscreant who threatened or hurt those you love.'

'Mayhap. Let us hope the day ne'er comes that I be put to the test.' Seb stood and fished in his purse for coin to pay for their ale but Thaddeus waved it away.

''Tis on my account, if you get those notes written up for me, in full, by the morn.'

'I shall and get them to you, first thing. Now, I have a solemn task to accomplish in Holbourne. God give you good day, my friend. Come, Gawain.'

## The Three Feathers Inn, Lambeth

'You've a visitor, milord,' the innkeeper, discourteous as ever when money was owing, shouted up the stairs.

'Well, don't delay, you great oaf; show him up.' Lord Pierpoint yelled back without stirring from his chair.

Walter sighed. His lordship was losing all sense of propriety and matters had deteriorated since the boy, Will – as he'd said was his name – had run away. After the first realisation that the child was gone, when his anger and disbelief had subsided, the old man had shrugged, muttering about youngsters today not appreciating what was best for them. Then, to Walter's dismay, he'd simply concluded that they would buy another fair-haired lad, as though children were but pairs of shoes to be replaced as and when.

The man who came up did not require escorting.

'Sir Marcus,' Walter bowed, 'I'm so glad you've come.'

The man was tall, broad of shoulder and, perhaps, about two-score years or so in age. His blond hair was greying around his ears. Clean-shaven and distinguished in feature there was, even so, some familial resemblance betwixt the visitor and Lord Pierpoint.

Much to Walter's relief, Sir Marcus was clad in attire befitting a prosperous citizen, not his lawyer's robes – the mere sight of the latter would likely have set the old man off on another rant against all members of the legal profession whom he detested. His hatred grew from the simple fact that the wretched profession had 'stolen away' his second son – Sir Marcus.

All had been well until his lordship's elder son and heir, Lord Henry, had been killed in a riding accident five years before. His lordship had been overcome by grief and then by anger when Sir Marcus, now the heir, had refused to abandon his lucrative legal career to become a minor lordling with virtually no income and fewer prospects; just a ruinous manor and a dwindling estate mortgaged away to pay mountainous debts.

But Sir Marcus did not forget his filial obligations. If not for his fat purse and skilful management of matters of law, his penniless father might well have been in court before now for non-payment of those debts. Yet Lord Pierpoint remained ignorant, perhaps wilfully so, of his son's efforts on his behalf. Hence, his insane desire to purchase a new heir!

Even as Walter approved Sir Marcus having discarded his usual lawyer's garb, a new difficulty arose.

Lord Pierpoint looked his visitor up and down, frowning.

'Well, sir? Introduce yourself. Who the devil are you to

interrupt my affairs?'

Sir Marcus looked surprised.

'I am your son, sir. I'm aware you have disowned me but you must know who I am, surely?'

'I don't know you from the King of the Indies. If it's money you want, you can get out now. I'm not in a charitable mood.' The old man waved Sir Marcus away and stared out of the window instead.

'Wine, Sir Marcus?' Walter offered, hoping his lordship would regain his wits and his memory shortly, as was often the case.

The lawyer declined. Although he had paid for the wine by settling his father's reckoning with the innkeeper just now, he had tasted The Feathers' vinegary offerings before and did not intend to repeat the experience.

'Father,' he said softly, approaching his lordship's chair. 'You know me. I am Marcus, your son. Your only son.'

The old man turned and looked at him. Sir Marcus bent low, so that father and son were eye to eye. For a moment, there seemed to be a flash of recognition in those faded blue eyes but then it was gone.

'I know you not. Stay away from me.' The old man shoved his son away with such force, he lost his balance and landed on his backside among the grubby rushes on the floor.

Walter held his breath, fearful of what Sir Marcus might do in retaliation for the insult. But Sir Marcus got to his feet, brushed himself down and turned to Walter.

'He is worse than I thought. When you told me of his deterioration, I hoped you were exaggerating the case. The truth is sad to behold: that the father I admired and respected is reduced to this.' As he spoke, Sir Marcus was shaking his head, watching as Lord Pierpoint sat, humming to himself and purposefully enlarging a moth-hole in his gown, tearing it until he could fit his hand through it. 'A sorry, sorry state of affairs, Walter. What is to be done with him? He cannot remain in this disgusting inn. I'm aware you care for him and deserve every gratitude but receive none. He must be a burden and a grave responsibility for you to bear...'

'But I would not have it otherwise, sir,' Walter interrupted. 'Having served him all these years, in good times and bad, I would not desert Lord Pierpoint now, when he needs me more than he ever did. If I may speak over-boldly, sir: I am his only friend.'

'You're a good man, Walter. Even so, things cannot go on this way...'

'Cease your confounded chatter!' Lord Pierpoint burst out. 'Get about your duties, you idle pair, or I'll dismiss you both. Alan, see to my horse. Bartram, get back to the kitchen, or I'll take my whip to you.' The moment passed and he returned to gazing out the window.

'I shall make some more fitting arrangements for him,' Sir Marcus continued, 'But fear not, Walter, you shall serve him for as long as you wish. I just pray he does not drive you to distraction also.'

# Holbourne

Passing by Newgate, Seb saw Mistress Fletcher standing at the door of The Hart's Horn. She waved a greeting which he returned, but his thoughts were all upon how best to break the ill-news to Edward Robbins' family, which words might be most kindly. Only later did it occur to him: Mistress Fletcher had given him the first small clue long ago, concerning the Robbins family, when she had told him of some white-haired children once dwelling at Holbourne. She had proved correct, so it seemed, and they lived there still, according to the school ledger.

Seb made his way up Snaws Hill, beyond St Sepulchre's Church and The Saracen's Head Inn, onto Seacole Lane. Where

Cock Lane – the city's haunt of loose women and all breeds of ne'er-do-wells – joined the way from the east, Seb hastened westerly, avoiding the unsavoury place, turning up Holbourne Hill by the Cross there. He paused to catch his breath and allow Gawain to lap cool water in the trough at the conduit – better that than have the creature attempt to drink from the River Fleet; you never knew what horrors might lurk 'neath its green-scummed surface.

As he looked down from Holbourne Bridge, Seb was surprised to see the swift-flowing waters, cutting deeply through the land, sparkled clean and wholesome. A watermill turned nearby, tossing diamond droplets as it creaked and splashed, labouring at its task. A glistening streak that was an otter dived from the far bank, slithering down through riverside reeds to enter the water silently. A pair of moorhens busied themselves upon the margin. No wonder the local folk called this stretch Turnmill Brook, mayhap attempting to disown the foetid midden that was the Fleet River downstream.

St Andrew's Church was upon the left hand, its short squat tower catching the late afternoon sun and a chaffinch called his ever-repeating phrase of song from a hazel bush beside the lych gate. It seemed piteous to spoil so pleasant an afternoon as the bearer of sad tidings but it could not be helped.

A few paces beyond the church, a paling fence enclosed a small yard where Seb could see stacks of willow and hazel withies, bundles of reeds and water-filled tubs in which such items could be put to soak. Upon low stools before the door of a neat cottage, there sat three people, each weaving some kind of basket. From eel-traps to trugs, egg baskets to hucksters' trays, the finished wares teetered in lop-sided piles, here and there. A handcart was ready laden with wares for sale on the morrow, in the city. Seb knew this was the Robbins' place forwhy he recognised the man he had seen at the mummers' play with the white-haired lass upon his shoulders. That same child was now treading down split reeds in a tub of water, her hair shining like a saint's halo. Although John Robbins' hair was dark, streaked with grey, 'neath his cap and a woman – likely his goodwife – had her hair tucked away, the third weaver upon his stool was a young lad with hair the same bleached colour as the little lass. Basket-making, it seemed, was the family business.

At that moment, just as Seb came through into the yard, the lad looked up and Seb was nigh stunned, taking a step back, for here was the very face of the deceased that he had drawn. It was like seeing Lazarus arisen from the dead. There could be no mistake: he had found Edward Robbins' family.

Courteous greetings were exchanged, remarks concerning the fine weather and introductions made. The little lass even insisted on making Gawain's acquaintance. Then Seb could delay no longer.

'I fear, Master Robbins, that my visit will bring you and your family no joy. I have to inform you that I found your son, Edward, upon the morn of Palm Sunday, at my place in Paternoster Row. There was naught to be done to aid him but I saw to it that he had the consolations of a gentle priest, Father Thomas of St Michael le Querne church.' Seb had decided there was no need to tell them the lad's soul was departed and his body long since cold when first discovered.

'Our Ned? Why did you not send for us?' the woman shrieked, throwing aside her half-finished basket.

'Mistress, I would have done so, believe me, but he was beyond telling his name. I knew not who he was. If 'tis any comfort to you, I believe the lad was struggling to get home to you when cold and fatigue o'erwhelmed him and he could go no farther.'

'But even then, he had been missing for a fortnight. Where had he been?' The woman's distraught expression changed upon an instant to a scowl of anger. 'What did you do to him? Why was he at your place and why did he die? You kept him locked away. You starved him to death, you Devil's spawn; you filthy toad…' She pounded Seb's chest with her fists.

'Nay, I pray you…'

'Hold off, Mildred.' Master Robbins pulled his goodwife aside, pinning her arms until she subsided, sobbing in his embrace. 'Accept my apologies, Master Foxley. Clearly, there is far more to tell but my wife is in no fit state to hear it. Come you within.' He turned to his lad. 'Gregory! Take your sister to Weller's house and leave her there, then fetch Mother Goodrich to tend your Mam. Make haste.'

It was more than an hour later that Seb left Holbourne having told John Robbins as much as he knew of his son's abduction, what came to pass after and the details of the funeral and interment. He refrained from describing the gruesome cause of their son's death, implying he had died of cold and exhaustion upon the night of the storm. It seemed kinder. He promised to show them the site of his burial marker as soon as was convenient for them. Master Robbins had insisted on paying him the costs involved in the burying and Offices for the Dead in full before he left.

The telling had drained Seb utterly. His ribs were sore, bruised by the poor woman's fists. It was as well that the walk home was downhill.

As they were close to The Hart's Horn, Gawain stopped, turned around, facing back the way they'd come. His ears were flattened and a growl rumbled deep in his belly, his teeth revealed in a snarl.

Seb looked behind. Twilight was descending. There was naught untoward that he could see. A cat, mayhap. Gawain had no liking for any of their kind other than Grayling, who was his companion at the hearth and partner in crime, on occasion.

'Come, Gawain, I would be home for supper.'

They trudged on, Seb's left hip beginning to ache. They were held up at Newgate by a crowd of folk, hastening home to the outlying suburbs, leaving the city afore the gate closed at dusk. At last, they were through and into the Shambles. Gawain turned aside to nose through some vile-looking remains of the day's trade, stinking in the gutter.

'Come away!'

But the dog was alert of a sudden, turning as he had done earlier. The noisome butcher's leavings were forgotten as he snarled, quivering, wolf-like.

'Gawain! Cease your foolishness. There be naught.' Even as he spoke, Seb thought he glimpsed a shadow that did not belong and he shivered, feeling the hairs on the back of his neck rise. Weariness was causing him to see things, imagining what was not there. However, despite his eagerness to be home, his feet avoided turning down the narrow short cut that was Ivy Lane. Rather, he kept to the wider thoroughfare, into Bladder Street, afore turning back upon himself by St Michael's, taking the longer way to Paternoster Row. Gawain seemed calmer, too, once they had passed the entrance to Ivy Lane.

Seb had his own reasons for disliking that dark lane with Lovell's Inn lurking there, menacing the very airs – a place of fearful memory for him. Yet why did Gawain seem to hate it also, having no such memories? It must be, Seb thought, that the dog sensed his master's distrust and behaved likewise. But why, then, had he done the same by The Hart's Horn? Seb liked Mistress Fletcher's inn, her decent ale and fine food – Gawain having appreciated the latter in the past. The inn was not a place of foreboding, yet the dog had acted most strangely.

## The Foxley House

After a disorganised supper, what with Nell Warren having to go home to get some rest but ordering that Emily was not to be left alone, instead of sharing ale in the kitchen or taking his turn at Em's bedside, Seb went to the workshop.

He lit two candles and set out his writing stuff to begin

copying out the notes of the interview with Will Thatcher, in full, in a proper secretary hand. That took him a deal of time, longer than expected, forwhy he had not realised quite how extensive were the notes he had made. Then he made sketches, using his own knowledge, of the woman known as Bessie and the others associated with The Mermaid, as far as he knew. The likenesses would aid Thaddeus in making the arrests when he served the warrant, that he could be certain of apprehending the true culprits.

The candles were burning low, the workshop growing chill as the warmth of the day and brazier basket faded and night brought a frost with a cloudless sky. Seb lit another candle and chafed his cold hands afore taking up his pen once more.

Throughout supper, he had been thinking over the walk back from Holbourne, Gawain's disquiet and his own. Mayhap, it had not been mere foolish fancy; mayhap, they were being followed. It was not the first time, of late, that he had felt that prickle of apprehension betwixt his shoulder blades. He took up his pen once more and began to write.

'Still at work? Aren't you in need of sleep?' Adam came into the workshop, taper in hand. He put a cup on Seb's desk. 'Thought you might need ale. The hour grows late indeed.'

'You go to your bed,' Seb said, without raising his eyes or ceasing the motion of his pen upon the page. 'I shall come when I have completed this letter.'

Nell Warren, as midwife, had this day banished Seb from the marital bed until such time as Emily's confinement was over. Meanwhile, he must share Adam's chamber.

'Letter? To whom do you write at this time of night? Can it not wait?'

''Tis to Thaddeus Turner in his capacity as City Bailiff.'

'But you'll see him in the morn, when you give him those notes. Can you not tell him then, in person?'

'This be not for the morrow, Adam.'

'Then, why the urgency?'

'Forwhy I know not when – nor if – it may be needed.'

'What's it concerning?'

'Better you know not. All I shall say to you is that it will be inside my pigment box, safe from prying eyes and mice. If aught untoward befalls me, Adam, at any time in the future, see it given into Thaddeus' hands, that he may act upon it, or do naught about it, as he sees fit. It will be up to him to determine the consequences of this information.'

'If aught untoward befalls you? What do you mean by that?'

'I think you know full well. Of late, I have come to believe someone has been following me.'

'Who?'

'You do not doubt me then, cousin?'

'Should I?'

'Nay, for Gawain has sensed it also.'

'But why would they and who is doing it?'

'I cannot be certain on either score but I have my suspicions. I first thought someone was stalking me, as a huntsman stalks his quarry, after Tom's body was found. I think the two occurrences be connected. And if that be so… I have written everything in this letter.' Seb took a sip of ale, an action that reminded him. He opened his purse and found among the groats, pennies, ha'pennies and farthings the scrap of paper he'd put there for safe-keeping when he had gone to question the priest at St Andrew-by-the-Wardrobe in Knightrider Street. He had forgotten the bloodied filament from a peacock's feather until he had been about to pay for the ale at The Panyer earlier, when Thaddeus had forestalled him.

He resumed writing, this time explaining how, when and where he had found the feather and why it might prove to be an important piece of evidence.

Adam fetched his stool and watched, wishing he could read upside down.

At last, Seb signed his name at the foot of the third page of neat script before sanding the wet ink. Then, having included that odd little scrap of paper, he folded the sheets with utmost care and melted a stick of red wax in the candle flame. Using a blob of wax, the colour of blood, to affix the folds closed, he pressed the Foxley seal, with its fox's head, into the wax. The task was done.

As he had told Adam he would, Seb wrapped the letter in a square of waste linen, used for wiping brushes, and fitted it into the lid of his pigment box. He closed the lid and sighed.

'Let us get some sleep now, Adam. But first, I must see that Emily be in need of naught, or whosoever be keeping vigil at her bedside.'

'Rose took first watch. Peronelle is likely taking her place about this time.'

'What hour be at hand then?'

''Tis long after midnight; the watching hour passed. St Martin's will be ringing the Matins bell before long. You've done a day's worth of work since supper. Come on, Seb; you too, Gawain.'

Tired though he was, Seb could not sleep. He closed his eyes but thoughts raced around his head. He kept going over the wording of the letter to Thaddeus. Had he omitted any vital detail, any relevant fact? Did it make sense? Would the bailiff even believe what he had written and, if so, could it serve in any way to bring a villain to justice? The more he dwelt upon this last, the less he thought it could. The rogue would get away with murder – yet again. On the other hand, he told himself, dead men tell no lies, as the saying went. Mayhap, they would believe his revelations, if he was found dead in an alley, as Tom had been. It was a harrowing thought, that he might perish that way. Little wonder, then, that sleep eluded him.

The morrow being Wednesday, he would go to church as usual but promised himself he would light a candle for Em and make a generous donation to the alms box for the needy of the parish, in the hope her forthcoming time of travail would be brief and not so arduous, since she had suffered greatly already.

Which recalled to mind the lock of St Margaret's hair he had purchased some days ago. He assured the women that it was meant to aid Em in her labours. As for himself, he would say a heartfelt prayer to St Christopher, defender against sudden death, to preserve him from whatever horrors might befall.

When at last he slept, with cockcrow nigh at hand, his dreams – nay, nightmares – were crammed with sinister shadows, flashing blades and cold corpses, such that he was relieved when Adam woke him, telling him it was time to leave his bed and begin another day.

# Chapter 16

## Wednesday, the fourteenth day of April

DESPITE SO little sleep, Seb made an especial effort with
his ablutions that morn. He was ever careful to wash
well and comb his hair afore attending Wednesday's office of
Low Mass but, since he had particular mercies to beg of the
Almighty, he forced himself to greater diligence than might have
been the case. He washed his feet as well as his hands, face and
neck – "cleanliness being next to godliness", as the saying goes
– then took a blade to the stubble on his chin. This last was no
easy matter when he had trouble keeping his tired eyes focussed
on the distorted image in the well-polished pewter dish they
used for the purpose. The clean linen of his shirt, nether clouts
and hose felt cold against his skin and lacing points was more
of a challenge than usual. Having decided to wear his Sunday
doublet and best shoes, he was ready to face the day. Later, after
having impressed the Almighty – so he hoped – he would come
home to break his fast and change into his workaday clothes.

# St Michael le Querne Church

He barely reached St Michael's afore the office began, having taken so long to wash and dress, but having dipped his fingers in the holy water stoop and crossed himself, he made for the tray of offertory candles, each one upon its pricket. Not for Em a cheap ha'penny tallow light. In a little wooden box lay three small beeswax candles. Seb selected the most perfect, the whitest of them, putting tuppence in the box for it. He lit it from a tallow candle already burning and pushed it down upon an empty pricket spike, to keep it upright and safe. Oblivious to both the priest and the congregation, he went on his knees before the little side altar, dedicated to St Mary Ever-Virgin, imploring her on Em's behalf. He beseeched the Lord Christ and his Blessed Mother to spare Em her suffering and pain, to bring forth the babe safely and without further delay, to give her a swift recovery after.

He was shocked when a hand upon his shoulder broke in upon his prayers, to find his face was wet with tears.

'You are in distress, my son. May I offer you consolation, Sebastian?' Father Thomas had a kindly face, wrinkled by the years, yet his eyes glowed softly with compassion.

Seb sniffed back his tears and wiped his cheeks with the sleeve of his doublet.

'Is the office done, then, Father? I fear, I paid it little heed; *mea culpa.*'

'Done some while since, my son, but you were deep in your devotions to Our Blessed Lady. You have been upon your knees too long.'

Seb realised the priest, who knew him so well, was correct: his hip was reluctant to straighten when he stood, his knees numb from the tiled floor.

'You were praying for Emily. Is she no better then?'

'No, Father, and the babe lies so heavy upon her. I worry for her... There seems to be so little a husband may do.'

'You have done the best you may, Sebastian. You have prayed for her. Mortal man can do her no greater service than that.'

'But it seems hardly enough when the womenfolk ne'er cease their efforts to aid her whilst I do naught but chew my thumbs and fret uselessly.'

'As I said, you have done your best, my son. Now go home and God blessings be upon you and all your house. *In nomine Patri et Fili et Spiritus sancti. Amen.* Go in peace, Sebastian.'

Seb left the church feeling quite out of sorts. He had a suspicion that prayer had not been all he had accomplished upon his knees. He wondered, guiltily, if he had dozed off for a while also, although he was unsure. Wandering outside, into a bright April morn, he quite forgot that he had intended to ask St Christopher to look to his care particularly, in case he was truly being followed and not just imagining some stalker lurking in every other doorway. He had also neglected to make a donation to the alms box, as he had promised in his prayers last night – or this morning, in fact, in the small hours. What he could not know, as the church door closed behind him, was that the draught extinguished the flame on one small beeswax candle.

## The Foxley House

Having enquired after Emily – there was no change, Rose said – he put on his working clothes and boots and broke his fast at last. Not that there was much left of the salted herrings. Nessie told her master that Jack had eaten a third helping and only shrugged when Seb asked for bread and cheese instead.

'All gone, 'til I get t' market, master. An' Gawain ate the last bit o' cheese. He likes cheese.'

'What of your other chores, Nessie?' Seb asked. 'Have you seen to the pig and the hens?' The kitchen was in such disarray. He suspected Nessie was becoming ever more slapdash about her tasks without Em there to chide and instruct her.

'Give me a chance. I on'y got one pair o' hands. I'll get to them soon.'

Seb went along the passage to the workshop, collected his scrip and the report and sketches he had completed last eve. It was a relief to find some, at least, were working.

Adam was in the shop, dealing with a customer – Heaven be thanked – and Kate was dusting the display of a few second-hand books, arranging them to best advantage. Some had been rebound for sale; a couple were intended rather as exemplars, to be copied out as new editions, if customers wanted them.

'Good day, Kate. Be you well?'

Kate nodded.

'Well enough, Master Seb, I thank you.' She looked up but there was no smile, no merry glint in her eye.

'You be making a fine show there, lass. The shelf has ne'er looked more neatly done.' Oh, how he hoped to coax a smile from her but she was downhearted these days. He knew not why. 'Good day to you, Master Kennet,' he greeted the customer. 'I see Vergil's *Aeneid* has appealed to you. 'Tis a fine copy you have chosen, done by Adam here.'

The customer agreed, handing over coins.

'Aye, my goodwife and I shall enjoy it together of an evening, now the days are drawing out. We like to sit in the garden after supper and share a book. I'm always impressed with your copies, Master Foxley. I've passed on the *Poems of Catullus*, the last book I bought from you, to my son and his family, knowing such good craftsmanship will last generations.'

'Thank you, Master Kennet. I trust you might spread our good name among your friends? We should greatly appreciate that, if you do.'

'We made a good sale there: a contented customer.' Adam

said, looking pleased with himself when Master Kennet departed. Seeing Seb wore his Sunday cloak, he asked where he was going, forgetful that Seb had lost his everyday garment at The Mermaid.

'I be away to Guildhall, Adam. Thaddeus requires these notes, as promised. I intend to be back for dinner, if Nessie can bestir herself to provide it.'

'I'll remind her... with my boot on her backside, if need be, the idle wench,' Adam said. 'Or we can buy something from Mistress Routledge's cookshop. She serves a decent oyster pie. I have a fancy for one right now.'

'As you wish, cousin.'

Seb pulled his cap on more firmly, seeing the breeze was rising, and went out into Paternoster Row by way of the shop door, Gawain at his heel.

# Guildhall

His walk to Guildhall was uneventful, save for narrowly avoiding a full barrel of salted fish that toppled from a cart on the corner where Catte Street met Aldermanbury. The carter was driving his poor nag far too fast to take such a tight bend and the barrel was unsecured. With a crash, the fish lay scattered across the street amongst the splintered staves. Two urchins straightway helped themselves to as much fish as they could manage and a barrel hoop each, to play with later. Housewives gathered up the rest of the spilt goods and a man with a barrow, half full of dung, carried off the broken wood for kindling.

By the time Seb had finished thanking the Almighty for his and Gawain's preservation, the street was cleared of debris. All that remained to show that there had ever been a mishap was the carter, red of face, shaking his fist at the disappearing backs of those who had plundered his goods and cursing his unfortunate horse for being the cause of his loss – not to mention Seb's thudding heart occasioned by the near-miss. He felt sympathy for the horse but none for the carter who had been at fault.

At Guildhall, Seb had to wait for Bailiff Turner who had been giving testimony before a magistrate, concerning another case: the theft of a noble lady's nether garments from a laundress. When Thaddeus returned to his chamber, they shared ale and laughed about the case. Seb suggested, in jest, that the culprit might be a fellow from Bankside who called himself Eleanor and dressed in skirts, if you please.

'The Marquis of Dorset is making much ado about his lady's loss, threatening to sue the Lord Mayor, if her garments are not recovered and the thieves caught and hanged. The laundress fears she will be blamed for it and charged the cost of replacing the items, something she can't afford since the clothes were of best Holland cloth and trimmed with silk ribbons. The things were taken as they lay drying on the grass at Moorfields. My sympathy is for the laundress. I'm sure the puffed-up marquis can buy his lady new clothes without straining his purse-strings too much, or King Edward will oblige his step-son, no doubt. But the laundress – a widow woman – will be left destitute if he forces her to pay.'

'What can be done?'

'Who knows? Mayhap, the lady will have to go naked beneath her gown.'

'I meant about the laundress?'

'I know you did, Seb, soft of heart, as ever. Now, you have my notes on the Thatcher case all written up? Ah, they appear to be evidence enough of criminal activity emanating from The Mermaid,' Thaddeus said, leafing through Seb's neatly-written pages. 'Oh, and likenesses too. They'll be a great help. But what of this one? A fine looking woman, indeed.'

'Not so,' Seb said with a grin, 'Though I admit that I too was misled. 'Tis a man; goes by the name of Eleanor, as I mentioned to you previously.'

'Well, he had me fooled. From your drawing, he's a handsome devil. Was he involved in the abduction?'

'Not that I was aware; Will did not mention him, did he? But, for certain, he must be breaking some law or another, making such a show of being a woman, accosting men on the street?'

'Confusing the customer, maybe? Obtaining coin by means of false pretences? Misrepresentation of wares for sale? In truth, Seb, I'd like to see him in the pillory – or should that be the thews, if he insists on being treated as a woman? The trouble is, mountebanks pretend to be women all the time and dress accordingly. There's naught illegal about that. If we catch him in the act, as it were, lying abed with another man, then the Church could bring a case, probably, but 'tis not against any civic statute I know of, unfortunately. The city simply hasn't legislated for such odd behaviour.'

'Oh, well, my shock and humiliation upon that encounter cannot be compensated then. 'Tis a lesson learned though.'

'When I have obtained the warrant, do you want to come along to Southwark with the constables and me to see it served?'

Seb thought for quite a while before answering:

'I think not, Thaddeus, but if you require notes be taken when you question the miscreants, I shall be pleased to oblige. The true nature of their activities troubles me but I would avoid the likely rough handling of the arrests. I yet have bruises enough from other mishaps, though I believe my black eyes have nigh faded, thankfully.'

As Seb closed the door upon the bailiff's chamber, someone called out to him.

'Master Foxley... if you please... to wait?'

Seb turned and doffed his cap.

'Lawyer Metcalfe. We meet again.'

'By intent, this time,' the Duke of Gloucester's lawyer wheezed. 'I thought I might find you here.' The elderly gentleman pulled a sealed letter from his sleeve. 'His Grace bade me deliver this to you, if I saw you. He requests that you attend him at your own convenience. This afternoon would suit, there being no sitting of Parliament then. The purpose is explained in the letter. Good day to you, Master Foxley.'

# Crosby Place

Having bought two large oyster pies from the cook-shop for dinner – since Nessie had failed to provide anything, as they'd feared would be the case – Seb and Adam walked to the Duke of Gloucester's residence of Crosby Place, nigh Bishopsgate. Sergeant Thwaites, as ever looking the very image of Hercules, stood guard beside the new iron gates.

'Well, if it ent Master Foxley?' Thwaites greeted them, recognising Seb from earlier times.

Seb bowed.

''Tis good to see you, Sergeant Thwaites. Is all well in the Northern Shires?' Seb asked.

'Quiet enough, 'til summer comes and them Scotch reivers start raiding o'er the border agen. Then we'll be having work to do, giving them a taste of English blades.' Thwaites rattled his halberd, grinning. 'And who's this?'

'Oh, forgive my discourtesy. Adam Armitage, my cousin, of sorts, and fellow scrivener. Adam, this be Sergeant Peter Thwaites, one of Duke Richard's most trusted men.'

'Any cousin of Master Foxley – even if only "of sorts" – is welcome here. Go you in.' Thwaites pushed open a smaller gate within the larger. 'Ot'shaw!' he bellowed, 'Escort Masters Foxley and Armitage to the Great Hall. His grace is expecting them. There, my good masters, young Ottershaw will see you're announced.'

'Thank you, sergeant. We be obliged unto you.' Seb touched

his cap, as did Adam, and they followed the servant, up the marble steps to the hall.

The hall was crowded but Ottershaw found the steward and gave their names.

'The duke is presently dealing with a matter, then the tall lawyer over there…' the servant indicated a sober man in lawyer's garb, '… has business with his grace, then the duke will see you. May I serve you with ale whilst you wait? Or wine?'

'Ale would be appreciated,' Adam said quickly, fearing Seb might decline the offer. 'We weren't treated so well as this on our previous visit, even though we brought a gift for the duke.'

''Tis Sergeant Thwaites's authority we have to thank. Last time, the gatekeeper was not known to me but the sergeant be an acquaintance of some years' standing.'

Ale cups in hand, they moved towards one of the great glazed windows that looked out onto the paved courtyard, hoping to avoid being jostled by the press of people and spilling their drink.

An elderly man sat upon the cushioned window-seat with the sober-looking lawyer on the one hand, sipping wine, and an anxious-faced servant on the other, holding a cup. The old man seemed to be staring up at the coffered ceiling, as well he might for it was a thing of beauty indeed.

Adam, too, gazed at the azure paintwork, spangled with golden stars.

'Your wine, my lord?' the anxious servant asked, offering the cup, only to be ignored.

Seb watched the old man and realised he was not admiring the roof beams but rather looking beyond them, at something far away.

'Do have some wine, my lord,' the servant coaxed.

'Leave it, Walter,' the lawyer said.

'But he's drunk nothing all day, Sir Marcus. I worry for him.'

'He'll drink when he's thirsty, no doubt.'

'Saddle my horse,' the old man roared of a sudden, coming to life, turning heads. 'We must be home by the dinner hour.'

'We've dined already, my lord,' the servant, Walter, said softly. 'Herrings, you remember.'

'I detest fish, as well you know. Who are you? Get away from me. I don't know you.'

''Tis I, Walter.'

'You're a thief! You took my purse.'

'But, Lord Pierpoint, your purse is yet upon your belt; quite safe.'

'For pity's sake, escort my father outside, Walter. I cannot have him making a scene in the presence of the duke,' the lawyer said.

But as Walter raised his lordship to his feet, the old man began shouting, trying to shove his servant aside.

'Where are you taking me? Remove your hands, you rascal. Let me be. Where is this place?' It was clear that he was not going to leave quietly, in a well-ordered fashion.

Hearing the name "Pierpopint", Seb and Adam exchanged glances, set their cups down on the window ledge and offered their aid.

The servant looked relieved and nodded.

'Come, your lordship,' Seb said gently yet firmly, 'Your horse awaits you outside, as you instructed.'

'Did I?'

'You did but a few moments since. 'Tis this way. And such a fine beast as I ne'er saw anywhere 'til now.'

They led Lord Pierpoint, smiling vacantly and nodding, to the grand doorway but then he hesitated, staring at the steps. Seb realised the difficulty – one he had suffered himself in the past.

'Let me take your arm, sir, and my cousin the other… there, now, but one step at a time… no need for haste… and the steps are soon accomplished.' Seb turned to the servant, eyebrows raised in question: what now?

The servant shrugged.

'Where is this place? I demand you tell me,' the old man raised his voice, elbowing Adam and trying to wrestle free of their restraining hands.

'A garden lies beyond that gate,' Seb said, pointing to the postern gate which opened onto a path, a shortcut to St Helen's church next door. Pretending a boldness he did not feel, Seb led the way through to the privy garden. He had walked here afore, with Lord Richard, when they had discussed the duke's portrait, and a few times since but never without permission. 'The duke will speak with us there, in a little while.'

'Who? What duke? York is it?' his lordship rambled. 'I know him. Good man, York. Fought at his side many a time, in France.'

'Nay, not York. Rather his son,' Seb said, not reminding the old man that York had been dead for nigh a score of years. He led the befuddled lord to a bench set in a vine arbour. For now, the vines were bare of leaf but the entwined stems shielded them from the wind better than naught. 'You be Lord Pierpoint, I believe?' Seb said when his lordship was comfortably seated with him and Adam on either side and Walter before him, to bar any attempt at escape.

'Who told you that? Why would you think it?'

''Tis true, is it not?'

Walter nodded when his lordship made no answer.

'I also know that you made arrangements to purchase a child: a lad by the name of Will Thatcher.'

Walter groaned, his face turned pallid.

'All ended well, you may wish to know. We found Will and took him home to his parents but we would appreciate hearing your side of the tale.' Seb realised then that Lord Pierpoint's wits were wandering as the old man stared blankly ahead. The story would not be told by him. But Walter was sobbing, collapsed on a turf hillock close at hand. 'Whatever made his lordship think a lad could be bought and sold, like merchandise… and what was the purpose of it?' Seb went on. 'Tell us, Walter, I pray you.'

Walter blew his nose on his fingers and wiped them on the grass.

'You say, you took the boy back to his parents?'

'Aye, of course we did.'

'We never knew… we thought the lad must be an orphan or the child of one of those whores. The same with the first boy, the white-haired lad. I believed we were doing the youngsters a favour, giving them some sort of life, at least…'

'The white-haired lad? What of him?' Seb prompted.

'Well, Lord Pierpoint said he wanted a pale-haired boy. They brought the youngster with white hair a few days later but his lordship refused to pay, saying the boy's hair was too pale; it must be fair but not white. The second lad was perfect. Lord Pierpoint was delighted and paid them what they asked.'

'Why did he want such a particular child?'

Walter sighed.

''Tis a long tale…'

'But we would hear it, all the same,' Seb insisted. 'Would we not, Adam?'

Adam agreed.

'Well, 'twas like this: Lord Henry Pierpoint was a fine man with a prosperous estate, by Hurst Pierpoint in the county of Sussex, not far from Arundel, close to St Nicholas Priory, if you know it? He had a beautiful wife, Yolande, three sons and two daughters. And I had the honour to serve him as his esquire, being but a few years younger than my lord. We went to France with the Duke of York and to Ireland with him. Life was fair in those days for us. But fifteen years back, or thereabouts, an itinerant chapman brought plague to Pierpopint Manor. Lady Yolande, her daughters and the middle son, Ambrose, all perished, along with half a dozen servants. It was a time of such grief but my lord, his eldest son, Henry, and youngest son, Marcus, survived, God be thanked.

'Yet naught was the same after that. Young Henry, always – if I'm honest in speaking – somewhat of a wayward child and now a man grown, spent my lord's coin as though its source was infinite as the stars in the heavens and my lord indulged him. Meanwhile, Marcus, never a favoured son, preferring book-learning to any knightly pursuits, had begged to go to the Inns of Court, Lincoln's Inn to be exact, to study for a lawyer. Lord Pierpoint, content to see him go, agreed.

'Then, five years ago, a further tragedy came to pass. Young Lord Henry, heedless and reckless as ever, tried to take his new steed over a hedge at full gallop. The beast, not yet used to its rider, refused. Henry was thrown, landed awry, his neck broken. My lord's favourite son and heir was dead. By the time his debts were settled, much of the estate had been sold off, the coffers emptied. And, perhaps worst of all, Lord Pierpoint, inconsolable in his grief, suffered an affliction of the mind.

'Sir Marcus, now a flourishing lawyer, became the heir but he wants no part of it: a bare title with little standing and a ruinous estate... who can blame him? In truth, though 'tis Sir Marcus's coin that keeps a roof above his father's head, clothes upon his back and food upon the board. Yet my lord does not acknowledge any of this and has long since disowned his only surviving son, hating all lawyers for some half-remembered reasons of his own. But he desires an heir for what he believes is still an honourable title and grand estate with a fine manor, numerous servants, horses and hounds. Yet he has but one remaining servant: me.

'We came to Lambeth because Lord Pierpoint still receives the king's summons to attend Parliament and 'tis but a ferry's ride from Westminster. Quite what they expect of one who is either witless and rambling or staring at nothing, I know not, but it is so. One eve, at our lodging house, The Three Feathers, his lordship was raving about his dire need of a pale-haired boy, aged betwixt ten or twelve years. I knew he was simply longing for a son that looked like Young Henry. But someone overheard. A man with a scarred face told my lord that in Southwark – but a mile away – anyone could be had, for a price, young lads included. My lord was, of an instant, beside himself with excitement and implored the fellow to bring him a pale-haired, blue-eyed boy.

'A few days after, the man and a woman brought a child for my lord's approval but the lad's hair was too pale and my lord refused him. I know not who the child was or what became of him...'

'He was Edward Robbins. He suffered sorely, mortally injured at some point,' Seb said. 'He died, poor soul.'

Walter looked horrified.

'Oh, what a woeful end, by all that's holy. What a fearful thing. We didn't know, upon my oath, we didn't. How did such a thing come to pass?'

'We know not. Not as yet, leastwise, but the City Bailiff be serving an arrest warrant at The Mermaid Tavern in Bankside even as we speak. Mayhap we shall learn the truth of it when he questions the women.'

'The Mermaid?'

'Aye, 'tis where this devilry began. The woman, Bessie, and the man with the scarred face, Cain, dwell there. Cain, though, will trouble no one any longer and be beyond punishment in this world but 'twas he who stole the lads away, taking them off the street, on their way to St Paul's School. I trust Bessie will be made to pay for their crimes.'

Walter looked most sorrowful.

Lord Pierpoint stared at a clump of sweet violets, although whether he heard and understood what was said, or even saw the tiny purple blossoms, none could tell.

The servant, Ottershaw, came then, flushed and breathless.

'I've been searching for you, Master Foxley,' he gasped, 'His Grace will see you now. He is waiting.'

'Apologies, apologies. We will come.' Seb and Adam nigh ran to the hall. It did not do to keep Duke Richard waiting. An unforgivable discourtesy. On the way, they passed Sir Marcus, who looked as content as any man of law ever does. His discussions with Lord Richard must have gone as he'd hoped.

Fortunately, the duke also appeared to be in a fair humour.

'Ah, Master Foxley, may God give you good day,' he said, smiling in that way which lit up his eyes. 'You have come as I requested. I pray you rise. 'Tis good of you and Master Armitage to oblige me so. Come to the solar, away from this crowd. I have some sketches of mine own concerning this coat-of-arms I would have you construct. They be but the poorest examples of draughtsmanship when compared to yours but will give you some idea of what I wish.'

Seb and Adam hastened in the duke's wake, entering the more private solar where Seb had once spent long hours, painting Lord Richard's portrait. He noticed that the hangings were not those he remembered from that time. Previously, the tapestries had depicted hunting scenes. The new ones had a theme of ancient times. Then he noticed a wheeled horse outside a walled city and realised he was looking at the famous Siege of Troy.

'I knew you would observe my new hangings, Sebastian,' the duke said. 'Your sharp eye could not miss such fine workmanship, the bright coloured wools and intricate details. They are a gift from my sister in Burgundy, of Bruges make. Do you espy the fair Helen upon the battlements of the city wall? So small a figure, yet every drape of her gown, her veil, her lovely face be perfectly done. In truth, if I may speak boldly, she calls to mind your beautiful Emily, London's famous archeress.' Lord Richard smiled at the memory of the May Queen, who had nigh bested him in an archery competition long ago. 'I trust your goodwife be well, Sebastian?'

Seb was unsure how to answer.

'Emily be great with child, your Grace. She be somewhat out of sorts, at this time.'

'Oh. 'Tis a sore worry to you then. I shall pray for her safe confinement, that she soon be mended, God willing.'

'Thank you, my lord. I shall tell her so.'

'Now! To business. Come to the windows where the light is better. See here my efforts with pen and charcoal… Sir Robert, if you would set those cups to keep the parchment from rolling up? You recall Sir Robert Percy, do you not?'

'Of course, my lord. How can a man of so modest mien e'er be forgotten?'

They all laughed at Seb's witticism, seeing that Sir Robert was six feet and a good hand's span in height, nigh as wide in the shoulders and topped out with a mop of fiery red hair no hat nor bonnet could ever quite contain. He was, indeed, a man hard to miss and impossible to forget. He and Seb were friends of old.

'No doubt the field of the escutcheon will give you little difficulty, Sebastian. 'Tis simply King Edward's arms – quarterly, first and fourth, the fleurs de lis of France with the second and third showing the royal lions of England. But it must be differenced, of course, with a three-point label of ermine, each point charged with a canton gules. See here? I have drawn it: these small red marks upon the ermine points. And atop I would have the ducal coronet with strawberry leaves of which you will make a far better likeness, I know. And at the foot, the Order of the Garter in blue and gold. What I have not so much as attempted to sketch are the supporters of the arms. I would have my badge of a white boar on either hand.'

Seb took out his paper and charcoal and, in as few lines as possible, indicated a boar, tusked and upright upon its hind legs, that it might support the shield.

'Somewhat like this, my lord?' He held out the sketch.

'Aye. A fine beast,' Lord Richard said.

Sir Robert looked over the duke's shoulder.

'The eyes seem too small...'

'I could draw them larger, if you wish, but pigs have small eyes for their size and a larger eye would give the beast a seemingly more friendly countenance.'

Sir Robert laughed.

'And we can't have that, can we? We have far too many petitioners, sycophants and fools plaguing his Grace as it is. What we need is an image to deter visitors. Can you make the beast's tusks bigger and more fearsome?'

Seb obliged with a judicious line of charcoal here and there.

'Better. That beast will put off all but the most stout of heart, will it not, Dickon? And a pair of them should keep Crosby Place free of time-wasters for good.'

''Tis an excellent figure, Sebastian. I knew you were the right man for this commission.' The duke touched Seb's arm in comradely fashion. 'As to the carpentry of my coat-of-arms, it must be possible to remove it from the gate arch when I am not in residence, since I do but pay rent to Dame Crosby for the use of her fine house when summoned to London. Can you arrange it thus?'

'Aye, my lord. When we have determined the dimensions, Emily's father, Stephen Appleyard, be a carpenter of great skill. He will cut and shape the wood and design some means of affixing it where required, such that it can be unhooked and lifted down, as need be. Will you want the coronet, fleurs de lis, lions and the garter fastenings in gold leaf or gold paint, the latter being a little cheaper? Or yellow orpiment would be somewhat less costly still.'

The duke said naught but gave Seb such a look.

'Gold leaf it shall be.' He should have known better than to ask. 'And what of your motto, my lord? That would look well inscribed upon a scroll across the bottom: *Loyaulte me Lie.*'

'Indeed. I had not considered that. Aye, it sounds well. I shall leave the design in your capable hands, Sebastian. As to cost, I propose a sum of twenty marks, if you deem that sufficient for materials, your time and labours and those of Stephen Appleyard, also?'

'As ever, your lordship be more than generous. Unless you require something of extreme proportions, such that it would take many men of Sir Robert's strength to put it up and take it down, I can achieve it for less than half that sum, gold leaf notwithstanding.'

'And you, Sebastian, be too honest for your own good. A

craftsman with a growing family must make a profit. Twenty
marks it shall be. Lawyer Metcalfe will draw up the contract.
Shall we seal our agreement with a jug of best ale? I recall you
prefer it to wine, as do I before supper.'

Contract in hand, Seb and Adam departed Crosby Place,
well content with the afternoon's proceedings.

'I shall make a brief visit to Thaddeus, at Guildhall,' Seb
said as they turned off Bishopsgate, into Broad Street. 'I want
to know if he made those arrests at The Mermaid and I can tell
him of Lord Pierpoint's involvement.'

'In which case, I might go home by way of Distaff Lane,'
Adam said, grinning.

'What be amiss this time? A tangled lacing or a disobliging
latch or a stuck window, mayhap? You made a fair job of
mending Rose and Kate's window when Jack could not do it.'

'I don't think he tried very hard; a bit of lard and a hefty
shove fixed it no time. But, as far as I know, there are no tasks
for me at Mistress Hutchinson's today.'

'Then what of her good name? You said you would only visit
her when there was a purpose to it.'

'I know but she draws me like a lodestone. Even that scamp
of hers, young Nicholas, cannot put me off.'

'Continue thus, cousin, and you will have to make an honest
woman of her. How long has she been widowed?'

'Her goodman died upon the last day of May, never knowing
she was with child again. Her babe is called Edmund, after the
father he never knew.'

'How did he die?'

Adam considered a while.

'What? You will not tell me?'

'Well, if you must know, he drowned in a boating mishap.
The boatman was either incompetent or drunk. They collided
with another, larger vessel and had the worst of it. The boat

capsized; Edmund Hutchinson was flung overboard. He knew not how to swim.'

'Have I not warned you, repeatedly, that boats are ne'er to be trusted?'

'That's why I was reluctant to tell you.'

'Did they find his body?'

'I don't know. Is that important?'

'If there be not a body, then Master Hutchinson will be accounted as missing, rather than dead. In which case, his wife will be considered as married to him still. A man must be missing for seven years afore he can be declared dead, making a widow of his wife and, therefore, able to wed another.'

'Seven years! Why so long?'

''Tis the law, Adam.'

'Oh, damn the law! Mercy has never mentioned a grave. I'll have to ask her. I cannot wait seven years, Seb.'

'Unless her husband has had a proper burial, you may have to. Elsewise, it will be termed a bigamous marriage, if that be what you intend? You have been acquainted for a matter of days only.'

'But I knew within hours; she's my soulmate, Seb.'

'And she be of like mind?'

'Aye, and we wouldn't wed until a year is past, come the summer, after her goodman's year-mind… if there is one. Oh, Seb, you've overturned all my hopes and plans, you wretch.'

'Not me; rather the law, cousin. But all may be well, if he lies in the churchyard. Now, I be bound for Guildhall, this way.' Seb gestured towards Old Jewry. 'May God speed your cause, Adam. I shall see you at supper.'

# Chapter 17

## Thursday, the fifteenth day of April

DESPITE HAVING sat at Em's bedside for hours last night, to give Rose some respite from her vigil, Seb rose early, at cockcrow, having been unable to sleep. His heartfelt prayers, the candle lighted, seemed to have done little good.

Upon her arrival in time for breakfast, Nell Warren, the midwife, assured them the patient had somewhat improved but Seb could make out no change. Em's face was puffy, her hands swollen, her body bloated as ever. She might make no complaint but her great discomfort was evident as her fever came and went, much as before. That morn, he realised, he no longer recognised the fair lass he had wed. What ravages the sickness had wrought. He wondered if she would ever look as she had afore this.

Only one appeared in the least merry as they broke their fast on yesterday's bread and the last of the ale: Adam.

'Edmund Hutchinson lies buried in St Augustine's by Paul's Gate,' he declared, eyes bright. 'His corpse washed up on one of the starlings of London Bridge, so all is well.' To anyone who had not been party to his conversation with Seb last afternoon, his pleasure seemed perverse.

'A relief to you, then,' Seb said.

'Puts a fair face on the day, I tell you. When I asked, Mercy told me everything concerning it, though it brought a tear to her eye, remembering. There will be no seven years of waiting.'

Seb nodded and finished his ale, coughing on the lees in the bottom of his cup, it being the last of the brewing.

Adam felt peeved at so little reward for his joyous tidings. 'Well, don't all congratulate me at once. Mercy Hutchinson and I are to be wed come summer. Is that not wondrous?'

'Matters have progressed so far so soon? I would advise a little caution,' Seb said, departing the board.

'Your great delight knows no bounds, I see. Is anyone pleased to learn of our forthcoming nuptials? What a dismal crowd you are that you can't even pretend a little gladness for my sake.'

'Forgive me, cousin. Tiredness had robbed me of my capacity for being glad. I be delighted, as are we all.'

Kate, Jack and Nessie nodded agreement.

'Wondered 'ow long you'd play the prickless monk, didn't I?' Jack said.

'Don't say that,' Kate cried, 'Master Adam knows how an honourable man should behave.' She flung aside her napkin and fled towards the workshop, knocking over two empty cups in her haste.

'I should never have mentioned it,' Adam said, ruefully. 'And what's amiss with our Kate these days?'

When all was arranged in the workshop for the day: Kate to attend customers and Adam preparing new cloth and board covers to enclose a repaired Book of Hours, Seb was relieved to find Rose in the kitchen, Dickon in her arms, looking weary but discussing with Nessie the marketing that needed to be done.

'The larder is empty, Nessie,' Rose said, wondering at the bare shelves. 'What did you do yesterday? Anything?'

Nessie's bottom lip protruded in a sulk.

'Did me chores. Fed the pig and the hens, like Master Seb told me to.'

'You shouldn't need telling. You've lived here longer than any of us. You ought to be capable of running this household without any instruction by now.' Rose set Dickon in his special chair and gave him the remains of a crust to chew on. 'Have you cleaned out the pigsty this morn? Collected the eggs? I see there were none for breakfast. Shift yourself, Nessie and do some work.' Rose looked in dismay at the crumbs of bread on the board and the empty ale jug. 'And naught left for Mistress Em or me. What a piteous state of housekeeping. Bread, cheese, ale, worts, parsnips, onions, leeks, bacon... we need them all. Go now, Nessie. Take both baskets and no lingering. We must have a goodly dinner to compensate for so little breakfast. See if there is any honey for sale to tempt Mistress Em. Oh, and butter and lard for pastry.'

Nessie grabbed her cloak, took up the baskets and slammed the kitchen door hard, only to return to demand coin for her purchases. She slammed the door again, even louder, and stormed off to Cheapside.

'I suppose it's down to me, then, to see to the livestock and collect the eggs,' Rose sighed. 'Without even some ale to begin the day.'

Seb had observed all from the passageway.

'I shall fetch you some fresh from The Panyer,' he said, taking the empty jug. 'You be doing the work of three women, at present, I know. Em's sickness be wearing you to the bone. If I may do anything...' Seb put his arm around Rose's slumped shoulders.

'Nay. Peronelle should be here soon. She has been a godsend of late. You know she took all our laundry home with her on Tuesday to help us. It was she who collected the eggs late yesterday and made the omelettes that you might have a decent supper last eve. Nessie is worse than useless without Em instructing her every hour. I keep forgetting to tell her what's next to be done when most of my concern is for poor Em. Oh, Seb, I feel I'm nigh at my wit's end.' She leaned her head against him and his arm held her closer.

'You be working miracles, Rose, keeping us all fed and in

clean linen, caring for little Dickon and constantly tending to Em. Matters will improve once the babe arrives. Em will be her old self again, giving orders and threatening all with her broom; you will see. Now, I best fetch that ale afore we all die of thirst.' Despite his words, Seb was slow to move away from Rose, reluctant to relinquish that small sense of comfort as he held her near, as was she.

It was Peronelle's arrival, a gentle knock upon the kitchen door, that forced them apart.

Seb helped her, bringing in two canvas bags over the threshold, full of clean sheets, towels, shirts and shifts before he hastened to The Panyer for the ale.

# Guildhall

All the way to Guildhall, Seb was afflicted by guilt. He didn't dare admit, even to himself, the consolation, the warmth, derived from holding Rose close for those few moments. Until now, he had not realised how lost and alone he felt without Em ever chiding him. It was a strange sort of love betwixt them but he felt abandoned without her complaining about his every deed. He even tried to explain all this to Gawain as they walked – as if the dog might sympathise with his master. At least he looked up at Seb with those deep dark eyes that seemed to hold a measure of understanding.

He also felt at fault forwhy he spent so much time away from Paternoster Row of late. Once young Will Thatcher was found, he should have left any investigating to Thaddeus but he had not, continuing his involvement in the case – as now.

Questioning the women from The Mermaid was not his concern and yet he had volunteered to take notes for the bailiff. It was merely an excuse. He wished to see the matter through to its conclusion, he told himself but that was not the whole truth. He had a manuscript to transcribe and every moment spent upon it was a penance. For once, he was finding his work irksome and avoiding it like a resentful apprentice.

But that was not all, either. He could not bear the smell of sickness that pervaded every corner of home, the essence of pain and suffering that hung like invisible cobwebs over everything. And worse was the suspicion of an unwanted intruder, lurking at hand. He hardly dared give it a name but felt its presence every time he entered the house: hooded in darkness, armed with a scythe... waiting.

Any distraction from these things was most welcome.


Seb followed Thaddeus down a flight of stairs, into the vaults below Guildhall. It was another world down here. In truth, it looked forbidding, even to a free man. How must it put fear into the prisoners who were kept locked in the cells, awaiting interrogation? Its only saving grace was that it was not so bad as Newgate. No one in this place was yet condemned. Once questioned, they would be sent to the appropriate prison, depending upon who had made the arrest, the crime of which they would be accused and tried, whether by a magistrate, a jury, or by the Crown, if upon a charge of treason. Those taken by the sheriffs were sent to The Counter.

The women from The Mermaid were housed in two cells. One of the bailiff's constables unlocked a door with a set of jangling keys on a large ring.

'Out you come, ladies and gentle damsels,' he mocked, 'Time to speak with Bailiff Turner. I know you can hardly wait.'

Four women were led out.

Seb recognised Bessie; the wench who had pretended to be an innocent lass, fresh from the countryside and Colette, the Bretonne. The fourth woman, a pale but voluptuous creature, he did not recall.

The so-called country lass saw Seb, marched straight up to him and slapped his face.

'You called me a hussy in the street, you bloody rakehell,' she screeched as the constable grabbed her and pinned her arms in a bear-like embrace.

'Peaches! Don't make matters worse,' Bessie ordered.

Seb supposed she had likely been called worse things than "hussy" in the past but was expressing her anger at being arrested and spending a night in a cell. Nonetheless, his cheek stung as he felt it gingerly, checking with his tongue that no teeth had been loosened. She was a woman of much strength, more than he had reckoned.

Thaddeus took them to another chamber in the vaults. Within was an anteroom where he bade the constables wait with Peaches, Colette and the fourth woman whilst he and Seb took Bessie through to an inner room, furnished with a chair, table and two stools. Thaddeus, as City Bailiff, took the chair at the end of the table, indicating that Seb should draw up one of the stools and use the rest of the table as his desk. Seb took his pens, ink and paper from his scrip and prepared to write.

'Sit down,' the bailiff told Bessie nodding towards the other stool. 'Name?'

'Elizabeth Moring,' she answered, taking her seat.

Seb wrote it down, thinking how respectable the name sounded.

'And you run your, er, business at The Mermaid Tavern in Bankside, Southwark?'

'I am the proprietress, aye. The girls are my apprentices to the craft of 'broidery. We also have the Bishop of Winchester's licence to sell ale, to earn extra coin,' she said. ''Tis all legal. I can't think why we're here, being treated like felons.'

At that moment, Seb glanced up as he dipped his pen. His eyes met hers for an instant. Her words were smooth, ordinary-sounding, but her eyes were icy with contempt.

'A man known as Cain worked there also,' Thaddeus

continued. 'Tell us about Cain.'

The woman did not reply straightway, staring at her hands, which were clasped demurely in her lap.

'Cain is my brother. We run the tavern together,' she said at last.

'No longer. Cain is dead,' Thaddeus said, hoping to shock the woman. His strategy didn't work.

'Indeed? I hadn't seen him for some days. I feared he had come to grief. Always reckless, my Cain. It was bound to end so, sooner or later.'

'Cain stole two children off the street. I believe you were a party to that crime.'

'Never. I wasn't Cain's keeper. How should I know he took those lads?'

'I didn't say they were boys. So you were involved. And you and Cain together took young William Thatcher to an inn at Lambeth, sold him to Lord Pierpoint for two marks. You can't deny it. Both the boy and his lordship's serving-man have told us quite independently.'

And so the questioning went on; Seb scribbling frantically, trying to keep up.

Seb's imprisonment at The Mermaid was dealt with in detail, although she denied putting a powerful sleeping draught in his food.

At last, Thaddeus asked about what happened to the white-haired lad, Edward Robbins. By this time, the woman was tired, likely having slept but little in the cell. She made no effort to deny anything and simply told how it came to pass.

'I didn't know where Cain found the lad. I had nothing to do with that. We kept him for a few days, at the tavern, quietening him for he was loud and unruly. Once he was calmer, we took him to Lambeth but the stupid old man said the boy wasn't right for him – some customers can be most particular. We were returning to The Mermaid with the lad. I thought, if trained, he could well serve some other purpose but he broke away from

Cain. My brother, ever reckless, as I said, threw his knife to bring him down. Cain said he'd aimed for the lad's feet but he was struck in the side.

'The wound bled but didn't seem so deep. It should've healed but, after a while, it began to fester. The lad kept saying he wanted to go home. He was fevered and complaining, so we let him go. He was no use to us like that.'

'You let him go? A sick child? And upon the night of that great storm, too.'

Bessie shrugged.

'What of it? It was a risk but whatever he said, nobody would believe him, thinking he was out of his wits with fever and that he'd imagined it all. A greater risk would have been having a dead body to deal with.'

Seb ceased writing. So heartless? Did they care more for their own situation than for a dying child? Tears sprung to his eye. Saying nothing, he began to tidy away his stuff into his scrip.

'I shall see that you have the notes by the morrow, Sir Bailiff,' he managed to say.

'But we haven't finished…' Thaddeus said.

'I have.'

Seb walked out, collecting Gawain from the constables in the anteroom.

'The bailiff requires a clerk,' he told them.


Now, the whole wretched story was known to him. He had expected that learning all the facts would close the case for him, give him peace of mind, but it didn't. Edward Robbins' end distressed him greatly and he kept going over the events of that Palm Sunday morn, remembering when he found the sorry little body in his workshop. The lad had been trying to get to Holbourne, home, through that fearful storm. What courage it must have taken but it was far too far… his dwindling strength could not carry him much beyond St Paul's. Mayhap, he hoped to take shelter in the school there, it being so familiar to him, but the place would be closed up of a Saturday eve. Paternoster Row was as near to home as the poor child could struggle, to die alone... in the dark... in a stranger's house.

Seb wiped his eyes repeatedly.

A little beyond Friday Street, where it joined Cheapside, was a gap betwixt two buildings. Less than an alleyway, little wider than a gutter. Strong hands seized Seb and hustled him into the narrow way. A sack was pulled over his head and ropes were wound around him, all in a matter of moments. He was flung down, landing on wood and straw and then lifted at his feet. A wheel clacked on cobbles. He realised he was being trundled along in a handcart. He tried to call out but sacking filled his mouth. More straw was piled on top, shutting out the last vestige of daylight. His befuddled mind was a cascade of questions: Who? Why? How? But uppermost was What? What of Gawain? The dog had made no protest. Not a single bark.

# The Foxley House

At least dinner was proving a more substantial meal, making up for a breakfast of scraps. A hearty pottage of bacon and peas, manchet bread and apple fritters sweetened with honey and served with cream was enough for all to have a second helping. However, some had not even come for their first helping. There being no sign of Seb and Gawain, Adam had taken it upon himself to say grace before the food went cold and spoiled.

'Business at Guildhall must be dragging on,' Adam said, holding out his bowl for more pottage. 'If Seb doesn't hasten, there'll be naught left for him.'

'Indeed there will,' Rose said, 'I've set a large helping aside for him.'

Peronelle and Mistress Warren had joined them for dinner whilst, briefly, Nessie was entrusted to keep watch at Mistress Em's bedside, warned to summon them upon an instant if the patient awoke or even stirred in her sleep. It didn't do to permit Nessie any element of judgement in this matter, fearing she might overlook some quite serious change of circumstance. Therefore, even at meat, the women were alert to any sound from above stairs and none could be at ease to enjoy the meal.

Seb was lifted out of the cart, still blind inside the sack. Unseen hands set him upon his feet and he was told to walk, being led along.

'Three steps up are before you,' said a voice. It was a London voice and seemed familiar to Seb but it was hard to tell through the thickness of sacking. Upon the first step, the dust of the sack and the straw caused Seb to sneeze and hands held him fast, as though fearing this to be the opening ruse of an attempt at escape. It wasn't. Just a sneeze. But Seb felt a warm body press against his knee; heard the sound, half whine, half whimper, that Gawain made whenever things occurred that he could not comprehend, expressing his puzzlement. Seb felt relief that the dog was yet with him but mystified as to why the creature made no objection to his master's rough handling by strangers. Unless they were not strangers? In which case, who of his acquaintances would treat him thus?

They were within a building, walking on flagstones at first, and then on woven matting above floorboards before descending stone steps. Seb could hear doors being opened and closed behind them. Then the sounds became more echoing. He sensed they were in an undercroft or cellar, probably vaulted and large, to judge by the hollow echo.

He was pushed onto a stool and his ankles tied, each to a stool leg. The ropes that had been wound around him were removed, the sack lifted away, the further disturbance of dust making him sneeze again.

'Where is this place? What do you want with me?' Seb asked, once his fit of sneezing subsided. He hoped his questions implied demand for information, not pleading. He looked around, attempting to see his captors but they stood directly behind him. He had worked out that there were two of them. But in turning his head, he realised there was a familiarity to the surroundings, viewed in the flickering glow of two torches in their sconces. Afore he and Emily were wed, he had rescued her from this very undercroft: the heaps of rusted armour and broken weapons were much as he remembered them. Mayhap, even the cobwebs were the same. He answered his own query: 'This is Lovell's Inn in Ivy Lane, is it not?'

'You know this place?' the somewhat familiar voice asked, sounding surprised.

'Aye. I have been here once, long since. It has not changed. Why have you brought me here? What does Lord Lovell want of me?' The realisation that he was at the little-used residence of his nemesis, Francis, Lord Lovell, was a worrying one.

'We know no more than you.'

'Then why...'

'He pays well.'

Of a sudden, like a shaft of sunlight breaking through cloud, Seb recognised the voice.

'Jonathan Caldicott, I thought better of you than this. What have I ever done to you to earn your enmity?'

'Money is all. My goodwife is ever discontent with our lot. She persuaded me...'

'And me,' said a second voice Seb had not heard 'til now.

Jonathan stepped into view, now concealment no longer served a purpose.

'You have been following me for some while, have you not?

'Some of the time. We had to await our chance,' Jonathan admitted. 'So often you were with Adam. His lordship paid us to bring you here. I was his choice because I know you by sight… and your dog knows me for a friend. A piece of cheese bought his silence, as I knew it would. Lovell says he must talk to you but means you no harm, Seb. He promised me that.'

'And you believe him? Come, Jonathan, 'tis not too late: this matter can be undone. Let me go and I shall say no more of this… this aberration of yours. It will be forgotten as though it never came to pass. You know of my situation at home; Emily's sickness… I pray you, do not make it worse for her.'

''Tis too late, already. Mary has spent Lovell's money. If me and Martin fail to do as Lovell wants, it will mean naught but trouble for us.'

'You do not think there will be trouble in any case? Your participation in Lovell's schemes means you know too much. That is a danger to him and, therefore, to you both. The flash of a blade in a dark alley would ensure his safety and end your lives.'

'He isn't going to do that. Why should he? He only asked us to bring you here so he could talk to you. Why should we be in danger for that? We haven't hurt you.'

'If all he wants is to talk with me, why did he not send a messenger with an invitation? I tell you why: he knows I would not come. Lovell be a dangerous man, Jonathan, more than you suppose. If he kills me, I shall not be his first victim nor, likely, his last. You are entangled in the Devil's coils now. I fear for us all.'

'What's done is done.' Jonathan sighed and looked towards the door at the head of the steps as it creaked open. 'Too late to change things now.'

Francis, Lord Lovell, resplendent in his favoured blue velvet hat with its peacock plumes, looked down with pitiless eyes. A serpent's eyes.

'Out!' he ordered, coming down the steps. He remained silent then, until Jonathan and his fellow had scuttled past him, up and through the door. He stood before Seb, hands on hips, feet set wide in an intimidating stance, every inch the high-born lord. 'Foxley,' he snarled. 'Ever the bane of my life. I should have slit your miserable gizzard the first time you meddled in my affairs.'

'But we came to an understanding then,' Seb said, trying to keep his voice from faltering. 'You would do me and mine no harm and I should ne'er reveal what I knew of your nefarious activities.'

'Indeed. And I kept my part of the bargain.' Lovell took his knife from its bejewelled sheath at his belt and began cleaning his nails with its wickedly pointed tip.

Seb watched, fascinated, wondering that the man did not slice off a finger end.

'And I have maintained my silence, as I promised. Why have you brought me here? I have done naught against you.'

'No, but you thought to make money from your knowledge of me. That was a grave mistake, Foxley, threatening me.'

'But I have done naught of the kind.' Seb did not add that there was yet a possibility he might do so in the future.

'This!' Lovell produced and held a crumpled piece of paper under Seb's nose.

Seb had no chance to read what was written upon it but he knew the hand that had held the pen.

'Tom Bowen wrote that...'

'At your instruction and sealed with your bloody fox-head seal. And then you send that young imbecile to collect the money.' Lovell laughed without humour. 'Well, he got what he deserved and it was cold steel, not silver. Now it's your turn, you damned foolish peasant. You think a stupid scribbler could get the better of me? Me: friend of kings and princes? Think again, Foxley. It'll be the last thought you ever have.'

'Hold!' Seb cried. ''Tis not like that. I had dismissed Tom Bowen from my service. You recall him? He was the apothecary's apprentice. Did you think he died in that explosion? He did not and has been working for me since. But when I ended his employment, he robbed me of one of my seals along with writing

318

stuff. He knew as much of your activities back then as I did, maybe more. It must have been his own idea to write that letter to you, demanding money forewhy he was now penniless. I knew not of his doings; I make my oath upon it.'

'So you say... now he can't tell it otherwise.'

''Tis true, every word of...' Seb gulped, holding his breath as Lovell's knife grazed his neck below his left ear. Though his hands were free, he was tied to the stool. Such an encumbrance made any act of defence unlikely to succeed. 'W-What of the Duke o-of G-Gloucester?' he managed to say.

'What of him?' Lovell's knife remained in place but wasn't pushed home.

'The duke will wonder at my sudden disappearance. He gave me a commission only yesterday.'

'Did he pay you?'

'Aye, ten marks: half the sum in advance.'

Lovell snorted.

'Then he'll realise you took his money and ran.'

'He will not believe that; his grace knows I will honour the commission.'

'Lives in a world of make-believe that one; thinks every man is to be trusted like a bloody saint. One day he'll realise we're all in it for ourselves. Survival is all that counts... and power, if you use it as you ought – a skill he might learn, if he lives that long. I'll tell him I saw you taking ship for Flanders. Which of us do you think he'll believe then? Me? His trusted confidant of many years. Or you? A pen-pusher of no account. Eh?'

'I-I have evidence...' Seb said, forced to roll his final die. 'In the event that I disappear... or my body found... my evidence shall be made known to Thaddeus Turner, the City Bailiff, serving Lord Mayor Richard Gardyner. Bailiff Turner has authority; Lord Mayor Gardyner has power. They both know full well how to use it, as you say.'

'What evidence? You're lying, you miserable worm.' This time, the knife broke the skin. Seb felt hot blood trickle down his neck.

'You dare not take the risk that I speak truly. 'Tis all explained in the letter: everything I know of you. If I give the letter to the bailiff now, it will simply be a matter of your word against mine but, if I be dead... a dead man's testimony carries all the weight of the grave with it. Your crimes will be made known; your villainy unmasked. The duke will realise what manner of man he has called "friend" all these years. You want that?'

'Every word a lie!' Lovell sounded desperate. The knife blade wavered.

'As I said afore,' Seb continued, 'I have maintained my silence, as I promised unto you. Our previous agreement can yet stand, if you desire it? You swear to do no harm to me and mine – and I believe that must now include my kinsman, Adam, and that misguided neighbour whom you paid to abduct me – and I shall hold my peace.'

'What of the letter, this so-called evidence, if it even exists?'

'Indeed it does.'

'You must bring it to me that I can see it destroyed once and for all.'

'Nay, my lord. That will not be the way of it. You have to trust me. We trusted each other until now but you killed Tom Bowen, lately my journeyman. That broke your side of our unwritten contract. The letter ensures my safety from a man who has just admitted to murder. Whatever you think of me, I be no man's fool.'

'No. You're a conniving bastard and I don't trust you farther than I can spit. But...'

'But like a cat and a dog sharing a warm hearth, we come to an accommodation? Our mutual destruction would benefit neither.'

Lovell stood considering for what seemed an hour to Seb but was likely no more than a minute or two. At last, he bent down and sliced the ropes around Seb's ankles with the blood-stained blade.

'You betray me, Foxley, you won't even live long enough to regret the day. And all your kinfolk will join you in Hell before your body goes cold. You have my word on that. Now get out of my sight before I change my mind.'

# The Foxley House

'Seb! Where have you been? We were beginning to worry,' Adam said when Seb entered the kitchen. Gawain came in behind him, head and tail down.

'I was delayed. A business agreement required confirmation.'

Adam folded his arms and gave Seb a look askance.

'What kind of business involves straw in your hair, blood on the neck of your shirt and a dog who looks as sorry for himself as any creature ever did?' Adam picked some straws from Seb's hair and the back of his cloak.

'Gawain be in disgrace. I reprimanded him for failing in his duties. My neck was a mishap, a scratch merely. As for the business, 'tis none of any man's but mine. I pray you, do not ask.' Seb hung his Sunday cloak upon the peg behind the kitchen door. It looked somewhat the worse for wear.

Adam shrugged.

'Rose left your dinner keeping warm on the hearthstone. And there's a piece of cheese for Gawain.'

'No cheese for him. He deserves no reward, especially not cheese. Meanwhile, I have a task afore I dine.'

Seb went through to the workshop and Adam followed, returning to his desk with a cup of ale. Kate was in the shop. Seb went to his desk and removed the troublesome astrology text from the exemplar stand.

'I shall be gone but a few moments,' he said, tucking the book under his arm. 'Gawain, stay! I do not want you by me in this.'

Seb went out of the shop door, into Paternoster Row. It was less than a dozen paces to his neighbour's house. He hammered on their door, venting his temper on the oak.

Mary Caldicott opened the door.

'Master Foxley. Good day to you. How may I help? More towels, perhaps?'

'You can take this back, mistress,' Seb said, thrusting the book at her. 'I will work on it no longer and, if you cannot understand why that be the way of it, I suggest you enquire of your husband. I want no more of your custom.' For once, even courtesy was dispensed with. With that, he turned and strode back home, though his actions had done little to sweeten his humour.

Adam was wise enough not to ask.

Seb helped himself to ale and sat at his desk. His ordeal had made him bone-weary and his neck was sore. No doubt his shirt was bloodied somewhat but, for the present, he did not care, too tired to change his linen. He made the wordless excuse that the womenfolk had more washing to deal with than they could manage as it was and it was a kindness not to add to it. This, despite knowing full well that the longer the stain dried upon the cloth, the more difficult it would be to soak out, was his reasoning.

His eyes strayed to the vacant exemplar stand at his left hand. The astrology text was gone and he should have felt relieved but rather he had to acknowledge it to be his failure. It had been a problematic text from the start but he had managed to transcribe such works in the past, refusing to be defeated by scribal intricacies. That this one had got the better of him was a concern. Was his eye less keen or his mind less sharp? He hoped not. This was an anxious time for the household and Mistress Caldicott's insistence upon haste had not helped. Then the hours... days of searching for Will Thatcher were a great distraction... Tom's murder... the need to put a name to the white-haired lad... Em's sickness and whatever ailed young

Kate… Little wonder he could not concentrate upon his work.

But upon the morrow, he determined, he would commence Duke Richard's commission with renewed heart and vigour. Aye, upon the morrow, he thought as his eyelids grew heavy and he fell asleep at his desk, head pillowed upon his folded arms.

# Chapter 18

## Friday, the sixteenth day of April

SEB WAS, once again, in the workshop promptly, long before everyone else had bestirred themselves. But no, that was not entirely true: Rose had been keeping watch at Emily's bedside for most of the night and was there yet. He had taken ale to her and asked after Em. She passed a quiet night, Rose told him.

Now, determined to attend to his proper work, he set out his drawing stuff and paper, his notes concerning the duke's requirements for the coat-of-arms, clearing his desk of all other clutter that might prove a distraction. It being Friday, he often attended Low Mass at St Michael's before breaking his fast but he did not want to waste this burst of enthusiasm for the new project.

He began at once with a preliminary sketch, to be certain every part might sit in harmony with another, to give a balanced whole. Then he would make a full-size plan of the outline shape for Stephen Appleyard, that he might prepare the wood. Finally, he could spend time upon the detailed drawings of the quarterings, the coronet, the garter, the supporters and the motto scroll. After that, once Stephen had cut and shaped the wood, it would require layers of whitening with fine plaster and constant smoothing to give a perfect ground for the gold leaf and pigments.

Kate should be shown how to do these things. She could prick out the design of his original cartoon. He would demonstrate how to rub red chalk through the pinholes, transferring the details precisely to the ground before applying the gold leaf. These intricate procedures were what he most enjoyed; where his skills lay.

And the painting itself, of course, giving colour and vibrancy to what had been but plain wood. It was always something of a lesser miracle, knowing it was God's hand, working through a man's God-given talent, that brought about such change. Seb never forgot that. Without the aid of the Almighty, his skills would serve for naught but daubings and scribbles.

His preliminary sketches were already being combined into a coherent design of sorts when Kate sought him out and summoned him to breakfast.

Seb said grace right swiftly and accepted a platter of food but his mind was upon pigments he might need to purchase, pumice to smooth the surface of the plaster, new brushes. Would he need to order more gold leaf from the goldsmiths, or did he have sufficient in the secret aumbry behind the image of The Virgin, wherein their valuables were kept safe? The aumbry was in the bedchamber where Em lay, so with the place ruled by women, this was not the time to check. But soon. The leaf must be laid on before the pigments and he wished to avoid delay once the plaster ground was prepared.

'Did you hear me, Seb?' Rose's voice cut across his considerations of gold leaf.

'Forgive me; my thoughts be elsewhere.' He saw his untouched pickled herrings upon the platter and took up his spoon.

'I said that Mistress Warren thinks Em's labours have begun at last. The herbs are finally proving effective.'

'That is well.' He broke off a piece of bread to soak up the piquant juices.

'Do you realise, the new babe could arrive today?'

'What?'

'Sebastian Foxley! Men! I despair of you all.' Rose tried to push her escaping locks of dishevelled hair back under her cap but to no avail. She looked exhausted, shadows black as bruises beneath her eyes. 'I'm going to leave little Dickon in your hands. I shall rest awhile in my bed, catch up with lost sleep whilst matters proceed calmly. Later, we will all of us have much to do, as Em's time draws nigh. You menfolk will have to fend for yourselves.'

'We can do that,' Adam assured her, 'So long as a woman is available to change Dickon's tail-clouts as needs be. We've proved inept in the past. 'Tis not men's work, after all. You can't expect us...'

But Rose only sighed and left the board, making her weary way up the stairs, hoping to sleep until her aid was required in the birthing chamber.

'Nessie, wash the dishes and don't forget the pig and the hens,' she called out as an after-thought halfway up. 'And prepare the worts for dinner to go with a pie from the shop across the way. And we'll need more ale as there will be many thirsty women coming to support Mistress Em... and you'd best get some sweetmeats for them too.'

Nessie stamped her foot when Rose was gone.

'And she expects me to do all that! I can't remember everything.'

'I'm off,' Jack said. 'I ain't staying in an 'ouse full of women. I got me carpenterin' to do, ain't I?'

'Tell Master Appleyard I shall call upon him later, concerning an escutcheon for the Duke of Gloucester,' Seb said.

'A wot? Never heard of a scutcher.'

'Es-scutch-eon. No matter. Just say I shall visit him, most likely afore dinner.'

Kate was awaiting customers in the shop. Little Dickon sat upon his blanket in the midst of the floor there, playing with his rag ball. He had discovered a fine game: if he threw the ball, however aimed awry, Gawain would fetch it back for him. There was such gurgling and chuckling and sounds of merriment that customers were attracted into the shop – women in particular. Even Kate's voice sounded more cheerful than of late.

Adam left his book-binding every now and then to see that all was well in the shop. He watched Kate complete the sale of a small volume of poetry, bound in gilded calfskin leather, smiling and making her courtesy to a well-dressed lady.

Seb was engrossed in his work, brows drawn down in concentration, streaks of charcoal dust upon his nose and down his old jerkin. Adam knew, if the workshop caught afire, Seb wouldn't notice until the flames reached his desk and burned his precious drawings.

He settled down to his own tasks and the malodorous stink of heated rabbit-skin glue soon filled the air. He would use it to affix the new covers to the end-papers of the repaired Book of Hours. Of course, Seb remained oblivious to the smell.

At length, Seb laid down his charcoal, blew away the loose black dust and rolled up the large sheet of paper before putting it in his scrip. It was overlong and protruded from the bag.

'That has the outline pattern done,' Seb said, 'And it had better not be raining, else it will ruin it.' He wrinkled his charcoal-smudged nose, 'Have you been glueing something, Adam?'

'Aye. The Book of Hours has its new cover. When it's dry, I'll do the gilding and it can go for sale. I think it will look very fine upon the shelf.'

'Excellent. Well, I be away to Stephen's place, to discuss the duke's commission.' Seb fetched his Sunday cloak and swung it about his shoulders. He took up his scrip. 'Gawain seems to be amusing little Dickon well enough, so I shall tell him to stay.'

'You've got a smear of charcoal…' Adam called aloud but Seb was gone, out into Paternoster Row. Adam had forgotten how single-minded his kinsman could be when an important project was in hand.

Soon after Seb had departed upon his errand, something

occurred in the bedchamber above the shop. Kate came hastening into the workshop, struggling with little Dickon, who hadn't wanted to be taken from his game and was protesting loudly. Gawain followed on, ears back.

'Oh, Master Adam,' Kate said, her eyes wide, 'I fear something amiss upstairs. Do you not hear the cries?'

Adam had heard but thought – nay, hoped – it was someone shrieking in the street outside.

'I wouldn't have Dickon upset by such sounds,' Kate added.

Before Adam could reply, Dame Ellen burst into the workshop. When had she arrived, he wondered.

'Where's Sebastian?' she demanded.

'Gone out upon a business matter but…'

'Trust him to be absent when he's needed. You'll have to go.'

'Go where, good dame?' Adam asked.

'To fetch Surgeon What's-his-name, of course?'

'Surgeon Dagvyle?'

'Aye, him.'

'But why? Childbirth is women's business, surely?'

'Don't argue. Just do as you're bidden. Now run! And you, Kate, go to St Michael's. Tell Father Thomas he's needed and to bring… everything.'

Adam and Kate exchanged anxious glances. Kate had tears in her eyes. Both grabbed their cloaks and dashed off with their messages, leaving Gawain like a nursemaid, sitting beside Dickon.

Dame Ellen shook her head and with much creaking of joints and grimacing, she picked up the child and kissed him.

'And they rush off and discard you, little one. No sense of responsibility, young folk these days. Oh, and you're soaking wet, poor mite. Does no one attend to their proper duties anymore? I would ne'er have left my son in such a case. Come with grandmother and she'll put you to rights – if I can find where they store your clean tail-clouts. Then you shall have a sweetmeat. And as for that father of yours… I'll be giving him a piece of my mind when he dares appear.'

Kate returned with old Father Thomas puffing in her wake. The house was becoming more crowded by the minute with women gathering to gossip, console, or encourage each other, as appropriate, but the priest was ushered through and up the stairs to the heart of the matter.

Dame Ellen was in command, doing her best to captain a rudderless ship in a storm of chaos. The kitchen was full of folk, all aiming for the ale jugs and trays of wafers that had appeared as if by magick, donated by some thoughtful soul or other.

'Ah, Kate, this child is in need of a dry tail-clout,' the good dame said, handing over the damp toddling. 'Then take him and that wretched dog outside. They're getting under everyone's feet and there's hardly room enough to stand as it is. And where's your master? He ought to be here.'

'Master Seb went to Appleyard's carpenter's shop, I believe,' Kate said, finding a tail-clout in a pile of folded laundry someone had shoved under the table.

'Aye, well, Stephen should be here too. He will want to see his daughter…' She wiped her eye upon the hem of her pristine apron. 'So when you've done changing the child's clouts, take him and the dog to fetch them both back.' Dame Ellen turned away, dabbed at her eyes again then cleared her throat. 'Ah! Peronelle. The midwife will need more towels,' she said briskly. 'And tell that idle wench to cease her bawling and wash out the empty ale cups. Mistress Barnes, Agnes, take that jug of hot water upstairs and where's Mary Jakes? I saw her but a moment since…'

Adam returned, accompanied by both Stephen and Jack.

'Where's the surgeon?' the dame demanded.

'He's setting a child's broken arm. He'll be along as soon as he has finished the bone-setting and splinting.'

'Did you impress upon him the urgency of this case?'

'Of course, but he was annoyed that I could give him no details…'

'Where is my daughter?' Stephen interrupted. 'What's amiss with her? Is the babe come?'

'Master Appleyard... Stephen,' Dame Ellen said, lowering her voice to a seemly whisper and putting her hand on his arm. 'I fear you must prepare yourself...' She pushed him through the folk, milling about, to the foot of the stairs. 'Go up. The priest and midwife are with her.'

A look of panic crossed Stephen's homely face. He nodded and made his way.

Dame Ellen turned her attention to Adam and glared at him. 'And where's that ne'er-do-well husband of hers, eh?'

'I called for Stephen on my way back from the surgeon. Seb was supposed to be there but Stephen said he'd already gone upon some other errand.'

'Then find him! Or do I have to do it myself? What a pack of knaves and fools you all are. You men are less use than bottomless buckets. Find him, I tell you.'

Adam obeyed swiftly, eager to escape Dame Ellen's eye, feeling like a schoolboy reprimanded by the master.

# Cheapside

Seb was pleased with his morning's accomplishments: the preliminary sketches for the duke's commission were done; he had given an outline pattern and explained his requirements to Stephen Appleyard, so the woodwork was all in hand. Stephen had even spoken encouragingly of Jack's progress in carpentry, which was good news indeed. Seb had then gone farther along Cheapside, to the goldsmith's shop of Alderman Shaa. Fearful of disturbing Em in the bedchamber by going to their concealed aumbry of valuables, he had decided to purchase more gold leaf. If it were not required after all for the coat-of-arms, it would not be wasted. Gold did not rust nor spoil, so could be kept for some other future commission. He spent more time with the goldsmith, admiring a pearl, sketching possible settings for the gem as a brooch, thinking it would make a splendid gift for Em upon her recovery. Having agreed a price and paid one and a half marks to secure the contract, he departed in good spirits.

Still smiling, he came to Cheap Cross, where Old Symkyn sat upon the steps, as usual, his begging bowl in hand.

'God give you good day, my friend,' Seb called out and came over. 'Be you in good heart?'

'Aye, as are you, I see. Did that business of the missing lad turn out well?'

'It did, for the Thatchers, at least. 'Tis quite a tale. Come, let me buy us a jug of ale and I shall tell you all.'

Seb led the old man into The Cardinal's Hat, close by, and ordered bread, cheese and ale. The proprietor recognised them and served them courteously, having heeded Seb's warning, concerning his licence, upon the previous occasion.

'Where's your dog today?' Symkyn asked.

'Somewhat in disgrace. I left him at home.'

As they claimed the bench by the hearth so Symkyn could warm his aged limbs, three fellows in motley took their positions in the centre of the floor. One held a lute, one a recorder and the third a flute. With the ease of long practice, the lute-player tuned his instrument and the minstrels began to play. Merry country airs soon had customers' feet tapping and fingers drumming the rhythm, some joining in the refrains and choruses.

The lute-player had a fair, strong voice but when they played *The Nut-Brown Maiden* – Seb's favoured song because it reminded him of Em afore they wed – he could not help but sing along.

His voice was famed throughout the city as he often sang in Paul's choir. He had sung *Jubilate* as a solo upon Easter Day to much acclaim by the congregation, if less so by the precentor. At the time, he was yet suffering the after-effects of that potion administered at The Mermaid, though they denied it. Thus it was that Seb feared he had not sung at his best then but, urged on by the minstrels and customers alike, once they heard his voice, he now sang song after song, some with the musicians playing, others unaccompanied. The Cardinal's Hat soon had folk coming through the doors to listen, the innkeeper, tapsters, and pot-boys barely able to cope with so much custom, scurrying to and fro.

Plied with free ale to keep his throat moist, Seb entertained them for nigh an hour, enjoying himself full well.

Coins were pressed upon him but he told folk to give them to Old Symkyn. By the time his knowledge of suitable songs was exhausted, Symkyn's begging bowl was heavy with silver. Reluctant though to have the fine entertainment end, everyone insisted Seb must repeat *The Nut-Brown Maiden* one last time.

Out in the street, Adam was hastening by upon his frantic search when he heard Seb's unmistakable voice raised in joyful melody. He couldn't believe it – now of all times for his cousin to be making merry.

'For Jesu's sake, Seb!' Adam dragged his errant kinsman out into Cheapside. 'I've been searching half of London for you. Em's taken a turn for the worse.'

'Worse?'

'Aye. We must hasten. They've sent for Father Thomas and Surgeon Dagvyle whilst you've been swilling ale.' Adam stopped their hasty steps abruptly and turned Seb so they were face to face. 'Tell me true: you're not drunk, are you? Say you're not.'

'Nay. But I admit to drinking more than I should.' Seb shook his head and blinked a few times. 'I be somewhat befuddled...'

'Well, you'd better be sober by the time we get home, or I've a mind to throw you in the water trough. The trouble you've caused, Seb. Dame Ellen will have you boned, jointed and diced in pieces when she sees you. And you'd best brace yourself...'

the tidings aren't good.'

They resumed their race along Cheapside, crowds parting like the Red Sea before Moses at the sight of their grim faces.

# The Foxley House

But no one, not even Dame Ellen, took the trouble to berate Seb when they entered the kitchen. Like the folk in Cheapside, everyone made way, standing aside, so he could go upstairs, falling silent as he passed.

He approached the bedchamber at the end of the passage, much as a man would go to Tyburn gallows, aye, and the walk seemed as far. He hardly dared open the door. The womenfolk stepped back, as did Father Thomas. Someone left the stool at Em's bedside and he was pushed towards it. Murmuring a prayer, he sat, reluctant to look. It took a deal of courage to turn his gaze upon the bed.

Emily lay still, paler than the sheets, her eyes closed. He was too late! But, no. She took a breath.

'Emily,' he said softly, taking her hand in his. Her flesh already felt coffin-cold. ''Tis me, Seb. Hold fast, sweetheart, I pray you.'

Her eyes flickered open, God be thanked.

'I'm so frightened,' she whispered, her voice husky and quite unlike her own. 'They sent for Father Thomas… I don't want to die. Hold me. Don't let me go.'

'I have got you, Em, dearest.' He lifted her from the pillow, damp with fever sweat, and drew her close, holding her to his chest, hoping to calm her. 'I shall not leave you, Em. I love you, you know that. You be more than my own life, my soul, to me. Dearest Em… I cannot be without you. Hold fast, dear one. Stay with me…' The knot of emotion in his throat silenced him.

He held her, counting every breath she took.

Folk departed and others came into the chamber; he did not notice.

Em shuddered in his embrace and he looked down at her. Her eyes were open, her lips moved.

He put his ear to her mouth, that he might hear her words.

'I knew you'd come to me. I have ever loved you and ever will... my beloved... my Gabriel.' These were her last words, uttered upon a sigh.

Seb closed his eyes, staring at the red darkness behind his lids. Silent tears leaked as he felt her slip away. His dearest was gone, leaving him with a final sword thrust to the heart. Someone gripped his shoulder.

'Come, Seb. You have done your part.'

'No...'

'Father Thomas and Master Dagvyle must do their work now. Come away, Seb,' Rose said. She helped him to ease Emily back upon the pillow then led him from the chamber. Like one entranced, he went silently.

Folk spoke to him in the passageway, upon the stairs and in the kitchen. Where had so many come from? They were all murmuring soft phrases of consolation, but he could not make out their meanings. One word alone echoed in his ears, drowning out all others. It had been the quietest of whispers, a sigh, but it was as loud and clear to him as a shout from the rooftop.

'Gabriel!'

Her last thought had been of another man. She was in delirium, he told himself, knowing not what she said, mistaking him for another. But his heart would not be convinced. The truth was an agony he could hardly bear: Seb Foxley meant naught to her.

# St Michael le Querne Church

Somehow, time had gone missing from his life: erased, as though he had ceased to draw breath, an aeon betwixt heartbeats. How he came to be upon his knees, his face resting against the gilded carving of the rood screen, he was unable to recall. His throat ached. Tears. He remembered. So many tears.

Strong hands gripped his arm.

'Come, Seb. Enough. Let's take you home now.' Adam's voice was firm.

They raised him. His feet lacked feeling; his knees remained bent but his companions bore his weight – Adam on his right hand; Jack upon the left – until strength and use returned. They guided him as a blind man back out into the fading light of day.

'What hour is it?' Seb asked, although he may as well have enquired of the day, the month, the year even, for all he knew.

'You need to eat something,' Adam said. 'A mouthful or two, at least. Come, we'll take you home. 'Tis quieter there now and all is clean again.'

They went along Paternoster Row, pausing to let a laden dray rumble by and a group of urchins shouting and yelling. Adam led Seb and Jack up the alleyway to the side gate of the house. Unlike the street beyond, the yard was silent. Neither pig nor hens made any sound. Even the breeze passed through the apple tree and the herb garden without a rustle of leaf or sigh of blossom. The kitchen door stood ajar but the usual murmur of conversation within was lacking.

On the threshold, Seb stopped. He could not go in. This was not home as it should be. Something was terribly wrong. And then it struck him; Em was gone. All was amiss without her.

Adam nudged him.

'Go on in. You haven't seen the babe yet.'

'Babe? You mean Dickon? Aye, the motherless lamb. His

Papa should be there for him.'

'Indeed, he should, but I was speaking of the new babe. She was saved.'

'Saved?'

'She lives still, Seb, and we have engaged a wet-nurse for her already. Come now. Come and meet them both. You will recall Mercy Hutchinson?'

Seb saw a pleasant-featured woman sitting by the hearth and recalled having seen her somewhere but could not place her. She held a plump, healthy child to her breast.

'Is this...'

'Bless you, no, Master Foxley,' Mercy Hutchinson answered. 'This is Edmund, my own babe. Your daughter sleeps in the cradle there. Fear not, I have milk enough for both.'

Seb peered into the cradle, seeing naught but blankets.

Rose came and lifted the coverlet away, revealing the tiniest face Seb had ever seen. Bright red and wrinkled like a dried plum, it didn't look human.

'Is it... all as it should be?' he asked.

'Aye, small but perfectly formed,' Rose said. 'Shall you hold her? She's a feisty little lass. Nell Warren was surprised at the strength of her cries and she has such a grip when you offer her your finger.'

Seb shook his head.

'Nay. I shall not disturb her sleep.' He looked at Rose and she saw the pain reflected in his eyes. This child had robbed him of his beloved wife. He would find that hard to reconcile.

Rose couldn't know that his own birth had, likewise, caused a cherished wife's death with fearful consequences for him, the innocent babe – as he had learned not so long since.

'Father Thomas baptised her as soon as she was...' Rose searched for an appropriate word to describe the babe's advent, being cut from her mother's still-warm body. '...brought into the world. Peronelle and I stood as her godmothers, Adam as her godfather. We thought it best not to trouble you.' Indeed not, when the mother lay there, a violated, bloody corpse, emptied of its burden. 'We had to choose a name... we chose Julia. Em had mentioned to me how she thought it a pretty name, if the babe was a little maid. I hope you approve, Seb?'

'What of E-Em?'

'She lies upstairs. Dame Ellen and Peronelle are keeping vigil for now. Master Appleyard sat with her a while but he went home to make her coffin with his own hands. He will not see her using the common parish coffin. Oh, Seb, the poor man be distraught, so much so, Jack offered to aid him, though his assistance was refused, but we fear he'll not see through his tears to wield hammer and saw safely.

'Do you want to see Emily? All is quite seemly in the bedchamber now.'

Did he want to see her one last time? He did not know. Mayhap, it was a sense of duty, knowing it was expected of him, that drew him to the stair foot, one step following another, until he stood within the darkened chamber. Dame Ellen and Peronelle left to wait without. Candles burned at each corner of the bed, dried rose petals and herbs perfumed the air. The shrouded figure lay, neatly wrapped, the head upon a pillow, the spotless linen ghostly white in the candlelight.

Rose turned back the face cloth.

'She is at peace now, Seb, her pain ended.'

He looked upon the face of a sleeping woman but it was not his Emily. Not Emily of the sapphire eyes and hair of every autumnal hue. This one was colourless as wax, dreamless eyes forever closed, tresses hidden within the winding-sheet. This had naught to do with his beloved wife for she had left him long ago, replaced by a fickle, unloving creature. And yet he mourned her passing all the same. Was it grief or melancholy concerning his own situation: a widower with two motherless infants? Two small children denied a mother's love and tender care. He would weep for their loss, not his own.

'Will you kiss her one final time?' Rose asked softly.

'She would not want that,' he said.

Rose might have contradicted him but didn't. She simply replaced the face cloth. She was about to ask if he would spend time alone with Emily but, having murmured a single prayer for a soul departed, he crossed himself and left the dead to slumber.

He knew not what he felt any longer, nor what he ought to feel. A sense of abandonment was uppermost in his mind and deep within his heart.

## Saturday, the seventeenth day of April

A kind of solemn chaos ensued – if such a thing was possible. Folk moved about on tip-toe, speaking in whispers, but confusion ruled the day in the Foxley household.

Rose set out platters of bread, ham, cheese, cold smoked eel, pickled herrings and tiny fishcakes upon the kitchen board. If any were hungry, they could help themselves. Cooking a proper meal was impossible with so many comings and goings and Nessie was of less use than a knife made of paper. Her bouts of weeping were overloud in a house of mourning, so Rose had sent her to market, to purchase additional provisions for after the funeral this eve, telling her not to hasten back. Nessie would spread the word abroad: the whole of London would know of Emily's passing by suppertime.

Kate helped Rose in setting out the board, saying naught – as silent as Nessie was raucous. Dame Ellen sat by the fire, the grey cat curled at her feet, dabbing her eyes with her apron every now and then, sometimes seeming to doze. The elderly woman was exhausted after the long night of fraught activity followed by a vigil; she was too tired to walk home. Peronelle and Nell Warren were now keeping vigil in the bedchamber above stairs.

Mercy Hutchinson sat opposite Dame Ellen across

the hearthstone, holding the tiny new babe to her breast, encouraging it to suckle with gentle words, stroking its face with a fingertip. It mewed, kitten-like, but then seemed to taste the milk and began to nurse.

While the women kept to the kitchen, coping with a continuous succession of visitors, offering condolences and wanting to see the babe that had, miraculously, survived its mother's fatal ordeal, the shop remained closed up, as was respectful.

Thus, Adam had no employment and went to Appleyard's workshop, to offer his services, to assist in the making of the coffin. However, Stephen had aid enough from his son, John, Emily's brother, and Jack also, so Adam decided to go in search of Seb and, maybe, some ale along the way.

As the bereaved husband, Seb ought, by right and for courtesy's sake, to have been at home, to accept the condolences of friends, neighbours and kinsmen. However, he had not been seen for some while, along with little Dickon and Gawain. Adam, though, had an idea where he might have gone.

## The Horse Pool

Seb sat on the damp turf 'neath his favoured oak tree. Dickon and Gawain played in last autumn's fallen leaves around the trunk. The child babbled and chuckled in delight, an incongruous sound, utterly out of place upon such a day. Seb had nigh reprimanded him until he realised the little lad had no understanding of the doleful events.

He gazed at the waters of the Horse Pool, watching the sunlight dance along the wavelets, stirred by a soft breeze. Primroses turned their smiling faces to the sun. Windflowers spangled the grass in pale profusion, nodding their heads, as if to the musick of the birds that sang their joyous hymns to the spring. How could the world be so beautiful still? How could nature be so full of joy? Did they not know of his loss; this darkest of times?

'I thought you would be here.' Adam came across the grass. 'I bought ale, knowing you would be in need.'

Seb did not need ale. More than that: he did not need nor desire company. He wanted to sit in silence, in peace.

Having left the ale-skin beside Seb, Adam sat a little way from him and began entertaining Dickon, making grass-blade whistles that pierced the quiet air with their shrill piping.

Seb got up and walked away, wandered around to the far side of the lake. The noise was too much. He needed to be alone. Since Adam now had care of the child, this was his chance for solitude and long may it last – forever, mayhap.

At the farthest end of the water, the hedgerow grew close. There was just room enough betwixt the spiky quickthorn bushes and the yellow irises at the water's margin for him to sit, unobserved, so he hoped. His throat still held the ache of tears but he could weep no more. His was a silent grief now.


Little Dickon grew tired of playing. Even being swung high in the air by Adam could no longer distract the child from the fact that he was hungry. He demonstrated his need by sucking his thumb and grizzling, so it was fortunate that his father returned.

Seb said naught but, when Adam suggested it was time to go home, he nodded and took the fractious toddling in his arms, making for the lane back to Newgate. Dickon fell asleep, his head snuggled against his parent's shoulder. It was a silent little procession: two sombre men, a sleeping child; even the dog trotted quietly at heel.

Adam did not expect others to have heard of a death in their household, but it seemed word had reached Mistress Fletcher at The Hart's Horn. She came forward to offer her condolences along with a tray of small fruit turnovers for the funeral repast later. News had also come to the gatekeeper's ears at Newgate somehow. As they passed by, the old fellow removed his cap and bowed his head in respect. Adam acknowledged the courtesy with a nod. Seb, though, seemed unaware, his eyes kept low, his brow furrowed deeply as a new-ploughed field. What solemn thoughts were hidden behind such an expression, Adam could well suppose.

Along the Shambles, down Ivy Lane and into Paternoster Row, folk did likewise. Anyone who did not yet know of Emily's departing saw what others did and followed their example. Only afterwards, with caps replaced, did they enquire for whom they paid their respects. Londoners never remained ignorant of ill-tidings for long.

'We're right sorry to learn of your loss,' Jonathan Caldicott stepped from his door to address Adam as Seb walked on. Mistress Caldicott followed her husband, apron at the ready to dab her tears.

'Aye, but a daughter was born, we hear,' the goodwife interrupted, elbowing her man aside. 'But what of Master Seb? Is he pleased to have a daughter? Jonathan was delighted when our Joan was born, after three sons. Were you not, Jonathan? Has she been baptised yet? It would be as well, wouldn't it? She was born afore time. Emily told me the other day she had yet a month or more to wait. What have you named the tiny mite? Who is to be her wet-nurse? When may I see her?'

Adam held up his hands to restrain the flow of questions.

'Her name is Julia, mistress, and mayhap, upon the morrow, you may see her.'

'Does she take after her mother? Or does she bear a resemblance to Master Seb?'

'You may determine that for yourself at some time hence. Now please excuse us. There is much to do before this eve of obsequies.'

'How discourteous!' Mistress Caldicott complained loudly, so her neighbours might hear. 'That Adam Armitage is no Londoner, that's for certain. Do they teach them no manners in Norfolk, or wherever he hails from?'

'Come now, Mary, he was civil enough. Their household is bereaved. You must make allowances. Besides, he spoke the truth: no doubt they have much to do, to arrange for torch-bearers, alms-giving and prepare the funeral meats. You are too hard on our neighbours at this time. Besides… Seb has no cause to be polite to us, remember. We owe him our abject apologies.'

'You do; not me! He let me down and yet owes me coin, so do not berate me, Jonathan Caldicott, or there will be no bed-sport for you, even though the Lenten fast is done at last. I don't care that you have been continent for forty days; you can wait another forty, if you dare chide me thus. Now, go mend that henhouse, as you should have done long since, before my hens wander off again.'


It was the case that, elsewhere, even next door in Paternoster Row, life went on as it always did. Only for Seb had the world, as he knew it, come to an end, destroyed by a single word uttered upon a last breath. Gabriel.

# Chapter 19

## Saturday eve, the seventeenth day of April
## St Michael le Querne Church

A SOFT, WET mist shrouded the little churchyard. It was as if the weather itself was mourning the passing of a young wife and mother. The obsequies had been done and now the relatives, friends and neighbours were leaving in solemn, torchlit procession to the Foxley house. There, they would partake of a light supper whilst reminiscing upon the all-too-short life of the departed.

Adam touched Seb's arm. Throughout the funeral, he had stood like a sleep-walker, staring down, seeing naught. Adam wondered if he had heard a word of Father Thomas's kindly eulogy or the commiserations offered by those gathered at the graveside.

'Come, Seb. I fear you must play your part. I know how hard this is for you, but at least try to acknowledge the condolences given. Folk are whispering that you are too drunk to know what you're about.' Adam took a torch from a pauper who had been paid two pence to carry it in the procession with the promise of a meal after. 'Go on with the rest,' Adam told the poor man. 'I will bring Master Foxley home.'

Seb went with Adam, wordless as they walked the few yards along Paternoster Row. Adam tried to give him encouragement, telling him the hour would soon pass and everyone be gone home. In the flickering light of the torch, Adam did his best to read Seb's expression but his face seemed as blank as new parchment. In truth, it was as if he accompanied only the empty husk of the man he loved as a brother, as though Seb's heart had gone with Emily into the cold earth. Tears he could have consoled; an outpouring of grief could be understood and allowances made, but this silence; the unseeing eyes, Adam knew not how to deal with these.

Rose played the part of the gracious hostess and Stephen Appleyard took it upon himself to thank everyone who came. Disapproving glances were cast at the new widower, who did not so much as trouble to greet a single mourner. Mayhap, they would excuse the discourtesy as the result of shock and an excess of grief; then again, mayhap they wouldn't.

Mercy Hutchinson had taken little Dickon and the new babe home with her own children. A house of mourning was no place for the little ones. Besides, Nicholas, the toddling, was behaving badly, shouting and bawling and making his brother Edmund cry, which, in turn, was upsetting Dickon, who appeared to sense that something had changed for the worse in his young life.

When only the household remained, having said farewell to Stephen and his son, John, who departed together, Rose, Kate and Nessie began to collect up platters and cups and put them to await washing up in the morn. Jack felt he had suffered more than enough woe and misery for one day and took himself off to the attic he used to share with Tom. Having a room to himself was a novelty still: nobody snoring or farting or complaining if he did the like.

Adam sat in the parlour with Seb, also eager for his bed but reluctant to leave his cousin alone. But as his eyelids drooped and he found it a struggle to keep them open, he relented.

'I'm that weary, Seb. Will you want to share my chamber again? Come, I'll light our way up the stair.'

Seb did not move nor make answer, only stared into the embers of the fading fire in the hearth. His ale cup was in his hand, still full.

'I'll stay with him,' Rose said.

Adam nodded.

'Not too long now.'

Rose removed the cup from Seb's hand for fear he might spill it and stood it upon the hearthstone. She fetched a stool and sat close to him, but not so near that they touched. Under her breath, she began reciting her nightly prayers: the *Paternoster,* a novena of *Ave Marias* and her private plea for blessings upon this house and upon Seb in particular. This was not because of his loss this day; she always prayed for him especially. When first she had come to dwell under his roof, she had prayed out of gratitude because he had saved her from her old life; rescued her from working as a tavern wench, ill-used by any man who took a fancy to her whilst the owner of The Pewter Pot kept the few coins she earned. Abused by her father and his apprentices even before that, Seb was the first man ever to treat her as a woman of value. He made her feel clean again and deserved every prayer for that. But even had he not achieved that marvellous change as to how she viewed herself, she would call down every blessing upon him for his kindness, his gentleness. Seeing him now, her heart ached for him.

## Sunday, the eighteenth day of April
## The Foxley House

'What came to pass last night, Rose?' Adam asked as the household prepared for church. 'If Seb doesn't hasten, we'll be late.'

'I dare say he's weary after last eve,' Rose replied. 'I know not what time he went to bed but I was alone in the parlour when I awoke. He left me to sleep undisturbed on the settle.'

'Well, he did not come to share my chamber. He must be in his own lonely bed: a brave thing indeed. I'll go wake him.' Adam sprinted up the stair and along the passage to bedchamber that overlooked Paternoster Row. The shutters were yet closed. 'Come, Seb, bestir yourself.' Adam opened the shutters, letting the milky dawnlight in through the diamond panes, illuminating the room. He turned, preparing to shake his cousin awake, if need be. But the bed was empty; the covers undisturbed.

Adam raced back to the kitchen.

'He's not there. Must be in the workshop.'

'Master Seb's not there,' Kate said. 'I left my cloak there yester eve and went to fetch it.'

'Then where can he be? He must have forgotten the day.' Rose wrung her hands in her apron, screwing the linen into a ball of creases. 'Might he have gone to Mercy Hutchinson's, to collect the little ones? Oh, Adam, he was so forlorn last eve, I fear for him.'

'Mayhap, he is at church before us? Aye, that must be the way of it. Seb has gone to St Michael's already. Prayer will be his only consolation, Rose, you know how he is.'

'Aye, a far longer penance might appeal to him but I wish he had said.'

'Seb is ever a man of few words, especially in his grief. I misdoubt he spoke more than two words to any who attended the obsequies last eve. His lack of courtesy drew comment.'

'Poor Seb. His mind must be in turmoil,' Rose said. 'I shall light a candle for him.'

When they returned from church, Seb was in the workshop. He said naught of where he had been but now he was grinding pigments in readiness for Duke Richard's commission, no matter that it was the Lord's Day.

When Adam dared remind him, he was ignored and seeing the wild look in his cousin's eye, he said no more.

346

# The Epilogue

## Thursday, the twentieth day of May, Ascension Day

It was a holy day. The shop in Paternoster Row was closed in honour of the day Our Lord Jesu ascended into Heaven to sit at His Father's right hand.

Emily's month-mind had passed a few days before. The house had been crowded again but Rose had organised everything, even hiring two men to act as servitors, fetching, carrying and presenting the dishes at the feast. Extra pewter platters, bowls, spoons and napkins were also hired and wine purchased with the option of returning what wasn't consumed, along with the cups, after the day was done.

The memorial to Emily could hardly have been done better, Seb acknowledged that, but he would have preferred to spend the day working. Duke Richard's coat-of-arms had likely saved his sanity these last weeks. He had immersed himself in the commission, working from dawn 'til dusk. Sundays and holy days, such as this, proved a trial indeed when labour was not permitted. Sometimes he had ignored them and worked anyway. Idleness was a widower's worst enemy, Seb discovered, allowing too much time for remembering, bringing to mind all that he most wanted to forget. Not that he could recall anything of the funeral itself. He'd been like one both sightless and deaf that eve, although he had a remembrance of feeling rain upon his face or, mayhap, it had been tears.

He was also aware that he was proving a trial to everyone else these days, not hearing folk who spoke to him, forgetting tasks he had promised to do and being short of temper with others for the least of reasons.

But they bore his tiresomeness without complaint. He must try to make amends somehow.

And now the commission was complete. The escutcheon could be polished and dusted no more. Every area of gilding was burnished to perfection, every bright colour of the quarterings gleamed, more like stained glass than paint. The ducal coronet caught the light just so, such that it appeared real and ready to adorn the royal brow, rather than a flat image. The Order of the Garter seemed likewise, prepared to adorn the noble thigh. And the motto scroll at the foot might almost lift and be blown away upon the wind. Seb was pleased with the result of his handiwork yet wished it was not done. How could he occupy his mind now, warding off dire thoughts and dismal contemplations?

'Seb, you've made a fine job of that,' Rose said when he called her to the workshop. 'The duke will be delighted with it, I know. Such workmanship as I've never seen...'

''Tis right heavy now, what with all the plaster and gold. I must parcel it up for safety's sake... I'll have to borrow a handcart to get it to Crosby Place upon the morrow.'

'Then you can have a well-earned rest from your labours. You've been working so hard since...'

'Aye. A-and what shall I do then?'

Rose noted the catch in his voice, saw the glint of tears in his eyes. His query concerned far more than simply his work. He looked forlorn indeed. She stepped towards him, coming betwixt the man and the fruit of so much time and effort.

'Start afresh; some new project. Make a new beginning.' Rose touched his pigment-stained fingers. 'I could help you,' she said softly. 'We could do it together if you wish?'

# Author's Note

Emily's sickness is based on the symptoms of eclampsia. Even today, pregnant women can suffer from pre-eclampsia – the precise cause of which remains unknown – but the baby is delivered by caesarean section before the mother develops full-blown eclampsia and, with modern medical techniques, there is usually a happy outcome. In times past, a caesarean operation was only performed as the mother lay dying or dead because, for her, there was no chance of recovery but the child just might be saved.

There really was a Pierpoint family who owned the manor of Hurst Pierpoint near Arundel, in Sussex, but the old man is fictitious, as are the events concerning him. The best result for Lord Pierpoint would have been for Sir Marcus Pierpoint to purchase a corrody for his father and the faithful Walter. A corrody was the medieval equivalent of a residential arrangement made for the elderly by their family, paying for them to live as permanent guests in a monastery. The closest to Hurst Pierpoint was St Nicholas Priory. There the two old men could have lived out the rest of their days in comfort, together, cared for by the good brothers.

Elizabeth Moring was a real person. Better known as Bessie, she used to take on girls as her apprentices, supposedly to train them as embroiderers but instead prostituted them to "friars and chaplains" in particular. She was tried at Guildhall, found guilty of turning innocent girls into whores and a tavern into an unlicensed brothel. She had to suffer punishment by being put in the "thews" – a special kind of stocks designed for female offenders – before being taken to the nearest city gate and forced to "foreswear the city", meaning she was banished from London forever.

There is no record of what happened to the girls. Their names are fictitious with two exceptions: Cherry-lips existed and was punished as a prostitute; John Rykener [aka Eleanor] was also real. Renowned for dressing as a woman, he used to consort with clerical gentlemen, in particular, including a few Oxford scholars, one of whom was a certain William Foxley – by coincidence. However, only in this tale was there any connection between Bessie and the cross-dresser.

Later, John is recorded as claiming to have "obliged" housewives too but said he never charged them for his services. He even confessed that he had "married" a man and lived as his wife for a number of years. When arrested, having been found *in flagrante* with a man in a stable, John appeared in court, still wearing a dress. The authorities didn't know what crime to charge him with – homosexuality wasn't illegal in medieval England – so they fined him for misrepresentation, a regulation that usually referred to selling counterfeit goods and fakes. Who knows: we may meet John again in a future novel?

# More in this series

For readers who may wish to read of Seb's first encounter with Francis, Lord Lovell, that story is told in the first Sebastian Foxley mystery, *The Colour of Poison*.

Rose's story begins in the third mystery, *The Colour of Cold Blood*. And Seb's scary experiences in the tunnels beneath the Tower of London are recounted in the fifth mystery, *The Colour of Murder*.

Other books in the series are number two, *The Colour of Gold* – a novella telling of Seb and Emily's wedding.

Number 4, *The Colour of Betrayal* – a Christmas novella.

Number 6, *The Colour of Death* – a novella set at Foxley village in Norfolk.

Number 7, *The Colour of Lies* – novel set during St Bartholomew's Fayre in London.

All titles are available from MadeGlobal through Amazon as paperbacks and Kindle downloads. *The Colour of Poison* is also available as an audiobook.

Seb's next adventure, his ninth mystery, will be *The Colour of Evil*.

OUT SOON

# THE COLOUR OF EVIL

ENJOY THIS PREVIEW...

# *Prologue*

I F EVER there was a hell-on-earth, this was it, in the city's very heart.

In the rats' nest of alleyways south of Tower Street, Furnace Court was more noisome than most. Sunlight never dared trespass among the soot-encrusted walls, nor tip-toed into the confines where fire burned, smoke choked and the din of metal on metal rang out, assaulting the ears. Yet a man made his living here. Bare-armed and brawny, smut-covered, the smith toiled at his anvil in the near darkness, working by the flickering light of the devil's flames. Sweating, he hammered and quenched, reheated and shaped, forcing his will upon the metals at his mercy. No iron could resist his power.

But such heavy labours were not his sole employment. Elsewhere, in the secret darkness beneath the streets, he had a second, smaller furnace. A more lucrative trade was to be had here, furtive and treasonous, undermining the prosperity of a kingdom. Hamo cared not a jot. In supposed-silver coins, struck with a die stolen from the nearby Tower Mint, there was money to be made – literally.

As the instigator, the greedy genius behind this crime, spread more of the gleaming, underweight groats and pennies throughout the city, strangers began to notice. Such coins undermined their livelihood and must be traced back to the source.

Thus it was that two men, speaking English with a foreign sound, came to a shop, just as the owner was closing the shutters at day's end, demanding to be told the origin of the coins at fault. When no answer was forthcoming, the pair resorted to torture: scores of small cuts, none fatal, but each draining the victim's strength a little more. Every time they paused, removing the rag from the victim's mouth, they repeated the question:

'Who makes these coins?'

The victim did not know the answer. He had but borrowed them to pay what he owed. Exchanging a debt to one for a debt to another.

The cuts continued until the strangers were certain the victim spoke true by which time only death awaited but they would not deliver the fatal cut. Time would do that. But it was necessary that a clear message be left. And it could not be spoken by the victim. For fear he might name them, they split his tongue in twain – to warn the devious serpent lurking behind the counterfeiting business that they would hunt him down. Then, to show how much they knew of it, they covered the victim's right hand – the guilty hand that passed the fake coins – in shiny pigment, brought for the purpose. And to end the message: that there was no escaping their retribution, they nailed the dying victim's hand to his workbench and left a bag of the false money behind.

The new-minted coins, used to pay debts to the strangers, shone even brighter than silver: the colour of evil.

# *Chapter 1*

## Friday, the eleventh day of June in the year of Our Lord 1479
## The Foxley House in Paternoster Row in the City of London

I RETURNED HOME with my purchases of quills and ink, Gawain at my heel. I could have asked Kate or Nessie to buy them, although, in truth, such items were not needed in the workshop. The errand was simply a means of escape. I entered the kitchen but the sense of something – someone – missing assailed me, like an icy hand clutching my heart, as it always did these days.

Rose sat stitching a pair of gloves of lavender-dyed kid leather, her work so delicate, the stitches were nigh invisible. Little Dickon was at her feet, playing some unknown game with a bunch of straws and a few twigs. Nessie stood at the board chopping fresh sage from the garden, the kitchen filled with its earthy scent. 'Twas a scene of domestic tranquillity, yet utterly amiss.

My Emily was not there.

I could not get used to the lack – a black hole in my soul that I feared naught would ever fill entirely.

I lifted Dickon from the floor. He laughed, showing off his few perfect white teeth.

'Does my little man fare well?' I asked him. A string of dribble down my jerkin was the answer to my query.

'He does very well,' Rose said. 'Dickon, show your Papa how you can play at peep-boo.'

The child put his fists over his eyes then took them away of a sudden, shrieking with delight. I took up a table napkin to assist his game, covering my face with it. He pulled it aside, shouting 'Boo!' It was a merry jest indeed and one he seemed unlikely to tire of in the near future. I had work to do but what of that? Merriment was hard to come by of late. Thus, I would play with my son a while. He would attain his first commemoration of his birth date in the week to come: the first significant day in his life thus far. I prayed daily that he would see many, many more, as so many infants do not.

'Mercy is coming to dinner,' Rose said, 'That you may see Julia.'

I nodded.

Julia was my daughter, born two months since upon that most sorrowful of days. The widow, Mercy Hutchinson, was the infant's wet nurse but having three sons of her own, including Edmund who was a little older than Julia, she had taken the new babe to live with her in Distaff Lane until she was weaned. Mercy's other children were Simon, a scholar at St Paul's School, and that scamp Nicholas – a toddling who was trouble upon two legs. I remained uncertain of the wisdom of having Nicholas visit too often, fearing Dickon might copy the elder child's bad habits – biting people being his most recent undesirable trait. But Mercy and my kinsman Adam were betrothed, so I had to make the best of it: Nicholas would one day become a member of the family.

Neither was I able to determine for certain quite how I felt about Julia. Born too soon, she was the cause of my beloved Emily's death. Yet she was an innocent. My own father once admitted that he had found it difficult, at first, to forgive me because my mother had died of a fever some days after my birth. I refused to blame my tiny daughter in like manner but realised now how hard it was to form an affection for the cause of so much grief. But Mercy and Rose were determined I should learn to love the child. Hence the nigh-daily visits when they expected me to take the babe in my arms and hold her close, whether I wished it or not.

When Mistress Hutchinson arrived with three children – the two babes being in slings, one upon each hip – with Nicholas held firmly by the hand, I had hardly begun my morning's work. In truth, since the completion of Duke Richard's coat-of-arms which had engrossed me and filled the bleak days after Em's passing, I found enthusiasm lacking for any new project. This was an experience quite new to me and one I prayed would end swiftly.

A man with a household and children to provide for cannot afford to shirk his duties, idling away the hours, wasting his efforts on inessential tasks. I had tidied the storeroom and checked the inventory so many times. I dusted shelves and swept the shop and workshop – tasks for the lowliest apprentice – rearranged my desk over and over and compiled endless lists. How frequently I sat down to work, all determined, prepared the ink, dipped the pen or brush and then... did naught. I could not settle. Inspiration was there none; my imagination dried up and shrivelled as last autumn's leaf-fall.

I greeted Mistress Hutchinson in the kitchen. As usual, she smiled and handed my tiny daughter into my arms.

'She's grown, has she not, Master Seb? She feeds and sleeps well. You should be pleased with her progress.'

'Aye. You be doing right well in caring for her, mistress. I be grateful indeed.' The mite in my arms looked plump enough but what did I know of babes?

'She'll be waking soon for her feed. Nicholas! Let the kindling wood be, for heaven's sake.'

As usual, Nicholas was up to his tricks. The wood stacked by the kitchen hearth had caught his eye and before anyone could prevent it, he grabbed a piece from the bottom of the pile and brought the heap tumbling down upon himself. There was not so much that he was harmed, merely startled, but began to bawl. The noise roused both babes, Julia and Edmund, as well as upsetting little Dickon, all of them joining in, howling.

How did women ever put up with such din without running mad?

My daughter was wailing now with great enthusiasm, so I handed her back to Mistress Hutchinson right eagerly.

'If you could distract Nicholas, Master Seb, that would help,' she said. 'He likes you.'

I was unconvinced that Nicholas liked anyone and wished Adam would come to rescue me from his future stepson but my kinsman was working. It was as well that one of us yet earned his bread and disturbing him would serve no purpose. Thus it was I had two toddlings to keep amused and out of harm's way.

Dickon was ever biddable and easy to distract with clapping games, foolish songs or his favoured rag ball. Nicholas was another case entirely: cast your glance elsewhere for an instant and he would be causing mischief. Only yesterday, he had succeeded in opening the gate into the pigsty. It took Adam, Kate and me – much hampered by Gawain who thought it a right merry game, barking and getting underfoot – to catch the escaped piglet, keep Nicholas from playing with the dung and prevent Dickon from copying him. Nicholas' face and hair were plastered in pig ordure and it seemed all too likely he had eaten some of it. I did not envy his mother having to clean him up after and wondered at the possible consequences of swallowing dung. As it was, he seemed none the worse for it this morn.

During my earlier inventories of the storeroom, I had espied the old sand tray. It had not been used since I first attempted to teach Jack his letters, writing them out in the damp sand with a finger, to learn the shapes and the correct order of strokes in their formation. A waste of effort that had been; Jack was never meant to be a scrivener. But now it might serve to amuse the little ones. Their attempts could hardly be any worse than Jack's, even at their young age.

Having first checked that the pigsty gate was secured, having learned a lesson yesterday, I set the tray down in the yard and tipped the fine sand into it. Nicholas began flinging it around even afore I had moistened it with water from the trough. Dickon received a face-full and some got in his eye, causing him to weep – the best thing since it would wash out the sand but he required consoling. Finally, the sand was evenly spread and dampened and I demonstrated how to draw marks in it with my finger and make imprints with my hand.

Dickon became quite enthralled, poking his finger into the sand, making numerous holes, chuckling all the while. Gawain joined in – whether he intended to or no – making a large paw print and a nose print in the midst of the tray. But Nicholas surprised me, drawing circles and swirls and patterns of lines, all most pleasing to the eye. What a revelation, that the little scamp could be creative! I regarded him anew.

Had I been unjust in thinking him ungovernable? Mayhap, he misbehaved for why he had naught else to do. His mother was much concerned with his younger brother, Edmund, and now Julia. His elder brother, Simon, had school to think on. Without a father, none had much leisure nor interest in Nicholas. Could that be the cause? I vowed to give the toddling greater consideration. In truth, he looked to be earning it: an hour passed and still he sat content, making marks in the sand, long after Dickon had turned his attention to ants among the cobbles of the yard and Gawain had gone to investigate the denizens of the hedgerow at the nether end of the garden plot.

The difficulties arose in persuading Nicholas to leave the sand when we were summoned to dinner. Then battle ensued over the washing of hands. Oh, well, a man can only achieve so much in a single morn. I thought I had not done too badly, playing my part as a mother hen.

After dinner, as I was ruling margins in readiness for some project, at yet undetermined, Kate came hastening to call me into the shop. Her eyes were wide as Sunday platters, her fingers knotting themselves in her apron.

'Whatever is it, lass?' I asked. 'I heard no commotion.'

'A messenger, master, asking for you in person. An-and he wears the king's livery.'

I was into the shop faster than a cat with its tail afire, then paused. It would not do to appear flustered. I smoothed my hair 'neath my cap and pulled my jerkin straight. My sleeve-ends were ink-stained but 'twas no time to remedy that. I entered the shop at a measured pace much belied by my racing heart.

'Sir.' I bowed to the messenger, removing my hat.

He greeted me likewise.

'You are Master Sebastian Foxley?'

'I am, sir. How may I serve you?'

'The King's Grace, the Lord Edward, has a commission for you. He has seen your work and approves of it. He would have a book to send as a gift to the Lord of Florence, Lorenzo de Medici. A trustworthy merchant is to serve as the English ambassador in Florence and he must impress this Medici who is said to be learned and cultured, as well as much interested in the fine arts of war.

'Therefore, the King's Grace would have a luxurious and elegant Latin copy – and accurate, of course – of Vegetius' De Re Militari to be presented upon arrival. The merchant sails at the end of July. The book must be ready well in advance, that the king may inspect and inscribe it. You will oblige His Grace?'

Oblige, I thought? As if I dare refuse the king?

'I shall be honoured, sir, to serve King Edward in any way.'

'That is well. And here are the requirements...' The messenger took a small roll of parchment from his official pouch and passed it to me. It was tied with red ribbon. 'I bid you good day, Master Foxley.' With that, he touched his cap, turned upon his heel and departed the shop.

Supposing the requirements were unclear? What if an unforeseen difficulty arose? Of whom should I enquire? I undid the ribbon and unrolled my set of instructions.

At first glance, they appeared sufficiently comprehensive but one matter remained unmentioned. Neither had the messenger broached the subject: money. How and when would I be reimbursed for my expenses, the cost of materials and the hours of labour needful to complete the commission? The Duke of Gloucester always paid me at least half the agreed sum in advance and the remainder was ever settled swiftly when he received the finished piece. It appeared that his royal brother did not do likewise. In truth, no remuneration whatsoever was referred to in my instructions, no sum agreed beforehand. It gave me pause, considering how best to proceed. I should discuss the matter with Emily...

Oh. I closed my eyes and breathed deeply. I had forgotten for a moment. Mayhap, Adam could advise me? Or Rose? Or my old master, Richard Collop?

In the workshop, Adam set down his pen and looked to me, an eager glint in his eye.

'A king's messenger, eh? What did he want, Seb? You're not in any trouble, are you?'

'Nay.' I gave him the instructions. 'We have received a commission from King Edward.'

'Well! What a fine feather in our caps that will be. The name and reputation of Foxley can go no higher. We must celebrate.' He read the parchment. 'Vegetius... in Latin... do we have an exemplar for this?'

'We do not.'

He watched me for a moment.

'Is that the reason for your expression of woe, cousin? Aren't you delighted to be working for the king himself? Or do you not approve Vegetius? Do you fear the Latin will be difficult?'

'My old master, Richard Collop, has a Latin version of Vegetius and I be certain he will permit us to borrow it since we have so illustrious a customer. And I have copied parts of that same treatise when I was Master Richard's apprentice: the text presented few problems, as I recall.'

'Then why the long face?'

'Payment, Adam: neither the messenger nor those instructions make any mention of how or when or by whom we will be paid for our work.'

'But it's the king... he can afford any and every luxury he has a fancy for. Paying us will be no hardship.'

'Ah, Adam, mayhap you have not lived in London long enough to have heard the merchants, the grocers, the vintners and the fishmongers all griping and moaning about the Exchequer, the Royal Wardrobe and the Privy Purse failing to settle their reckonings. 'Tis well known that the king's coffers are ever bare and he be the worst debtor in the city... in England, for all I know. Many merchants truly fear receiving an order for goods from Westminster, knowing they may wait years for payment and yet they do not dare refuse. 'Tis as if the king believes the honour of being of service to him be compensation enough to atone for loss of coin.

'Thus, you be correct regarding the gilding of our reputation but what of the cost for so elaborate a volume? We could be the losers in this commission, Adam, and I be uncertain whether the possibility of it inspiring future, lucrative orders from other customers will make good such losses. The bejewelled binding alone, as per the instructions, could cost us a small fortune. That be the reason why my delight stands tempered by caution.'

Adam sighed, his shoulders drooped.

'I hadn't realised getting payment might be a problem. But you'll still accept the commission?'

'Of course. How may I refuse the king? 'Tis a royal command, no less. The matter requiring most thought though is... do we do the work to a reasonably high standard but trim our use of materials to reduce costs? Or do we oblige our sovereign to the utmost of our abilities, stinting naught, and pray that it so impresses him he actually hands over coin for it? I do not know if we even dare send him the reckoning? What be the etiquette for asking money of the king?'

'Who might you ask about such delicate matters, Seb? There must be someone who can advise us afore we begin ordering the finest parchment, gold leaf and lapis lazuli?'

'Aye: Master Collop. I trust his judgement in all things regarding business.'

'But not in his choice of a second wife, eh?' Adam laughed. This had been a source of mystery, aye, and mirth to many of our fellow stationers in recent years. 'She's a dainty piece but hardly a suitable spouse for the Warden of the Stationers' Guild, being barely one third of his age. She was giving me the come-hither look across the tablecloth at the Whitsun feast, the saucy wench. If I was Warden Collop, I wouldn't trust her an inch or take my eye off her for one moment.'

''Twas but your imagination, cousin, I be certain. Mistress Collop may be young but a good wife for all that. Master Collop would not have wed her elsewise.'

Adam grinned and chuckled.

'You're innocent as a newborn lamb, aren't you, Seb? When it comes to women, at least.'

'That be untrue. I be no fool, cousin.'

He simply laughed all the more, the knave.

# Master Richard Collop's
# stationer's shop, Cheapside

Later that afternoon, we made our way to Master Collop's shop along Cheapside, to the north end of Soper Lane, opposite the Hospital of St Thomas Acon. How many times had I made my way here in my youth from my father's house by St Martin-le-Grand, lame and leaning upon my staff, to learn my craft as a scribe, illuminator and book-binder?

Richard Collop had been a good and kindly master to me, realising my talent as an artist early on. Not so my fellow apprentices who made mock of my affliction at every opportunity. Had it not been for Mistress Collop's keen eye – she who had been the master's first wife – my years served there could have been an enduring penance but she succeeded in shielding me from my fellows' worst taunts much of the time. Only occasionally did the eldest of we three apprentices – Guy Linton by name, I recall – manage to hurt me with his words as well as deeds. But that was in the past; matters are quite different now.

'Good day to you, Sebastian, Adam.' Master Collop greeted us as we entered his shop. It was twofold larger than our premises at least and I noted an impressive array of handsome volumes, set out upon new book shelves that I had not seen afore. 'Come you through to the parlour and we may share ale and wafers and speak in comfort.'

As we passed the workshop doorway – once so familiar to me – I could not help but glance in. There, at the desk where I used to sit, I glimpsed a dark, tousled head, bent low over a ruled page. It might have been me... until the lad glanced up. The snub nose and a thousand freckles scattered like ochre pigment powder across his face were never mine. Then I saw he held the pen cack-handed, as they say, in his left hand.

'That's young Hugh Gardyner, the Lord Mayor's nephew,'

Master Collop said, seeing the direction of my gaze. 'God be praised, he's a promising lad and a hard-working apprentice. Unlike so many,' he added, sighing.

Did we not all make that discovery where youngsters were concerned?

'You may recall your fellow: Guy Linton?' master continued.

Indeed I did: one who would avoid labour whenever he might.

'He came to see me last eve, asking after you, your whereabouts these days.'

'Oh? Did he give a reason?' I asked. 'I cannot imagine why he should. We were never close in age or fellowship except for both being in your service when our terms overlapped – a matter of months only.'

'He never said.'

'I misdoubt he was concerned for my welfare. It must be a matter of business. 'Tis quite an odd happenstance. I pray you, good master, should he ask after me again, if you would kindly enquire of him the reason.'

Master Collop led us to a well-appointed room. A tapestry hung upon the wall. I remembered it: 'Jason and the Argonauts', although lowly apprentices were permitted in the parlour but rarely.

'To what do I owe this pleasure?' our host enquired once we were settled upon a cushioned bench, ale cups in hand. 'You did not come simply to ask after my health and discuss old times, I know.'

I felt a surge of guilt. I ought to visit him more often. His hair remained thick as ever but was now bleach-white at his forehead and around his ears, marking the passing years.

''Tis true, master, for which I apologise sincerely. I have come in need of your sound advice upon a delicate matter.' I sipped my ale, watching my master discreetly over the cup rim.

'Hence why you did not ask me at the guild hall meeting yesterday.'

'The matter did not arise until an hour or two since.'

'Urgent then? Well, tell me of this business that is of such import.'

I delved into my purse and retrieved the little roll of parchment tied with red ribbon. I passed it to my master.

''Tis a commission from King Edward, no less,' I explained.

He undid the bow and unrolled my instructions. He read it silently but his lips formed each word. He frowned once or twice and nodded approval at the end. The parchment re-rolled itself as he set it down.

'The instructions appear to be clear enough but it will be an expensive volume to produce as the king requires. He means it to be an impressive gift indeed. Who is his intended recipient of such an elaborate work?'

'The messenger mentioned the Lord of Florence, or some such.'

'Lorenzo de Medici,' Adam said, having remembered the name better than I had.

'The expense be my main concern,' I said. 'You will have noted there is no mention of any payments to be made.'

Master Collop read the parchment once more.

'I see your difficulty, young Sebastian.' Almost word for word, as I had explained to Adam earlier, my master reiterated the problem: to make a good copy, well bound, and trust it was found acceptable to the king; or fulfil every last, lavish detail of the commission and pray that we were paid the price eventually.

'Can you advise me, master?' I asked, retying the ribbon and replacing the parchment in my purse. 'For this piece will empty our coffer, if we follow the instructions precisely.'

He rubbed his brow, turning his gaze to the painted roof beams, deep in thought.

We waited, drinking our ale. Adam helped himself to another wafer and a marchpane-stuffed date. I was too concerned for my master's words of wisdom to have any interest in sweetmeats.

'It would be tempting to suggest you complete the work to a good standard but spend no more than is necessary to make it appear that you have followed the instructions to the letter. No one outside the craft will be able to tell lapis lazuli from the cheaper alternative, azurite. The jewels need not be rubies and amethysts when coloured glass may serve as well. Once the book is in Florence, in some rich man's collection, who will notice if the colours fade forty years hence?

'However, you and I will know. Deceiving the king... it is a serious step to take. You are a man of conscience, Sebastian: could you be easy in your mind, knowing of the deception?'

Master Collop had come upon the heart of the matter. Did I follow the dictates of my conscience or my purse? He knew me well indeed. And there was always the possibility that the king would pay after all.

'I fear I could not, master.'

'Then I believe you have answered your own query. Do you have an exemplar of Vegetius' treatise? You will need an accurate version. It will save you time and trouble, although I know you are more than capable of correcting any errors in the previous scribe's Latin grammar as you copy it: the fewer mistakes, the better, else they may require the layout of the pages to be changed.'

'We have an English version of the most popular Book Three. This we sell as a separate booklet: five copies sold so far this year. Which brings me to the second purpose of our visit...'

'You wish to borrow my complete Latin copy.'

'If 'tis not in use, I shall be most grateful for it.'

'None has worked on it since you left, Sebastian. As you say, the English version sells more readily these days. I will instruct young Hugh to dust it off and bring it along to you at Paternoster Row in the morning. I know he will be glad to have time away from his desk; any errand is welcome.'

I set down my cup and rose to my feet.

Adam did likewise, though he was yet chewing a sweetmeat.

'I thank you, master. You have made my decision for me. I should ever suffer sleepless nights if I fail to follow the king's instructions as required.'

'Aye. I believed that would be the case.'

'And I shall be pleased to see Hugh Gardyner upon the morrow.'

Master Collop came with us to the parlour door but held my sleeve to detain me. 'If money becomes a problem in this instance,' he whispered so Adam could not hear, 'Officially, the guild has funds to lend out at a most reasonable rate, if required. Unofficially, I also have coin available. And for my best apprentice, this would be loaned at a further reduced rate of interest: that is to say, naught but the capital need be repaid at a time to suit ourselves. Don't let this commission cause you hardship, Sebastian.'

'I be most grateful, Master Collop, both for your advice and your generous offer. Fare you well.' I touched my cap courteously and bowed my head so he might bless me. Kindly, he also bestowed his benediction upon Adam.

'What offer was that?' Adam asked as we returned along Cheapside. I explained about the possibility of borrowing money though, in truth, such an action would be utterly against my nature.

'I hope and pray that it never comes to such a pass,' I said.

'We're going to make the most extravagant book, then? Cost no object?'

'Aye. Something of the kind. Master Collop was correct: I cannot give less than my very best in working for the king. Mayhap, that be why we were chosen. If our workshop was recommended to His Grace by the Duke of Gloucester, think what he would say, if he e'er discovered I had given his royal brother a shoddy piece and called it craftsmanship. I cannot do that, Adam. I am a better man than that – as are you. We are no charlatans. Together we will do justice to the king's commission and show ourselves worthy of his patronage and our own fair and goodly reputation. I wonder that I had dared consider, however briefly, doing otherwise. Come. Let us tell Rose, Kate and everyone our good tidings.'

Toni Mount, a member of the Crime Writers' Association, earned her Master's Degree by completing original research into a unique 15th-century medical manuscript. She still studies history and is the author of several successful non-fiction books for Amberley Publishing and Pen & Sword Books, about the lives of ordinary people in the Middle-Ages. Toni's detailed understanding of the period allows her to create accurate, atmospheric settings and realistic characters for her Seb Foxley medieval murder mysteries. Toni's first career was as a scientist, which enhances her knowledge and brings an extra dimension to her novels. She writes regularly for both The Richard III Society and The Tudor Society and is a major contributor to MedievalCourses.com. As well as writing, Toni teaches history to adults, co-ordinates a creative writing group and is a popular speaker to groups and societies.

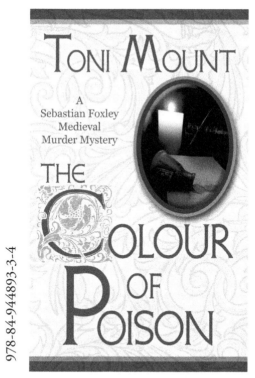

TONI MOUNT

A
Sebastian Foxley
Medieval
Murder Mystery

THE

COLOUR

OF

POISON

978-84-944893-3-4

**The first Sebastian Foxley
Medieval Mystery by Toni Mount.**

The narrow, stinking streets of medieval London can sometimes be a dark place. Burglary, arson, kidnapping and murder are every-day events. The streets even echo with rumours of the mysterious art of alchemy being used to make gold for the King.

Join Seb, a talented but crippled artist, as he is drawn into a web of lies to save his handsome brother from the hangman's rope. Will he find an inner strength in these, the darkest of times, or will events outside his control overwhelm him?

Only one thing is certain - if Seb can't save his brother, nobody can.

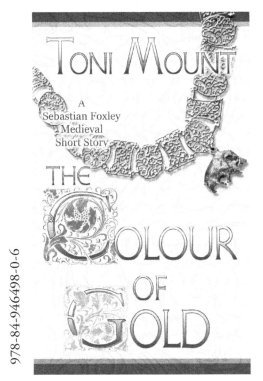

978-84-946498-0-6

**The second Sebastian Foxley
Medieval Mystery by Toni Mount.
A short story**

A wedding in medieval London should be a splendid occasion, especially when a royal guest will be attending the nuptial feast. Yet for the bridegroom, the talented young artist, Sebastian Foxley, his marriage day begins with disaster when the valuable gold livery collar he should wear has gone missing. From the lowliest street urchin to the highest nobility, who could be the thief? Can Seb wed his sweetheart, Emily Appleyard, and save the day despite that young rascal, Jack Tabor, and his dog causing chaos?

Join in the fun at a medieval marriage in this short story that links the first two Sebastian Foxley medieval murder mysteries: *The Colour of Poison* and the full-length novel *The Colour of Cold Blood.*.

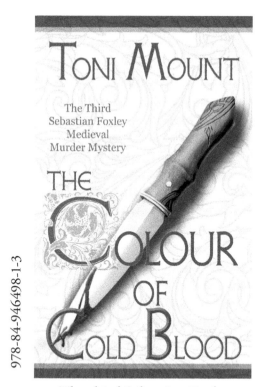

TONI MOUNT

The Third
Sebastian Foxley
Medieval
Murder Mystery

THE COLOUR OF COLD BLOOD

978-84-946498-1-3

**The third Sebastian Foxley
Medieval Mystery by Toni Mount.**

A devilish miasma of murder and heresy lurks in the winter streets of medieval London - someone is slaying women of the night. For Seb Foxley and his brother, Jude, evil and the threat of death come close to home when Gabriel, their well-liked journeyman, is arrested as a heretic and condemned to be burned at the stake.

Amid a tangle of betrayal and deception, Seb tries to uncover the murderer before more women die – will he also defy the church and devise a plan to save Gabriel?

These are dangerous times for the young artist and those he holds dear. Treachery is everywhere, even at his own fireside...

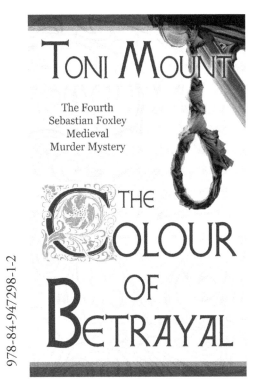

# TONI MOUNT

The Fourth
Sebastian Foxley
Medieval
Murder Mystery

## THE COLOUR OF BETRAYAL

978-84-947298-1-2

**The fourth Sebastian Foxley
Medieval Mystery by Toni Mount.
A short story**

Suicide or murder?

As medieval Londoners joyously prepare for the Christmas celebrations, goldsmith Lawrence Ducket is involved in a street brawl. Fearful that his opponent is dying from his injuries, Lawrence seeks sanctuary in a church nearby.

When Ducket is found hanging from the rafters, people assume it's suicide. Yet, Sebastian Foxley is unconvinced. Why is his young apprentice, Jack Tabor, so terrified that he takes to his bed?

Amidst feasting and merriment, Seb is determined to solve the mystery of his friend's death and to ease Jack's fears.

TONI MOUNT

The Fifth
Sebastian Foxley
Medieval
Murder Mystery

THE COLOUR OF MURDER

978-84-946498-0-6

**The fifth Sebastian Foxley
Medieval Mystery by Toni Mount.**

London is not safe for princes or commoners.

In February 1478, a wealthy merchant is killed by an intruder and a royal duke dies at the Tower. Neither case is quite as simple as it seems.

Seb Foxley, an intrepid young artist, finds himself in the darkest of places, fleeing for his life. With foul deeds afoot at the king's court, his wife Emily pregnant and his brother Jude's hope of marrying Rose thwarted, can Seb unearth the secrets which others would prefer to keep hidden?

Join Seb and Jude, their lives in jeopardy in the dangerous streets of the city, as they struggle to solve crimes and keep their business flourishing.

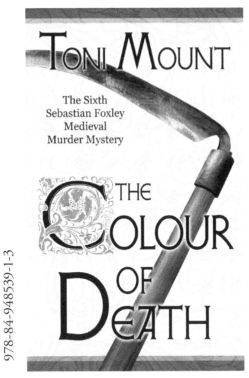

TONI MOUNT

The Sixth
Sebastian Foxley
Medieval
Murder Mystery

THE
COLOUR
OF
DEATH

978-84-948539-1-3

**The sixth Sebastian Foxley**
**Medieval Mystery by Toni Mount.**
**A short story**

Seb Foxley and his wife, Emily, have been forced to flee medieval London to escape their enemies. They find a safe haven in the isolated Norfolk village where Seb was born. Yet this idyllic rural setting has its own murderous secrets and a terrible crime requires our hero to play the sleuth once more.

Even away from London, Seb and Emily are not as safe as they believe - their enemies are closer than they know and danger lurks at every twist and turn.

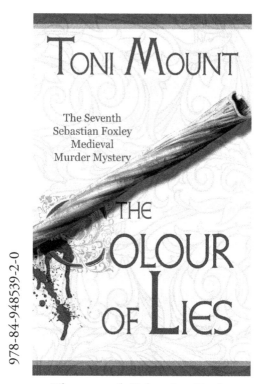

# TONI MOUNT

The Seventh
Sebastian Foxley
Medieval
Murder Mystery

## THE COLOUR OF LIES

978-84-948539-2-0

**The seventh Sebastian Foxley
Medieval Mystery by Toni Mount.**

It is late summer and London is all a-bustle for St Bartholomew's Fayre, with merchants arriving from faraway lands. When an old friend returns with fabulous items for sale, it can only mean one thing: trouble. As thievery, revenge and murder stalk the fayre, Sebastian Foxley – artist and sometime-sleuth – has mysteries to solve. In uncovering the answers, he becomes enmeshed in a web of lies and falsehoods. His greatest dilemma means having to choose between upholding honour and justice or saving those dearest to him. How can a truly honest citizen of London practise deceit and yet live with his conscience?

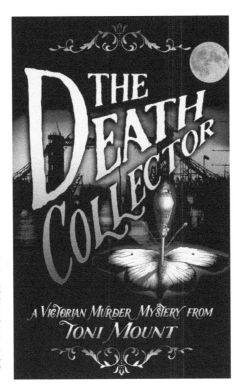

978-84-948539-4-4

More dastardly than Jack the Ripper; more vile than a London Particular, an arch-fiend prowls the Victorian city streets. Nobody is safe from his experiments, whether peer or prostitute, preacher or policeman in this murderous melodrama. Will Inspector Albert Sutton, aided by his wife Nell and her cat, be able to unmask and apprehend the heartless killer, or will they become the next novelty specimens of the Death Collector?

In this riveting novella, Toni Mount explores the darker side of Victorian London, creating a gripping thriller packed with shocking murders, unexpected twists and chilling suspense.

Read it if you dare …

Greetings, my name is Sebastian, my brother Jude and I are from Foxley, a small village in Norfolk, just a few miles north west of Norwich.

I was born in 1453, the year our lord king Henry, the sixth of that name, lost his reason; Jude is nearly three years my senior.

I'm an illuminator and Jude a scribe and we work near St Paul's Cathedral in the city of London, producing illuminated manuscripts. Most people in our trade work around here; stationers and bookbinders even store their paper in the cathedral crypt.

Why not come to see my website and discover more about my adventures?

# www.SebastianFoxley.com

# Get your FREE BOOK!

## Historical Fiction

The Sebastian Foxley Series - **Toni Mount**
The Death Collector - **Toni Mount**
Struck With the Dart of Love - **Sandra Vasoli**
Truth Endures - **Sandra Vasoli**
Cor Rotto - **Adrienne Dillard**
The Raven's Widow - **Adrienne Dillard**

## Historical Colouring Books

The Mary, Queen of Scots Colouring Book - **Roland Hui**
The Life of Anne Boleyn Colouring Book - **Claire Ridgway**
The Wars of the Roses Colouring Book - **Debra Bayani**
The Tudor Colouring Book - **Ainhoa Modenes**

## Non Fiction History

The Turbulent Crown - **Roland Hui**
Anne Boleyn's Letter from the Tower - **Sandra Vasoli**
Jasper Tudor - **Debra Bayani**
Tudor Places of Great Britain - **Claire Ridgway**
Illustrated Kings and Queens of England - **Claire Ridgway**
A History of the English Monarchy - **Gareth Russell**
The Fall of Anne Boleyn - **Claire Ridgway**
George Boleyn: Tudor Poet, Courtier & Diplomat - **Ridgway & Cherry**
The Anne Boleyn Collection I, II & III - **Claire Ridgway**
Two Gentleman Poets at the Court of Henry VIII - **Edmond Bapst**

# PLEASE LEAVE A REVIEW

If you enjoyed this book, *please*
leave a review at the book seller
where you purchased it. There is
no better way to thank the author
and it really does make a huge
difference! *Thank you in advance.*

Lightning Source UK Ltd.
Milton Keynes UK
UKHW041829010920
369159UK00014B/180